Praise for *The Pataala*

'Doyle creates a world of fa
mythology, action and suspen.. ....gether to weave a
thriller that keeps you spellbound to the very end.'
—*The New Indian Express*

'*The Pataala Prophecy: Son of Bhrigu*, another riveting series
which creates an enchanting world of fantasy and adventure,
blending mythology, action and suspense.'
—*Deccan Chronicle*

'There's a "chosen one", there's a secret society, and philosophical
ideas from the Vedas, the Bhagavad Gita and the Srimad
Bhagavatam have been quoted – Christopher Doyle's latest,
The Pataala Prophecy: Son of Bhrigu has it all.'
—*Sunday Mail Today*

'The story…keeps you on the edge of your seat…the atmosphere
crackles with energy.'
—*Sakal Times*

The Mists of Brahma

Christopher C. Doyle is a bestselling author who transports the reader into a fascinating world where ancient secrets buried in legend blend with science and history to create gripping stories. His debut novel, *The Mahabharata Secret*, featured among the top ten books of 2013 and was nominated for the Raymond Crossword Book Award, 2014. His 'The Mahabharata Quest' series features the bestselling novels *The Alexander Secret* and *The Secret of the Druids*.

Son of Bhrigu, Book 1 of 'The Pataala Prophecy' series was published in April 2018. It went on to become a bestseller and won rave reviews from readers.

An alumnus of St Stephen's College, Delhi and IIM Calcutta, Doyle had a successful career in the corporate sector before embarking on an entrepreneurial journey, running a firm which helps companies to achieve exponential growth. He is also one of India's leading CEO coaches. He lives in New Delhi with his wife and daughter.

He can be contacted at:

Website: www.christophercdoyle.com
Email: contact@christophercdoyle.com
Facebook: www.facebook.com/authorchristophercdoyle
The Quest Club: www.christophercdoyle.com/the-quest-club

Also by Christopher C. Doyle

The Mahabharata Secret (2013)

The Mahabharata Quest Series
Book I: The Alexander Secret (2014)
A Secret Revealed: The Mini Sequel to the Alexander Secret (2016)
Book II: The Secret of the Druids (2016)

The Pataala Prophecy Series
Book I: Son of Bhrigu (2018)

The Pataala Prophecy Book II

The Mists of Brahma

Christopher C. Doyle

First published by Westland Publications Private Limited in 2019

1st Floor, A Block, East Wing, Plot No. 40, SP Infocity, Dr MGR Salai, Perungudi, Kandanchavadi, Chennai 600096

Westland and the Westland logo are the trademarks of Westland Publications Private Limited, or its affiliates.

ISBN: 9789387894679

10 9 8 7 6 5 4 3 2 1

This is a work of fiction. Names, characters, organisations, places, events and incidents are either products of the author's imagination or used fictitiously.

Typeset by Jojy Philip, New Delhi 110 015
Printed at Thomson Press (India) Ltd.

This book is dedicated to my mother,
whose strength and determination are an inspiration.
For teaching me to be strong even in the face of adversity.
For all the nights you stayed awake, caring for me,
so I could sleep.
For your love, blessings,
and years of prayers for my success and well being.
For everything you have taught me and given me.

Prologue

Five Years Ago

New Delhi

Maya tossed and turned in her sleep. The nightmare had her in its steely grip and would not let go. Her body stiffened, her muscles tensed, as her brain responded to the horrifying scenes that were playing out in her mind. Her hands clutched the bedsheet as if trying to gain purchase, the movements of her fingers betraying a sense of desperation.

She screamed; a sound filled with terror and despair.

The sound of her own shriek jerked her awake and she sat bolt upright in her bed.

She was sweating profusely.

The door to her room crashed open and a figure rushed in, looming in the darkness.

Maya shrank back against the headboard, cowering under the quilt.

The lights came on, flooding the room with a sense of comfort and assurance, a shield against the darkness and the things that hid beneath its cloak.

'Maya!' It was her father, Naresh Upadhyay, roused by her scream. He looked anxious. 'What happened?' he asked gently.

Maya closed her eyes. Unbidden, the images from the nightmare rushed back into her mind. She saw the black, shadowy shapes as clearly as if they were real. The intense cold that had permeated the dream still clung to her bones.

And the voice … the voice …

Whispering to her, the words unintelligible. It had been a hoarse rasp with a chilling edge to it that made her hair stand on end even now, when she was awake.

What the dream meant Maya couldn't fathom, but it had ended with her being sucked against her will into an infinite darkness that enveloped her. She had tried to scream but no sound came out. Desperate to escape the clutches of the living darkness that drew her into its fold, she had scrabbled wildly for something to hold on to, to no avail.

The cold voice had seemed to beckon to her, drawing her deeper into the darkness, wrapping itself around her. Even now, she could feel its slimy touch, as if it were a living thing, folding her in its embrace, stifling her consciousness.

Then, suddenly, she had found her voice. And screamed.

That was when her father had woken up and rushed to her room.

Maya shivered involuntarily. Her eyes were still wide with terror and glazed with confusion. She snuggled up against her father, as he sat next to her on the bed and put a protective arm around her. She struggled to tell him what she had seen.

'It's alright,' Naresh Upadhyay murmured. 'It was only a nightmare.' His voice was calm and comforting, assuaging her fears. 'It wasn't real. Those things weren't real. Nothing but a nightmare.'

'Mmm … hmmm.' Maya snuggled closer to her father, safe in his protective presence. Her breathing returned to an even rhythm. Nothing could harm her as long as her father was with her. Not even the shapes from her nightmare.

'Dad, I won't be able to go back to sleep,' she said tremulously.

'Don't worry, my dear,' her father told her with a smile, as he stroked her head. 'I am going to recite a very powerful mantra that will not only help you go back to sleep but will also ensure that you do not have any more nightmares tonight.'

'Dad!' Maya was not reassured. 'How can a mantra help?'

'It will. I promise you. Now, lie down and close your eyes. I'm turning the lights out.'

Ten minutes later, Naresh Upadhyay shut the door of Maya's room behind him. His forehead was creased with thought. He made his way to his study and sat at his desk, lost in contemplation.

A little over a month ago, Maya's dreams had begun. She had had them every night since then, but they weren't the usual dreams of a ten-year-old's fertile mind. She had described them to him as slow, lazy dreams filled with peace and happiness. Nice things happened in them, though she never remembered what they were about once she woke up. But she always rose in the morning with a smile on her face and a strange, joyful sensation inside her head.

Then, exactly one month after the dreams began, she had had her first nightmare. Like her earlier, nicer, dreams, she was unable to remember what her nightmares were about, but she would wake up with an unpleasant feeling of unease the next day, and tell her father about it at breakfast.

Tonight was the first time he had been roused by her reaction to a nightmare.

Naresh realised that the nightmare Maya had experienced tonight was no ordinary one. What really worried him was that, for the first time, she had vivid recollections of it.

Why had her dreams suddenly turned? And what was special about tonight's nightmare?

Naresh hadn't given much thought to the dreams over the last month, but if he was right, they would continue. Unless he was able to figure out the source of the nightmares, he would not be able to do anything to stop them from recurring.

Still lost in thought, he rose and walked to one of the bookshelves that lined three walls of his study. He studied the books along one of the walls and, after a few moments of searching, found what he was looking for. An old leather diary, well thumbed and worn.

He flipped it open and glanced through the pages which bore inscriptions, written by hand.

When he reached a particular page, he found a loose sheet of paper that was covered with inscriptions. He frowned and sat down at his desk, reading the inscriptions. A few moments later, he closed the book and sat for some time, lost in thought.

The conclusion was inescapable. He had been wrong.

So, so wrong.

Everything he had done had been for nothing.

Now, he had a choice to make.

He had already sacrificed a lot. But the decision that he was confronted with called for something greater.

He knew what had to be done. But he couldn't bring himself to confront the reality of what it would mean. For him. And for Maya.

Naresh sat there for a long time, considering the possibilities. But there seemed to be only one way forward.

He knew Maya would never forgive him for this.

But he had no choice.

Present Day

'The setback is only temporary, O Wise One.'

Shukra had been lost in deep thought. He stirred and eyed the Naga who had spoken, an enormous being more than ten feet tall and all muscle, who towered over him as he sat brooding in his secret cavern.

Encouraged by Shukra's silence, the Naga continued, 'Garuda will not stay at the Gurukul for long. His place is near his Lord, near Dwarka, the place where Krishna lived in Bhu-lok. If he hasn't returned yet to his island, he will, and soon. There are more Gurukuls spread across Bharatvarsha. How many will Garuda defend?'

'There are the *sadhs*,' a second Naga, equally massive, added. 'We now know the Sangha is weak. If we spread out among the sadhs, we can take Bhu-lok by ourselves.' He allowed the hint of a snigger to escape him. 'We won't need the Daityas or Danavas or even the Mahanagas.'

'Kuhaka, Kâlya,' the third Naga, who had been silent so far, addressed the two Nagas who had just spoken. He was the largest of the trio, standing head and shoulders above the other two giant reptiles, and spoke with a tone of authority and superiority. 'You do not understand the thoughts of the Wise One. The Gurukul we attacked is where the One of the prophecy resides. We will achieve nothing if we create chaos and panic among the sadhs or destroy the other Gurukuls, as long as Yayati's scion lives. And Garuda will defend *that* Gurukul with his life. We have to be realistic. We have to find a way to get the boy.'

'No, Takshaka.' Shukra spoke finally, as he rose to his feet. 'You are correct about the boy from the prophecy residing in the Gurukul. But he is weak. He is not ready. I do not see him as a threat. He means nothing to me.'

'Then what do you wish us to do, Son of Bhrigu?' Takshaka asked. 'The ranks have been restless this past week. They have not taken their defeat well. None of them had gone to the Gurukul expecting to be routed. Shall we mount another attack and finish off the boy before he has the chance to fulfil the prophecy?'

Shukra shook his head. 'No, Takshaka. If I wish to kill the boy, I won't need the Nagas to help me. Even Garuda cannot protect the Gurukul if I bring my powers to bear against it. But there is always a cost. Even for someone like me. And, right now, that cost is not worth it. I have much work to do before my plans come to fruition. And I have learned what I needed for now. But you have raised a valid issue. Your troops need to be satisfied.'

He paused.

The three Nagas waited for Shukra to continue.

'Here's what I want you to do,' Shukra began. The Nagas listened attentively.

'You can't be serious, Wise One!' Takshaka exploded as Shukra finished.

'You must listen and obey,' the Son of Bhrigu commanded, his voice stern. 'What I have asked you to do is the only way forward for me.'

Takshaka and his companions stood uncertainly for a few moments. Then, with one accord, they bowed and left the Son of Bhrigu alone with his thoughts.

Chapter One

Terror in Corbett National Park

The Gurukul at Ramganga
Corbett National Park
Uttarakhand

16:00 Hours

The classes had just begun to disperse and the clamour of loud conversations filled the air. Students threaded their way out of the classrooms and towards the Gurukul's archives or to their dormitories.

Not far away, the lazy rays of the sun glinted off the slow flowing Ramganga river that skirted the Gurukul as the day marched towards twilight and the embrace of darkness.

A few Mahamatis stood in groups of twos and threes, talking animatedly.

A normal day at the Gurukul located within Corbett National Park. Or any Gurukul for that matter.

Until now.

Abruptly, the sky darkened, the sun blotted out by extraordinarily dark clouds.

Everyone looked up, surprised. There had been no forecast of rain or a thunderstorm; or any climatic disturbance of any kind.

Curiosity turned to shock.

Then fear.

For, hovering above them was no ordinary cloud. It was a seething mass of black shapes writhing within tight coils, flying in from the west and hovering above the Gurukul.

A shout went up. 'The Nagas are attacking!'

The cheerful hubbub was instantly replaced by a tumult born of fear and horror. Everyone had heard about what had happened at the Gurukul in Panna just over a week ago.

Mahamatra Vishesh, the Maharishi who led the Sangha as the head of its council, stood calm and composed in the midst of the pandemonium. He knew what he had to do. But he was not sure if time was on their side.

Already, the black cloud had begun to disintegrate into individual reptiles who descended to the ground, surrounding the Gurukul from all sides with guttural roars and grunts.

They sounded angry.

They *were* angry.

And they wanted revenge.

Vishesh realised this. But the Gurukul would not go down without a fight. He gestured to Pradeep, who was a member of the Sangha Council—the five leaders who governed the Sangha.

'Call for help,' he urged Pradeep. 'We don't have much time.'

Pradeep nodded, fully aware of their predicament, and hurried away.

All around, orders were being shouted. The students were being rallied and instructions given to defend the Gurukul.

The chant of mantras grew louder as reinforcements were put in place to strengthen the defence of the Gurukul. The Sangha had never seen an adversary as powerful as this before.

Vishesh could only hope that help would arrive in time. Otherwise, they were all doomed.

Chapter Two

Where's Maya?

The Gurukul
Panna National Park

Life was back to normal at the Gurukul in Panna, after its near destruction nine days ago. Ever since the rout of the Nagas, the place had been a hive of activity. Help had descended upon the little hamlet in the form of Rishis and Kshatriyas and Maharishis from across the country; some were Mahamatis from other Gurukuls and others were members of the Sangha, who were teaching at educational institutions in different parts of India.

Everyone had come to help rebuild the partially destroyed Gurukul. As a result, within just a few days, the boys' dorms and the guesthouse, along with some of the other installations, which had been attacked and destroyed by the Nagas, had been swiftly rebuilt and were now as good, if not better, than before. The girls' dorms had been untouched; Garuda had arrived before the Nagas had had a chance to have a go at them.

The common room was a cacophony of loud chatter, even louder laughter, and shouts, as some of the residents indulged in rough games.

Arjun sat at a table, laughing at one of Varun's jokes.

A sudden, fierce knocking at the door of the cottage made everyone jump.

One of the boys ran to open the door.

Kanakpratap, Arjun's uncle, his face dark as thunder, stood on the doorstep.

In one swift motion, Arjun rose and scurried to the door.

Kanakpratap pulled him outside and slammed the door shut, leaving Arjun's friends and the other boys surprised.

'Where's Maya?' Kanakpratap's tone was urgent.

Arjun almost asked, 'Why?' but restrained himself just in time. His uncle's tone indicated that he would not take kindly to a question at this moment.

'Probably with Maharishi Satyavachana,' Arjun replied, again repressing the urge to ask why Kanakpratap was looking for Maya. His uncle rarely had any work with Maya, so something must be up for him to be searching for her with such a grim visage.

'Can't find him anywhere either,' Kanakpratap responded in a tone of steel that indicated he was restraining his fury with great difficulty. 'Can't imagine where they could have disappeared to.'

Arjun didn't have an answer. But he didn't want to say so either.

'Have you checked with Adira and Amyra?' It seemed logical to Arjun that the two girls who were Maya's closest friends in the Gurukul might know where she was.

Kanak shook his head. 'I did. They don't know either.' He gritted his teeth in exasperation.

Arjun was now sure that something was seriously wrong. It was not like Kanakpratap to get worked up over small things.

'What's the matter, Uncle?' He couldn't help himself finally. 'Can I help in any way?'

Kanakpratap put a hand on his shoulder and gripped it firmly. A bit too firmly for Arjun's liking.

He looked Arjun in the eye. 'The Nagas have attacked the Gurukul on the banks of the Ramganga river in Corbett. We just received an SOS from them. They can't hold off much longer.'

Finally, Arjun understood his uncle's urgency. Maya was the only one in the entire world who knew where to find the nemesis of the Nagas. The saviour who had rescued their own Gurukul, just a week ago.

'Let me look for her,' he offered, but Kanakpratap stopped him.

'You stay here, Arjun. Just in case she turns up. There are enough people scouring the Gurukul as it is.'

Arjun stood there and watched his uncle walk away, a deep foreboding in his heart. The memory of the assault of the Nagas was all too fresh. The Gurukul's deliverance had hung upon a slender thread.

And Maya.

Who was nowhere to be found.

Where could she be?

And what would happen to the Gurukul on the Ramganga?

Chapter Three

Kapoor's New Case

Police Commissioner's Office
New Delhi

Raman Kapoor fidgeted as he waited outside Commissioner of Police Ramesh Vidyarthi's office.

He wondered what bug had bitten the Commissioner. It had been only three weeks since he had been assigned the Trivedi murder case. And he had still not solved it. So why this sudden urgency? He couldn't understand it. Even if his boss wanted an update, surely he should have given him a week or two more to investigate? Especially since Kapoor had been all set to travel to Allahabad to try and unearth clues there.

The Commissioner's aide came up to Kapoor. 'Sir will see you now.'

Kapoor followed the man into the office and stood before the Commissioner's desk. Vidyarthi smiled at him from under bushy eyebrows and a mop of white hair.

'Ah, Kapoor, my man! Come on in, sit down.'

Kapoor took a chair. The door shut behind him, as the aide left the two men alone.

'What's the update?' Vidyarthi asked him, getting to the point immediately. 'I haven't had a proper report from you yet.'

Kapoor bit back a retort about not having had enough time to investigate, leave alone write a report.

'No conclusion yet, sir,' he replied instead. 'I'm still working on some leads.'

'Ah.'

Kapoor didn't like the sound of that 'ah'. He waited. He knew there was more.

'What does it look like, Kapoor?' Vidyarthi sat back in his chair and observed him keenly. 'Going anywhere? Or will it be a dead end? That would be a first for you!'

'I don't know yet, sir. I wanted to follow up a few leads to see if I could find something concrete.'

'Don't bullshit me, Kapoor. I know you well. And I knew when I gave you the Trivedi murder case that it looked pretty hopeless. But if there was anyone on the force who could solve it, it was you. And yet, if you haven't got anywhere in three weeks, I don't know if you ever will.'

Kapoor said nothing. He, too, knew his boss well. The two had worked together several times before.

'It's okay,' Vidyarthi said, pushing some photographs towards Kapoor. 'Those murdered school teachers aren't going anywhere for a while. The case can wait. And I've figured out a way to keep the media out of it. So forget it for now. There's something more urgent. Something that the media have got their hands on already.'

Kapoor looked at the photographs curiously. They were all images of the same girl. A teenager, probably sixteen or seventeen years old. And she looked dead. But there was something strange about the photographs. Kapoor couldn't quite put his finger on it.

'Dead,' Vidyarthi clarified. 'But no signs of sexual assault. The autopsy came out clear on that.' He switched on the television in his room.

Kapoor flinched. On the screen was a news anchor, talking at the top of her voice, as if she was trying to broadcast to the world without the aid of the television camera trained on her.

Vidyarthi switched the television to mute. But Kapoor couldn't escape the words flashing in bold red letters on the screen, in full caps: BREAKING NEWS: DELHI UNSAFE FOR KIDS. UNUSUAL MURDER OF YOUNG TEENAGE GIRL.

'This kid?'

Vidyarthi nodded. 'This kid.' He leaned forward. 'And you know what? She was missing for almost two weeks. Yet her parents didn't file a missing persons report. Now why would they do that?'

Kapoor was mystified. That didn't make sense. 'How do the parents explain it?'

Vidyarthi jabbed a finger in the air. 'Good question. We don't have the answer. The parents aren't to be found anywhere. They've disappeared as well. Apparently they left town as soon as the body was handed over to them.' He leaned back in his chair. 'What kind of parents would not report their daughter missing for almost two weeks?'

'Cause of death, sir?'

'That's the other reason I'm giving you this case. Seems to be right up your street after the last one with the school teachers.' He smirked. 'First the school teachers, then the school kids.'

A horrible feeling caught hold of Kapoor. He fervently hoped he was wrong.

'We haven't told the media yet, otherwise there would be mass hysteria.' Vidyarthi rolled his eyes. 'You know.'

Kapoor knew. But he didn't say anything. His boss's words implied there was a mystery. Now he knew why he had been summoned with such urgency. And why he had been chosen, despite being on a big case that was still unsolved.

'The autopsy revealed a mystery that's difficult to explain,' Vidyarthi said, pursing his lips as he looked at Kapoor across the desk.

Kapoor waited.

'It seems that the girl actually died well before the time of death indicated by the decomposition of her body.'

'I don't get it.' Kapoor shook his head in disbelief. 'You mean to say that decomposition did not start immediately after her death?'

'That is correct,' Vidyarthi said. 'Both decomposition and rigor mortis set in much later than they should have. And, according to the autopsy, there is no identifiable cause of death.'

'How can that be, sir?' Kapoor was mystified.

'That's for you to find out, Kapoor. So here's the mystery. The girl is dead, that's for sure. Her body was beginning to decompose when it was discovered. All the physical signs of death. But it seems that she died much earlier. Talk to forensics, they'll give you the details. It appears she died a good two weeks before rigor mortis set in,' he finished, leaning back in his chair.

'It's almost as if she died, then came back to life before dying again.'

Chapter Four

Oh, There She Is!

The Forest
Unknown Location

Maya walked a few steps gingerly, uncertainly, then stopped and stood still, looking around in the darkness of the forest that surrounded her.

The trees closed in, stifling her.

There was no breeze in this forest.

Where was she?

Nothing was visible in the pitch black darkness that surrounded her.

She heard a noise to her left and spun around.

She heard it again.

A gurgling, rasping sound.

It was unearthly.

What was it?

Maya could hear another sound now. The sound of something scraping against the ground. Something heavy being dragged …

'*Vidyutate!*'

But the ball of light refused to materialise even as the gurgling, dragging noises came closer.

She screamed, nearly in tears now, terror gripping her very soul.

'Tch, tch.' A disapproving voice was heard as a glowing sphere of light appeared, revealing the form of Satyavachana. He stood barely two feet away from her, shaking his head.

Maya jerked her head to the left, trying to identify the source of the noise she had heard in the darkness.

But there was nothing there.

'Sorry,' she said in a small voice. 'I was trying very hard to practise what you taught me.'

'I know.' Satyavachana's voice was gentle and understanding. 'I don't believe for a moment that you didn't try. I didn't expect you to be able to cast off your sadh qualities in the course of a week. Especially when you have been disturbed all these days by the phenomenon you described to me. Most strange. I wish I could understand what was causing it.'

In the midst of the general bedlam of rebuilding the Gurukul, Satyavachana had begun his lessons with Maya as promised. During the day, he would take her through the training she needed to develop into a Rishi. At night, while the Gurukul slept, Guru and student would take to the skies as *atmas*, and Satyavachana would instruct Maya in the science of atma travel.

In the beginning, he would walk with her to the practice field allocated to the aspiring Rishis of the Gana, and teach her there. Unlike the Kshatriya practice field, which had been decimated by the Nagas, the other field had survived unscathed. Whether it was because of its proximity to the remains of the Dandaka forest or because the Nagas simply did not have enough time to reach it, Maya did not know. But it remained a puzzle to her that the Nagas had not even attempted to attack the Gurukul through the Dandaka. Especially since she knew that the forest had been created by Shukra thousands of years ago.

And *that* was when it had started, on the very first day of her lessons.

The same feeling that she had experienced on her first night at the Gurukul, after she had walked through the rock and been led to the guesthouse.

That particular night, three weeks ago, as she struggled with her beliefs about the inefficacy of mantras and rituals, and the battle she had witnessed in the clearing outside the Gurukul entrance, she had felt almost as if something was calling to her. It had been an invisible attraction that pulled at her; a gnawing sensation she could not understand or explain. It was almost as if there had suddenly developed within her an inexplicable longing for something unknown.

Day after day, as Satyavachana instructed her, the feeling persisted. It made Maya uncomfortable and she found herself floundering at her lessons.

'What's the matter, child?' Satyavachana had asked her this morning, having observed her discomfort for the past nine days. 'You are clearly distracted. Come now, tell me what's on your mind.'

Maya had been unable to explain. How could she when she didn't know what was troubling her?

Satyavachana had frowned, his bushy white eyebrows meeting. 'This won't do,' he had proclaimed. And he had immediately transported her to this forest, where he had proceeded to teach her for the entire day, the lessons broken only by a simple meal of fruits and nuts. This forest, the Maharishi had explained, would be their venue for the lessons from today onwards.

'Now,' the Maharishi said, 'let's go over it again. Explain the theory to me and then we'll have another go at practising it.'

Chapter Five

A Strange Case

Raman Kapoor's Office
New Delhi

'Okay,' Kapoor told the two policemen standing at his desk. 'We have a new case. I want to get cracking on it immediately and get some leads ASAP. The Trivedi–Upadhyay murder case goes on the back burner until then. Commissioner's orders.'

Ajit and Harish nodded. Kapoor had selected these two men to aid his investigations simply because he considered them to be the brightest men in his team. They had served him well in earlier cases and had pulled through every time, in the toughest circumstances. It was only in the Trivedi case that the two men had floundered a bit—but so had Kapoor—and he knew that it was unique. He had never come across anything like it in his career. All the more reason to go back to it as soon as he solved this one.

He motioned to them to sit down and spread out the photographs that Vidyarthi had handed over to him with the case files.

'So here are the photographs of the murder victim,' Kapoor said, after giving his men a quick briefing on the facts of the case. 'A teenager. We don't know how she died. The autopsies could not pinpoint the cause of her death.' He decided not to say any more. Vidyarthi had been unnecessarily dramatic, in his opinion, in describing the fate of the girl.

'So here's what we're going to do,' he continued. 'I'm going to talk to forensics and get more details about the autopsy. There's more to this than meets the eye. You two will find out more about this girl. Her background, who she knew, who she met, who she spoke to. Get her mobile records from the telco for the last few months and go through them with a fine-tooth comb. See if you can find anything there. Most called numbers, an obsessive boyfriend, anything. Check her apps. Blue whale, black whale, I don't know, anything could be linked to her death. You know the drill. Got it?'

Both men nodded.

'Good. Keep me updated.'

As the two men filed out, Kapoor sat lost in thought. He didn't like the fact that there was still an unanswered question about the case. The question of the difference between the time the girl was supposed to have died, clinically speaking, and the physiological indications of death.

He made up his mind and picked up his landline receiver. 'Get me Suresh,' he barked, referring to his contact in forensics.

The phone rang.

'Suresh? Kapoor here.'

'Yes, sir. I heard that you are on the case now. What can I do for you?'

Kapoor took a deep breath. 'First explain to me this whole business of the difference between when the victim supposedly died and when she actually died. I still don't understand.'

'Sir,' Suresh replied. 'When the body was first found, the time of death was established to be around forty-eight hours prior to the discovery of the body. The standard procedure for establishing time of death is based on physiological factors like rigor mortis, decomposition, eye condition, skin condition, blood pooling, body temperature and other such indicators.' He paused.

'Go on,' Kapoor said. 'I'm with you so far, though not particularly interested in the technicalities,' he added, knowing Suresh's inclination to get into the details.

'During the detailed autopsy, however, the discrepancies began to emerge,' Suresh continued. 'Brain decay had occurred two weeks prior to the time of death, a sure sign that blood flow to the brain had ceased. This normally happens at the time of death, when the heart stops beating and circulation is affected. It starts almost immediately after death, beginning with certain areas of the brain that are responsible for our thinking and higher activities. It's irreversible.'

'Ah! That's what I want to know. How did you figure she was dead for two weeks?'

'Subcutaneous fat analysis, sir,' Suresh replied. 'If a person does not eat for a long time—two weeks is long enough—it affects the subcutaneous fat as the body starts drawing down its energy reserves. Sometimes, as with this victim, the body begins to digest muscle tissue as well.'

'She could have starved for two weeks. She could have had a stroke of some sort that blocked the blood supply to the brain and then starved to death.'

'That is a possible explanation, yes, but for the fact that there was undigested food in her stomach that was around two weeks old. Even with a stroke, part of her brain would have continued to function and her internal organs would have continued to work.'

Kapoor sat, stunned, trying to reconcile what he was hearing with his understanding of reality.

'This fact,' Suresh continued, 'combined with the presence of brain decay, makes it apparent that the girl died two weeks before her body was found.'

'That still seems like a bunch of assumptions.' Kapoor was sceptical.

'There were other indicators in the case, sir. The girl had symptoms of pneumonia as well as an internal fungal infection. And there were toxins in the tissues that only accumulate when there is a total lack of oxygenated blood supply to those tissues.'

'And that indicates that she died earlier?'

'It's like she suffered a total systems shutdown two weeks prior to the start of decomposition,' Suresh replied. 'Her brain, heart, liver, kidney, stomach and immune system, all shut down at the same time. That is the only conclusion one can reach on the basis of the physiological indicators. Moreover, the stage of progression of the illnesses—pneumonia and the fungal infection—indicated that the infections set in around the same time, or shortly after the brain decay began.'

'Her immune system would have collapsed when she died,' Kapoor mused. 'Which was much earlier. That would have allowed the infections to spread without a problem. I get it now. But it doesn't make sense. And what about the cause of death?'

'Sir,' Suresh's voice sounded strained now. 'I have nothing to add apart from what is in the autopsy report.'

'No, no,' Kapoor clarified, 'this question is off the record. How do *you* think she died?'

Suresh hesitated. 'You're asking my personal opinion?'

'Correct. I know that what you put down in the official report has to stand legal scrutiny. I'm not interested in that. Tell me your gut feel.'

'Well, sir, this case is strange. It will be a problem to establish that she was murdered, though my instinct tells me that she did not die a natural death. We'll need to wait for the detailed visceral report to come in, but I doubt that it will shed any additional light on the case.'

'So what do you think happened?' Kapoor pressed Suresh. He needed an answer even if it was a guess. 'She couldn't possibly have been murdered twice! And it seems unbelievable that she could have died of natural causes and then suddenly come back to life only to die again.'

'It really looks as if that is exactly what happened.'

'But that's pretty much impossible, isn't it?'

'Totally impossible. There's no scientific explanation for it.'

'You mean there could be a non-scientific explanation? Come on, Suresh, don't tell me you are going superstitious on me.' Kapoor felt a sense of deja vu. He remembered having a similar conversation just a few weeks ago.

But Suresh's next words chilled him.

'I'm not superstitious, sir. But there's no explanation that makes sense. The only way to explain it is that she had her soul sucked out of her.'

Chapter Six

Revision

The Forest

Maya's brow furrowed as she concentrated on recalling the lessons that Satyavachana had been giving her the past few days. It had been difficult for her to concentrate when he had been teaching her at the Gurukul, with the mysterious pull on her mind and her senses, but she had tried her best. Even meditation at the Gurukul had been difficult; today was the first day she had been able to meditate effectively and practice the concentration techniques that the Maharishi had taught her, to banish her base emotions and control her mind so that it focused on what was important rather than what was material.

'Start with the concept of a sadh,' Satyavachana urged her.

'Um, all humans are born equal, without any differentiation,' Maya began. This was the easy part. Jignesh had taught her this on her very first day. Hearing it from Satyavachana had simply reinforced it. She had no problem explaining the concept.

'We are all sadhs when we are born, with no special powers,' she went on. 'None of us is born superior to any other human or inferior to others. It is the attachment to the material world and its distractions, or the lack of it, that sets a person on the path to remaining a sadh or breaking free. Another way of explaining it is that those of us who cannot control the baser aspects of human nature—which we share with animals—remain sadhs, attached to the materialistic world, capable of using only the basic mantras and that too, without much effect. But those of us who can express the nobler aspects of human nature can use the higher mantras. Both aspects of our nature are present in all of us at birth. It is the aspects that we stress upon and develop through our lives that determine what and who we become eventually.'

'Very good. It is important to remember that no one is born a Rishi or a Kshatriya. Or, for that matter, a president, a prime minister, an Olympic gold medallist or a successful businessperson. Go on.'

Maya hesitated. This was the part at which Jignesh had stopped. She remembered that she been bored during that first lesson and least interested in the process by which people acquired yogic powers in Kaliyuga. She had wanted to get on with it and learn the mantras and other techniques that would enable her to acquire those powers.

If she could.

Jignesh, with a perspicacity that she had not understood at the time, had sensed her disconnect and had moved on to talk about mantras, which had immediately restored Maya's interest in the lesson. She realised now that, on that occasion, she had missed out on an important part of her education; something that was critical to her achieving the goal that she had set for herself on entering the Gurukul. Which was becoming a Rishi that her father, a Maharishi himself, would have been proud of.

Aware that Satyavachana was waiting for her response, she continued hesitantly, hoping that she remembered correctly what he had taught her, even if her understanding was not complete.

'Each one of us has an innate power that we are not aware of. And this power is based on the karma that we accumulate during our past lives.'

'And?'

'While the karma of our past births determines the circumstances of our present lives, what we make of our lives depends on the karma that we earn in our present life. So, even if we remain sadhs, we can become whatever we want to, depending on our decisions and actions in our present lives. Our success, or failure, depends wholly on us.'

'Excellent. See, I knew you were paying attention. Go on—how do you leave the state of being a sadh and become a Rishi? In the earlier yugas, *tapasya* was the means to acquire the *siddhis*. In today's material world, in Kaliyuga, what is the method we use in the Gurukuls?'

Maya paused to gather her thoughts. This was the difficult part. She thought she had understood the concept, but it had been so difficult to put into practice even after spending almost the entire week meditating on letting go of the old and embracing the new. That old doubt returned to nag her.

Was she really cut out to be a Rishi?

She pushed the thought aside almost as soon as it surfaced, and blurted out the answer to the Maharishi's question.

'First, we must understand that the material universe is a whole and we are all integral parts of it, connected in ways that we do not know and cannot even begin to imagine. Our manifested material world provides the illusion that distinct entities inhabit the universe. But deep down, at the very foundation of all things—living and non-living—there is a state of interconnectedness. It is invisible, and in many ways immaterial, but it is palpable. Not on the surface, in the forms and shapes that we see in each other and around us, but in the way our actions affect other people and other objects.' She paused, unsure if she had articulated the lesson correctly.

'Hmmm, not bad for a sadh,' Satyavachana remarked. 'Continue.'

'Second, it is not sufficient to understand that this remarkable oneness exists. In order to attain the siddhis, it is important to *become* one with the universe. To fold oneself into the implicate order that is unseen and unfelt. Without this ability to meld with the material universe, we can never move to the third step, to achieve our yogic powers.'

'Very good. Spot on. And what is the third step?'

'To activate the inner power that each one of us is born with—the fruit of the karma earned during our past rebirths.'

Satyavachana smiled at Maya.

'Full marks, my child. Now, what does that mean in practice? What did you do wrong when you heard the sound that you could not identify?'

'I panicked. I was terrified.'

'And what should you have done?'

'I should have focussed on repressing my fear, my emotions. Instead of freaking out, I should have tried to become one with the forest around me, the animals in the forest, the source of the sound.'

'Correct. That is exactly the point. You cannot fear something that you are connected to, that you are a part of.'

Maya nodded. 'I get it. But in the heat of the moment, it's so difficult to remember and put into practice.'

'That's understandable,' Satyavachana assured her. 'As I said, I don't expect you to be able to respond spontaneously so soon, let alone master the suppression of your emotions and the process of becoming one with the universe. Especially when something has been troubling you these last few days. We will keep trying until you become adept at it. Shall we give it one more shot now, and then call it a day? It's getting late and we really should head back to the Gurukul soon.'

Chapter Seven

The Creature

The Forest

Maya nodded. She knew she had to keep trying, however disheartening it seemed at times.

'Good.' Satyavachana smiled at her and the ball of light winked out, the darkness swallowing the form of the Maharishi and enveloping Maya once more.

To her surprise, this time the darkness faded slowly, as if the sun was rising above the horizon. She could make out the trees around her, within a radius of around ten feet or so. But Satyavachana was nowhere to be seen. She was alone.

She fought back the rising panic. This was just an exercise, she told herself. Nothing was going to happen.

Without warning, she heard a loud *plop* and ragged breathing, accompanied by a fetid stench that assailed her nostrils.

Maya froze, her blood running cold. A sense of terror filled her as she fought to control the urge to run, and slowly turned around instead.

The sight that met her eyes was out of her wildest nightmares. In the gloom, the creature stood not more than three feet away from her.

It was around five feet tall, misshapen, withered and ugly. Its hairless head had one eye and its jaw was elongated, with fierce, pointed teeth that were black with decay. Where its nose should have been were two holes which produced the breathing she had heard, as air passed through them. Its skin was like dry parchment, stretched tight against the bones of its face—so they stood out in stark relief—and its hard, wiry muscles. Although it looked thin and emaciated, it emanated an aura of immense strength.

She realised that it was the same creature she had encountered just a short while ago in the darkness of the forest. It had only one leg and one wing, a leathery cape stitched onto thin bones that ended in hooked claws. Its wing dragged across the ground as it walked, creating the horrible scraping, dragging sound she had heard.

She knew what it was. Her father had read stories of these mythical creatures to her when she was a child.

Only, this one wasn't in a story.

A *pisacha*. More specifically, a *vartika*.

The vartika stared balefully at Maya with its bloodshot eye and snarled at her. As its mouth opened, something red and viscous trickled out of one corner, along with a thick yellow fluid.

Blood? And was the yellow stuff digestive fluid? Bile?

Yuck.

One thing was for sure. The pisacha didn't have good intentions. If it liked blood, then Maya had plenty to offer. And if it ate flesh, it was in for a treat.

Maya backed up a couple of steps and the creature hobbled forward on its single leg and wing, once again producing the sound that made Maya's hair stand on end. She tried hard to focus, to remember Satyavachana's words, but how could anybody feel as one with this thing?

Nope, it just wasn't working. It was all very well to pontificate about being one with the universe, but *that* universe didn't include creatures like this.

She desperately looked for a way to quell her fear, reminding herself that the creature had been conjured up by Satyavachana; that it wasn't real.

Suddenly, the vartika let out a piercing screech and launched itself at her.

Maya screamed, unable to keep her terror in check any more. She felt the hot, fetid breath of the pisacha on her face, and then suddenly it was gone.

The ball of light winked on again and Satyavachana reappeared.

'How did I do?' Maya asked shakily. She had not yet recovered from the shock of the final moment before the pisacha disappeared, but tried to put up a brave front.

'Better. Now let's return to the Gurukul. They must be wondering where we are.'

Chapter Eight

In the Dorm

The Gurukul
Panna National Park

'A pisacha!' Adira could barely contain her excitement. 'I've never encountered one in any of my projects. I've heard they are horrible creatures. Ags had a run-in with a couple last year. He found them quite disgusting.'

The two girls were sitting in the common room. Maya was telling Adira about the day's lessons.

'Disgusting? That's an understatement.' Maya made a face. 'I freaked out. When it came for me, I thought I was done for.'

Adira laughed. 'We all go through this phase,' she told Maya. 'Only, your experience is different from mine because I'm training to be a Kshatriya and you're training to be a Rishi.'

'To *find out* if I can be a Rishi,' Maya corrected her. 'They still have the option of sending me back.' A hint of bitterness crept into her voice.

'Don't be silly.' Adira took Maya's hand in hers to comfort her. 'You're the daughter of a powerful Maharishi. The genes do get passed on, you know.'

'The trouble is,' Maya said, 'that it isn't just the genes. It's also the ability to break free from the state of being a sadh. I keep doubting if I will ever be able to do what it takes to rise above the state in which I have spent my life so far, and tap into the power that I was born with.' She sighed. 'You Kshatriyas have it so easy. For you, the genes are more important. Strength, speed, agility, and training to hone it all.'

'Hey, we need to use mantras too!' Adira was indignant. 'It isn't that easy to be a Kshatriya. There are lots of sadhs who call themselves Kshatriyas. But can they fight off the creatures of the darkness like we do?'

'True. I didn't mean to belittle your efforts,' Maya said contritely.

There was a loud banging on the front door of the cottage and both girls jumped. Someone was in a major hurry.

Adira rushed to the door and opened it.

Arjun stood there, panting as if he had just run a mile. 'Hey, is Maya here?' he asked, still panting. Adira pointed wordlessly to her friend who was sitting inside.

'There you are,' Arjun wheezed. 'You're wanted. In the Assembly Hall. Right now. The Mahamati Council is there. And so is Maharishi Satyavachana.'

Wondering what was happening, Maya hurried out of the cottage, down the Central Avenue and towards the Assembly Hall.

She had returned from her practice with Satyavachana a short while back and almost immediately the Maharishi had been whisked away by Kanakpratap. She had guessed that the Council needed to discuss something with him.

But what did they want with her?

Chapter Nine

Maya's Mission

The Assembly Hall

Maya stood before the five Mahamatis of the Council. Satyavachana, Kanakpratap and Yajnaseni were also present. Everyone wore a grim expression.

Something was wrong.

Something had happened.

Maya's heart sank.

What was it now?

She waited.

'We need your help, Maya,' Mahesh began. 'The Gurukul on the banks of the Ramganga river in Corbett National Park was attacked a while ago. We received a call for help.' He paused, struggling to find the right words. 'We've been trying to call them for the last one hour now and there's been no response.'

Maya knew that, while internet and mobile connections were non-existent in the Gurukuls, they were all connected by satellite phones.

If the Gurukul in Corbett was not responding, that could mean only one thing.

But what could she possibly do?

'You did a great job with Garuda,' Usha took over from Mahesh. 'If our Gurukul is safe today, it's because of you.'

'We don't have time for this,' Jignesh cut in sharply. 'Look, Maya, here's the situation. The Gurukul in Corbett was attacked by the Nagas. There's only one being that can save them. And there's only one person who knows where he can be found. You. We need you to go back to Dwarka and solicit Garuda's help once again.'

'I'll come with you.' Satyavachana spoke up. 'You'll get there faster with my help and you know where to find Garuda. We'll bring him back with us to Corbett.'

Maya tried to digest all of this. She had often wondered why Satyavachana had not gone to solicit Garuda's help himself, that night when the Nagas attacked the Gurukul. Surely it would have been easier and faster if he had used his powers to travel to Dwarka, locate the island and bring Garuda back? But the venerable Maharishi had insisted that Maya be the one to perform the task. And, though she had come perilously close to abandoning the mission, she had eventually succeeded.

Maya understood the importance of her role tonight, and anyway, this was not the time to figure out what her guru's motives may have been. The lives of hundreds of people were at stake.

And only she could save them.

'Let's go,' she told Satyavachana. 'I'm ready.'

Chapter Ten

Dwarka Again

The Assembly Hall

The others had left, leaving Maya with Satyavachana in the hall

'Now,' the Maharishi said, 'I am going to teach you the mantra that I used to transport us from the Gurukul to the forest today. It is one of the most important mantras—a mantra so secret that few people know it. It taps into one of the siddhis and will enable us to travel to Dwarka more swiftly than by any other means.'

Maya wondered what the mantra was. Earlier in the week, the Maharishi had very clearly told her that he would not teach her any mantras until she had mastered herself; until she was ready to learn. She knew that Satyavachana was making an exception tonight, not because he believed Maya was ready, but because the situation demanded it.

But that only increased her self-doubt instead of bolstering her confidence. If it was such a powerful and secret mantra, how would she be able to use it? Her experience in the forest that evening had already demonstrated that she was far from capable.

Satyavachana guessed her apprehensions. 'Clear your mind of all doubts, my child. I know you can master this mantra. It is the same mantra that Rishi Vyasa had imparted to Yudhisthira and which Dharmaraja, in turn, imparted to Arjuna when he sent him to Deva-lok to obtain the celestial weapons that Arjuna would use in the war of Kurukshetra. Remember, neither Arjun nor Yudhisthira were Rishis. If they could master the mantra, so can you. Never forget that you mastered a mantra that few could—the one that gained you access to the Gandharva valley.'

The Maharishi lost no time in teaching Maya the mantra and getting her enunciation right.

'Now,' Satyavachana said, when he was satisfied with the way Maya was reciting the mantra. 'This is not a mantra to be uttered.'

Maya looked at him in surprise. If she could not say the words out loud, how would she be able to use its power?

'Use it as you did when you searched for Garuda earlier,' Satyavachana told her. 'Remember, you were travelling in your atmic form and could not recite the Garuda mantra aloud. What did you do then?'

'I ... I don't know,' Maya stammered. She recalled wondering how she would use the mantra without the sound necessary to activate its power. But she had managed.

Memories of that night flooded back to her mind. She remembered her dilemma as she hovered over Dwarka, struggling with her lack of confidence. Her father. His diary. And her resolve.

That night, Maya had resolved that she was going to be a Rishi, no matter what it took. There was no way she would spend the rest of her life as a sadh. That resolve returned now, and was strengthened by the challenge at hand.

Maya thought hard. She remembered concentrating, focusing on what she had gone to Dwarka to achieve.

She closed her eyes and focused her entire being on the purpose of her mission—to find Garuda and save the Gurukul in Corbett. Nothing else mattered. As she meditated on her purpose, the other distractions slowly faded away, until a tight knot of resolve was all that remained in her mind; her sole goal.

In her mind, she recited the mantra that Satyavachana had taught her. To her surprise, the words flashed through her brain as if they were a part of her.

She focused hard on her destination—the hidden island in the midst of the ocean—and on the two of them, as instructed by Satyavachana, since they had to travel together.

After a few moments, she smelt the salty fragrance of a sea breeze and opened her eyes to find that they were both hovering over the ocean in the darkness of the night.

They had reached their destination.

In the Sky over Western India

Maya hovered in mid-air and stared at the vast black expanse that stretched below her.

Just like the last time she'd been here.

But tonight was different, quite apart from the fact that there was no moon and the stars were obscured by a cloud cover.

For one thing, she was not alone. Satyavachana was with her.

For another, she was not travelling in her atmic form. Both the Maharishi and she were physically hovering over the sea.

It was not something she would have believed was possible if it wasn't actually happening.

As she gazed at the ocean below her, she recalled her dive into its depths on the last occasion and her exploration of the ruins on the seabed, allowing herself a split second of distraction before she turned her attention to the task she had come here to accomplish.

Slowly, she recited the mantra that Satyavachana had taught her the last time she had made this trip—the mantra that would locate Garuda.

'*Om namo bhagawate garudaya trayambakaya sadhsttvastu svaha.*'

Chapter Eleven

Ramganga

The Gurukul at Ramganga
Corbett National Park

Darkness flooded the landscape below them, while dark clouds stretched across the sky. Silence reigned unbroken. With the *Pratismriti* mantra in effect, Garuda didn't need to use his wings and there seemed to be nothing else around to disturb the stillness of the night.

A cold foreboding gripped Maya's heart.

Nothing moved beneath them.

'*Ujjvalam vidyutate.*' Satyavachana broke the silence with his mantra and a bright glow spread out over the forest below them, lighting up the treetops.

And a scene of devastation.

Slowly, the trio descended to the forest floor, taking in the horrific sight that greeted their eyes in the artificial light.

It was hard to believe that a Gurukul had once stood there. There was no structure standing, only rubble and debris littering the forest floor for miles around.

The Gurukul had been entirely obliterated.

As they descended, Maya could see dark shapes scattered on the ground in all directions. As they touched down, she realised with a shock that these were bodies.

Humans. Animals. Birds.

Nothing had been spared.

It wasn't just the Gurukul that had borne the brunt of the Nagas' wrath.

Tears filled Maya's eyes as she gazed upon the corpses around them. Blood soaked the ground on which the Maharishi and she walked. Garuda had already taken to the skies to see if he could spot any signs of life from the air.

But there seemed no chance of finding anyone alive. The inhabitants of the Gurukul, and the forest around it, had been savagely attacked; bodies had been ripped apart and the pieces flung in all directions. Some of the corpses had limbs or heads missing; all had been mutilated in some way.

These people hadn't stood a chance against the brute savagery of the Nagas, Maya realised. Without the protection of Garuda, even the powers of the Sangha had been inadequate to protect them. If she had not fetched Garuda in time, the Gurukul at Panna too would have suffered much the same fate nine days ago.

Satyavachana turned to face Maya. 'There isn't much we can do here,' he said sombrely. 'We came too late. I was hoping that somehow they would have been able to hold off the Nagas until we got here. But the Sangha was not created to face adversaries from Pataala-lok. When even the Devas found it difficult to battle them, how can mere humans hope to defeat them?'

The flapping of Garuda's great wings came nearer and the celestial bird descended to the ground close to them.

Satyavachana bowed to Garuda, speaking to him in Sanskrit. 'O Garuda, we are thankful for your help. We cannot do more for the ones who lived here. We are returning to our Gurukul now and will arrange for the last rites of the dead.'

Maya understood every word, having learned Sanskrit from her father in her childhood.

Garuda responded, also in Sanskrit, 'O Maharishi, it grieves me that I could do nothing to save these people from my half-brothers and enemies, the Nagas.' Maya thought she could discern tears in the great Garuda's eyes. 'I will return now to my island and resume my devotion to the Lord.'

Maya bowed to Garuda, following Satyavachana's example, and Garuda bowed in return.

Then, with a rush of mighty wings, he was gone.

'Come,' Satyavachana told Maya. 'We must be on our way as well.' He looked at her. 'You go on to the Gurukul. Inform the Council about what we have seen and tell them what must be done.'

'You are not coming back to the Gurukul with me?'

'No. You know the *Pratismriti* mantra now. You have no need of my help.'

'But don't you need to meet the Council as well?'

Satyavachana shook his head. 'It won't take the two of us to convey the message. I have work to do. I have been extremely remiss. We left Shukra unobserved after the attack of the Nagas. I fear that I too became complacent and believed that Shukra would measure his steps after that defeat. None of us anticipated this.' He gestured at the devastation around them.

'What will you do?' Maya pressed him. 'Can I help?'

'No, my child. You have a long way to go before you can do what I plan to do.'

Maya understood what Satyavachana had in mind. The memory of another night came back to her from a couple of weeks ago; the night just before the attack on their Gurukul by the Nagas. She remembered how Satyavachana had bound her atma to his and they had both observed Shukra opening the gates to Mahatala and the Nagas emerging from it.

She also realised something that she had missed earlier. Clearly, Shukra had been under surveillance before the attack on the Gurukul. From the Maharishi's confession of complacence, it was obvious that it was he who had been keeping a watch on Shukra's movements. How else could he have known that Shukra was releasing the Nagas that night? It hadn't struck Maya then, but it was too much of a coincidence that the Maharishi had taken her to watch the entry of the Nagas into Bhu-lok on exactly the same night that they did emerge from Mahatala.

'You're going to spy on Shukra and the Nagas, aren't you?' she blurted out.

Satyavachana smiled. 'You really are persevering, child. And perspicacious too. Something strange has happened here today, which I cannot understand. Unlike the attack on your Gurukul, where the Nagas waited until it was dark to make their final assault, here they attacked in broad daylight, even before twilight fell. That is unusual. Shukra is clearly planning something big. And I want to find out what that is. So, yes, I am going to spy on him and the Nagas. And that is why you cannot come with me. You are still terribly clumsy while travelling as an atma. You will not be able to hide yourself or your thoughts from Shukra. Remember, he is also a Maharishi, and a powerful yogi, much more powerful than I am. He would spot your atma in an instant.'

'But I have seen Shukra earlier, with the entire *bhutagana*, the very first time my atma travelled, though I thought it was a dream at the time,' Maya protested. 'And Shukra didn't notice me then!'

'Hmmm.' Satyavachana looked thoughtful. 'That's strange. But you say that the entire bhutagana was present there. There must have been thousands of spirits like yours floating around and Shukra may not have noticed one new spirit among them. Whatever the explanation, we cannot count on there being enough spirits to camouflage your presence this time around. I, on the other hand, have the knowledge and ability to cloak my atma even from the eyes of a powerful yogi like Shukra. So I will be quite safe.'

Maya was silent. She knew that Satyavachana had a point. There was nothing to be gained by taking a chance. But she so badly wanted to help. Especially after tonight, after the failure to help the Gurukul at Ramganga.

'Go along now, my child,' Satyavachana patted her shoulder. 'No lessons in atma travel tonight. I'll see you in the morning, in the forest. And this time, I will not come to fetch you. You can find your way there by yourself.'

Maya nodded and bowed. She closed her eyes and opened them again, meaning to ask the Maharishi how she would find her way to the forest when she didn't know its name or location. But he was gone.

Maya was alone in the darkness.

She wondered if the spirits of the people who had died here tonight had already found a new life. Or had they also been imprisoned by Shukra?

Shrugging off these awful thoughts, she closed her eyes once more and the mantra unfolded in her mind.

Then she was gone and a deathly silence returned to shroud the forest.

Chapter Twelve

Visitors

The Gurukul
Panna National Park

Maya stood on the balcony of her dorm and breathed in the cool, sweet night air. Four days had passed since that fateful night when she had travelled to Corbett National Park in the company of Garuda and Satyavachana. Four nights since she had witnessed the horrific scene of death and destruction by the Ramganga river.

Ever since she had returned to Panna, she had kept to herself. She still had her morning lessons with Satyavachana, though her lessons on atma travel had not yet resumed; the Maharishi was apparently continuing to spy on Shukra during the night.

Maya had still not got over the shock of the carnage she had seen.

No one had.

But she had taken it especially badly. She couldn't help but think that if she had been in Panna, instead of in a remote forest practising her lessons, she may just have been able to help save the Gurukul. News of the Naga attack had reached Panna long before Satyavachana and she had returned. They had lost precious hours because no one knew where the two of them were or how to reach them.

Precious time that could have helped them avoid the carnage at Ramganga.

And all this had happened because of the strange tug, the mysterious attraction of something unknown that reached out to her, calling out to her, drawing her to itself.

As she stood on the balcony, savouring the peace and the scents of the night, she realised that the eerie sensation, the inexplicable magnetic attraction that she could not identify or understand, had ceased to matter while she was away from the Gurukul, in the forest where she received her instruction from Satyavachana. For the last few days, it had not troubled her at all.

But now, it was back to haunt her.

Maya shook her head, as if the action would help her get rid of the uneasiness that accompanied the feeling.

There was a sudden commotion as Adira and Amyra burst into the dorm.

Maya turned, surprised, the uneasiness dissipating as if it had never been there. She laughed as the two girls rushed out onto the balcony, their eyes shining with excitement.

'Maya!' Adira gasped, breathless, as if she had run all the way here without pause. 'Something is happening!'

'Come with us!' Amyra chimed in, as Adira stopped to catch her breath. 'There's a big meeting happening in the

Assembly Hall. The Mahamati Council and the visitors have gathered there.'

The Gurukul had had visitors today. The Sangha had not been sitting idle since the destruction of the Gurukul in Corbett. Word had spread among the students of a stunning new development.

Two key members of the Sangha Council—Mahamatra Vishesh and Sanghanetra Pradeep—had been victims of the Naga onslaught at Corbett. Both had had to be replaced and, more importantly, a new Mahamatra had to be elected. Subsequently, Jignesh and Amba had been nominated to the Sangha Council and, to everyone's astonishment, Jignesh had been elected the new Mahamatra. All this had been accomplished within a day of the Naga attack on the Corbett Gurukul. The Sangha, for once, had shown great urgency in making these important appointments.

Since Jignesh continued to stay at the Gurukul in Panna and teach there, the students had had to suddenly get accustomed to calling him Mahamatra instead of Mahamati. Most of them still had to get their head round it and often found themselves saying 'Mahamati ... oops, sorry, Mahamatra.' Jignesh had been surprisingly good-natured about it and patient with the students each time they flubbed his new title.

The reconstituted Sangha Council had lost no time in getting to work and performing the last rites of those who had died at Corbett. Special mantras had been chanted to try and protect the souls of the departed from Shukra's power. The site of the Gurukul was swiftly cleared and all signs of the devastation hurriedly erased so that the tragedy would never be known to the sadh world. Within two days, there was no sign that a Gurukul had ever stood on the site or that a group of people had lived secretly in the forest, away from prying eyes.

Today, the three other Sanghanetras had arrived, accompanied by two strangers, and all five visitors had been whisked away to the guesthouse before any of the students could lay eyes on them.

'I wonder what they are discussing,' Maya said, half to herself.

'Are you thinking what I am thinking?' Amyra squealed, unable to contain her excitement. 'Do you think they could be discussing ways to find the other two parts of the prophecy?'

'I suppose so.' Maya smiled at Amyra's exuberance. 'But don't get your hopes high. With Mahamatra Jignesh in charge, I think it's extremely unlikely that we'll get to be involved. There's no way he'll buy the theory that we are the *Saptas*.'

'That's why we're here,' Adira said cryptically. 'Come.' She turned and ran for the stairs without waiting or looking back to see if Maya was following. 'Arjun's got an idea.'

Amyra took Maya's hand as they followed Adira down the stairs. 'Quick!' she urged Maya. 'You have to hear Arjun's idea.'

Wondering what bright idea Arjun had come up with now, Maya allowed herself to be led by the excited novice down the stairs and to the front door of the cottage.

The Assembly Hall

'A girl called Diya Chaudhry, who was a member of the Gana has been found dead,' Jignesh informed the small gathering. 'Both her parents are Sangha members and have since been relocated to the Gurukul by the Yomgo river in Aalo. The police wanted to question them and we could not allow that.'

'Not Diya!' Yajnaseni was horrified. 'She was in Arjun's school! What happened?'

Jignesh's face was grim. 'She was murdered.'

'Impossible!' Kanakpratap interjected. 'I knew the girl. She had amazing powers. In just a couple of years she would have graduated to become a member of the Sangha. Dhruv was very fond of her and used to talk a lot about her potential. No sadh could have harmed her in any way.'

'Maharishi Ratan believes it was not a sadh who killed her,' Jignesh replied. 'He thinks it was a *vikriti*.'

'How did she die?' Anasuya, a Sanghanetra asked. 'Maharishi Ratan must have good reason to believe what he does.'

'Our sources in the police department tell us that no discernible cause of death could be established. She had a complete internal system breakdown.' Jignesh looked around. 'And the strangest part is, according to the autopsy report, her body did not decompose for two weeks after it shut down. You know what that means.'

Anasuya covered her face with her hands in horror. 'No! Poor girl!'

'Who could be responsible for this?' Mahesh wondered aloud. 'It has to be someone with highly developed siddhis.'

'Vikritis do not have the ability to do something like this,' Diksha, another Sanghanetra from outside the Gurukul said. 'The pancha vikritis were the last of their ilk to have the powers that we possess. The vikritis of today are a shadow of those Maharishis.'

'True,' Mahesh agreed. 'We have confronted vikritis of different hues and always found them to be weak.'

'If it was not the vikritis,' Jignesh replied, 'who else could it be?'

Chapter Thirteen

Arjun Has an Idea

The Gurukul

Arjun was waiting outside the door, along with Tanveer, Agastya and Varun, hopping from one foot to another. His face wore an expression of undisguised impatience.

'What's the matter with you guys?' he complained as the three girls burst out of the door. 'You took forever!'

Adira frowned at him. 'Tell Maya.'

'So here's the deal.' Arjun got straight to the point. 'They're holding a Sangha Council meeting. Which means they're going to be discussing the prophecy, Shukra and us. Right?'

'I don't know, AJ.' Maya was trying hard to control her excitement. 'I really doubt if they're going to be talking about us. But I guess they'll tell us later, won't they, if it involves us?'

'That's just the point,' Varun chimed in. 'They'll tell us only what they want us to know. The rest will be censored. You know how the Sangha works!'

'I have a plan,' Arjun told Maya. 'But you have to agree.'

'Oh no.' Maya could see where Arjun was going with his idea. 'You can't be serious!'

'Of course! That's the only way we can get to know exactly what they are saying about us!'

'No way, AJ! We'll get into trouble!' Maya didn't know what horrified her more: the fact that she had guessed what Arjun's idea was or that Arjun could have come up with such a wild idea in the first place.

'The first time you and I are in agreement,' Agastya chimed in. 'I told him the same thing. Mahamatra Jignesh will have our heads if we are discovered. Remember that he leads the Sangha now.'

'But there's no way they can find out!' Arjun persisted, looking at Adira and Amyra for support, his eyes urging them to persuade Maya.

'Will anyone be able to see you, apart from Maharishi Satyavachana?' Adira asked Maya. 'I'm sure he wouldn't give you away—he's a decent sort.'

Maya thought for a moment. 'I don't think anyone else in the Gurukul can,' she replied, 'but I don't know about the Sangha Council. Suppose they can?'

'Come on, Maya.' Amyra slipped her hand into Maya's. 'We'd love to get a first-hand briefing on what's happening in there. And you're the only one who can do it.'

'Ringside seats,' Varun added with a chuckle. 'Can't ask for more.'

'I don't know,' Maya said unhappily. Part of her wanted to do it. And part of her was vehemently opposed to the idea. If they hadn't been invited to the meeting, they were not supposed to be there. So how could she justify being an uninvited, and probably unwanted, presence at the Council?

She looked at Tanveer. She still didn't know him too well, but whatever she had seen of him in the last few weeks told her that, even though he didn't speak much, he was sensible.

'What do you say, Tanveer?'

The archer shrugged. 'I'd say we are breaking the rules, but,' he broke into a grin, 'I have to admit I'm curious.'

Maya sighed. 'Fine, I'll do it.'

'Yessss!' Arjun was jubilant. 'You're a true sport. We'll be waiting here for you.'

Maya shook her head and re-entered the cottage, heading towards the dorm. Adira and Amyra took up positions on the floor outside the door to the dorm to ensure that no one disturbed Maya while she slept.

Chapter Fourteen

The Sangha Council

The Assembly Hall

Maya found herself floating high above the gathering in the Assembly Hall. The five Sanghanetras sat in a semicircle, with Jignesh in the centre, flanked by Amba and the three visitors from the other Gurukuls.

Facing them sat the three other members of the Mahamati Council—Mahesh, Usha and Parth—along with Kanakpratap and Yajnaseni. Ratan Tiwari had returned to Delhi, his job of chaperoning Maya now over. As a senior Sangha member, he had responsibilities to fulfil in his job at the university.

On either side of the Sangha Council, between the Sanghanetras and the others, sat the two strangers who had arrived earlier today at the Gurukul. Maya wondered who they were.

She had heard that the structure of the Sangha allowed the Sanghanetras to perform a dual role—as members of the Sangha Council and also as members of the Mahamati Council at their Gurukul. As a result, Jignesh and Amba served on both councils after their elevation.

Maya guided herself upwards until she was close to the highest point of the conical roof. Until now, all that she had been capable of doing was transporting her spirit from one point to another using thought, but Satyavachana had shown her how to guide her atma and manoeuvre it so that she could navigate away from, or towards, or even around anything. Maya had learned fast and was getting better at it by the day.

Satyavachana was missing. Maya wondered where the Maharishi was. Surely he knew about the council meeting. Whatever the reason, Maya was relieved since she could eavesdrop without the fear of anyone knowing she was there.

An animated discussion was in full flow below her. Maya realised they were talking about Shukra and his plans. She had clearly missed part of the discussion.

'We must not underestimate Shukra, Sriram,' Jignesh was saying, with his customary asperity, addressing one of the Sanghanetras. 'He is a powerful and highly intelligent Maharishi. Remember what Lord Krishna said about his intellect and wisdom. For too long has the Sangha underestimated Shukra. And we have seen where that has got us. For once let us be realistic!'

'We have to consider all possibilities, Mahamatra,' Anasuya spoke up. 'We never thought that he would send the Nagas to attack a second Gurukul. We cannot rule anything out.'

Jignesh was resolute. 'I do not believe that he will unleash the Nagas upon the sadhs. If that had been his objective, he would have done it already. It would have been far easier to decimate the sadhs than fight the Sangha. If he had let the Nagas loose upon Bhu-lok earlier, we would have all been caught by surprise and unable to muster our resources in time.'

'Then we must be ready for an attack on one of the other Gurukuls,' Diksha interjected. 'Isn't that a real danger ?

Instead of answering, Jignesh looked at the roof, directly at the spot where Maya was hovering. He frowned, and Maya immediately rose higher, clinging to the ceiling. Did Jignesh have the ability to see her atma? She wouldn't have thought it possible. Then he turned his attention back to the discussion and Maya floated lower, to hear more clearly.

'We must not forget,' Kanakpratap joined the conversation, 'that Shukra is bent on killing Arjun. He knows about the prophecy and surely he will do everything to destroy the One who is destined to lead us against him?'

Jignesh shook his head. 'If that was the case, he would have led the Nagas himself against us. He has attacked this Gurukul twice, but was not present on either occasion. It would have been far easier for him to overcome us in person. Why send Vishwaraj and the Nagas? Poor replacements for Shukra, surely. He knew that we would not have been able to defend ourselves against his power. So his absence doesn't make sense.'

'He could have been testing us,' Yajnaseni suggested. The other members of the Mahamati Council nodded in agreement, recalling their conversation about this very possibility on the night that Arjun and Maya had arrived at the Gurukul. It was Yajnaseni who had brought it up then too. 'Shukra may have been wanting to see how strong we are; what resources we have at our command. Whether we are capable of fighting his proxies and how we respond to their assault on the Gurukul. He could not have foreseen that we would find deliverance. Now he knows that we have a defence against the Nagas.'

'That is possible,' Jignesh agreed. 'But it doesn't explain why he attacked the Gurukul in Corbett. He knew we had Garuda to bank upon. Yet he unleashed the Nagas a second time. We never anticipated that. We thought that the fear of Garuda would restrain the Nagas from any further attacks. How could Shukra and the Nagas be so certain that we would not be able to call Garuda in time to save the other Gurukul? It would have made more sense for him to attack the sadhs rather than another Gurukul.' He paused. 'We're going round in circles. We're back to where we started and we're none the wiser about Shukra's motives.'

Even as he spoke, the doors to the Assembly Hall flew open.

All eyes turned towards the entrance.

It was Satyavachana.

And he didn't look happy at all.

Chapter Fifteen

Arguments

The Assembly Hall

'It is useless to sit here and speculate about Shukra and his motives.' Satyavachana began speaking even as he strode from the entrance to the small group at the opposite end of the hall. 'We need to act. And it seems that we have a window of opportunity, however small it may be, to begin our work.'

'What do you mean, Maharishi?' Jignesh asked. 'What window of opportunity?'

'The reason I am late for this Council is because I have been spying on Shukra,' Satyavachana announced. 'I have had him under surveillance for the last few days. And what I have witnessed today only goes to prove that we simply cannot predict what he will do next.' He paused to give his next words greater effect. 'Shukra has sent the Nagas back to Mahatala.'

Surprise and bafflement registered on everyone's faces. Even Maya, floating above them, was taken aback.

'I don't understand.' Mahesh was the first to break the silence, echoing the thoughts of every person present there. 'Why should the Nagas return to Mahatala? Why would

Shukra release them only to send them back?' He shook his head. 'It just doesn't make sense.'

Jignesh frowned. 'There's something wrong,' he mused. 'I cannot put my finger on it, but it seems to me that Shukra is playing a deeper game than we can understand. If he was testing us, then what was he testing us for? The strength of our power? Our resources? Our knowledge of the means to fight the inhabitants of Pataala-lok? No, no, no! There's more to this than meets the eye.'

He paused and held Satyavachana's gaze, wagging his index finger for emphasis. 'It is not an exercise in futility to try and understand Shukra's motives. They may hold the key to our survival, and that of humanity.'

Jignesh turned and looked at each of the Sanghanetras in turn. 'We must find out what Shukra is really after. What he wants to achieve. Why he has returned after 5,000 years.'

'Isn't his aim to open the gates of the five levels of Pataala and allow the Nagas, Asuras and Rakshasas to take over Bhu-lok?' Kanakpratap looked puzzled. 'I thought that was obvious. That's what he tried to do 5,000 years ago, when the Saptarishis and Devas stopped him.'

'Maybe.' Jignesh had a thoughtful look in his eyes. 'Maybe. But I can't help feeling that the attacks on the Gurukul were not solely because of Arjun's presence here. And that there is a deeper motive that underlies everything that Shukra is doing. We need to find out what that is. We cannot stop him unless we know what he is planning.'

Sriram nodded. 'There is reason in what you say, but we have no way of figuring it out.'

'Look at the pattern,' Jignesh replied. 'Shukra has surprised us every time we thought we knew what he was going to do. He has been highly unpredictable. After Allahabad, he disappeared for fourteen years, then suddenly resurfaced in Delhi at Dhruv's house. What was he doing for fourteen years? And how did he know where to find Dhruv? Then, he sent his monster army against our Gurukul. When that failed, he opened the gates to Mahatala and released the Nagas, inflicting them upon us. After we sought, and obtained, the help of Garuda, instead of retreating, he sent the Nagas against a second Gurukul, despite knowing that we have access to Garuda.'

'There is no pattern, Mahamatra,' Diksha said.

'Exactly.' Jignesh jabbed a finger in the air. 'There is no pattern. But there should be. If he was solely concerned with finding and opening the gates to the five levels of Pataala-lok that matter to him, there would be a pattern. Why isn't there one?'

'That's a lot of speculation, Mahamati,' Satyavachana addressed Jignesh. 'You may be correct about Shukra's motives. But you may also be hopelessly wrong about them, you know.'

Maya noticed that Satyavachana had not once used the honorific titles for either Jignesh or the other members of the Sangha Council. He addressed Jignesh only as Mahamati. She found it curious and wondered why.

'Who among us here can hope to be absolutely certain of what is correct?' Jignesh's voice could have cut through steel. 'But we need to do something. We cannot sit and wait for Shukra to take us by surprise yet again.'

'We need to push ahead swiftly with our plan,' Anasuya asserted. 'We have had fourteen years to prepare and this is the time to move.'

'True,' Satyavachana responded. 'Yet, what have you achieved after all your preparation? Shukra is stronger than ever. And we have no means to defeat him, not yet. You had planned for Vishawaraj to partner with Arjun, hadn't you? The young Rishi joining forces with the One to defeat Shukra. Well, that plan lies in tatters now. Your young saviour has gone over to Shukra, hasn't he?'

Silence greeted him. He had apparently touched a raw nerve.

'Oh yes,' Satyavachana continued, without waiting for them to respond. 'I too have heard the legends. About the third part of the prophecy—the one hidden in Deva-lok. I may have left the Sangha to live by myself in my ashram two centuries ago, but I know how the Sangha thinks. I don't need to be actively involved to know your plan. You have tried to plan events in such a way that they match the legends. Is that not correct?'

Maya was taken aback. Satyavachana had left the Sangha two hundred years ago? She hadn't thought he was a day over sixty. How old was he then? Her mind boggled.

'That is so, Maharishi,' Sriram replied after a moment's hesitation, having overcome his initial surprise at Satyavachana's accurate divination of the Sangha's plan to counter Shukra. 'I agree that we did not anticipate that Vishwaraj would desert the Sangha. But all is not lost. We still have Agastya. He may not be as powerful as Vishwaraj, but there is no other young Rishi in the Gana who can match up to him. We will yet forge a partnership between Arjun and Agastya that will fulfil the third part of the prophecy.'

Chapter Sixteen

Farewell, Now

The Entrance to Mahatala

The last of the Nagas had disappeared into the gaping portal that served as the gateway to Mahatala-lok. Only Kuhaka, Kâlya and Takshaka remained outside the portal with Shukra.

The three Nagas bowed to the Guru of the Asuras.

Takshaka gave him a quizzical look. 'We obey your command, Wise One,' he said. 'I am no one to question your intentions and plans. But I still do not understand. Why ask us to return to our world? We had forgotten what it was like to walk free in Bhu-lok. Wouldn't it be easier to decimate the humans who inhabit this world and rule it ourselves? These are not the humans that we mingled with in Dwapara-yuga. Those were noble beings, powerful and upright. These humans do not deserve the freedom and luxuries they enjoy in Bhu-lok.'

Shukra shook his head. 'No, Prince of the Nagas,' he replied. 'Not yet. The time will come when you will have the run of Bhu-lok.' He looked around. 'Soon ... soon. The power of Kali grows stronger. I can feel it.'

He looked at the three Nagas. 'This is not the time,' he repeated.

'Then why open the gate to Mahatala at all, Wise One?' Kâlya asked. 'What purpose did that serve? Why bring us back into Bhu-lok only to send us back?'

'I told you earlier,' Shukra replied patiently. 'I needed to know if the Sangha was ready and prepared. They are not. And I wanted to send them a message, which I have. Now, I need to get back to the work that is necessary to carry out my plan.' He folded his hands in a polite dismissal. 'So you must bide your time. Be patient. The time will come. That is my promise to you.'

Takshaka nodded. 'We will wait, Son of Bhrigu. We know that you will fulfil your promise to us. You will not let us down. Farewell, now.'

The three Nagas bowed again and strode through the portal without a backward glance, disappearing as they passed through it. When they had all vanished, Shukra looked thoughtfully at the portal for a moment, then waved his hand in a swift motion across the open gate and the darkness beyond it, the mantra for sealing it unfolding in his mind.

The portal snapped shut and was gone.

The Son of Bhrigu lingered for a few moments, his forehead creased in thought. He was not happy. Things were not going according to plan.

He had to work out a new strategy now.

Then he too disappeared.

Chapter Seventeen

A Plan

The Assembly Hall
The Gurukul
Panna National Park

Maya was surprised to hear that Vishwaraj had been groomed to partner with Arjun. She knew that when projects were assigned by the Gurukul, the prospective Gana members always worked in pairs—one Rishi and one Kshatriya—their skills, powers and mantras complementing each other. But she had never realised how important Vishwaraj had been to the Sangha and how devastating his apostasy had been. She was equally surprised to hear that Agastya was the Sangha's choice to replace Vishwaraj. While she knew that Agastya had highly developed yogic powers and was one of the brightest stars in the Gana firmament, she didn't quite like him. She had found him to be brusque, rude, condescending, and, worst of all from her perspective, always kowtowing to the Sangha.

'Rubbish,' she heard Satyavachana say, intruding on her thoughts. 'You do not have the time for that. You have spent the better part of the last decade grooming Arjun and Vishwaraj, have you not? That was when Shukra was not around. Now, Shukra has reappeared. This is no time to be training anyone to face him. Whoever battles him now must be fully prepared, fully trained and ready. Arjun may be a scion of Yayati, but he is far from ready to take on the role of leading us against Shukra.' He looked at Kanakpratap. 'Isn't that so, Kanak?'

'He will be ready soon,' Kanakpratap admitted grudgingly.

'Soon. But will it be soon enough?'

No one spoke.

Satyavachana was not finished yet. 'As for your plan to pair Arjun and Agastya, you are going out on a limb on the strength of speculation. What if the legend about the third part of the prophecy is wrong? What then? It is just a legend, after all. We have no time to make any more mistakes.'

Jignesh fixed him with a steady gaze. 'I agree with you, Maharishi. I have always felt that the Sangha has been shooting in the dark for the last fourteen years. Yes, we had a plan, but clearly, it hasn't worked. Today, let's face it, we are woefully unprepared to face Shukra. The One is not ready and we have not yet found the weapons from the prophecy.'

Satyavachana bowed. 'Thank you, Mahamati. Your candour is refreshing. I cannot say the same about the other Mahamatras I have encountered in the last three hundred years.'

There was a moment of silence.

Maya's mind boggled even more. So Satyavachana, *her* teacher, was more than three hundred years old? What was his true age?

'We need to find out what Shukra is planning,' Jignesh repeated. 'Unless we know that, we are only guessing. Like we have been for the last fourteen years.'

Satyavachana shook his head. 'No, no, no.' He looked at Jignesh. 'Just when I thought there was something we agreed on!'

Maya was amused. She had always liked the Maharishi, having got over her initial fear of his power and temperament; and over the last few days she had grown fonder of him. He was the exact opposite of what she had expected in someone who was supposed to be the most powerful Maharishi alive. He was patient, understanding and fun, yet firm, and she loved his quirky sense of humour. Unlike Jignesh, who was stern, forbidding and unbending.

'What do you have in mind, Maharishi?' Jignesh asked him.

Satyavachana stared back at him, unblinking. 'You already know,' he said, lowering his voice. 'You were there when I told the Sangha Council fourteen years ago.'

'There was never any evidence for the existence of the *Ranakarman Parva*,' Diksha intervened. 'And there is none even today.'

'The practical problem with your plan has not gone away either,' Sriram joined in. 'We cannot travel to Deva-lok to retrieve the part of the prophecy that is hidden there, forget about searching for it. And the Gandharvas would never permit us to mount a search in Gandharva-lok for their part of the prophecy. Finding the remaining two parts remains impossible.'

Satyavachana was silent for a few moments.

'Nothing is impossible,' he said finally. 'We are limited only by our thinking, by the boundaries that we set for ourselves. Is that not what you teach the novices who come to the Gurukuls? Then why are we limiting our own capabilities?'

Maya wondered what the *Ranakarman Parva* was and why Satyavachana had not addressed Diksha's argument. But Satyavachana was speaking again.

'There is a way to carry out my plan. And, contrary to what you think, there is evidence today that I was right all those years ago. But I will tell you only if you are ready to believe what I say. I will not be humiliated the way I was fourteen years ago.'

Chapter Eighteen

Discovered

The Assembly Hall

Jignesh leaned forward in his chair, his eyes boring into Satyavachana. 'What is that evidence, Maharishi? You have my word that we will hear you out.'

Before Satyavachana could reply, however, Jignesh abruptly looked up again, directly at her. 'Wait,' he said, holding up a hand. 'I've been sensing a presence here in this hall for a while now.' He looked sharply at Satyavachana. 'Do you not feel it?'

Satyavachana nodded but said nothing.

'Is this another ploy of Shukra's?' Jignesh's tone was hard now. He rose.

All of a sudden, Maya sensed a thought reaching out to her. *'Go, Maya, flee now! Stay no longer! You are in grave danger!'*

Maya realised that it was Satyavachana warning her. Jignesh was going to do something that would put her in peril. Thankful for the Maharishi's warning, she turned her thoughts to her dorm and was back in her own body in an instant.

She jerked awake roughly as her atma re-entered her body. Driven by Satyavachana's alarm, she had failed to practice the 'soft landing' as Satyavachana called it—the gentle and calm re-entry of the atma into the body. It was not easy to master but Maya had at least learned to stop waking up with a jerk after she returned to her body; the technique also helped her to swiftly overcome the lassitude that normally overcame her after a bout of spirit travel.

Maya lay in bed for a few moments, listless and drained, then fought to stand up and stagger to the door. She opened it and Adira and Amyra sprang up. They quickly supported her and began guiding her back to her bed.

'No, no,' Maya insisted weakly. 'I'll be better soon. Let's catch up with the boys. We need to talk.'

Chapter Nineteen

Satyavachana Explains

The Assembly Hall

'It's gone.' Jignesh sounded baffled. 'I sensed it all this while and then suddenly it was gone.' He returned to his seat and turned his attention to Satyavachana. 'You were going to present us with some evidence.'

'Indeed.' Satyavachana sat down. He had been standing all this while.

The others waited.

'Let me jog your memory a bit first,' Satyavachana began. 'When I first told the Sangha Council, fourteen years ago, about the *Ranakarman Parva*, I also told you what it contained. Of course, it is a different matter that none of you believed me at the time, except for Dhruv. I will reiterate now that the book contains mantras that the Devas used during their decisive victory against the Asuras and the Nagas. Now, the big problem that we have always faced is that we have no way of knowing where the gates of Pataala-lok are located. Only Shukra knows that. And even if we did know their location, what could we have done? There is no mantra powerful enough to seal the gates against Shukra's power to open them. My plan was, and still is, to find the parva and use the mantras contained in it to defend ourselves against the Asuras and the Nagas, whenever they are released by Shukra.' He paused and looked at the others to emphasise the point he was about to make. 'If we had found the book—and we had fourteen years to do it—we would not have lost a Gurukul and all the people in it.'

There was a hushed silence as the import of his words sank in.

'And the evidence?' Jignesh pressed him.

'As I said, Maharishi Dhruv was the only one who believed me. He told me, in private, that whatever the Sangha said— and we all know that the Sangha had a lot to say to me at that time—he would search for the book. And he did. I believe he found the book. But he told no one about it. Why, I do not know.'

'The diary!' A sudden realisation dawned on Kanakpratap. 'The verses in *Brahmabhasha*! Of course! That makes sense. The *Ranakarman Parva*, if used by the Devas, would have had mantras in Brahmabhasha.'

Satyavachana smiled. 'My thoughts exactly. That is why the diary was so special. Maya told me that Dhruv asked her to pick up only one thing from the house before she fled. The diary. Why? Because he wanted to keep it away from Shukra. He knew it was the only thing that stood between us and the doom of humanity.'

'You may be right, Maharishi,' Sriram said. 'And if that is the case, this will indeed be a powerful weapon in our defence.

But how are we to know that you are right? We have no way of reading the verses.'

'As I said before, there is a way to carry out my plan. The means exist today to decipher the verses in the diary and find the remaining parts of the prophecy. We also need to know what we have to do in order to find the weapons to counter Shukra. Just having a defence against him is not sufficient.'

Satyavachana leaned forward and lowered his voice.

'I have a plan,' he said.

Chapter Twenty

Shukra Reflects

Shukra's Cavern

As Shukra returned to the darkness of the cavern, he realised that someone else was already there. His mind evoked the need for light and the cave was immediately illuminated by an unseen source, revealing a young man of around nineteen or twenty years, seated on a rock.

He rose as Shukra appeared and bowed with his hands folded in a silent namaskar. '*Pranaam*, Poorvapitamah,' he greeted Shukra.

Shukra raised a hand in benediction. '*Bhagavadanugraha-praaptirastu*, my child.'

'You summoned me, Poorvapitamah?'

'Indeed, I did.' The light in the cavern grew brighter, illuminating their features. 'You have done well. Your leadership of the Nagas was commendable and your powers grow by the day. I am proud of you. But now, I have more work for you.'

The boy smiled at the praise and bowed his head slightly in acknowledgement. 'It is your blood that runs through my veins, after all, Poorvapitamah.'

Shukra gazed upon his descendant, noting the change that had taken place in the young man in just two weeks. He remembered how he had had to convince him to lead the Nagas to attack the Gurukul in Panna just two weeks ago.

Vishwaraj had looked up at Shukra, his face troubled, when Shukra had given him his instructions. 'But is it necessary to allow the Nagas to kill all those people? They were my brothers and sisters when I was with the Gana.' He shook his head. 'It will be difficult for me to watch the Nagas slaughter them mercilessly, as I know they will. The Gurukul stands no chance. They …'

Words had failed him.

Shukra had advanced and held the boy by his shoulders. There was affection in the gesture, and warmth.

'I know how you feel, Vishwaraj.' Shukra's voice had been gentle. 'But it is inevitable.' He looked Vishwaraj in the eye. 'This is war, my son. And the Sangha is the enemy. It is your dharma, and mine, to fight them, even if they were related to us by blood; just as Arjuna fought his own cousins, the Kauravas, and his Guru Drona on the fields of Kurukshetra. That was *his* dharma. And if they have to die, well, that is ineluctable, isn't it? You have chosen your side. You must stand by what you believe is *your* dharma, come what may.'

'I understand, Poorvapitamah,' Vishwaraj had replied. 'But it is difficult. Just like the death of Diya. I didn't mean for her to die!'

Shukra had nodded. 'I know, my child, I know. That was an unfortunate outcome. Whether you were too powerful for her or she was too weak to withstand the strain of being possessed by your atma, she died the moment you used your siddhis to take over her body. But you did what you had to. And you succeeded. That is important. Nothing else matters.'

Vishwaraj had stood silent for a few moments and Shukra had allowed him to ruminate. The boy was young, though powerful in the siddhis, and he would learn that life was rough, especially in Kaliyuga. But he would pull through. Everyone did.

Finally, Vishwaraj had looked up from his silent musing. 'I will do your bidding, Poorvapitamah. And I will come back victorious!'

'I know you will, my son,' Shukra had told him. And, true to his word, Vishwaraj had delivered. If it had not been for Garuda's wholly unexpected appearance, the Gurukul in Panna would have been annihilated. Just like the one in Corbett.

And now, Shukra reflected, just two weeks later, the young man had not only accepted his dharma but was yearning to prove himself a worthy descendant of the Son of Bhrigu.

'What is your command, Poorvapitamah? Tell me and I will do as you instruct.' Vishwaraj bowed to Shukra and waited.

'I have lost more than three weeks,' Shukra told him, his brow furrowing with concern. 'I found the boy, and now know that there is no threat from him, but that distraction has cost me time. Time that is extremely valuable.'

'But what is three weeks, Poorvapitamah? You have waited 5,000 years. In comparison, three weeks is just a blink of an eye.'

Shukra shook his head. 'You do not understand, child. The power of Kali grows rapidly. I must be ready when his power is at its peak. Otherwise everything—my tapasya, my careful planning, the long wait—will all have been in vain.'

'Then why send the Nagas back?' Vishwaraj wanted to know. 'There is so much more that we could have done, so much that they could have helped us with. The Sangha would have been powerless if we had allowed the Nagas to spread out across the country. Especially with the powers that you have helped me acquire.'

'You know why I released the Nagas,' Shukra replied, frustration lining his voice. 'I needed to search their world and needed them gone for a while. While they were busy with the Gurukuls, I travelled the length and breadth of Mahatala, searching high and low for the missing mantras, but in vain. I have to continue the search now, and the Nagas would only have been in the way. I had to send them back.'

He looked directly at Vishwaraj. 'And remember, the use of force and violence to achieve one's goals is the refuge of the weak or the desperate. When I can get what I want through the use of intelligence, cunning and guile, why should I resort to brute force and mayhem?' He shook his head. 'No, I have to find the exact location of the mantras. There is no other way.'

He clenched his fists. It was extremely frustrating. He knew where his eventual destination lay, but the means to reach it eluded him. There had been a ray of hope when he had received assurance from his mysterious source—the one who had introduced him to Vishwaraj—that the key to executing his plan was within reach. But then his source had suddenly vanished without a trace, which meant that Shukra would have to continue on his path by himself. The one consolation was that he had learned a lot from reading Dhruv's mind before the Maharishi died. He knew it was possible to find what he needed without help from the mysterious source who had deserted him.

Difficult, but possible.

'So you want my help with locating the mantras?' Vishwaraj guessed. 'But how will I do that? If you haven't succeeded, how can I hope to find them?'

Shukra shook his head. 'No, my son. I need you to do something else.'

Vishwaraj waited as Shukra outlined his plan.

The boy's eyes widened when he finished. 'Truly, there is no intelligence greater than yours, Poorvapitamah.' His eyes shone with unabashed admiration and devotion. 'I bow to you. I will do what you ask, though it will take some time to accomplish. Victory will be yours.'

'Do your best,' Shukra told him, 'but time is one thing I do not have. Kali's power will reach its peak soon. I cannot say how soon. It could be ten years or it could be two years. But I have to be ready by then.'

The boy nodded and folded his hands. 'I will start today. Now. *Pranaam*, Poorvapitamah.'

He vanished.

Shukra gazed into the distance, the light in the cavern dimming as he ruminated on his plans. There was so much to do and so little time. It was good in a way, he reflected, that his meditation had been disturbed by the birth of the boy. He had been interrupted just in time. A few years more, and the most opportune time would have passed. He would still have been able to achieve success, but it would have taken more effort, more time, and all his power. As it turned out, he was now in a position of great strength.

The Sangha was not ready.

The One was woefully unprepared.

The power of Kali was about to peak.

Nothing could stop him now.

All he had to do was find what he had been searching for these past fourteen years.

Chapter Twenty-one

The Council Agrees

The Assembly Hall
The Gurukul
Panna National Park

'What you propose is outrageous!' Jignesh fulminated as Satyavachana finished explaining his plan. 'I promised we would hear you out, and we have. But your plan is … is preposterous!'

Satyavachana said nothing, but sat staring back at Jignesh, his face impassive. He had expected this outburst.

'Do you really believe that the girl will survive exposure to the Mists?' Anasuya asked, sounding doubtful. 'She is a sadh. Maybe she has some powers. But so far, from what I have heard, there is no evidence that she has what it takes to be a member of the Gana.'

'She cannot recite even the basic mantras, forget mantras for the manipulation of matter,' Jignesh snapped. 'I have worked with her.' He looked at the Maharishi. 'So have you. What has your experience been?'

Satyavachana nodded. 'I agree with your observation. But how do you explain the fact that she can use the highest class of mantras like the *Pratismriti* and *Gandharva* mantras?'

There was no response.

'I believe,' Satyavachana continued, 'that she is able to tap into some yogic power that enables her to use the higher mantras. Somehow, this is possible even though she does not yet have the ability to use any of the lower categories. I cannot explain it. I have never seen anything like it before. But there it is. She used the *Pratismriti* to travel with me to Dwarka and then to return to Panna after Garuda left us.'

'The *Pratismriti* can be used by Kshatriyas as well, if taught properly,' Diksha said. 'It is not essential to have yogic powers to use it. You taught Maya the mantra and she was able to use it. That makes her a bit more than a sadh. But not much. It really doesn't prove anything.'

'There could be something to what Maharishi Satyavachana says,' Amba said slowly. 'I remember that Maharishi Ratan had made a revelation the night Arjun and Maya first arrived in this Gurukul.' She looked at Jignesh. 'Do you remember, Mahamatra, what he told us about Maya's knowledge of mantras?'

Jignesh looked thoughtful. 'I do,' he admitted. 'He said that she knew the *Narsimha* mantra without having been taught how to recite it.' He shook his head. 'But that's preposterous. Remember, Maharishi Ratan was only speculating. He could have been wrong.'

'The girl is capable of atma travel,' Amba pointed out, 'without having been taught how to do it.'

Satyavachana shrugged. 'There's only one way to find out. If I am right, then Maya may be the key to unlocking the secrets of Dhruv's diary. The Mists of Brahma may help.'

'No one has been into the Mists since Tribhuvan,' Sriram interjected. 'And that was almost 4,000 years ago.'

'I have entered the Mists,' Satyavachana said, his voice low. 'A few centuries ago. It is not an impossible task.'

'It is dangerous,' Jignesh persisted. 'Why *you* entered the Mists, I don't know, but you were either brave or foolhardy. There is a fine line between courage and foolishness. No one in the Sangha would consider it prudent to enter the Mists after the Devas proscribed it for humans. Maya is just a child. And a sadh at that. It is the responsibility of the Sangha to protect humanity, not put sadhs in grave peril to achieve our purposes.'

'This is not something for the Sangha to decide,' Satyavachana said quietly. 'I am not asking for permission. I am only telling you my plan. It will help the Sangha and all of humanity. But, even if you forbid me, I will go ahead and do it. Remember, I renounced the Sangha a long time ago. Just because I have returned to confer with you and aid you does not mean I am returning to the fold. If I assist you now, it is only because the very future of humanity is at stake.'

There was silence again. Everyone present in the room knew that the Maharishi was dead serious and meant every word.

'There is something I know about Maya that none of you do,' Satyavachana continued, not waiting for a response. 'Five years ago, when she was just ten years old, Dhruv contacted me. He and I had been in touch because he was searching for the *Ranakarman Parva*. He told me something about Maya that I cannot disclose to you because he swore me to secrecy. But it is on the basis of this knowledge that I believe that Maya might brave the Mists and survive; and in doing so, perhaps find us the key to decipher the Brahmabhasha verses in the diary.'

'And if you are wrong?' Jignesh looked at the Maharishi. 'You say "might" and "perhaps". If you are wrong, you know what will happen to her. Are you prepared to take that risk and live with that decision?'

'I will spend sufficient time over the next few months preparing her for the experience,' Satyavachana replied, holding Jignesh's gaze. 'She will not go unprepared. I will ensure that she is equipped to deal with the Mists before I take her there. I will be with her all the way.'

Usha shook her head. 'You cannot go into the Mists with her. That would defeat the very purpose of taking her there. She will have to enter the Mists herself.'

'I know that,' Satyavachana replied calmly. 'I will accompany her there. Once she enters the Mists, she will be on her own. As I said, I will prepare her well, so she will know what she must do.' He paused. 'I believe that I am right. But, if I am wrong, what happens to Maya will be the least of our worries.'

Chapter Twenty-two

Disappointment

The Gurukul

The three girls made their way outside the cottage where the four boys were waiting. Maya had almost fully recovered by the time they reached.

'Well?' Arjun demanded, as he spotted them. 'What happened?'

'I got thrown out,' Maya admitted sheepishly. 'Mahamatra Jignesh couldn't see me, but he could sense my presence. Maharishi Satyavachana warned me to leave before I got into trouble.'

'I told you she shouldn't have gone,' Agastya broke in. 'We could all have got into a lot of trouble. Remember our last jaunt to the Gandharva valley?'

'Come on, Ags, don't be a wet blanket,' Varun chuckled. 'Look, nothing happened. No one knows she was there, except for the Maharishi. And I'm sure he's cool about it.'

'I do have some news,' Maya said. 'Let's walk down to the classroom block, shall we?'

The seven children made their way past the Assembly Hall and towards the classrooms. No one ventured there at this time, so they were by themselves.

'Okay, so spill the beans.' Arjun was beside himself with impatience.

Maya told them what she had heard while she was inside the hall.

Varun chuckled when she got to the part about Arjun and Agastya being groomed to pair up together. 'Never thought I'd see the day,' he said, clapping the two boys on their shoulders. 'Fancy that! You two fighting together!'

'So that was the Sangha's plan,' Arjun said slowly, once Maya had finished. 'And Vishwaraj put an end to it.' He looked at Maya. 'And you didn't get a chance to hear what the Maharishi's plan was?'

Maya shook her head. 'No idea. All I know is that it involves the book I told you about—the *Ranakarman Parva*—and the two missing parts of the prophecy.'

'I think part of the plan will involve finding the missing parts of the prophecy,' Tanveer spoke up.

'Well, we know that Visvavasu, at least, thinks that is the way forward,' Adira said. 'That's what he told Maya, isn't it?'

Maya nodded. 'But I don't think we are part of the plan,' she said. 'At least, it didn't seem that way. The Sangha will probably want to find the missing parts of the prophecy by themselves.'

'And if Arjun and Agastya are pairing up, what happens to the rest of us?' Amyra asked in a small voice. 'What about the Saptas?'

'From what Maya has just told us,' Adira replied, 'it doesn't seem like the Saptas are top of mind for the Sangha.'

The seven children looked at one another, wondering what lay ahead for them.

Had they been wrong? Were the Saptas going to emerge from somewhere else in the Sangha? Or the Gana?

Chapter Twenty-three

A Decision is Made

The Assembly Hall

'Will you tell Maya what you have planned? About the Mists? About the dangers she will face?' Yajnaseni spoke up now. Maya had practically grown up in her house in Delhi and Yajnaseni had always treated her like she was her own daughter.

'Of course!' Satyavachana sounded mortified at the very thought of concealing his intentions from Maya. 'I do not plan to deceive the girl.' His voice was hard.

'I am glad you will be honest with her,' Yajnaseni replied, her tone steely in response, the implication clear.

'I know how you feel about the child,' Satyavachana said more gently, understanding Yajnaseni's concern. 'I will tell her everything. I will need to, if she is to be prepared for the journey.'

'And what if she refuses to go?' Kanakpratap asked.

Satyavachana shook his head. 'She won't. If *we* are eager to decipher the verses in that diary, she is impatient to do so. Remember, she went all the way to the Gandharvas, without permission from the Sangha, to solicit their help in deciphering the verses. No, she will be more than willing to explore any opportunity that appears promising. And the Mists are as promising as it gets.'

'Promise me,' Yajnaseni said, fiercely, 'that you will not force her or persuade her by any other means to go there against her wishes.'

'I promise.' Satyavachana held her gaze. 'I will not coerce her. If, for any reason, she declines, I will not try to persuade her. Do you take my word for it?'

There was a moment of silence.

'I believe you,' Yajnaseni said finally. 'But if any harm comes to that child, remember this. I will never forgive you. Gandhari's curse felled the divine Lord Krishna. I may not be Maya's mother but, believe me, I will be as unforgiving as Gandhari was.'

Satyavachana bowed. 'I take full responsibility. And, if I fail, you can curse me with anything you wish. I will humbly accept it.' He looked at her. 'Will that be sufficient?'

Yajnaseni nodded. 'For now. But make sure you do not fail.'

'I cannot,' the Maharishi replied simply. 'The world depends on Maya's success.'

Chapter Twenty-four

The Rest of the Plan

The Assembly Hall

'Now that the matter is settled,' Jignesh said, 'and Maharishi Satyavachana will prepare Maya for the Mists, it is time for us to talk of the rest of his plan to counter Shukra.'

Kanakpratap nodded. 'While Maharishi Satyavachana prepares Maya, we have to work on preparing Arjun and Agastya to work as a team. I will take care of that. I will need help from a Rishi, though.' He looked around.

'I will help you,' Usha volunteered. 'I have taught Agastya and know the boy well. I will work with you.'

'Very well,' Jignesh said briskly. 'We need people to search for the prophecy in Gandharva-lok. I suggest that we form a team from the group gathered here today. We will lose time if we search for volunteers from across the Sangha.'

The others nodded in agreement.

'I'm in,' Amba said. 'It would be useful to have Kanakpratap on board, since the Yayati clan has always been close to the Gandharvas, but I guess he will be busy with Arjun and Agastya.'

'We do need people who can persuade the Gandharvas to allow us to search for the prophecy in Gandharva-lok,' Yajnaseni agreed. 'I volunteer. I may not be a descendant of Yayati but I am married into the family. The Gandharvas know me well.'

Jignesh and Satyavachana nodded at her.

'I will join the team,' Mahesh offered. 'I have had some interactions with Visvavasu. It may help.'

'You need one more Maharishi,' Sriram said. 'I will join you.'

'Great,' Amba said with grim satisfaction. 'Shall we start tomorrow at first light?'

The others nodded their assent.

'What about the part of the prophecy that is hidden in Deva-lok?' Anasuya asked. 'We have no way of finding it. Deva-lok is out of bounds for us.'

'We will cross that bridge when we come to it,' Jignesh said. 'Our immediate concern should be to convince the Gandharvas to mount a search for the part of the prophecy that is hidden in their world. That will be no easy task. We know they are wary of allowing humans a free run of their world.'

'It is possible,' Satyavachana added, 'that the second part of the prophecy, once found, may point the way to retrieving the third part of the prophecy. And who knows what the diary contains? Maybe there is a solution there as well?'

'That's speculation, Maharishi,' Jignesh said sharply. 'I cannot allow the Sangha to plan based on uncertainties. We must do what we can. And what we can't must be discarded and new solutions found. That is the only way forward.'

He looked around at the group. 'Are we all in agreement?'

There was a chorus of 'Agreed' from the group.

'Right then,' Jignesh said, 'let us turn our attention to the third plank of our plan.' He looked at the two strangers, a man and a woman, who had been silent spectators until now.

'Mahakshapatalika,' he addressed the man, who bowed his head in acknowledgement. 'Maharishi Satyavachana believes that the Sangha archives may contain information or even clues to the location of the *Ranakarman Parva*.'

'Or documents relating to the location of the two remaining parts of the prophecy,' Satyavachana added. 'I told the Sangha this fourteen years ago, when Shukra first appeared.'

'We have lost valuable time,' Jignesh agreed. 'We need to initiate a search, on a war footing, for anything that can help us in our quest. We don't know what Shukra is planning. It may be that he will be back in a day or two. But I fear that he is engaged in some activity that will spring yet another surprise for us. And we cannot be caught unawares again.'

The Mahakshapatalika bowed but did not reply. Instead, a thought suddenly filled the minds of all those present in the hall.

We will marshal all our resources. Every single Akshapatalika will be briefed and this will be our top priority. But we will need help.

Jignesh nodded in response. 'I know what you need, Mahakshapatalika. We will scour the Gurukuls for the most advanced or promising students who are in line to join the Gana as Akshapatalika sahayaks and place them at your disposal. You will have the numbers you need to expedite the search.'

The Mahakshapatalika bowed again and, once more, a thought flashed through the minds of the assembly.

Thank you, Mahamatra. That will be of immense help to us in our efforts.

Jignesh nodded and turned his attention to the woman on the other side.

'Mahashastrakar,' he addressed her by her title, 'you said you had something to show us tonight.'

Chapter Twenty-five

Something Special

The Assembly Hall

'Yes,' the woman replied. Her glance swept the group. 'You all know that we have been working for several years on a new type of armour for the Kshatriyas; one that is tougher and smarter, and which can be worn swiftly in case of an emergency.'

'Yes,' Kanakpratap agreed. 'All three attributes are the need of the hour. With the kind of adversaries we are up against, our existing armour is inadequate and takes too long to don. When we battled Shukra's army, almost one month ago, in the clearing outside the Gurukul, our Kshatriya students had to rush into battle without their armour because there was no time for them to wear it.'

The Mahashastrakar nodded. 'We used your experience in the battle with Shukra's army and the battle with the Nagas to incorporate additional features into the designs that we were already working on. And we have a prototype ready.'

Jignesh raised an eyebrow. 'When will you show it to us?'

The Mahashastrakar smiled. 'Now.'

Jignesh frowned. 'You haven't brought anything with you,' he said.

'I didn't need to.' The Mahashastrakar stood up and walked to the centre of the group. '*Virachayati kavach*,' she intoned.

Instantly, her bare arms were sheathed in a smooth, dark cladding that seemed to emerge from her skin, all the way to the tips of her fingers. Her head and face disappeared under the dark attire that had emerged from her body—it seemed that she was covered from head to toe in the armour.

A voice echoed in the heads of all those who were watching, startling them. With the Mahakshapatalika, as with the Akshapatalikas, they were accustomed to telepathic communication—that was how the Keepers of the Archives communicated. It was their inborn gift that set them apart and marked them out for their future career within the Sangha. But this voice was a female voice—that of the leader of the Weapon Forgers.

Well? What do you think?

'Impressive,' Kanakpratap said. He looked at Parth. 'What do you think?'

'Amazing,' Parth agreed, nodding. 'But is it robust enough to protect us against the kind of weapons that Shukra's army might have?'

The Mahashastrakar's voice floated through their minds again.

It may look delicate but that's because we've made it flexible enough to accommodate every possible movement of the human body. But it's as tough as nails. We haven't been able to test it against the Nagas, but I am confident that it will survive even their poison. It has been strengthened and reinforced by special mantras that we've developed over the last few years. Basically we've rediscovered the secret of Karna's kavach. He was born with it; it was a part of his body. When Indra asked for it, Karna had to cut it off his body in order to hand it over. That's what this kavach is. Literally body armour. When summoned by the mantra, it grows on the body of the Kshatriya who is wearing it. And you can communicate with individuals or an entire group of Kshatriyas using the telepathic powers conferred on the armour by another set of mantras. The head and the face are better protected and the nature of the material used—it's organic—allows the warrior to breathe freely although the face is fully covered. Our Kshatriya forces can now face stronger enemies than in the past without fear.

'Is there some way to control who receives the telepathic communication?' Jignesh asked. 'If we come up against vikritis, for example, how do we ensure that *they* don't receive the thoughts of our Kshatriyas?'

The Mahashastrakar nodded. '*Yes, Mahamatra. We had the same concern. The communication needs to be targeted either at an individual or a specific group, using the thoughts of the user of the armour. The power of the mantra does the rest. Opponents cannot receive the telepathic communication unless it is specifically directed at them. It will require some training for the Kshatriyas to get accustomed to this, but it will not be difficult. It is as simple as using the name of the person you are addressing while speaking.*'

Jignesh nodded, satisfied with this clarification.

'How soon can we roll this out across the Sangha, the Gana, and all our Gurukuls?' Amba wanted to know.

'*Vahate kavach*,' the Mahashastrakar intoned and the armour disappeared, seemingly sinking back into her body. 'If we start tomorrow, with the Council's permission, we can cover the entire Kshatriya force within a month.'

'Very good,' Jignesh said. And how much longer before the new defences for the Gurukuls and the new weapons the shastrakars have been working on are ready to deploy?'

'The defences will be ready within a week, Mahamatra,' the woman replied. 'The new weapons may take a little longer. It has been only three weeks since we were asked to develop them based on the requirements which the Sangha Council provided us with.'

Jignesh nodded. The shastrakars had been tasked with developing new weapons after the fight with Shukra's army of monsters, on the day that Arjun and Maya had arrived at the Gurukul. Upon realising the new danger they were confronted with, the Sangha Council had decided that new and more powerful weapons were required to fight creatures like the ones the Gurukul had battled on that night.

'We are working as fast as possible,' the Mahashastrakar assured him.

'I know,' Jignesh told her. 'I do not believe otherwise.'

The institutions of the Akshapatalikas and the Shastrakars went back four thousand years, to the time when the Sangha had suppressed the vikriti rebellion and organised itself into a formal structure—the organisation as it existed today. They were the two pillars of the Sangha that supported the Maharishis and Kshatriyas to fulfil the purpose for which the Sangha had been created, with their knowledge aggregated over thousands of years and the continuous development and evolution of weapons and mantras.

He had no doubt that they would both do their utmost to achieve the objectives the Sangha had set for them.

But would they be able to do it in time?

And would it be enough?

Chapter Twenty-six

Denied

The Guesthouse

Arjun stood before his uncle, his face betraying his emotions. He was upset.

And angry.

As soon as his uncle had emerged from the Assembly Hall, Arjun had cornered him, insisting on a private conversation. The two of them had come to the guesthouse and closeted themselves in the living room.

'What did you guys decide?' Arjun blurted out as soon as the door was shut. 'Are we going to look for the prophecy in Gandharva-lok?'

'Hold on, hold on,' Kanakpratap laughed, amused at his nephew's excitement. He didn't know what had led Arjun to ask the question. 'Yes, *we* are going to look for the prophecy.' He proceeded to tell Arjun what the Council had decided.

'But how can you leave us out?' Arjun protested after hearing that neither he nor any of his friends were part of the team. 'We're the Saptas! We're the ones who should be looking for it!'

Kanakpratap's face grew serious. He realised what was happening here. 'Arjun, you don't know for sure that you are the Saptas. The prophecy only mentions the Saptas in passing. It doesn't provide any way of identifying who they are or will be. They could be anyone from the Sangha. The only thing we know for sure from the prophecy is that you are clearly identified as the One.'

'Then shouldn't I be a part of the team?' Arjun demanded. He didn't think the Council's decision was fair at all.

'No, Arjun.' Kanakpratap's voice was gentle but firm. 'You are not ready. We have decided to partner you with Agastya. Both of you need plenty of practice together before you can call yourselves a team. Once you are ready, you will get your projects.'

'When will that day come, Uncle?' Arjun asked despairingly. 'I've been training for seven years now. Everyone says that I've made great progress since coming here. Isn't it time yet?'

'You've spent less than a month in the Gurukul,' Kanakpratap replied. 'Not enough time for you to hone your skills to a level where you can undertake a project that carries risks. And you must remember that time moves more slowly in the Gandharva world than in ours.'

Arjun remembered the first day he had stepped into the Gandharva valley. When they had entered, it was early morning in Bhu-lok. When they left, it was evening in Panna, even though they had stayed in the valley for only a couple of hours.

'Visvavasu may not look it,' his uncle continued, 'but he is thousands of years old. He has been mentioned in the Mahabharata; that's how old he is. We don't know how long the search for the prophecy will take. Even if it takes a week or two in Gandharva-lok, months would have passed in our world before you return. That would take away precious time that could be used for practice and to get better prepared to take on your role of the One when the time comes. And that time will come sooner than we think.'

Kanakpratap hesitated before he continued, 'Do you know that a member of the Gana has been found dead in Delhi? She went missing suddenly and then her body was found under strange circumstances. She was a powerful member of the Gana—more advanced than anyone in this Gurukul.'

Arjun's eyes widened at this news.

'It was someone you know, Arjun,' Kanakpratap continued. 'Diya Chaudhry. She was a prefect. Twelfth grade. Sanskrit topper.'

Arjun didn't know what to say. He was shell-shocked.

'And you want to dive into danger before you are ready for it!'

'Who killed her, Uncle?' Arjun finally found his tongue.

'The Sangha is investigating. We suspect the vikritis. The nature of her death indicates a power that no sadh possesses. And, even though Sangha rules forbid the practice of our powers in the presence of sadhs, this girl would have been able to defend herself if attacked by sadhs for any reason.'

Arjun was mystified. 'How was she killed?'

Kanakpratap was silent for a moment, debating with himself the extent to which he should expose Arjun to the dangers in the outside world. He decided Arjun was old enough to know. And if he had to become more independent, he had to understand what he was going to be dealing with.

'We can't be sure because we were unable to examine her body. She had died two weeks before her body was found, according to the information we were able to gather through our connections in the police. And her parents—both Sangha members—wished to hasten her last rites so that her atma could continue onward to its next birth. But it seems that her body was possessed by someone else for two weeks. She probably died when the possession took place, unable to withstand the shock.'

'How is that even possible?' Arjun cried.

'Ordinarily, it would be impossible. But some of the vikritis may have mastered the secondary siddhis. One of those siddhis is the ability to enter into the bodies of others.' His uncle shrugged. 'It is difficult to believe that any of the vikritis could be that powerful, but we cannot think of any other possibility at the moment.'

'But why would anyone even want to do that?' Arjun still could not get over what he was hearing.

'We don't know. But that's not the point. What I am trying to tell you is that there are dangers out there—outside the security of the Gurukul—that you have no idea about. You still have a long way to go before you are ready to face them.'

But Arjun was still not convinced. He had lived his entire life in a gilded cage, protected and pampered, and yearned to break free.

'I think I am ready, Uncle,' he insisted.

'And the Sangha thinks you are not,' his uncle retorted. '*I* think you are not ready. And that is how things stand, whether you like it or not.'

A thought struck Arjun. 'Uncle, Gandharva-lok is not Bhu-lok. There are no vikritis there. There is no danger there.'

Kanakpratap would have been amused, if he was not so irritated by his nephew's determination to be obstinate.

'That doesn't matter,' he told Arjun. 'You don't decide these things. The Sangha does. And I've told you what they decided. Now go and get a good night's rest. Our practice will have to be even more intense tomorrow onwards, if you want to be ready soon!'

Chapter Twenty-seven

Midnight Meeting

The Gurukul

Adira opened the door of the cottage and cautiously peered outside.

It was past midnight and the Gurukul lay under a cloak of darkness and silence. Nothing stirred, not even the animals in the forest.

'The coast is clear,' she whispered to Maya and Amyra, who were standing behind her.

The three girls slipped out and made their way towards the Kshatriya practice field where they planned to meet the four boys. It was a cloudless night and the faint light of the stars was sufficient for them to find their way to the field.

Arjun, Varun, Tanveer and Agastya were waiting for them.

Upon the arrival of the girls, Agastya created a soft glow of light, very unlike the bright orbs that lit up the Gurukul during the evening.

'What happened?' Adira asked in a hushed whisper, even though there was no one around. Arjun told his friends about his conversation with his uncle.

'They didn't even mention us in their meeting,' he concluded bitterly.

'Maybe they don't believe we are the Saptas,' Adira said. 'After all, we haven't proved ourselves in any way.'

'I find it hard to believe that the seven of us came together by sheer coincidence,' Arjun insisted, frowning. 'There has to be a reason for our association. None of us knew each other from before, apart from Maya and I. It cannot be by chance!'

'I'm inclined to agree with you,' Tanveer said.

'Of course,' Varun said. He looked knowingly at Adira. 'I know you feel the same way.'

Maya thought she saw Adira flush in the light of the orbs that were suspended above them. She wondered why.

'How do we prove ourselves when there is no way to decide if we are the Saptas?' Varun frowned. 'Arjun's uncle was right. The prophecy doesn't say who the seven will be or how they will be recognised. We simply assumed that, because there are seven of us, and we had a role to play in the defence of the Gurukul, we are the Saptas of the prophecy.'

'We could be wrong,' Agastya agreed. 'Just look at us. None of us has made it to the Gana yet. Amyra is a novice and Maya still has to prove that she is not a sadh. Maybe the Saptas will turn out to be seven members of the Sangha and not us.'

'No,' Arjun said, fiercely. 'I don't believe that, Ags. There is a reason we all came together. We worked as a team, right from the day we entered the Gandharva valley without permission from the Sangha. I believe that we are the chosen ones mentioned in the prophecy.'

'So what do we do?' Tanveer asked, ever practical. 'The Sangha is clearly not willing to allow us to search for the remaining parts of the prophecy. Even if we *are* the Saptas, how do we move forward without the guidance of the Sangha?'

There was silence as they contemplated the dilemma.

'We act without their guidance,' Arjun said slowly, breaking the silence.

'Huh? What?' Agastya looked at him in surprise. 'Are you out of your mind?'

'No,' Arjun said, more firmly now. 'We don't need the Sangha. If they don't want to help, then we will search for the remaining parts of the prophecy by ourselves. If we succeed, we will have proved beyond doubt that we are the Saptas of the prophecy.'

Maya stared at Arjun. Her old childhood friend had changed so much in the course of barely four weeks. She could hardly believe this was the same Arjun who, less than a month ago, was clutching her hand in the SUV as they drove, surrounded by pretas, through Panna National Park. The same scared boy who had been glad to be comforted by her.

Today, however, he sounded different.

Looked different.

His tone had changed. She knew that Arjun had always been rebellious. In school he had constantly rebelled against authority. But he had always got away because he was an outstanding sportsman and won accolades for his school.

What she was seeing today was something else. It was an attempt to break free. Standing before her was a boy who was confident enough to take his own decisions and stand by them.

She saw before her not the Arjun she had known in school but an Arjun who was determined to do what he thought was right to save the world.

Tonight, she had got her first glimpse of the scion of Yayati.

Until now, she had wondered how Arjun would play his part in the scheme that had been described by the prophecy.

Now, she knew.

How had this sudden transformation come about? Was it his genes? She wondered. Passed down the generations, all the way from Yayati?

But then, genes were not everything. Wasn't that what they were taught at the Gurukul? That it didn't matter if you were born a sadh? That you could determine your own life's journey and destination by your own actions?

She saw that truth in play now. Arjun had the genes. But he had also made the change that was required.

Tonight, she realised he was no longer a sadh.

Tonight, she believed that he could be the One.

She wondered if she could make the transition like he had. No, she corrected herself, not if but *when*.

Chapter Twenty-eight

Trouble

The Kshatriyas' Practice Field

Arjun looked around at the others. 'What do you guys say?'

'With you, buddy,' Varun said immediately.

'I'm in,' Tanveer responded.

'Done.' Adira sounded determined.

'Oh, yes, of course,' Amyra said enthusiastically.

'Maya?' Arjun looked at his childhood friend. 'I'm assuming you're in.'

Maya hesitated. Was *she* doing the right thing now? She didn't know. All she knew was that she had to speak her mind. And, for the first time in her life, she was not going to take her friend's side.

'No, Arjun,' she said softly, trying to hide the rough edges that her answer carried. 'It would be wrong.'

Arjun stared at her in disbelief.

'The Sangha operates by its rules,' Maya continued. 'We are a part of the Sangha, whether we have qualified to be part of the Gana or not. We must live by its rules. And we have already broken the rules once, when we went by ourselves and without permission to the Gandharva valley. Also, don't forget that the Sangha will have a team, which includes your mother, in the Gandharva valley. How can we land up there as well? What justification will we have? It will look like the Sangha itself is divided. We cannot allow that to happen. And your uncle ... your uncle has spent the last seven years training you to get to where you are today. Shouldn't we respect his opinion? No, Arjun, I cannot bring myself to do this. I'm sorry. I really am.'

Arjun said nothing, but his silence carried more meaning than any words could.

'I can't believe it,' Agastya said. 'For once I am not alone in saying that we shouldn't do crazy stuff like this.' He looked at Arjun. 'Maya's right, you know. Drop it, Arjun. Let's not do it.'

A heavy silence hung over the group.

Maya watched as Arjun stood there clenching his fists. Whether in anger or frustration, she couldn't tell, but he was clearly upset that two of his friends were opposing him.

She could understand how he felt. He had locked horns with his uncle, arguing that his friends were the Saptas and should be treated as such. It was natural for him to feel let down now.

But she didn't regret taking a stand against his idea. It was just plain wrong.

With a great effort, Arjun composed himself and spoke. 'I can't believe you guys don't want to look for the prophecy. I really don't understand it.'

Maya realised that Arjun hadn't been listening to them explain their positions. His attachment to his own idea blinkered his understanding.

'It isn't that we don't want to search for the prophecy,' she tried to explain. 'It's just that we don't want to go against the decision of the Sangha.'

'It's the same thing,' Arjun insisted. 'They don't want us to look for the prophecy either.'

Maya was nonplussed. For the first time in her life, she didn't know how to get through to her friend. It was like a chasm had suddenly opened up between them—a chasm that she had never believed possible.

'Fine, then.' There was a strange undercurrent in Arjun's voice. 'We'll drop the idea. We can't do it without the two of you. We can't get into Gandharva-lok without Maya since only she can recite the mantra that opens the portal. And Ags is the only Rishi in the group. We need him along. If you two are dropping out, the rest of us don't have a choice.'

He turned and walked away towards the dorms without another word.

The rest of the group cast apprehensive glances at each other, then followed him.

Chapter Twenty-nine

A New Angle

Raman Kapoor's Office
New Delhi

Kapoor sat at his desk, looking at Ajit with a perplexed expression.

The last four days had been spent frenetically poring over mobile phone records of the dead girl, talking to neighbours, school teachers, her friends, examining the girl's medical history, and speaking to doctors who had treated her for any kind of ailment in the last few years.

One thing had been established. The girl—her name was Diya Chaudhry—had been in fine fettle before she disappeared. She had definitely not been suffering from any kind of sickness or infection.

Ajit had made another discovery, which he had just reported to Kapoor. A discovery that was wholly unexpected, but not one that made the case simpler.

Diya Chaudhry had been in touch with Naresh Upadhyay just a few days before the history teacher was murdered. And she had studied in the same school as Upadhyay's daughter and Virendra Singh's nephew.

'Are you sure about her having been in touch with Upadhyay?' Kapoor asked Ajit.

'One hundred per cent, sir,' Ajit replied.

'Not that it means that there is any connection between the two cases,' Kapoor muttered, rather unconvincingly. 'But it doesn't help us either.'

'I just thought you should know, sir,' Ajit said.

Kapoor nodded. 'You did the right thing. Now go out there and get some more clues.'

'Sir.' Ajit rose, saluted and left the room.

Kapoor sat staring into space for a few moments. Then he picked up the phone. 'Get me forensics,' he said. 'Suresh.'

In less than a minute, the phone rang.

'Suresh,' Kapoor said,' do you have the fingerprints of Diya Chaudhry?'

'Yes, sir. They'll be in the files.'

'Good. Then listen carefully. Here's what I want you to do.'

After giving Suresh his instructions, Kapoor put the phone down and paced the room, thinking hard. He had acted on a hunch, asking Suresh to compare the fingerprints. He really didn't know what he was trying to achieve. He only knew that his instinct had never failed him.

The phone rang.

It was Suresh.

'Sir!' Suresh's voice carried an unmistakable ring of excitement. 'You were right.'

'But that doesn't make sense,' Kapoor said. 'Ajit was very clear that he saw a man go into Upadhyay's house. Not a girl.'

'Ajit must be mistaken, sir. The prints match. There can be no doubt that the person who opened the gate to Upadhyay's house was none other than the victim—Diya Chaudhry!'

The Forest
Unknown Location

'What you did last night was unacceptable.' Satyavachana's face was grave as he looked at Maya. 'Eavesdropping, that too on a Council meeting! Whatever were you thinking, child?'

'I'm sorry, Mahamati,' Maya said with downcast eyes. 'I ... I was curious to know if the Council would discuss the Saptas.'

'The Council does not believe in the Saptas,' Satyavachana sighed. 'Sometimes I think they do not believe in the prophecy itself.'

'I will not eavesdrop again,' Maya said.

Satyavachana nodded. 'Fine,' he said. 'Last night you were in real danger. If Jignesh had uttered the mantra that I thought he was going to unleash, you would have been in real trouble.'

'I understand, Mahamati.'

'Come, now. Let us proceed with our lessons.'

Chapter Thirty

Kapoor Follows Up

Raman Kapoor's Office

Raman Kapoor rose and greeted the rotund little man who bustled into his office.

'Professor Ratan Tiwari?' Kapoor proffered his hand, which Tiwari shook with a firm grip. 'Thank you for coming to meet me. I thought it would be more discreet than my visiting the university.'

Tiwari nodded and sat down. 'No problem, sir. But I am curious about why you wanted to meet me.'

Kapoor sat at his desk and nodded. 'Of course. I wanted to ask you some questions about a case that I am investigating at the moment.'

Tiwari looked at him inquiringly. 'Oh,' he said. 'I'm not sure how I can help, but I'm happy to try.'

'Thank you, Professor. Now, you must have seen and read about the girl who was found dead under mysterious circumstances. It's all over the news and social media.'

'You'll have to be more specific, sir,' Tiwari said. 'I don't watch a lot of television, especially not the news, and I stay away from social media. And the newspapers are filled with bad news about children being killed almost every day.'

'True,' Kapoor agreed. He opened a drawer in his desk and took out the photographs of Diya Chaudhry and handed them to Tiwari, observing him keenly as the professor looked at the photographs one by one.

Finally, Tiwari handed the pictures back to Kapoor and nodded. 'I remember these,' he said and shuddered. 'A terrible thing to have happened.' He hesitated. 'So, I guess you know that I knew Diya. Is that why you called me here?'

'Yes, Professor. We examined Diya's mobile phone records and found that you are one of the people with whom she was in touch quite often. Tell me what you know about her.'

'Well.' Tiwari pursed his lips and shrugged. 'She came to me for Sanskrit tuitions. I'm a Sanskrit scholar and professor, as you know. She was a very intelligent student and a hard worker. Quite good at Sanskrit too, and one of the toppers in her school. But I'm afraid that's all I know about her.'

'Did she ever mention anything that you feel may be important and has a bearing on this case?' Kapoor pressed.

Tiwari thought for a moment, then shook his head. 'I can't think of anything of that nature,' he replied. 'I'm sorry I'm not being of much help.'

'That's alright, Professor.' Kapoor rose and held out his hand. 'Thank you, once again, for coming over. And if you do happen to remember anything, please let me know.'

'I will definitely do that.' Tiwari shook Kapoor's hand, then bustled out of the room.

Kapoor gazed thoughtfully at Tiwari's disappearing back. The man was hiding something. Of that he was sure.

But what was it?

Harish appeared at the door.

'Well?' Kapoor looked enquiringly at him.

'It's a positive identification, sir.'

'You're sure of it.'

Harish nodded vehemently. 'I'm sure. This is the man who arrived at Panna National Park with the girl and then met up with Virendra Singh and his family.'

'It was sundown. There was insufficient light for you to have seen his features properly. And you were at a significant distance from the car.' Kapoor's face was grim. 'That's what the defence will say, if it gets that far.'

Harish shook his head. 'I'm one hundred per cent sure, sir. There's no doubt about it. He's the one.'

'Well then, get a tail on him. I want to know what he does, where he goes, who he meets.'

'Sir.' Harish saluted and left the room.

Kapoor leaned back in his chair and grimaced. He seemed to be going round in circles. No matter what lead came up, it led back to the same place.

A part of him exulted. It seemed that this case was inextricably linked with the Trivedi and Upadhyay murder cases. The girl, Diya. The involvement of this man, Tiwari. His presence in the park where Virendra Singh had met him. It all meant that the leads in his earlier case had not gone cold, and the two cases were possibly connected.

There was something big happening.

The key to that revelation had eluded him so far. But Kapoor was determined to find it.

For the umpteenth time, he pulled out the sheet of paper he had found beneath the desk in Upadhyay's house and studied it.

A flaming sword.

A sword on fire?

What did it mean?

Chapter Thirty-one

Arjun Reflects

The Gurukul
Panna National Park

Arjun sat and reflected.

He had still not got over the shock of the previous night. Somehow, he had been able to understand and forgive Agastya; the two boys had not exchanged a word last night in the dorm when they retired for the night, but by this morning, Arjun had calmed down and was able to think things through more rationally.

Agastya, as long as Arjun had known him, had played by the rules; he would the last one to go against the grain. It didn't matter if the rules made sense or not; for Agastya, they were sacrosanct. They existed, therefore they had to be followed. Without question.

But, try as he might, Arjun could not understand why his oldest and closest friend from childhood had deserted him at the moment when he needed her support the most.

It was very unlike Maya. She had always found a way to agree with him when they were growing up. It wasn't as if they never had disagreements or fights, but they had always found a middle ground to make up. Their friendship had ensured a healthy respect for each other, even when their ideas differed.

Last night was different. Maya had shot down his idea without a second thought. She had acted like Agastya, only she was not Agastya. Far from it.

He had been stunned.

Maya had always been cool, level-headed, logical, and willing to see sense. Why had she not supported him this time?

The two missing parts of the prophecy had to be found. That much was clear. All that Arjun wanted was the chance to be able to prove that he and his six friends *were* the Saptas.

Was that too much to ask?

Apparently, according to the Sangha, it was.

But that didn't rankle as much as the fact that Maya didn't think the way he did. She too felt that the Sangha's decision was not to be questioned. She didn't seem to mind that the Saptas would have to sit on the sidelines instead of being in the thick of the action as the first part of the prophecy had predicted.

Arjun had spent the entire day moping over Maya's behaviour last night.

By now, however, a strange loneliness had begun to creep up on him.

His mother had left with the rest of the team deputed by the Sangha to search for the prophecy in Gandharva-lok. The day had been spent with Agastya, under the supervision of his uncle and Mahamati Usha, learning and practising. It had been tough and intensive and he had had no time to think.

But when he returned to the dorm after practice, something seemed to be missing. He felt the absence of his mother keenly.

And, despite his misgivings about Maya's behaviour, he missed her too.

He rose abruptly, making up his mind.

There was something that he had to do.

Chapter Thirty-two

Maya Explores

The Gurukul

Maya looked around. The dorm was unoccupied. Adira and the other girls were probably in the common room.

She flopped onto the bed, exhausted. Satyavachana had been putting her through her paces and it had been both difficult and enervating.

Ever since Satyavachana had taught Maya the *Pratismriti* mantra, she had been using it to travel to the forest and back to the Gurukul. Initially Satyavachana had accompanied her, both to ensure that she was safe and also to give her the experience of taking someone else along with her while using the mantra. But after a couple of days, he was satisfied that she was quite capable of making the trips herself.

The sun was setting and darkness was slowly creeping up on the Gurukul, like a black wall separating it from the world of the sadhs. The glowing orbs of light that illuminated it at night began winking on, keeping the darkness at bay.

There it was again.

Cutting through her excitement and happiness, the familiar tug was back, calling out to her.

It was like an argument that you knew you could not win. At some point, you would have to give in to it.

Maya slid off the bed.

She had to know.

Where was this coming from? What was its source?

She stole down the stairs of the cottage, past the other dorms, creeping past the open door of the common room where some boisterous game was in progress, accompanied by much squealing and laughter. She stepped outside and quietly shut the door of the cottage behind her.

The Central Avenue was deserted at this time, students and faculty alike having retired to their dorms or cottages.

Maya decided to follow her instinct. The tug seemed to be coming from beyond the classrooms.

But there was nothing there. Just the practice fields for the Kshatriyas and the Rishis.

And the river Ken.

Was it coming from the river?

There was only one way to find out.

She walked down towards the Assembly Hall.

The tug did seem to get stronger as she walked. She was definitely moving in the right direction.

A sudden apprehension gripped her.

What was she going to do when she found the source of the feeling that had been plaguing her since she had arrived at the Gurukul?

Chapter Thirty-three

Dilemma

Lajpat Nagar
New Delhi

Vishwaraj threw a few things into a suitcase. He wouldn't need much; he was travelling light. Just the bare essentials.

He looked around the small, drab, flat.

A tiny bedroom with a single rickety bed and attached bathroom; a second bedroom just beyond, and a room that doubled as a sitting room and dining room with a cubicle of a kitchen attached.

It had never been comfortable, but he had more important things to worry about. There was a job to be done.

And he could not use this flat as his base any more. The Sangha knew about him now—they would have seen him in Panna, where he had used his powers to counter the protective mantras of the Gurukul, to enable the Nagas to advance on it unchallenged.

He had been reluctant at first, to play such a leading role in attacking the very institution that he had been a part of. But that feeling had not lasted long. The feeling of power, of dominance and invincibility that he had experienced once he started chanting the mantras had been unparalleled. Nothing he had ever done in the Sangha was comparable to that feeling. He had revelled in it.

Until Garuda had appeared and reversed the momentum of the Nagas.

Vishwaraj knew that the Sangha would come for him. They would search him out, produce him before the Sangha Council and pass judgment on him. He was powerful, but he knew he could not battle the might of the Sangha.

No, he could not stay here any longer.

Yesterday, the Son of Bhrigu had given him a new assignment. He had stressed its importance. And Vishwaraj had understood what Shukra was planning.

It hadn't been long since Shukra had first sought him out in Allahabad. Vishwaraj still didn't know how Shukra had known about him, or found him. He had simply appeared at Vishwaraj's school one day. The Son of Bhrigu had spoken to him and convinced him to be a part of his grand plan for Bhu-lok.

Vishwaraj had begun working with Shukra, training under him, learning powerful mantras that he had never known existed, even while being a part of the Gana.

Shukra had told Vishwaraj about the prophecy and about what had happened in Allahabad fourteen years ago.

Subsequently, Vishwaraj had also learned that Rudrapratap's son was still alive. And that Kanakpratap was living in Delhi under an assumed name.

Vishwaraj had left for Delhi immediately, but he had been unable to locate Rudrapratap's son. However, he had managed to locate Maharishi Dhruv, who was also living in Delhi under an assumed name, by using a member of the Gana—Diya Chaudhry.

He had used his siddhis to possess her body, but she had been unable to withstand the shock of possession and had died instantly. Guided by Shukra, Vishwaraj had used his powers to keep her body alive while his atma possessed it and had found out where Dhruv lived.

It was Vishwaraj who had approached Dhruv, in Diya's body, on the day that Maharishi Dhruv had died. As a precaution, in case anyone was watching, he had created the illusion of Shukra's appearance, complete with eyepatch, so no one would ever know that Diya had turned up at Dhruv's house. Once he had confirmed Dhruv's identity, he had vanished, using his power of instant travel, and Shukra had materialised inside the Maharishi's house.

Vishwaraj had then discarded Diya's body. It was no longer of any use to him.

But he also knew that his earlier encounter with Trivedi would send out warning signals to the Sangha. They would know that he had turned.

Finally, Shukra had told Vishwaraj about their own connection. Shukra had known immediately that Vishwaraj was his direct descendant, through his daughter Devyani. The relationship had made Vishwaraj proud. He had realised that he was unique. And it explained his immense power in the siddhis even at such a young age. He had always been one of the stars of the Gana, and would have shortly become a full-fledged member of the Sangha; possibly the youngest ever.

But that didn't matter any more.

The Sangha was impotent. It had outlived its purpose. The present and the future belonged to Shukra. His plan was grand. It was infallible.

And Vishwaraj would help Shukra succeed.

He looked around one last time.

Everything was packed.

Only one thing was left to be done.

He took two steps towards the second bedroom. It was tinier than the master bedroom.

The wail of a police siren burst upon him.

No.

Not now.

Not when he was on the cusp of leaving.

How had they found him?

What terrible timing. He grimaced.

Vishwaraj didn't have the inclination or the time to deal with the police.

He threw a second, wistful glance at the spare bedroom.

He had wanted to cover his tracks. Ensure there was no evidence. But that would take time.

And time was something he did not have now.

He had made a promise to Shukra. A promise that he was determined to keep.

The spare bedroom would have to be abandoned. The police would find what was there. It would incriminate him.

But what could they do?

Hang him?

He laughed to himself. That was a joke.

Actually, it would give the sadhs something to be puzzled about.

Forget it.

Vishwaraj picked up his suitcase.

And vanished.

Chapter Thirty-four

A Shocking Discovery

Lajpat Nagar

Kapoor alighted from the jeep and looked around as the sirens wailed.

A crowd had begun gathering, curious to know why a convoy of police vehicles had suddenly converged on the neighbourhood park.

'Barricades,' he ordered. 'Keep those idiots out of my hair. Let's move. Fast.'

The posse of policemen in the accompanying armoured trucks spilled out of their vehicles and took up positions outside the house that was their target.

'Second floor,' Ajit informed Kapoor, who nodded grimly.

'Follow me.' He strode briskly towards the gate, drawing his revolver, opened the gate, and sprinted up the staircase that led to the second floor.

Just a week ago, Ajit had made a stupendous discovery. One that promised to lead them to the bottom of the mystery at the heart of this case while simultaneously muddying the waters.

Along with Tiwari's mobile number, another mobile number had been identified from Diya's call records.

It was an outstation number.

Ajit was cast from the same mould as Kapoor. He had begun digging deeper, since Diya seemed to have made and received quite a few calls in the last two months from this number. Eventually, he had traced the number to Allahabad.

It belonged to someone called Vishwaraj.

When Ajit had informed Kapoor of this development, the DCP was initially unable to accept the serendipity of it all. It was too great a coincidence. Everything in this case had pointed to Allahabad so far. And here was one more piece in the puzzle, located in Allahabad, no less.

It *had* to be the same Vishwaraj who had spoken to Tiwari before he died and whom Updadhyay had taught in Allahabad.

And if it wasn't, he now had a chance to figure out just who this Vishwaraj was.

It had taken some time through the backchannels to identify a possible hideaway for Vishwaraj. Since there was very little concrete evidence, it would have been impossible to get a warrant to obtain the information from the telco. So Kapoor had to rely on his contacts and pull strings to obtain cell tower locations that were used primarily at night and triangulate to work out possible locations based on other cell tower data.

It had to be a nondescript colony where Vishwaraj could blend into the crowd without being noticed and lead an anonymous existence.

After several days and nights of speculation and brainstorming, they had managed to home in on this particular address.

And now Kapoor would find out if he had been correct.

If he was, he was going to turn up at Vishwaraj's doorstep. And give him a nasty shock.

The policemen, carrying assault rifles, clattered up the stairs behind him.

Kapoor knocked on the door. 'This is the police,' he announced. 'Open the door!'

Silence greeted his demand.

He looked back and nodded, then flattened himself against the wall of the staircase to allow two burly policemen to push their way past him.

The two men looked at each other and then, with one accord, flung themselves against the wooden door.

The lock gave way easily, and the two policemen tumbled into the sitting room.

'Spread out! Search the flat!' Kapoor ordered, even as he realised that there wasn't much room to spread out. It was a small flat, and obviously empty.

Damn! The bird had flown the coop.

Vishwaraj must have figured out that the police was on his trail and decided to disappear. There were no clothes or any other personal effects in the house. It was clear that Vishwaraj was not planning to return any time soon.

The one solid clue, the one link that Kapoor had thought was within his grasp, had just disappeared.

'Sir!' Ajit called from the doorway that led to the smaller of the two bedrooms.

Kapoor didn't like the sound of Ajit's voice. He sounded too much like Harish when he had called him from Panna on the night he claimed to have been hounded by demons.

'What's the matter?' Kapoor asked, still irritated that he had been unable to catch Vishwaraj. If only he had arrived sooner ...

He walked past Ajit and stepped into the tiny bedroom.

And sucked in his breath sharply.

A small bed, and not much else, occupied the room.

But it wasn't the size of the room, or the bed, that jolted Kapoor.

It was what lay on the bed.

Chapter Thirty-five

Unexpected Encounter

Maya's Dorm
The Gurukul
Panna National Park

Arjun smiled wryly at the squeals and laughter that could be heard even through the closed door of the cottage. Shaking his head, he knocked loudly.

There was no response.

He knocked again.

The boisterous noise inside suddenly stopped and he heard the sound of someone running to open the door.

It was Adira. She flung open the door, then stood there, stock-still.

For some reason, Arjun found himself fumbling for words. 'Er … um, Adira,' he said.

Then he found his tongue. 'I'm looking for Maya.'

There was a moment of silence.

Almost as if Adira was disappointed.

'Let me check in the dorm,' she replied, and hurried up the stairs.

Arjun waited.

'She isn't there,' Adira reported, as she jogged back to him. 'She's probably gone for a walk. You could try the classroom block. Maya goes there sometimes when she wants to be alone.'

Arjun nodded. 'Thanks,' he said, but made no move to walk away. It was as if he was rooted to the spot.

Adira stared at him uncertainly.

Arjun suddenly realised the awkwardness of the situation. 'I'd better go look for her.' His laugh was forced.

'Yeah,' Adira agreed, rather perfunctorily.

Arjun gave her a silly grin and walked away wondering what had come over him.

Behind him, the door of the cottage slammed shut and squeals and laughter floated out once more.

The Rishi Practice Field

'Maya!'

Surprised, Maya stopped in her tracks and turned.

It was Arjun's voice.

She waited, seeing him racing towards her, past the Assembly Hall.

'Hi,' Arjun panted. He stood with his hands on his hips, trying to catch his breath.

Maya stood watching him silently, patiently.

'Hey,' Arjun said finally, having got his breath back.

'Hey, AJ,' Maya responded.

The two stood there for a moment, looking at each other, each wondering what to say.

'About last night.' Both of them spoke together.

For some reason, they both found it funny and doubled up with laughter.

That seemed to ease the tension.

Arjun held up a hand. 'No, let me go first. I … I want to say that I'm sorry I took off on you last night. I didn't mean to blame you for anything. I was just … disappointed.'

Maya nodded. 'I know, AJ. But so was I.'

'But why? I mean, I'm not being unreasonable. The fate of the world is at stake. If we're the ones who are destined to find the prophecy, shouldn't we be the ones looking for it?'

Maya shook her head. 'We're not the ones who make the decisions, AJ,' she replied. 'A day will come when we will make the decisions. But not today. If the Sangha has decided something in their wisdom, we should either argue with them and try to change their minds or accept it. That is how disagreements should be settled. Agreeing to disagree and then acting independently is not the solution. This is the time that the Sangha and its members should be united. If we are divided, what chance do we have against Shukra?'

Arjun stared at Maya. She made sense, but he didn't want to give in so easily. 'What if they are wrong?' he demanded. 'Despite all their powers, they're as human as we are; as the sadhs are.'

Maya winced. She was still a sadh for all practical purposes. A gifted sadh, but a sadh nevertheless.

Arjun was oblivious to her reaction. 'Today they say that the Saptas don't exist. Or at least, that we are not the Saptas. Tomorrow, they will take some other decision without any justification. The least they can do is give us a chance to prove that we are the Saptas! Is that too much to ask? Am I being unreasonable?'

Maya said nothing. A part of her agreed with Arjun. But she couldn't bring herself to join a rebellion against the Sangha, which seemed to be the only thing standing between humanity and Shukra.

'I think the Sangha is too caught up in its own importance, in its role of protecting humanity,' Arjun carried on. 'They are not open to new ideas.'

Listening to him, Maya recalled what Satyavachana had said on the night when she had first met him; when she had travelled in her atmic form to his ashram and he had arrived on her balcony in the guesthouse. He had said two things. He had mentioned the Saptas and referred to her as one of them. And he had said that the Sangha were navel gazing. Clearly, there was no love lost between the Maharishi and the Sangha. She remembered how Satyavachana had refused to address either the Sanghanetras or Jignesh by their rightful titles. It was as if he did not believe in the institution at all. Maya wondered why the Maharishi had renounced the Sangha to live in exile in his ashram. Was it for reasons similar to those that had caused Arjun's disillusionment?

'AJ,' Maya ventured, once Arjun had finished railing against the Sangha. 'If I ever feel that the Sangha is wrong or that they are taking decisions that will vitiate our battle with Shukra, I will be the first one to stand with you. But today I don't feel they are either committing an injustice or disabling us from rallying against Shukra. I agree with them that you, I, and the rest of what you call the Saptas, are neither ready nor proven. Until we give them proof that we can do something substantial, something big, how can we assert ourselves? Killing a few pisachas here or there as part of Gurukul projects,' she shuddered at the thought, not having mastered this herself, 'is hardly a justification for what you are demanding. When we come up against Shukra, none of us will be able to stand against him. The Saptas will not survive more than a few minutes. I have seen Shukra's power. He murdered my father, who was a powerful Maharishi, before my eyes. That memory is indelibly etched into my mind. When I think of what he did to my father, I have no reason to believe that you, I, or any of us can stand against Shukra. I don't blame the Sangha for their lack of faith in us. They have too much at stake to place all their bets on a bunch of children who, let's face it, are greenhorns.'

She paused for breath.

Arjun took the opportunity to speak.

'Forget all that,' he said, coming to the point finally. 'I was looking for you because I wanted to say that I'm sorry. I … I just don't know what came over me last night. I shouldn't have acted the way I did. We've had fights before.' He grinned as a memory came back to him. 'Remember the time you didn't speak to me for a week because I made fun of the guy you had a crush on?'

Maya nodded, smiling at the memory. 'You were pretty beastly then, AJ. But you did turn out to be right. That guy was a loser. I don't know why I ever liked him anyway.'

'Doesn't matter,' Arjun said, hurriedly, afraid that the conversation would, once again, go off on a tangent. 'I was wrong to diss you last night. Whether I was right or not, that's not the way I should be treating my oldest friend.'

'You've changed, AJ,' Maya looked at him frankly. 'You're more … I don't know … commanding? And I guess you should be. You're the One. You have to lead us all into battle against Shukra. You can't do that if you start giving in to everyone. You need to have your own opinions, your own convictions, and follow through on them.'

'And I need to have friends like you who can tell me where to get off,' Arjun laughed. 'That's the mark of any great leader, isn't it? To be able to listen, to accept contrarian opinions and change course when required?' He shook his head. 'Fat lot of good it will do me if I cannot lead. I cannot impose my opinions on others. Either I have a convincing argument or I have to be flexible. That's something I have to accept and learn.'

'You're already learning that, AJ.' Maya smiled at him. 'Isn't that what you are doing right now?'

'So, you've forgiven me?'

'How can I not?'

'Go for a walk?'

Maya smiled happily at Arjun. Despite the darkness around them, the sun was shining brightly in her world once more.

Chapter Thirty-six

The Mystery Deepens

Raman Kapoor's Office
New Delhi

Kapoor glared at Suresh, who sat across the desk from him. He was seething. Every single clue, every lead that popped up in this case, seemed to be pre-destined to end in a blind alley. Like a matchstick that flickers briefly before burning itself out, every lead seemed to hold enormous potential before dying a natural death.

The latest instance was the man they had discovered in Vishwaraj's flat in Lajpat Nagar, five days ago.

When the police had burst into the tiny bedroom, they had found him lying prone on the bed, apparently dead. Rigor mortis had set in and the man clutched a sheet of paper in his right hand so tightly that it had been impossible to prise open his fingers and remove the paper to find out what it was.

An ambulance had been hurriedly summoned and the body transported to AIIMS where doctors confirmed the rigor mortis. However, to the surprise of everyone present, the medics at AIIMS had also detected a pulse and discovered that the 'body' was actually breathing.

Was there a possibility that the man was actually alive?

He was instantly admitted into the ICU under the care of a team of doctors who were specially summoned for the task.

But the case had baffled them too.

And now, after five days, Kapoor wanted answers.

'Well?' he demanded. 'You said you wanted to meet me and discuss the report in person.'

Suresh nodded. 'I did.' His voice was unusually soft.

'I'm waiting.'

Suresh cleared his throat uncertainly. He didn't know how to break it to Kapoor. 'Well, er,' he began, 'this case is similar in some ways to the Diya Chaudhry case.'

Kapoor groaned and buried his face in his hands.

Suresh waited.

'Don't tell me,' Kapoor said finally, 'that the man died two weeks before his body started decomposing.'

Suresh saw an opening here. 'Actually, no,' he said. 'That's where the difference lies. The man you found in the flat is not dead. He is alive, but in a coma.'

'But the rigor mortis? Doesn't that happen only after death?'

'Yes, and that's how it's similar to the Diya Chaudhry case.'

Kapoor frowned. 'Explain.'

'Um, as you just stated, rigor mortis happens after death. It is a temporary condition, usually lasting around 72 hours.' Suresh looked apologetic. 'I will have to explain some of the science for you to understand what has happened in this man's case.'

'Go ahead. I'm all ears.'

'So, after death, the membranes of muscle cells become more permeable to calcium ions. Living cells expend energy to transport calcium ions out of the cells. But after death, calcium ions flow into the muscle cells, causing muscle contraction through the promotion of the cross bridge attachment between actin and myosin, which work together in muscle contraction.'

'So what you're saying is that after death, due to calcium ions flowing into the muscle cells, they contract.'

'Yes, sir. Now, the energy molecule, adenosine triphosphate, or ATP, is required by muscle cells to pump the calcium out of the cells. So, muscle cells need ATP to release from a contracted state. Upon death, the reactions that recycle ATP cease and ATP reserves are quickly exhausted. When the ATP is depleted, calcium pumping stops.'

'And the muscle cells remain contracted, resulting in stiffening or rigor mortis. Ah, I see.' Kapoor nodded. 'So why is it temporary?'

'The actin and myosin fibres remain linked until the muscles start decomposing.'

'Got it. So decomposition causes the delinking of the muscle fibres and the contraction ends.'

'Yes sir.'

'But in this case, you say the man is alive.'

'Yes sir. There is a strong pulse and breathing is normal.'

'So how could rigor mortis have occurred?'

'Sometimes ATP depletion in muscle cells can happen due to extreme exertion or hysteria,' Suresh explained. 'In these cases, the ATP levels are restored by the base metabolism, since the person is alive. That is what happened in this case.

It's similar to the Diya Chaudhry case, in the sense that this is exactly what would have happened to her. When she died, rigor mortis would have set in, but somehow her metabolism was revived and the rigor mortis would have ended until her vital functions finally ceased.'

Kapoor rubbed his face with one hand, trying to digest the information. 'How is something like this even possible?' he asked.

Suresh shook his head. 'I've never seen anything like it before. I … I just can't explain it.'

Kapoor looked at him wearily. 'Nothing in this case is like anything we've seen before,' he told Suresh. 'And your explanation for this man is exactly the same as the one you provided me for the girl?'

'My personal opinion, sir?'

'Yes. The one about the soul being sucked out et cetera.'

'Well,' Suresh hesitated, 'this man is alive, so his soul is obviously intact. I personally feel that it is possible that there was an attempt to extract his soul, which could have caused the exertion or hysteria that led to the rigor mortis. It would have happened shortly before you reached the flat. In the girl's case, she died instantly, but in this man's case, he didn't die.'

'Good enough for me. Thanks.' Kapoor dismissed Suresh and the forensics expert scurried out of the room, glad that the conversation was over.

Chapter Thirty-seven

A New Development

The Gurukul
Panna National Park

Satyavachana looked solemnly at the group that had been hastily assembled in the hall.

It was close to midnight and the students had all turned in for the night. The orbs that lit up the Gurukul had been extinguished and darkness reigned over the forest.

The Maharishi had suddenly appeared, knocking on the door of Jignesh's cottage, insisting on an immediate gathering of the Mahamati Council. It was important, he had urged.

Wondering what the urgency could be, Jignesh had quickly woken up Usha, Parth and Kanakpratap, to hear what the Maharishi had to say.

'I hope you have a good reason to make us all stay up long beyond the hours that we should be awake,' Jignesh began the proceedings.

'I do,' Satyavachana said quietly. 'What I have to say is of great concern to the Sangha.'

'Well, let's hear it then,' Kanakpratap said, rubbing the sleep out of his eyes.

'You know that I have been keeping tabs on Shukra for the last ten days,' the Maharishi began, his voice even and low. 'I had told you six days ago that Shukra had sent the Nagas back to Mahatala. Well, something curious has happened since then. I have spent the last ten nights hovering around Shukra's hideaway. For the first couple of nights he kept coming and going—at least at night. Then, from the third night onwards, the cavern was empty. And it has been that way for the last seven nights. He has not returned.'

The others were instantly jolted awake by this revelation.

'He's definitely up to something,' Parth observed.

'Yes,' Jignesh said thoughtfully. 'The question is: Is this absence temporary? I mean, will he be back soon? Or has he disappeared once again, like he did fourteen years ago?'

'I cannot find him,' Satyavachana said simply. 'That means he has either taken on a different form or has disguised himself in some other way, using his powers of illusion.'

'That would mean that he will be gone for some time,' Usha commented. 'Such an effort to cover his tracks can only mean he is planning something big. But that will also take time to accomplish.'

'I will keep searching and checking on his hideout for the foreseeable future,' Satyavachana assured them. 'I will get to know if he returns.'

'Are the defences for the Gurukul ready yet?' Kanakpratap addressed Jignesh. 'The Mahashastrakar had indicated they would be ready in a week's time, the last time we met her. It is more than a week since that day.'

'I believe they will be ready in a day or two,' Jignesh replied. 'We have to ensure that the new defences are deployed immediately. And if Shukra does plan to disappear for some time, we need to double our efforts to achieve our goals.'

'True,' Parth agreed. 'We must make full use of whatever additional time we get while Shukra is away.'

He left unsaid the two thoughts that were uppermost in everyone's minds.

If Shukra had disappeared, it meant he felt confident enough that the Sangha was unprepared to do anything to stop him.

And if he was planning something big, what could it be? Would the Sangha be ready for it?

Chapter Thirty-eight

Grim Possibility

The Gurukul

Jignesh stared grimly at the other members of the Sangha Council who had assembled in Panna to take stock of the fresh developments that had come to their attention.

The new and stronger defences had been deployed at all the Gurukuls across the country. There would be no repetition of the tragedy at Corbett, at least in the foreseeable future. The Shastrakars were working on developing and advancing the new defences even further, keeping in mind the possibility that Shukra might release more of the inhabitants of Pataala-lok. If that happened, the Gurukuls had to be prepared. And, since the nature and powers of the inhabitants of the five levels of Pataala-lok were known to the Council, it was possible for the weapon forgers of the Sangha to anticipate future attacks and prepare their defences accordingly.

But it was the news from Delhi that had the Sangha troubled.

'First Diya, now one of the Akshapatalikas,' Kanakpratap murmured, looking deeply disturbed. 'What is happening?'

'What this means,' Usha said slowly, 'is that there is someone out there who has the power of the siddhis. If the Akshapatalika was possessed, someone had to have the capability of doing it. Someone who is on Shukra's side. But who could it be?'

'It can't be a vikriti,' Jignesh declared grimly. 'I cannot believe that.'

No one wanted to state the only alternative explanation.

Satyavachana voiced it for them.

'If it wasn't the vikritis,' he looked around at the group, 'there is only one other possibility. The Sangha has a traitor in its ranks.'

Chapter Thirty-nine

Kapoor Has a Plan

Raman Kapoor's Office
New Delhi

Raman Kapoor held the receiver to his ear, listening to the ring of the phone at the other end of the line. Finally, the call was picked up.

'Hello?'

'Is this SSP Dubey?' Kapoor enquired.

'Yes, it is.' There was a pause. 'Kapoor? Is that you?'

'Yes it is, buddy!' A smile crossed Kapoor's face. SSP Dubey and he had been batch mates at the Police Academy in Hyderabad. Dubey was now with the Special Task Force, or the STF as it was commonly known, for Uttar Pradesh and was based in Lucknow.

'Hey, good to hear from you,' Dubey said enthusiastically. 'How have you been?'

The two men exchanged notes for a few minutes before Kapoor decided to get to the point.

'The reason I called you,' he explained, 'is that I need your help.'

'Tell me what you want. The resources of the STF are at your disposal as long as the jurisdiction is UP.'

'Thanks, my friend. That is exactly what I was hoping for. I am investigating one of the toughest cases of my life. Every clue has led to a dead end so far. So I decided to follow the trail backwards and it leads to Allahabad.'

'Allahabad?'

'Yes.' Kapoor swiftly explained the background of the case.

'I see,' Dubey said when Kapoor had finished. 'So you want to go to Allahabad and poke around there to see what you can find.'

'Exactly.'

'Will a plainclothes driver and a sub inspector in an unmarked vehicle serve your purpose? I'll find a couple of chaps who are trustworthy and will be useful in case there is any trouble.'

'Dubey, that will be perfect. Thanks a ton.' Kapoor had a look of grim satisfaction on his face as he put the phone down and stared at the files that lay on his desk.

His new case was getting nowhere. The tail he had put on Tiwari, since their meeting eight days ago, had yielded no results yet. The Sanskrit professor seemed to live a very ordinary life. College, tuitions and home. He did have a few friends with whom he socialised on weekends but, as far as Kapoor could tell based on Harish's reports over the last eight days, there seemed to be nothing out of the ordinary about him.

Another blind alley.

And the only clues he had led back to Trivedi and Upadhyay.

He decided that he would return to pursuing that case. There were too many connections for it to be mere coincidence.

And now, he had a plan.

So far, the Trivedi and Upadhyay murder case had confounded him. With its multiple twists and turns, he had been outfoxed every step of the way. Every clue had ended in a cul-de-sac. Every step forward led two steps back.

A lesser man would have given up and relegated the case to the heap of unsolved cases that lined the filing cabinets of police posts around the country.

But not Raman Kapoor.

His decision to go to Allahabad had been quick and the rationale simple. Upadhyay himself had spoken of the friendship between the three men—Singh, Trivedi and Upadhyay—from Allahabad. Clearly, there was a backstory here that needed to be discovered.

And the only way he was going to be able to uncover that backstory was by going to its source.

Allahabad.

Chapter Forty

Kapoor Investigates

Allahabad

Raman Kapoor sat back in the Toyota Fortuner provided by the STF, lost in thought. His flight from Delhi had been uneventful and he had spent most of it going over his plans for generating leads in Allahabad.

He had never been to Allahabad before, but it wasn't the culture or history of the city that he was looking forward to savouring. Kapoor's entire focus was the case. It had taken him two weeks to wrap up things in Delhi, but he was now in the city where Upadhyay, Singh and Trivedi had lived their lives prior to migrating to Delhi.

And Vishwaraj.

There were several possibilities he had considered. The three men had got mixed up in something nefarious and fled to Delhi to escape the consequences. Or, they were afraid of something or someone in Allahabad and had taken flight to get away from that person.

But where did Vishwaraj fit in?

Kapoor's instincts told him that, while the two men he had met a month and a half ago had seemed normal and unassuming, the subsequent events—especially the mysterious murder of Upadhyay—pointed to a past that was questionable.

Well, he was here to question it.

And find some answers.

And while he was at it, he wanted to find out what part Vishwaraj had played in the entire matter.

Kapoor stared at the backs of the heads of the two policemen in the front seats of the vehicle.

Mishra, the driver, and Mirza, the sub inspector assigned to him by Dubey. Both were in plainclothes and Dubey had assured him of their reliability in case things took a turn for the worse.

'Mirza,' he addressed the sub inspector, 'where can we sit and discuss our plans?'

'Sir,' Mirza turned in his seat to face Kapoor, 'I am taking you to the guesthouse at police HQ. You had asked for accommodation that would enable you to keep a low profile and not draw any attention to your presence in Allahabad. The guesthouse is the best place—there are police officers constantly checking in and checking out—so you will be just another senior officer passing through. We can sit there and you can tell me what you need. My orders are to provide you with whatever information you need and coordinate with resources across the state for anything that you require.'

'Great.' Kapoor settled back and gazed out of the window.

Presently, the vehicle drew up at a nondescript house and Mirza jumped out, moving swiftly to open the rear door of the vehicle to allow Kapoor to alight.

'This way, sir,' he gestured, indicating a corridor that led to a staircase, as the two men walked through the main entrance.

They walked up two flights of stairs and arrived at a door. Mirza unlocked it before stepping aside, allowing Kapoor to enter.

Kapoor didn't waste time looking around. He sat down on a sofa and gestured to Mirza to sit down.

'Now,' he began. 'Here's what we are going to do.'

He opened his briefcase and took out photographs of Virendra Singh and Naresh Upadhyay, spreading them on the centre table between the two sofas.

'I need information on these two men,' Kapoor told Mirza. 'They lived in Allahabad, probably growing up here before migrating to Delhi.' He had decided not to divulge too much information. The case was complicated enough as it was and he didn't want to spook Mirza. He had already seen what Harish had gone through in Panna. He didn't want Dubey calling him up later, asking what he'd done to one of his best men.

'I'll begin working on it right away, sir.' Mirza picked up the photographs and studied them. 'Their names, sir?'

'Virendra Singh and Naresh Upadhyay.'

'Singh and Upadhyay are fairly common names in Allahabad.' Mirza looked at Kapoor. 'Anything else on them, sir? Something that can help us narrow down our search?'

Kapoor smiled. 'Yes. Both men spoke fluent English. Clearly, they studied in an English-medium school.' He looked at Mirza.

The sub inspector held Kapoor's gaze.

'Got it, sir. There are only two English-medium schools in Allahabad that these men could have attended while growing up. Boys' High School and St. Joseph's.'

'Very good. So here's a thought. Upadhyay told me that he taught at a school in Allahabad. It stands to reason that he would have taught at one of the schools you mentioned. It is worth checking on that angle as well. And Singh is a body builder. He owns a chain of gyms in Delhi.'

Mirza looked thoughtful. 'If Singh grew up in Allahabad and was into body building, then we will have to check with the *akharas* here. In the 1990s, there were hardly any gyms in this city. But there are a couple of akharas that were quite famous.' He grinned. 'And technology can help us with that, sir. There are WhatsApp groups for these akharas. We can circulate Singh's photograph on these groups and see what we come up with.'

Kapoor nodded. Mirza was smart. Dubey had meant what he said about the capabilities of the men he had assigned to him.

'So here's what we're going to do.' Kapoor leaned forward. 'You check with the akharas and try and figure out how to get into their WhatsApp groups. I will check with the two schools to see where Upadhyay taught. It shouldn't take us long to figure out where these two men lived and what their social circles were. Once we know that, we just have to interview people and get the information we need.'

'Yes sir.' Mirza nodded. 'Doesn't look like there's going to be a problem. We'll have you back in Delhi in a couple of days.'

'Brilliant.' Kapoor was now convinced that he had his dream team. His driver had not been tested yet, but he was sure that, if push came to shove, Mishra would prove every bit as useful as Mirza was proving to be at this moment. For the first time in more than two weeks, he felt upbeat. This case and its peculiarities had confounded him at every step. Now, he felt the mists clearing.

They knew what they had to do. Their plan would lead them to where Upadhyay and Singh had lived in Allahabad.

And, once there, he would find out what the two men had been involved in before they made a break for it and headed for Delhi.

He would not rest until this case was solved.

Chapter Forty-one

Frustration

Allahabad

Raman Kapoor stared glumly at the two photographs on the table.

It was one week since he had arrived in Allahabad; seven days since his first, sunny conversation with Mirza about what they needed to do to crack the case.

It had all seemed so easy then. Kapoor kicked himself for allowing himself to be beguiled into thinking that he had finally reached a stage where the case could move forward.

He had forgotten, or optimistically ignored, the fact that nothing in this case was as it seemed to be. You saw one thing but if you scratched deeper, you found something else. Or nothing at all.

It was the same now.

Mirza had begun searching for contacts who were on the WhatsApp groups for the akharas, while simultaneously talking to people at the akharas to find out about Virendra Singh.

In the meanwhile, Kapoor had sought meetings with the principals of the two schools Mirza had told him about: Boys' High School and St. Joseph's College.

Mirza had been confident of finding someone on the WhatsApp groups, since he had got some leads from people he had spoken to; leads for contacts who would have been active at the akharas fourteen or more years ago, when Singh would have frequented them.

But his inquiries about Virendra Singh had drawn a blank. No one he met had heard of a Virendra Singh who might have worked out fourteen years ago, at any of these places. A couple of people had said that the photograph looked familiar but had no further information to offer.

It had taken Kapoor a few days to meet the principals since they were travelling on work. But when he finally met them—they were extremely courteous and cooperative—he discovered he had been walking down a cul-de-sac.

His hopes had lifted when the principal of St. Joseph's confirmed that Vishwaraj had, indeed, studied at the school and passed out from there just two years ago. But Naresh Upadhyay was another matter altogether.

According to both principals, who had taken the trouble of checking their school records, no one by that name had ever taught in their school.

How was it even possible? Kapoor was stumped.

Had both the men lied about living in Allahabad?

Kapoor refused to accept this possibility. If Upadhyay had wanted to lie, there was no reason for him to admit that he had taught Vishwaraj in Allahabad. He could have simply said that he had met Trivedi in Delhi and had no idea about Vishwaraj.

No, Kapoor decided, Upadhyay had been truthful and sincere when he had spoken about Allahabad.

The two men *had* to have lived here all those years ago.

So why couldn't he find any trace of them?

Chapter Forty-two

Hopeless?

Allahabad

'Sir,' Mirza ventured, 'I have an idea.'

Kapoor stared at him through bleary eyes. He had not slept well last night. He had already spent too much time in Allahabad, having been away from his post in Delhi for over a week. He had to return today and he was not happy leaving the investigation at a dead end.

'What?' he barked.

'Maybe,' Mirza suggested tentatively, sensing Kapoor's black mood, 'if we can get photographs of both men, or at least one of them, from fourteen years ago, we might be able to make some progress. Their faces could have changed over the years, which is probably why people cannot recognise them from the photographs we have. We can try and connect with the alumni networks for these schools and see if we can get positive identifications. There are WhatsApp groups for the alumni. If we can get them to share these old photographs, we should get a hit.'

'Hmmm.' Kapoor considered this and cursed. Why had he not thought of it before? This was just the kind of thinking that had made his reputation in the force. He looked at Mirza with a newfound respect. Mirza was his kind of man. A younger Raman Kapoor.

'Brilliant idea!' Kapoor clapped Mirza on his shoulder. 'I'm going back to Delhi tonight. I'll work on getting us passport photographs or DL photographs from whenever they came to Delhi from Allahabad. That should get us somewhere.'

'Yes, sir. In fact, we could also check with the stationery shops in the vicinity of both schools once we have the photos. I am sure that one or more of those shops would have been around fourteen years ago and will be able to identify at least Upadhyay, if not Singh.'

Kapoor's spirits rose again. All was not bleak. There was always something that you could do, even if the situation seemed absolutely hopeless.

He would get the fourteen-year-old photographs, one way or another. Whatever it took.

What was he going to find out then, he wondered.

Chapter Forty-three

Maya Makes Progress

The Forest
Unknown Location

'Thought control,' Satyavachana told Maya, as they walked together through the forest that the Maharishi had designated as her practice area, 'is the most critical step to becoming a Rishi. It helps you to repress thoughts that chain you to your baser emotions. If you can control your thoughts, you can control your emotions and you will achieve peace. It is only then that you can take the first step away from your sadh life, become one with the universe, and discover your powers.' He looked at her. 'I do believe you are getting better at it, now that we are away from whatever it was that was disturbing you at the Gurukul. Since we began practising in this forest, one and a half months ago, you have definitely made progress.'

'Thank you, Mahamati.' Maya was pleased with the praise. Her mind reached back to when her lessons with Satyavachana had resumed. She had been unsure of how to address the Maharishi, but he had been quick to realise her dilemma and had suggested that she address him as she addressed Jignesh, since she was comfortable with the use of the title that was used for all the teachers in the Gurukul. Maya had been hesitant at first, since she knew that the Maharishi was not at all happy at being associated with the Sangha in any way, but he had appeared to be quite okay with her use of the title, so she had complied.

In the last month and a half, Maya had tried her best, while practising, to push all kinds of thoughts away. In the beginning, the memories of the carnage at Corbett would suddenly come rushing into her consciousness when she tried to meditate and she had to create a mental vacuum that banished them from her mind. Then, after the ill-fated midnight meeting where she had disagreed with Arjun's idea of rebelling against the Sangha, she had wrestled with the guilt and wretchedness she had felt afterwards.

It was only after Arjun had met her and made up with her that she was able to dismiss all thoughts from her mind and concentrate on what she had to do: control her emotions. And she had spent the rest of the last forty days after that working diligently on Satyavachana's instructions.

'We fear things that we do not understand,' Satyavachana had explained. 'Usually these are things that are different from us in some way—appearance, habits, speech. And emotions like fear, anger, apprehension or frustration take away our ability to become one with the universe. Look at the sadhs. They spend their entire lives trying to be different from one another, emphasising and highlighting their differences. What does that engender?'

'A lack of ability to understand other people, especially those who are perceived to be different,' Maya had replied.

'Correct. And that gives rise to suspicion, apprehension and fear. So, instead of becoming one with the universe and embracing their differences, sadhs move away from each other, weakening the forces of the universe that can help them accomplish so much. If you want to become a Rishi, you will need to let go of the differences in your mind between you and everything around you.'

Maya had nodded. 'I understand, Mahamati. But understanding and doing are two different things. When I meditate, I am able to control my thoughts. As long as I am focusing on the trees around us, the birds, the small animals scurrying through the undergrowth in the forest, I have no trouble. But I don't know what I will do if I see the pisacha again.'

'You won't,' Satyavachana had assured her. 'Not for a while. I revealed the creature to you only to see how you would react. So I would know what to focus on while teaching you. We'll get back to the pisacha once you have gained a certain level of control and are able to control your fear and revulsion on seeing the creature.'

Maya had nodded again. She resolved to work hard on her meditation to ensure that she reached this level as quickly as possible.

Satyavachana's voice intruded on her reverie.

'Now that you have begun making progress in thought control,' he said, 'it is time to start work on the next step.'

Chapter Forty-four

Maya Understands

The Forest

Maya waited, curious.

'Once your thoughts and emotions are under control, you must use your mind to move closer to oneness with the object that you decide to focus on, whether it is a person, a tree or a pisacha. That will lead you to oneness with the universe.'

'How is that possible, Mahamati?' Maya could not fathom how it was possible to overcome her revulsion for the pisacha she had encountered the last time, leave alone moving closer to oneness with the creature.

'Suspend your judgement,' Satyavachana said, wagging his finger. 'All of us humans are born with an innate capacity to make spontaneous and instinctive judgements about everything around us. We look at something and judge it as good or bad. And very often, we do this without even knowing much about whatever we are judging. Isn't that true?'

'Yes, Mahamati.' Maya remembered the time she had seen Ratan Tiwari for the first time. With a twinge of guilt and regret, she recalled how she had dismissed the possibility of his being her benefactor simply because of his appearance. Yet, he had been the one who had rescued her from the Metro station and delivered her safely to the Gurukul.

'Judgement emphasises differences. You need to find the similarities. And replace the tendency to judge with an ability to understand, to empathise. That will bring you closer to the object of your focus.'

'But how do I do that with a pisacha?' Maya couldn't repress an involuntary shudder as she thought about understanding or empathising with the vile-looking creature.

Satyavachana stopped and looked at her. 'Compassion, my child. That is the answer. If you are one with the pishacha, you will feel compassion for it. You will feel its pain and suffering. Remember, the pisacha is a soul trapped in a body that it hates. It takes birth as a pisacha not out of choice but as a result of the karma in its previous birth, which dooms it to suffer as a revolting creature that is destined to cause suffering to others. Would you like to be reborn as a pisacha?'

'No, Mahamati.'

'Then why hate the poor soul who has been reborn as one? Why feel disgust and revulsion for it when it cannot control what it looks like and what it does? If you understand this, then you will feel compassion for it. And that will make you one, even with a pisacha.'

'Then why do we kill pisachas, Mahamati?' Maya wanted to know. She didn't understand. If she had to be compassionate towards the creature, shouldn't it be allowed to live?

'Great question, Maya. The reason we kill pisachas is because of the compassion we feel for them.' He smiled as he saw Maya's puzzled expression. 'Let me explain. The pisacha is a creature that causes suffering to other living beings. There's no doubt about that. So it must be killed. Second point: the soul that is reborn as a pisacha is also suffering, living a life of misery. By killing the creature, we are putting that soul out of its misery and hastening its rebirth in another body. You must destroy the pisacha, but not in anger or hate. You should destroy it so that you can liberate the suffering soul locked up inside that body and move it forward in its cycle of rebirths. That is why we use a team consisting of a Rishi and a Kshatriya, especially when we encounter creatures like this. While the consecrated weapons of the Kshatriyas can destroy them, the mantras of the Rishi will speed the liberated souls of the creatures on their way to the next birth. It is the same thing with pretas and bhutas. They are both spirits, atmas of people who have not yet been assigned a new body in their next rebirth, but are being made to wait as a result of their karma in their previous birth. That is the reason pretas and bhutas try to possess living bodies. They remember the pleasures of having a physical body and want to experience these again, but cannot do so.'

'But we cannot kill pretas or bhutas.'

Satyavachana shook his head. 'No we cannot. They are atmas. They cannot be killed. That is where we Rishis come in. We use mantras to put their souls at peace so that they may hasten towards their next birth. And that is why compassion becomes so important. Compassion and empathy.'

Maya's face lit up with understanding. 'I get it now. I'm going to work on it.'

'Very good. Now let me show you something new. Something that you are going to love. Something that is going to leave you amazed.'

Chapter Forty-five

Maya Gets a Gift

The Forest

'I think it is time I introduced you to something that all Maharishis use,' Satyavachana told Maya with a smile. 'While you have a long way to go before becoming even a Rishi, I am curious to see how you will handle this. And it will be useful practice for your thought control.' He lowered his voice to a conspiratorial whisper. 'Just don't tell anyone in the Sangha. They will be very upset.' He chuckled. It didn't seem to matter to him that the Sangha would be upset.

Maya waited and wondered what the Maharishi was going to reveal to her.

Satyavachana stood with his hands outstretched and closed his eyes.

Maya jumped as something appeared in the palm of his right hand.

It was a long wooden staff of irregular width, crooked and bent in places, narrow for most of its length and widening near the top. Almost like a club, except the head was not bulbous. More like a walking stick, except this one was covered with obscure symbols and letters that were carved into the wood in some unknown script.

Satyavachana opened his eyes and rested the narrow end of the staff on the ground.

Maya stared at it, bewildered.

'This,' Satyavachana told her, 'is the instrument that Maharishi Vashishta used to confound Vishwamitra.'

Maya knew at once what it was. Of course! She had read about it in the Ramayana. The story of the battle between Vashishta and Vishwamitra where the latter had hurled all kinds of weapons including mighty celestial missiles at the Maharishi; Vashishta had nullified every one of them using his brahmadanda.

Her head was spinning. Was Satyavachana going to teach her how to use this device? A part of her felt apprehensive. Did she have the ability to use the brahmadanda to do all the wondrous things it was reputed to do? Her father had told her that the brahmadanda was even more powerful than the Vajra—Indra's thunderbolt. This was because the Vajra could blast only those objects or beings that lay within its immediate range. But the brahmadanda was able to smite whole countries and entire races across generations.

'This is for you,' Satyavachana told her, answering her unasked question. 'My gift to you.'

Maya was beside herself with delight. To be gifted an essential part of a Maharishi's armoury while she was still coming to grips with thought control and mantras was beyond her wildest expectations. She had no idea why Satyavachana was giving a weapon as powerful as this to a novice like her, but it didn't matter. If the Maharishi felt it was appropriate, she wasn't going to make a big deal out of it.

A thought struck her, dampening her excitement. 'But how will I take it back to the Gurukul?' she asked. 'Everyone will see it and they will know. Won't they take it away from me then?'

'No, they won't,' Satyavachana said, his eyes twinkling. 'You see, the brahmadanda has a curious but interesting property.'

'It is collapsible?' Maya ventured, her excitement getting the better of her.

Satyavachana frowned. 'No, child. Wherever do you get your ideas from?'

'It's the kind of thing that you see in the movies,' Maya said. 'I'm sure there is a superhero somewhere who has a weapon like this and it is collapsible, so it becomes a small stick which can be hidden away inside a haversack.'

'A superhero.'

Maya nodded.

'And where would you find this superhero, child?'

'Hollywood movies,' Maya replied, oblivious to the disapproving look the Maharishi was giving her.

'Western movies,' Satyavachana snorted violently, making Maya jump. 'The brahmadanda is thousands of years old— going back to the time of the Ramayana and even earlier. The stories from the Western world take place in the blink of an eye in comparison to the antiquity of the Maharishis. Next you'll be telling me that mantras were invented by the Western world.'

'No,' Maya replied. 'But they have magic spells.'

'Well,' Satyavachana said firmly, 'there is no such thing as magic or spells. Have you ever come across anyone who used magic spells in their everyday lives? No. But there are millions of people who use mantras every day of their lives. Mantras are real. They have power. Everything I have taught you, and will teach you, is about something much deeper, much more ancient than the stories of sorcerers and magic spells that you have come across so far.'

Maya nodded, chastened.

'Now, what was I saying?' Satyavachana frowned. 'Oh, yes, I was going to tell you about something curious about the brahmadanda.'

Chapter Forty-six

A Decision

The Gurukul
Panna National Park

Adira was in the dorm when Maya appeared suddenly, making her jump and drop the book she was reading.

'I wish you wouldn't do that,' Adira grumbled. 'I can never get used to you disappearing and reappearing like the Cheshire cat.'

Maya laughed. 'Dude, you're no Alice in Wonderland.'

Her smile abruptly disappeared as a sudden giddiness took hold of her.

'What's the matter, Maya?' Adira jumped off the bed with concern as Maya bent over double. There was no pain. Just a sudden surge of the now familiar call, so strong today that the world around her had spun.

'I … I'm fine,' Maya lied. She didn't know how to explain it.

'Just lie down, okay?' Adira made sure that Maya was comfortably in bed before she switched off the lights and left. 'I'll be in the common room if you need anything.'

'Thanks, Adira.'

Maya was grateful for the friends she had made at the Gurukul. She lay in bed for a while, trying to relax and get rid of the sensation that had made her feel ill. But it just wouldn't go away.

If anything, the call grew stronger, beckoning to her, urging her towards it.

Maya's mind went back to the day, almost a month and a half back, when she had made up with Arjun after their disagreement over acting against the Sangha's wishes. They had walked through the Rishi practice field, talking, when suddenly the strange tug had begun to grow stronger. Even though she had originally set out that day to find the source of the mysterious sensation, Maya had decided to turn back, not wanting to investigate further while Arjun was present.

She lay for a while, undecided. Then, her mind made up, she rose and made her way down the stairs.

Adira saw her pass the common room entrance and came rushing out.

'You should be resting,' she scolded Maya.

'I'm going out for a walk,' Maya told her. 'The fresh air will do me good.'

'I'll come with you.'

'No, no,' Maya protested. 'I'll be fine. I think I just need some time to myself after all the practice that Maharishi Satyavachana has been putting me through.'

'You sure?'

Maya nodded. 'Absolutely. I'll be fine.'

With misgivings, Adira backed off.

Maya made her way past the classroom block and walked down the length of the Rishi practice field. This was where the sensation had been the strongest during her walk with Arjun.

But where was this strange pull, this inexplicable tug emanating from?

What was it that was calling to her so insistently, every single day?

There was something happening that she could not understand. She had to know what it was.

Maya decided to experiment. She began moving in different directions, checking to see if the tug grew stronger or weaker.

Finally, she worked out the source of the mysterious sensation.

It was coming from the direction of the Dandaka forest.

Chapter Forty-seven

A Mystery

The Rishi Practice Field

Maya cut across the Rishi practice field and headed straight towards the forest.

The sun, a red ball of fire, hung low in the western sky and there was still enough light for her to see her way.

After a few minutes of brisk walking, the forest loomed ahead of her and she felt the familiar tug grow stronger the closer she got. It was almost as if the Dandaka was urging her to approach and enter.

A vague apprehension hovered at the back of her mind as she walked briskly towards the forest.

What was it about the Dandaka forest that was drawing her towards it?

Maya realised that no one ever talked about the forest. It was there. That was all. In plain sight, yet hidden away from everyone's sight by the simple device of being ignored.

She too had taken its presence on the Gurukul campus for granted within the first few days of arriving here.

Now, she wondered why it was out of bounds for the students. Was it dangerous? But why would that be? Wasn't this the very forest that Lord Rama, along with Sita and Lakshmana, had lived in during their exile from Ayodhya?

It couldn't be because there were wild beasts in it. The Gurukul itself was right in the middle of a forest. Wild animals roamed the campus, though she had never seen a tiger or any other animal that might pose a threat to the residents.

She recalled the fact about Dandaka that had struck her when Jignesh had pointed it out during her first tour of the Gurukul—the forest had been created by Shukra himself, thousands of years ago. It had been an act of rage, a curse.

Yet, Arjun had told her after the rout of the Nagas that even they seemed to fear the forest. They had besieged the Gurukul from all sides, except from the direction of the forest. Arjun had also told her that he had heard that the Nagas would never attack the Gurukul by traversing the Dandaka. It was a natural, protective barrier, apparently even more reliable and powerful than the mantras that kept the Gurukul safe.

Maya reached the boundary of the Rishi practice field, marked by a hedge that was five feet tall, at a safe distance from the forest. She began searching for a gap in the hedge that would allow her to approach the Dandaka.

Unable to find one, she finally decided to squeeze through, getting scratches on her hands as she protected her face with her palms.

Between the field and the forest lay a wild, grassy stretch of land that she had never noticed before. Whether it was because the hedge had blocked the view or her own lack of attention, she had never realised the vastness of the strip of land that lay between the practice field and the Dandaka.

The ground under her feet was uneven and rough, and she wondered if there were snakes here.

But the magnetic attraction of the forest drew her feet onwards.

After a short while, the forest was close enough for her to distinguish the trees. The Dandaka was dense—trees crowded together with barely any space between their trunks, their branches and foliage intertwining to form a thickly woven canopy that rose a hundred feet or more above the forest floor.

As Maya drew nearer, she noticed that the canopy of leaves was so thick that hardly any sunlight filtered through. From afar, the Dandaka had always looked like it was shrouded in darkness, even in the daytime. From up close, Maya realised this was because it was enveloped in a darkness of its own making. She wondered how any animals managed to live in it. How could the undergrowth survive in the intense darkness?

She walked closer. A few feet from the outer line of trees, she stopped and studied the forest intently.

Chapter Forty-eight

Friends

The Gurukul

Adira knocked on the door of the cottage housing Amyra's dorm.

The door was opened by a young novice who looked at her, awestruck. The novices and other students training for the Gana didn't really mix—Amyra's friendship with Maya had been an exception and only because Amyra had been persistent in seeking her friendship. The tales of Maya's exploits during the siege of the Gurukul had made the rounds of the novices' quarters, embellished as the story spread, with Amyra no doubt contributing much of the embellishment.

When it became known that Adira was a friend of the One as well as of Maya, her standing among the novices had gone up even more.

'I wanted to see Amyra,' an amused Adira told the novice.

'I'll call her,' the novice said, excited and shy at the same time, no doubt thrilled that one of the saviours of the Gurukul had asked her for help, however insignificant.

'Thanks,' Adira smiled at her and the novice's face glowed as she disappeared to call Amyra.

Adira didn't have to wait long before Amyra came hurrying to the door.

'Adira!' Amyra squealed. She was always delighted to see any of the Saptas. Then she noticed Adira's serious expression and sobered up immediately.

'What happened?'

'I ... I'm not sure.' Adira was hesitant. She really didn't know why she had come seeking Amyra. But now that she was here, it was time to put the novice to work. 'I need your help. It's about Maya.'

'Of course!' Amyra was always ready to help where Maya was concerned.

'I think something is wrong,' Adira told her. 'I can't be sure, which is why I want your help. Can you come to our dorm and run a check?'

'On what?'

Adira explained what she had in mind and Amyra nodded. 'I'm not sure if I can help,' she said, 'but I'll try.'

The two girls made their way to Maya's dorm and sprinted up the stairs. Amyra screwed up her face as soon as she was inside the room. She turned to face Adira.

'This is not good,' the novice said.

'What is it? What can you sense?'

'I don't know for sure,' Amyra's brow creased as she concentrated. 'It ... it is very fuzzy. I see Maya appearing in the room. You're there too. You make her lie down and then you leave the room. Then ...' the furrows on her forehead grew deeper, 'she feels something. I don't know what. I can sense the vibrations. There is something else in the dorm, but I can't feel it; I can't sense it. Maya gets up and leaves.'

Amyra looked at Adira. 'Whatever it was, it can't be good. Something compelled her to get off the bed and walk out that door.' She pointed to the entrance to the dorm. 'I don't know what it was, but I could feel it through space and time.' She clutched Adira's hand. 'What do we do?'

'We find her.' Adira's face was set. She looked at Amyra. 'Can you track her?'

'I think I can,' Amyra replied. 'The trace is quite recent.'

'Let's go then.'

The two girls hurried down the Central Avenue, past the Assembly Hall and the classroom block, towards the Rishi practice field.

But Maya was nowhere to be seen.

'Where could she have gone?' Adira wondered.

Amyra shook her head. She was trying to walk as fast as possible, following Maya's tracks with the use of her psychic powers. It wasn't easy. One step in the wrong direction and the tracks would disappear. She had to course correct continuously according to the vibrations through space and time that told her that Maya had passed this way recently.

Neither girl had any idea where they were headed.

It was only when they reached the hedge bordering the Rishi practice field that they realised where Maya had bent her steps.

Adira gasped. 'She couldn't have gone in there!'

Amyra nodded, a doleful expression on her face. The vibrations all pointed in one direction.

The Dandaka.

'She's mad!' Adira exclaimed. 'No one goes there! Whatever came into her mind to make her do this?'

Suddenly, they heard a scream.

And another.

It was Maya.

Chapter Forty-nine

Fear

The Dandaka Forest

The Dandaka was dark, formidable, brooding.

Not a leaf stirred. There was no breeze blowing through this forest.

From where she stood, Maya could see no undergrowth, among the line of outer trees at least.

The Dandaka was quiet as death, unmoving, impenetrable. Maya could not see how anyone could possibly enter the forest; there was no path to be seen between the trees and no space for anyone to squeeze through, even if they wanted to. She thought of the Nagas and their bulk. There was no way they could have marched through the forest to the Gurukul, even if they had mustered the courage to enter.

What was inside the forest that terrified the Nagas so?

Suddenly, she felt it again; the same nagging sensation. She had forgotten it in the wonder of being here, so close to the forest.

But now, it hit her with an intensity she could not have imagined.

Maya could *feel* the forest calling to her, drawing her closer to it.

An unseen force beckoned to her, urging her to enter the forest.

She did not feel uneasy or dizzy this time, but the urge was so strong that she felt it take hold of her feet, as if to propel her forward.

Shocked and alarmed, she forced herself back, trying to shake off the compulsion to move forward, to enter the forest. But it persisted.

A sudden doubt arose in her mind, sowing the seeds of panic.

Had she been wrong to disregard Jignesh's warning about the Dandaka? Had she committed a colossal blunder by coming here today?

For no reason, the thought flashed through her mind that the forest was alive, that it could consume her. Or drive her insane.

What was happening to her?

It was like being in a nightmare.

Panic finally took hold of her mind, bursting within as a deep darkness that washed away all her thoughts and filled her mind with terror.

Maya screamed.

Chapter Fifty

A Promise is Made

The Rishi Practice Field

Adira and Amyra struggled to push through the hedge that bordered the practice field. Finally emerging on the other side, they sprinted towards the Dandaka, unmindful of the dangers and the warnings that had kept students and faculty alike away from it.

For them, only one thing mattered at this moment.

The solitary figure standing near the trees at the edge of the forest, screaming with terror.

What had happened?

The two girls came running up to Maya.

'Maya!' Amyra was the first to speak, gasping as she tried to catch her breath.

'What is it, Maya?' Adira asked. She couldn't see any sign of danger.

'Help me!' Maya turned her face, contorted with fear, from Adira to Amyra and back. 'Help me!' Her mind was devoured by terror.

Amyra looked panic-stricken at Adira. What were they to do?

'Pull her away,' Adira ordered, thinking fast. 'Get her away from this damn forest. Something in the trees has frightened her.'

Unable to fathom what was happening, Amyra caught Maya by one hand, while Adira grabbed the other, and both girls tugged at Maya, pulling her away.

But she could not turn away from the forest; she was transfixed by the sight of the trees, the darkness, the gloom.

Adira and Amyra heaved with all their strength, trying to overcome some unseen, unknown force that seemed to keep Maya rooted to the spot. It was like she had suddenly developed superhuman strength and it took everything the girls had to drag her away.

Maya didn't stop screaming all the way across the stretch of land that lay between the forest and the practice field.

It was only when they were a safe distance from the trees that Maya felt the sensation ebb. She collapsed on the uneven ground, surrounded by the wild grass, sobbing.

Amyra was sobbing too, though without understanding why. She was terrified.

Adira stood, panting, and stared at Maya.

After a while, Maya recovered enough to get to her feet. Supported by her two friends, she was able to squeeze back through the hedge.

Slowly, the trio crossed the field and headed back towards the residential cottages.

The sun had gone down and darkness was beginning to spread across the Gurukul.

Adira glanced back briefly; the Dandaka had already disappeared with the onset of night, merging with the darkness, becoming one with it.

Glowing orbs lit up their path, hovering overhead.

'Promise me one thing,' Maya told her friends. 'You will tell no one about what happened this evening.'

'Fine,' Adira replied, 'but only if you promise you will never go back there again.'

'I promise,' Maya said, looking at both girls in turn. 'I promise.'

But deep down in her heart, she wasn't sure she would be able to keep her promise.

What if the strange sensation, the unknown tug, returned?

Would she be able to resist its lure?

The Assembly Hall

'It has been over a month,' Satyavachana said, addressing the same group that had gathered in this very hall more than one month ago, to hear the news about Shukra's unexpected disappearance. 'He has not returned.'

'There's no news from our team in Gandharva-lok,' Kanakpratap added. 'Though it is still early days. Less than a week would have passed in their world.'

'Whatever Shukra is planning,' Jignesh mused, 'it will be big. And it will happen suddenly.'

'Our defences are much stronger now,' Parth said. 'We are better placed than we were two months ago to resist any attacks. Even the new weapons are ready to be deployed. The Shastrakars have outdone themselves this time.'

'Whatever Shukra plans to unleash upon the Sangha,' Kanakpratap said, slowly, 'will be more potent than anything we have seen so far. You can be sure of that.'

'There is a silver lining, though,' Usha spoke up.

The others looked at her, wondering what could possibly be positive about the news that Satyavachana had just given them.

'If it is big, it will take time to plan and execute,' Usha explained. 'You don't think that freeing the Nagas is something that Shukra did on the spur of the moment, do you? For all you know, he had been planning that during the fourteen years that he was missing.'

'You may have something there,' Parth agreed. 'Although, if he is planning to open another gate of Pataala-lok, it may not take that much time. He may have already located all the gates in the last fourteen years. Perhaps that is what took him so long.'

'No,' Jignesh insisted, stubbornly. 'I don't think he's going to open another gate. That would be too obvious, too predictable. He's going to do something else.'

'What could that be?' Parth wondered.

'I don't know,' Jignesh replied. 'But it will be something that none of us can even imagine. Of that I am sure.'

Chapter Fifty-one

Progress

Police Guesthouse
Allahabad

It had been a mixed day, Kapoor mused, after the debriefing was over. He had flown to Allahabad that morning to discuss progress on the case with Mirza.

It had been over a week, almost ten days in fact, since he had approached his boss with a request to pull strings and get him the photographs, either from the passport office or the transport office. Or, better still, from both.

Bloody bureaucrats, he had chafed. But there was nothing he could do apart from wait.

The photographs and other documents had finally come through today and he had carried them with him to Allahabad.

He had placed the photocopies on the table once both men were safely ensconced in the guesthouse. 'These are copies of passports and driving licenses that the two men were issued fourteen years ago, when they first came to Delhi. The DL application forms and supporting documents are also attached. The passport photographs are the best identification leads we have on them after their departure from Allahabad.'

Mirza had picked up the photocopies and studied them. 'These are new passports,' he said. 'No prior passport numbers.' He looked at Kapoor. 'If they didn't have passports while they were living in Allahabad, we will need to use their photographs and search the DL database manually to find out where they lived. That is, if they had driving licences in the first place. Even the DLs are new and not transfers from UP, according to the application forms here.'

'Or,' Kapoor had countered, 'you can try using these photographs in the WhatsApp networks that you have identified.'

Over the last nine days, Mirza had managed to identify the WhatsApp administrators of not only the akhara groups but also the alumni of the two schools where they presumed Singh and Updadhyay had studied.

Mirza had smiled. 'Of course, sir. And I'm going to check out the stationery shops right away.'

He had struck gold. The owner of one of the stationery shops had recognised Upadhyay's photograph and helpfully informed Mirza that the man in the photograph had taught at St. Joseph's College. He did not know the name of the teacher he had identified, but he had no doubt about his identity.

This was a positive development. Upadhyay had told Kapoor that he had taught Vishwaraj in Allahabad. Kapoor had been told by the Reverend Father Oscar D'souza, the principal of St. Joseph's, that Vishwaraj had studied in that school. And now, there was a positive identification that Upadhyay had, in fact, taught there. All the facts matched.

And yet, if Upadhyay had indeed taught at St. Joseph's College, as the stationery shop owner insisted, why was he not in the school records?

Chapter Fifty-two

Happy Birthday!

The Assembly Hall
The Gurukul
Panna National Park

That it was a special occasion was obvious. The Assembly
Hall was decked up with wreaths and strings of marigolds and
a general celebratory air prevailed.

It was the birthday of five students today.

Including Arjun.

It was the day of the winter solstice.

The five children—Arjun, Maya and three novices—had
risen earlier than usual today. Their day had begun with an
abhyangasnan—a bath with an oil massage—followed by
offering obeisance to their parents and elders. The parents of
the novices had specially travelled to the Gurukul to shower
their blessings on their children. Since Maya had no living
parents, the Mahamatis in the Gurukul stood in for them
while Kanakpratap stood in for his late brother, Arjun's father.

This was followed by a public celebration in the Assembly
Hall, where all the residents of the Gurukul had gathered
after the morning assembly and prayers.

When the rituals were completed, the children were offered a sweetmeat each, and sweets were distributed to the rest of the community before they dispersed for their respective classes.

Maya caught up with Arjun before they parted ways—he for his training with Agastya in the Kshatriya practice field and she for her lessons with Satyavachana.

'So,' her eyes sparkled with happiness, 'how does it feel to be fifteen and starting on sixteen?'

Arjun grinned back at her. 'I don't know, but one step closer to being considered a real grown up, I suppose?'

'You aren't legally an adult till you are eighteen, you know,' Maya reminded him.

'What's two years? They'll fly past.'

'Arjun!' Kanakpratap's stentorian voice broke up their conversation and Arjun hurried away with a smile and a wink.

Maya looked around for Satyavachana. He had made it a point to be present as part of the elders' community to bless her. Knowing how uncomfortable the Maharishi was around anything to do with the Sangha, Maya appreciated his gesture from the bottom of her heart. Somehow, the Maharishi had filled a vacuum in her life; a hole that had been created by the loss of her father. While she knew that no one could ever replace her father, Satyavachana had become her rock: solid, reliable, and always there for her.

She spotted him and waved frantically to catch his attention.

The Maharishi smiled at her, a twinkle in his eye, and beckoned to her to join him.

Then he disappeared.

Maya smiled. The Maharishi was hundreds of years old, but he still behaved like he was a student at the Gurukul. Perhaps that was why she liked him so much. He was like one of the children rather than one of the Mahamatis.

She closed her eyes silently recited the *Pratismriti* mantra.

Then she too disappeared.

Chapter Fifty-three

Atma Travel

In the Skies above Satyavachana's Ashram
Madhya Pradesh

'So, where are you taking us tonight?' Satyavachana asked Maya.

They—or rather, their atmas—were hovering above the treetops that closed over the Maharishi's ashram. After a long break of almost three months—Maya knew Satyavachana had been spying on Shukra during this time—the Maharishi had finally resumed lessons on atma travel with Maya.

She didn't understand why Satyavachana had given up on his surveillance of Shukra, but welcomed the chance to learn more about atma travel. She had had just nine days of lessons before the Maharishi had suspended them in favour of watching Shukra's movements.

'Um ... I don't know,' Maya responded, communicating with Satyavachana purely through the power of thought.

'Let's spy on the Sangha, shall we?' Satyavachana suggested. If he had been in his physical form, Maya was sure this suggestion would have been accompanied by a chuckle and a wicked twinkle in his eye.

She loved his attitude. She now knew that he was several hundred years old—exactly how old, no one had been able to tell her, not even Maharishi Gurumurthy at the Gurukul archives—yet he was as impish and impulsive as a teenager.

'Yes, let's,' Maya agreed, delighted by the thought that no one in the Sangha could see her. So what if the Sangha had Maharishis? Maya could travel in spirit form and they wouldn't even know.

'But what will we spy on?' she wondered. 'Everyone will be asleep.'

'Not everyone,' the Maharishi told her. 'The Akshapatalikas will be up. They don't sleep much.'

'The *who?*' Maya hadn't the foggiest what he was talking about.

'So they haven't told you?'

'About the ... the Aksha pataalas? No.'

'The Akshapatalikas,' Satyavachana corrected her. 'The Keepers of the Archives.'

'I thought Maharishi Gurumurthy was the Keeper of the Archives.'

'Yes, he is. At the Gurukul, that is. But he is not an Akshapatalika. He is a Maharishi tasked with the responsibility of looking after the archives at the Gurukul, just like the Keepers of the archives at the other Gurukuls.'

Seeing that Maya still looked confused, the Maharishi continued his explanation. 'The archives at the Gurukul are meant for students. Children who have not yet qualified for the Gana. They contain material that helps you to graduate to the Gana. The Akshapatalikas, on the other hand, are the Keepers of the Archives of the Sangha. Their title came into being around 4,000 years ago, during the rule of the first Mahamatra, Tribhuvan, who organised the Sangha into the organisation that you see today. They are the ones who have, for the last 4,000 years, maintained the records and knowledge of the Sangha; archives which may be accessed only by members of the Sangha or the Gana. Students are not allowed there.'

Maya's mind boggled. She suddenly felt small. Here she was, hunting for clues to Brahmabhasha in the archives at the Gurukul, housed in two storeys of a cottage, when 4,000 years of knowledge were locked away in a much larger archive.

One that she would never be able to access.

Unless she graduated to the Gana.

Her determination to learn and succeed grew even stronger at this thought.

At the same time, the idea that she could, in her atma form, spy on these otherwise out of bounds archives, appealed to her.

And, if Satyavachana was suggesting it, who cared about the rules of the Sangha? If it was okay with him, it was okay with her.

'Let's go,' she said.

Chapter Fifty-four

Discovery

In the Skies above the Bhimbetka Caves

'That was very good,' Satyavachana praised Maya. 'It took you just one lesson to get it right!'

The Maharishi had explained to Maya that there was no fixed entrance to the archives. To maintain secrecy and the highest level of security, the entrance kept changing at random intervals. He had disclosed to Maya their destination—the current entrance to the archives, which lay concealed among the caves below them—and Maya had used her lessons to bind their atmas together and transport them at the speed of thought to their destination.

'Thank you, Mahamati.' Maya focused on the dark ground below, trying to make out the caves that Satyavachana had told her about. She had never heard of their existence before, but the Maharishi had informed her that they contained rock paintings that were 30,000 years old, rivalling the renowned rock paintings in France and Spain.

But there was one thing that Bhimbetka had, which the caves of France and Spain did not: one of the entrances to the Hall of Archives of the Sangha.

'Descend with me,' Satyavachana instructed her.

By now, Maya had learned to 'see' the Maharishi's atma, another feat that Satyavachana had praised her for. Apparently, only yogis whose siddhis were very highly developed were capable of this. Strictly speaking, Maya should not have been able to sense or 'see' any other atmas, but she could.

Maya could still not understand why she was able to accomplish feats like this while the ability to master offensive mantras, or mantras to manipulate matter, remained elusive. And while Satyavachana had acknowledged her growing abilities in atma travel, he offered no explanation for her inability to use certain classes of mantras. So, Maya had reasoned that the important thing, the fact, was that she could do it. And *that* was what mattered, eventually.

Maya followed the Maharishi as he whizzed off among the boulders, under the overhangs and through an open cave, until he came to a stop before a cliff wall that towered above them. All around was thick forest. Maya had observed that, in this part of the woods, only the tips of the tallest rocky outcrops were visible above the trees; so dense was the forest that hid the caves from the eyes of humanity.

'This is the entrance?' Maya asked.

'Indeed, it is. It is concealed using the same device as the one used for our Gurukuls, at least those that are built near a cliff or a mountain.'

Maya understood. This was how the sadhs never got to know what lay hidden in the midst of their material world. You needed a mantra to enter. And only the Sangha or Gana members knew the mantra.

'Should we return?' she asked, realising that they could go no further.

'Return? My dear child, aren't you curious to see the archives of the Sangha? The repository of knowledge carefully collected, curated and conserved for 4,000 years?'

'But how do we enter? Do you know the mantra, Mahamati?' Maya wasn't sure how he could, since he had, himself, long left the Sangha. But she felt sheepish even as she asked the question. After all, the Maharishi had known the location of the entrance to the archives.

If Satyavachana had been in his physical form, Maya was sure he would have snorted. 'Mantra? My dear child, we are atmas, not physical bodies. Have you forgotten that you can go where you like and nothing can stop you?'

'Of course!' Maya felt stupid. She had got so accustomed to re-entering her own body after a night of atma travel that she had taken for granted the fact that she quite easily passed through walls to do so.

A sudden surge of curiosity tinged with a strong sense of guilt took hold of her. She was about to see something that was supposed to be out of bounds for her. She was about to break the rules. But she was also dying to know what lay beyond the cliff wall.

'Right, then,' Satyavachana said. 'Here we go.'

Maya waited but, to her surprise, the Maharishi stayed put. He didn't move. She wondered if something was wrong with her senses; if she was seeing him even though he had passed through the wall.

She decided to enter the Hall of Archives herself.

'Wait.' The curt instruction stopped her in her tracks.

She had been right, then. Satyavachana was still here. He had not gone through the cliff wall.

What was holding him back? Why did he want her to wait?

'Can you sense that?'

Maya strained to understand what Satyavachana was referring to.

'Something's wrong.' The Maharishi's thought felt troubled.

Without warning, she felt herself bound to his atma and, before she knew it, they were both hurtling up towards the sky, away from the entrance to the archives.

Chapter Fifty-five

What's Happening?

In the Skies above the Bhimbetka Caves

'There,' Satyavachana said.

Somehow, Maya knew exactly what he was referring to, almost as though he was physically pointing to it.

When they had arrived here, there was darkness below them. Nothing had moved, nothing stirred.

But now, there was movement.

Blue and red lights. Advancing towards the caves.

'What are they?' Maya wondered.

'Vikriti lights.' Satyavachana's thoughts felt grim. 'Vikritis cannot create the pure golden lights that we do using mantras. They are worshippers of Kali, after whom Kaliyuga is named. Their mantras are dark and tainted by the influence of Kali.'

Maya realised what he was saying. The blue and red lights were being used by the vikritis to illuminate their way in the darkness.

'What are they doing here?'

'I don't know. They can't get into the archives even if they try. They cannot use our mantras. The portal will not open for them. One thing is for certain. They are up to no good. But how did they know where the entrance to the archives is located?'

'Shall we try to stop them?'

'No. It's too dangerous. Especially for you in your atmic form. We need to warn the others.'

Once more, without warning, Maya was swept away in a whirl of motion, travelling at high speed.

The blue and red lights disappeared.

Slowly the blurry motion around her began to coalesce into familiar forms and the Gurukul came into focus.

'Go,' Satyavachana instructed her. 'Return to your body and go back to sleep. I have work to do.'

Maya knew that his work was connected with what they had just seen in Bhimbetka.

She also knew that she would have no part in it. That was the reason Satyavachana had deposited her here.

She made up her mind.

She had done it before. She would do it again.

Maya waited.

The Assembly Hall

'I have to contact the Sanghanetras,' Jignesh said, his face registering shock. 'This is a matter for the Sangha Council.'

Satyavachana had reappeared at the Gurukul a short while back, rousing Jignesh from slumber and asking for an urgent meeting of the Mahamati Council.

When the familiar circle of faces had assembled in the hall, he told them what he and Maya had seen.

'There is no time,' Satyavachana said frankly. 'We need to act. Now.'

Jignesh looked at him. For the first time as Mahamatra, he felt tested.

'We do not have the resources to act,' he told Satyavachana. 'We are a Gurukul, not the Sangha. These are students, not accomplished warriors. I cannot ask them to face the vikritis when they haven't even graduated to the Gana!'

'Do we have a choice?' Satyavachana asked him. 'Even if the vikritis cannot enter the Hall of Archives, they need to be stopped.'

'You speak sense,' Jignesh acceded. 'We do not have time on our side.'

'But you have me on your side,' Satyavachana told him. 'It takes more than eight hours to drive to Bhimbetka from here. But if I go with you, we can get there in a matter of seconds.'

'In that case,' Kanakpratap spoke up, 'we should not lose any more time.'

'Your ward is not ready,' Jignesh told him.

'No one can ever be completely ready to face the unforeseen,' Kanakpratap shot back. 'And Arjun is no different. But he is well prepared. I am the one who has held him back. He has been champing at the bit, wanting to break free. How long will we protect him? If he is the true scion of Yayati, his blood will shine through tonight. And if it does not, then perhaps he does not deserve to lead us.'

'Very well, then,' Jignesh said. 'Rouse the students. But we will take only the eight with us. They are the only ones who are even remotely prepared to face the threat that we will encounter tonight.'

Chapter Fifty-six

Preparation

The Assembly Hall

Eight bleary-eyed children sat and gazed upon the quintet of Jignesh, Satyavachana, Kanakpratap, Parth and Usha. They had been hastily woken up and summoned to the Assembly Hall for a meeting with the Mahamatis.

'We have called you here at this odd hour,' Jignesh began, 'to prepare you for an urgent mission. You are the senior most students in the Gurukul. This is the moment that you have spent your lives training for. The moment of truth.'

Arjun's heart leapt as he listened. What was in store for them? Had the Sangha finally changed its mind about the Saptas? But then, why weren't Maya and Amyra present? And why were the three other Rishis here instead? Gopal, Anisha and Sonali were the Rishi partners for Varun, Tanveer and Adira respectively. He knew that.

'The Hall of Archives, where the records and documents encompassing 4,000 years of knowledge are kept, is under attack as we speak,' Kanakpratap explained. 'We will go there together to defend it. There is no time to assemble a larger force or alert other members of the Sangha. With the constant fear of another attack by Shukra or his proxies, we cannot spare any more members from this Gurukul. But we are the closest to the archives and the only ones who can get there in time, thanks to Maharishi Satyavachana.' He looked at the eight faces before him. 'It will be up to us to drive away the intruders.'

Jignesh fixed them with a stern eye. 'This will also be the final project for all eight of you. If you acquit yourselves well, you will be formally enrolled as members of the Gana once you return.'

Arjun was thrilled. He now understood why Maya and Amyra were missing. They still had a long way to go before they could become Gana members. But he did wonder what had made the Sangha change their mind.

'Do not take this project lightly,' Kanakpratap warned them, taking over from Jignesh. 'We are going up against the vikritis. This is not a practice run. None of you have fought vikritis before. But we believe that you are ready for the challenge. Never forget, even for an instant, that they are extremely dangerous. The cost of forgetting something so critical can be enormous.'

'If you fail, you may forfeit your life,' Jignesh added, his usual, blunt self. He looked directly at Arjun. 'We think the eight of you are ready for this trial by fire. It is now up to each of you to prove that you are, indeed, ready.'

'Any questions?' Kanakpratap asked.

'When do we leave?' Arjun countered.

'Now.' Satyavachana stepped forward. 'There is no time to lose!'

'Okay,' Kanakpratap said. 'Kshatriyas, equip yourselves. Do it now. We must leave here fully prepared.'

Arjun, Tanveer, Varun and Adira nodded.

'*Virachayati kavach.*' They all uttered the mantra simultaneously and were instantly sheathed in the special new armour that the *Shastrakars* had developed for the Kshatriyas of the Sangha.

Each one also silently summoned their respective weapons—Arjun, Varun and Adira calling for their swords and Tanveer his bow and arrows.

They turned to look at Agastya, Gopal, Anisha and Sonali, all of whom now stood beside them holding brahmadandas. Due to their seniority in the Gurukul, they were eligible to have their own brahmadandas, which was otherwise the sole prerogative of the Rishis who were part of the Gana and the Sangha.

Once the eight children were equipped with their weapons, Kanakpratap and Parth summoned their armour and swords.

The Sangha force was ready for battle.

Chapter Fifty-seven

Arrival

The Bhimbetka Caves
Madhya Pradesh

The small group of thirteen—the eight children, Satyavachana, and the four Mahamatis—materialised next to one of the rocky outcrops that lay strewn within the dense forest that surrounded them. It was in these outcrops that water, several millennia earlier, had carved out natural caves, which had then been used for shelter, and expressions of artistic creativity, going back thousands of years.

Arjun shook his head to clear it. When Satyavachana had told them that he was going to transport them to the Hall of Archives, he hadn't known what to expect.

But he certainly hadn't expected it to feel like being thrown into a whirlwind.

The journey had lasted just a few minutes. He was still in a daze.

From the expressions of the other children, it was evident that they too felt the same way.

Soft, intermittent *booms* came to their ears through the still winter air.

'What is that?' Arjun wondered aloud.

'The vikritis,' Satyavachana said grimly. 'When we saw them earlier, they were at the entrance leading to the caves that are open to the public. My guess is that they are moving fast and blowing up some of the caves as they go along.'

'It will take them some time to get here,' Usha said. 'There's over 1800 hectares to cover. And over 700 caves. Only a few of the caves are in open forest; beyond those that are accessible to the public, the forest thickens and the going will be slow for them, even with their destructive proclivities.'

'We need to spread out and encircle the entrance to the Hall of Archives,' Jignesh said. 'We don't know which direction they will approach from. But we can be sure that this is their target. There's nothing else here of importance for them.'

Arjun looked back at the sheer cliff face that towered behind them.

Was this the entrance to the Hall of Archives? He wondered what lay inside. What did it look like? He had never even heard of the place before tonight.

And how did the vikritis know where it was located if it was so hush-hush that even the students of the Gurukul didn't know about it?

Jignesh was speaking again. 'Each Mahamati will accompany a pair of you and take up positions.' He looked at Satyavachana. 'Maharishi, you are free to take up your position where you will.'

Satyavachana's face was grim. 'I'll be around,' he said.

Before anyone could say anything, he disappeared.

Jignesh frowned. He hated it when Satyavachana acted like this. But there was nothing he could do. At a gesture from him, the group split up into sets of three; each Mahamati accompanying a Kshatriya and a Rishi.

Kanakpratap stood with Arjun and Agastya while Jignesh took charge of Varun and Gopal, Usha went with Anisha and Tanveer, and Parth set off with Sonali and Adira.

Kanakpratap's voice floated into the minds of the others as they took up their positions. He was using his new armour to communicate telepathically.

Remember, Kshatriyas, that you can now communicate with everyone else, including the Rishis. If you need reinforcement at any time, call for it. Don't wait. The vikritis are dangerous and, unlike us, they fight to kill.

Arjun followed his uncle as the latter pulled him and Agastya into the shadow of one of the rocky outcrops.

'We have the advantage of surprise,' Kanakpratap explained as they huddled in the shadows. 'They won't be expecting to see us here. But we know they are out there and approaching us—if the entrance to the archives is their goal. The forest is quite dense, so it will afford us good cover. We will be invisible to them if we stay perfectly still.' He paused. 'But let us not forget that the forest cover works both ways. We know they're coming, but we won't see them until they are almost upon us.'

Above them, the clear winter sky was dotted with stars which failed to penetrate the thick canopy of leaves and afforded little light to those on the ground.

Arjun waited, wondering.

What was going to happen now?

Chapter Fifty-eight

Anticipation

The Bhimbetka Caves

Vishwaraj didn't like this at all. He preferred to size up his opponents, study the landscape, and then plan his course of action.

That was how he had always acted in the Gana.

He liked to know what he was up against.

But tonight was different. He was going in blind. And he hated it.

To start with, neither he nor his companions knew exactly where the entrance to the Hall of Archives was located. It had changed since he had last been part of the Gana. By a stroke of luck, he had managed to find an Akshapatalika whose body he had possessed in an attempt to learn the new location. But he had not had enough time; all he had been able to find out through his machinations was that one of the entrances lay somewhere here, among the Bhimbetka caves. Being a former member of the Gana, he knew the mantra that would open the entrance. At least that hadn't changed.

Vishwaraj wondered about Shukra's strategy. He didn't understand it. Power was meant to be wielded.

And Shukra had the ultimate power.

Why, then, was he creeping around, trying to stay under the radar, instead of using his power to demolish all the obstacles in his path?

True, Shukra had told him that he hadn't found all that he was looking for. But wouldn't it be easier to attack the archives, destroy their Keepers and then search among the ruins rather than sneak around trying to do things the hard way? It would have been so easy for Shukra to penetrate the Hall of Archives and find what he wanted.

But, no, Shukra preferred to use intellectual power rather than brute force to accomplish his objectives.

Anyway, Vishwaraj knew he had a job to do. He could only hope that the vikritis with him were up to it.

'Any luck?' he demanded, as a vikriti powered a ball of fire towards a lone monolith that shattered into fragments on impact.

'No luck,' the vikriti grumbled. 'There's miles and miles to cover here. It's going to take all night.'

'Then we'll take all night,' Vishwaraj told him. 'But we're going to find it. We have to.'

They had ignored the rock shelters that were open to the public and concentrated, instead, on checking out the others. It was time consuming, but Vishwaraj had figured that it was extremely unlikely that the entrance to the Sangha's archives would be among the caves that thousands of people gawked at every day, and where the forest cover was sparse.

No, the Sangha was smarter. They would have ensured that the entrance was located in a place that was inaccessible to the sadhs—deep in the forest, where the trees clustered thickly together and where the public was denied entry.

There was no way to determine exactly where the entrance lay, so they had employed the simple expedient of demolishing parts of, or entire, rocky extrusions. The idea was to get the Akshapatalikas to reveal themselves. If the natural formations that concealed the entrance to the Hall of Archives were damaged or destroyed, surely they would rush to defend it?

At least, that was the expectation.

And Vishwaraj was determined to complete the task he had been assigned.

Near the Entrance to the Hall of Archives

Arjun shivered. Not because of the intense cold—his armour kept him well protected against the winter chill, unlike the Rishis, who had to wear woollen robes to keep themselves warm.

It was the anticipation, the wait, that made him shiver. Especially since he didn't know what he was up against.

This was only his second live confrontation with the forces that the Sangha battled. The last time had been in the clearing outside the Gurukul entrance, against Shukra's army. There, he had had the advantage of seeing who, or rather what, his adversaries were. Tonight, he had no idea. And the forest around them would ensure that he wouldn't be able to see them until they were upon him.

All he knew was that, somehow, they were even more dangerous than the clumsy creatures he had faced that night in the clearing.

All right, everyone alert! They're here. They're advancing from our side. Kanakpratap's voice floated into Arjun's head.

He was instantly alert, scanning the night for any sign of the vikritis.

How had his uncle got to know that they were here?

Then he saw it.

Chapter Fifty-nine

Confrontation

Near the Entrance to the Hall of Archives

Vishwaraj frowned and held up an arm, signalling for the others to halt.

Something was wrong. He didn't know what it was but he could feel it in his bones. There was something different about this place. About the rocky outcrops that loomed before them.

It wasn't the shape or form of the rocks, which were virtually undistinguishable from the darkness of the forest around them. It was something else.

He snapped his fingers and the multicoloured orbs floating ahead, nimbly gliding between branches of the dense forest around them and lighting up their path, winked out instantly.

Was there someone out there?

It certainly felt that way. He was attuned to the vibrations given off by all things, living or inanimate. Everything in the material world had a natural frequency of vibration, and he was sensitive to these.

Until now, all that he had sensed was the vibration of rocks and trees.

Now, he could feel a distinctive warm hum of vibrations emanating from a certain kind of living being.

Humans.

Were they the Keepers of the Archives?

Had he and his band of vikritis succeeded in smoking the Akshapatalikas out into the open? Had the Keepers heard the sound from the demolition of the structures and emerged to see what was happening?

Vishwaraj had no way of guessing that there could be an ambush ahead. He could not imagine that the Sangha could have learned about his mission. He had gathered his band of vikritis quietly, without too much fuss. He didn't necessarily need forces that were skilled or had immense powers. All he needed was numbers to put Shukra's plan into action. No one, apart from the vikritis he had recruited, knew about his mission.

His mind reached out, searching for Shukra.

Where was he?

In the Shadow of the Rocky Outcrop

Arjun realised how his uncle had detected their enemy.

The blue and red lights had appeared suddenly, like glowing fireflies in the darkness. As his uncle had pointed out earlier, the tree cover was dense, adding a layer of shadows to the natural darkness of the night. If the vikritis had to pick their way through the forest, the lights that guided their steps would have to stay as far from the tree cover as possible. There was no other way they could see where they were going. The flip side was that the lights were also visible to the defenders of the archives.

Without warning, the lights suddenly disappeared.

Darkness reigned.

They know we are here.

Kanakpratap's warning echoed through Arjun's head, even as the young Kshatriya wondered how the vikritis knew of their presence.

We wait. Let them make the first move. Stay alert.

Arjun gripped his sword tighter and nodded, oblivious to the fact that no one could see him in the darkness.

Near the Entrance to the Hall of Archives

Vishwaraj made up his mind. If someone was indeed hiding in the forest ahead, his plan risked revealing their presence, but it was the best way to proceed without endangering anyone in his group.

He was sure of the plan. It was the ideal way to take whoever was up ahead by surprise and inflict some damage to their ranks.

Something was happening to him.

Something within him was changing.

The sense of power that he had felt when he was with the Nagas was returning. It was taking over, energising him, giving him a sense of invincibility.

He smiled to himself in the darkness.

He was going to enjoy this. If only he could see what was happening.

In the Shadow of the Rocky Outcrop

Arjun waited, the uncertainty beginning to weigh on him.

Everything was still and silent. Not a leaf stirred.

Were the vikritis still out there?

Why aren't they moving forward? He asked telepathically.

Parth responded. *They're planning something. Watch out for the unexpected.*

Kanakpratap agreed. *If they've detected us, they're going to use proxies. But if they do, at least we won't be taken by surprise.*

Arjun didn't like the sound of that. What proxies?

He didn't have to wait long to find out.

Suddenly, there was a sound of scrambling from the dense section of the forest ahead of them, accompanied by blood-curdling shrieks and a foul stench that seemed to pervade every molecule of the air they were breathing.

Every member of the defending team knew instantly what was going to hit them; the elders from several years of experience and the students from their lessons at the Gurukul.

Bloody hell! Varun's panicked thought rushed through Arjun's mind. *How many of these are there?*

Chapter Sixty

The View from Above

In the Skies above the Bhimbetka Caves

From far above the caves, Maya—or, rather, her atma—watched in horror at the scene unfolding below her. In her atmic form, she could see past the dense tree cover as if it were broad daylight and the forest was one large treeless plain.

After Satyavachana had left her at the Gurukul, she had not returned to her body, but had waited near the cottage where her dorm was located.

She had watched as Kanakpratap had roused the boys, and Usha the girls, and ushered them swiftly into the Assembly Hall.

Burning with curiosity, she had restrained herself from floating into the Assembly Hall to eavesdrop on the group's plans. It didn't really matter. She knew what was going to happen and she knew where they were going. There was no point in being discovered. If Satyavachana knew that she had disobeyed him, he was sure to be angry and would probably ensure that she was confined to her dorm.

All she had to do was bide her time.

So she had waited, knowing that Satyavachana would be transporting the defenders to Bhimbetka. That was the only way they could get there in time.

When she thought the coast was clear, she entered the Assembly Hall tentatively, to check if everyone had gone.

It was empty, though the lights were still on. Probably to ensure that the group didn't return to a dark hall.

The next moment, she was hovering in the sky over the dense forest that engulfed the Bhimbetka caves, watching as the vikritis made their way towards the entrance to the Hall of Archives, using explosive fireballs to blow up caves and rocks alike along the way.

She had watched as they stopped, and realised to her dismay that they had detected the presence of the defending force from the Gurukul. And then, as she looked on, she saw the vikritis unleash their weapons on the group from the Gurukul.

Maya's surprise and horror came from several sources. In the brief span of time that her lessons had lasted, she had learned from Satyavachana how amazing atma travel could be if you knew what to do and how. Since the atma had no physical limitations, all the constraints of the physical body were irrelevant. It had been simple for her to learn to control her atma so that she could see in multiple directions at the same time, observe things that were in close proximity or far away with the same clarity and focus, and have clear visibility whether it was day or night, clear or foggy. The laws of nature that applied to physical forms ceased to apply when she was in her atmic form. And there was more, the Maharishi had promised her, that she would learn in due course.

Despite her immense distance from the ground—primarily to ensure that she was not detected by the vikritis—and the darkness around, she could see clearly. She had already spotted the Mahamatis and their protégés in their positions around the entrance to the Hall of Archives.

But it was what she could see of the vikritis that had her worried.

The first thing that struck her was the presence of Vishwaraj. She had recognised the young man immediately. If Maya had been in her physical body, she would have rubbed her eyes in disbelief and probably thought she was imagining things, but it was less easy to deceive the atma than the eyes.

Vishwaraj was a vikriti?

She was confused. Vishwaraj had been a member of the Gana. How could he be a vikriti?

Yet, nothing else seemed to explain his presence here, among the vikritis.

The fact that he was here was terrifying, for Maya had seen how easily Vishwaraj had countered the mantras during the siege in Panna. If Garuda had not been there, the Gurukul would have been destroyed for sure.

And Vishwaraj would have had a significant role to play in its destruction.

Her fear of Vishwaraj was nothing, however, compared to the horror evoked by the sight of the creatures that bounded along the ground and floated through the air, advancing towards the Gurukul force, invisible to them in the darkness.

How were the Mahamatis and the students from the Gurukul going to protect themselves against them?

Chapter Sixty-one

The Battle of Bhimbetka

The Bhimbetka Caves

Abruptly, a number of large, brilliantly glowing orbs appeared in the forest, suspended just beneath the treetops. Some of the spheres cast a diffused light through the trees on the creatures advancing towards the defenders from the Gurukul. The others hovered above the group of vikritis who, caught unawares, scattered among the surrounding trees to escape their penetrating gaze.

In the light of the glowing orbs that lit up their path like a spotlight, the creatures unleashed by the vikritis appeared in stark relief against the darkness.

They were of two kinds.

One group, on the ground, bounded towards the entrance to the Hall of Archives. Fearsome to look at, they were tightly muscled though lean, with bulging eyes, red bodies and faces and fangs that dripped blood even as they sprinted towards their targets.

Pisachas.

The second lot were in the air. Pretas, who floated towards the defenders, their dark, sunken eyes staring at their intended victims, their jaws open in a silent scream which made them look even more horrifying than when Arjun had seen them in Panna.

It had to be Satyavachana who had created the orbs to light up the attackers. The defenders were quick to take advantage of the situation.

Jignesh, Usha, you go after the vikritis. Parth and I will handle the creatures. Kanakpratap issued crisp orders. *Arjun, Agastya, ready?*

Even as they watched, the pisachas split up, going in different directions, targeting all four groups of defenders.

Kanakpratap grimaced. This was not going to be easy. He knew what was going to happen next.

Near the Entrance to the Hall of Archives

Vishwaraj cursed as the glowing orbs suddenly appeared, negating the advantage of darkness. Some of the orbs were shining down right over his group, revealing their numbers and giving their position away.

He knew immediately that these were no ordinary orbs. Unlike the golden globes that lit up the Gurukul or those that the Rishis created to light their path in the dark, these were solar orbs created by a special mantra which invoked the power of Surya. Not only were they powerful and difficult to create, but they were almost inextinguishable by anyone other than their creator. Even he did not know the mantra to create the Surya Prabha orbs, as they were known. Only the most powerful Maharishis in the Sangha had this ability. Had the Sangha somehow discovered his plans?

A cold, uneasy feeling took hold of him for a split second.

Then his confidence returned and he pushed the thought away.

Whoever it was, it didn't matter. Vishwaraj had only just begun. And, if the Sangha had somehow learned about his plans, they were going to regret their presence here tonight.

He smiled to himself.

He knew that the number of defenders had to be limited. While the number and capacity of the vikritis too were limited, the bhutagana was different. And, even if there was a Maharishi on the other side who was formidable enough to create a Surya Prabha, Vishwaraj had confidence in his own power. He would relish using it against a powerful member of the Sangha.

He looked around at the vikritis, who were scattering, dispersing in all directions in panic as the spotlights searched them out.

Near the Entrance to the Hall of Archives

Remember, the pisachas have to be decapitated. Parth issued last minute instructions to the Kshatriyas before they launched into the advancing creatures.

Got it. Adira adjusted her grip and rushed towards the pisachas and pretas that were advancing toward them.

Sonali, the Rishi partnering Adira, was already reciting mantras against their attackers.

सहे पिशाचान्त्सहसैषां द्रविणं ददे ।
सर्वान् दुरस्यतो हन्मि सं म आकूतिर्ऋध्यताम् ॥

'Sahe pisachantsahasaishan dravinam dade,
Sarvaan durasyato hanmi sung ma aakootitridhyataam!'

This was the core foundational mantra used while embarking on a fight against pisachas. As they charged towards the attackers, Sonali continued her recitation.

Then the attackers were upon them.

Adira launched into them, slashing at the pisachas and pretas, even though she knew that her sword would have no effect on the latter, who were immaterial beings, no more than wisps of smoke, existing on a plane other than this material world. There was nothing she could do to harm them.

But, like all the others, she was wearing an amulet that would protect her from them.

As she fought the pisachas, she heard Parth tear into their ranks as well.

Both Kshatriyas engaged in a counter attack that was fierce and well coordinated, with Sonali backing them up with mantras that ensured that the pisachas stayed away from her.

The pisachas tore and scraped at Adira as they pounced on her. They were flesh eaters and nothing would please them more than a meal here and now.

Adira's sword flashed as it swung through their ranks like a blur.

She had a reputation for being one of the swiftest Kshatriyas in the Gurukul.

Three pisachas rushed at her.

'Udnayate! Vegita vriddhi!' Adira was instantly propelled at top speed above the heads of the attacking pisachas, so that

they were left grabbing at empty space. She latched on to a branch of a tree and somersaulted down behind them.

'Here, suckers!'

The three pisachas turned to face her. Before they knew it, she had swung her sword across their necks. Three hideous heads rolled to the ground.

Adira was not just the fastest Kshatriya in the Gurukul. She was also known for her accuracy. The deadly combination of speed and precision was her strength.

She paused to catch her breath.

'Adira!' she heard Sonali shout.

Adira swivelled around.

Her eyes widened as she took in the scene.

Chapter Sixty-two

Pisachas

The Bhimbetka Caves

Vishwaraj had sized up the situation well. He had not moved from where he stood, despite being revealed by the light that shone down on him. He knew that the first wave of attacks by the creatures he had unleashed would keep his adversaries busy.

As the pretas and pisachas reached those who lay in wait for them, the band of defenders came into the light and their scant numbers were revealed to him. As was the fact that most of them seemed to be children.

Vishwaraj laughed to himself, despite being the only one left standing in the light; the vikritis had all sought refuge in the dense forest around them.

Children.

Accompanied by adults.

Which meant they were unlikely to be members of the Gana. If that had been the case, they would have operated unsupervised.

They must be from some Gurukul nearby.

Students.

This would be less difficult than he had thought, even if there was a powerful Maharishi among his adversaries.

He saw two groups break away from the defenders and head towards him. One group was led by a woman, with a girl and a boy in tow, and the other group comprised two boys following a man.

Time to leave.

Vishwaraj vanished.

Near the Entrance to the Hall of Archives

Varun sprinted towards the vikritis who were closest to his group, slashing and cutting at the pisachas that stood in his way.

The pretas he could not do much about, so he ignored them, focusing instead on decapitating the pisachas, even as Gopal recited mantras to kill those that he was decapitating.

Jignesh was busy tackling the pretas, reciting mantras that would despatch them into oblivion.

ॐ नमो भगवते आंञ्नेयाय महाबलाय स्वाहा ॥

'OM namo bhagavate anjaneyaya mahabalaya svaha ॥'

ॐ नमो भगवते रुद्राय: कोशेश्वराय नमो ज्योति:
पंतगाय नमो नम: सिद्धि रूप रूपाय ज्ञपति स्वाहा ॥

'OM namo bhagavate rudraayah kosheshvaraaya namoh jyotiah patangaaya namo namah siddhi roop roopaaya gyapati svaha ॥'

By the time they reached the spot where they had seen the vikritis, there was no one there. They had disappeared into the forest, scattering in different directions.

Varun didn't know if that was good or bad. Scattering meant they had panicked. But it also meant they could regroup and attack from different directions.

Not far away, Usha was busy battling the pisachas, who seemed to have attacked her group with a vengeance.

Tanveer had been cutting the pisachas down, as they ran, with a flurry of well-aimed arrows that sliced off their heads, his hands a blur as he handled his bow with practiced ease.

But the closer they got, the more difficult it became.

Varun looked on as a group of pisachas swarmed over Tanveer even as he released arrow after arrow, decapitating several of them.

A bow and arrows were not of much use in close combat.

Need help, buddy? Varun asked Tanveer telepathically, through his suit of armour.

About time someone asked. Tanveer sounded wry.

Alright.

Varun looked at Jignesh. *They need help.*

Jignesh nodded in response and the three of them rushed towards Usha's group.

Varun charged into the group of pisachas who were trying to overwhelm Tanveer, cutting them down with a few swift strokes of his sword, even as Usha, Jignesh, Anisha and Gopal recited mantras targeting the pretas and the pisachas.

Look out! A silent shout went up from somewhere near them.

It sounded like Arjun, but Varun couldn't be sure.

All he could focus on for now was the mass of vikritis bearing down upon them.

Near the Entrance to the Hall of Archives

Arjun stared at the vikritis who had regrouped and were now returning to the fray.

It wasn't their numbers that had caught him off guard.

It was the person leading them.

Was that Vishwaraj?

He recognised the boy from his appearance in Panna when the Nagas had attacked the Gurukul.

He had just a split second to ponder this question before he was back to tackling the swarm of pisachas.

A group of pretas swooped down to surround him, their jaws open in silent snarls, frustrated at their inability to attack him and possess his body, repelled by the amulet he wore and the mantra within it.

'*Rudraayah   Kosheshvaraaya!   Anjaneyaya   Mahabalaya!*' A few well-aimed mantras from Agastya, and the group of pretas around Arjun disappeared, snuffed out, released from their suffering, their souls liberated.

Thanks, Ags. They were getting to me. Arjun grinned at Agastya, then realised that Agastya could not see his face. He realised that he was no longer petrified by the pretas, unlike the first time he had seen them, but he still hadn't got used to them. He put it down to his lack of experience.

What worried him was that there seemed to be no end to the ranks of the pisachas. They kept coming at him and the others as fast as the vanguard got cut down. And now, to make things more difficult, the vikritis were attacking.

From the corner of his eye, even as he neatly sliced off the heads of two pisachas who were attempting to leap onto him, he saw the vikritis break up into smaller groups of two and three.

They were operating to a game plan.

But what was it?

Chapter Sixty-three

Vikritis

Near the Entrance to the Hall of Archives

Vishwaraj had managed to regroup the vikritis. He had changed his location and somehow the glowing orbs of light had not followed, perhaps because it had happened so fast. They were still suspended in mid-air over the spot where he had stood some time earlier.

As a result, he had been able to marshall his forces and quickly convey a plan to the vikritis.

A plan that he knew would not go wrong.

Could not go wrong.

It was simple. They would break up into five groups, of two or three. The plan was to surround the enemy and reinforce the attack already under way by the pisachas and pretas.

It was only a matter of time before their opponents were overwhelmed.

He hadn't come here to battle anyone. That had not been among Shukra's instructions.

But if they wanted a fight, he would take it to them.

In the Skies above the Bhimbetka Caves

Maya watched from above as the battle continued. She had got over her initial surprise at seeing brahmadandas in the hands of the young Rishis. When Satyavachana had gifted her one, she had not known that other students in the Gurukul had them as well. Seeing the weapons in their hands gave her some comfort. For it meant that the defenders had one more weapon to battle the vikritis.

But would it be enough?

The defenders had done a good job of fighting off the first round of attacks. But now, not only were they facing unending waves of the creatures, but the vikritis, having regrouped, were using the bhutagana as a cover for their own attack. And they were being led by Vishwaraj.

A double whammy.

From her vantage point she saw Jignesh and Usha lead their protégés to meet the vikritis head on, leaving Kanakpratap and Parth with their wards to continue the fight against the pisachas and pretas.

But where was Satyavachana?

Near the Entrance to the Hall of Archives

Shukra stood, invisible, in the shadow of an enormous boulder perched on some rocks and watched the battle with great interest. Even though he was present in his physical form, he had used his powers to ensure that he could observe the clash of the two opposing forces, from his vantage point, without the dense forest cover obscuring his vision.

Unusually for a Gana member, Vishwaraj had well developed siddhis, no doubt a result of his past births. Shukra's blood coursed through his veins, and much of Shukra's power too.

What Shukra had not been able to gauge so far was Vishwaraj's ability to lead.

Shukra knew that, in order to put his plans into action, he needed someone to lead the Vikritis.

But was Vishwaraj capable?

He knew that this battle was unnecessary. It didn't advance his plans in any way.

But there were two things he would learn tonight.

The first was whether Vishwaraj could be the one to unite the vikritis. That would be a useful development for him. A unified band of vikritis operating under a single leadership would be an effective counter to the Sangha, enabling him to carry out his plan. In any case, the reason he had come here tonight was to move that plan forward, irrespective of Vishwaraj's abilities. But if he was capable, it would definitely help.

The other thing was, of course, that the ongoing battle would conclusively demonstrate whether the One—the boy who had so fortuitously escaped him twice—was actually going to pose a threat to him.

Shukra still believed that the boy was not ready to fulfil the prophecy. He didn't consider him a danger at all; just a minor irritant. But it would be good to see that conviction validated in the battle tonight.

One thing bothered him though.

He could sense another presence.

An atma.

And it wasn't one of the bhutagana.

This was a spirit that belonged to a living being, not a dead one.

It was travelling out of its body, which meant that it was the spirit of someone who had unusual powers.

It was at a distance, observing all that was happening on the ground.

But he could sense it nonetheless.

And there was something about it that was deeply disturbing. Even familiar. Like a memory from thousands of years ago. And he didn't know why.

Even as he pondered this, he saw it.

The atma that he had sensed.

It had been in the sky, hovering above them all.

And it was swooping down now, towards the ground. As it approached, he could see it clearly, flying straight towards the vikritis who were going in for the kill.

Chapter Sixty-four

Overwhelmed

Near the Entrance to the Hall of Archives

Jignesh and Usha, with their band of students, struggled to free themselves from the onslaught of the pisachas and pretas so they could focus on the vikritis.

They had just two Kshatriyas—Varun and Tanveer—between the two groups, and Tanveer was handicapped by the close combat conditions that reduced the effectiveness of his bow and arrows.

But they had to break free—they were the first line of defence against the vikritis, since the other two groups had only two Rishis between them.

Varun and Tanveer fought back-to-back, slicing and slashing at the pisachas, who kept up the assault relentlessly. Tanveer had resorted to grasping two arrows, one in each hand, wielding them much as one would wield knives. He used the sharp edges of the arrowheads to decapitate the pisachas as they got close to him.

The vikritis stopped their headlong rush and paused to hurl flaming spheres at their opponents. Jignesh and Usha, with one accord, raised their brahmadandas to counter the attack and absorb the energy of the missiles, which flew fast and furious at them.

Unknown to the defenders, three other bands of vikritis had circled around and were now positioning themselves to attack the groups led by Kanakpratap and Parth.

In the Skies above the Bhimbetka Caves

Maya watched with horror as three groups of vikritis—nine in all—sprinted around the frontline of defence mounted by Jignesh and Usha, and took up positions to attack the other two groups of defenders.

She realised the peril the six defenders were in. They had only two Rishis, and the enemy attack would be mounted from three directions. They would be defenceless on one flank. While the Kshatriyas were useful in despatching the pisachas, the vikritis had to be neutralised by the Rishis before the Kshatriyas could be effective against them. That was the reason the Sangha and Gana fought in complementary pairs.

As she watched the vikritis hurl fireballs at the defenders led by Jignesh and Usha, she realised the enormity of the danger they were in. She had seen the explosive power of these fireballs earlier tonight. Jignesh and Usha were using their brahmadandas to good effect, but they were fully occupied with the two groups of vikritis they were battling along with the pisachas and pretas that were still swarming around them. They were in no position to aid the others.

What Kanakpratap and Parth needed was a third Rishi with a brahmadanda, who could effectively help neutralise the vikritis that were now preparing to attack them.

Maya felt helpless. Even if she were to return to the Gurukul and reappear with her brahmadanda, it would be of no use, since she had no idea how to use it. Without the necessary mantras and siddhis to operate it, it would be no more than an ordinary piece of wood.

She made up her mind.

There was only one course of action available to her.

She knew it would mean discovery of her presence here and a severe reprimand, perhaps even punishment for disobeying her guru's instructions, but it didn't matter. Nothing was more important than the lives of her friends and teachers.

She knew exactly what she was going to do. There was no way of helping Kanakpratap and Parth, but she could help the other two groups battle the pisachas. If she could help free one of the Rishis, who could then rush to the aid of the other defenders, that would be good enough.

She had to try.

Without another thought, she dived towards the scene of the battle far below her.

Chapter Sixty-five

Identification

Near the Entrance to the Hall of Archives

Kanakpratap and Parth fought side by side, along with Arjun and Adira, both groups having come together when they saw the vikritis re-enter the fray. Agastya and Sonali hurled mantras, destroying the pretas and weakening the pisachas.

Still, the pisachas maintained their onslaught, never slackening, reinforcements appearing from the forest around them with each passing moment.

They're coming. Kanakpratap's warning flashed through the heads of the other five. They also realised what he had left unsaid, as they saw the nine vikritis, in three groups, taking up positions encircling the six defenders.

Sonali and Agastya took up defensive positions, brandishing their brahmadandas even as they kept reciting the mantras to destroy the pretas and keep the pisachas at bay.

Arjun's heart sank as he saw the third group of vikritis position themselves, with no defensive shield of Rishis facing them. He knew that Agastya and Sonali would fend off the attack from the other two vikriti groups; this was what his and Agastya's practice over the last forty days had been about, under the tutelage of Usha and Kanakpratap. Today's battle was what they had been preparing for, even though they had not known that it would upon them so soon.

But now, they were outflanked and outnumbered.

Was his birthday going to be his last day alive?

Near the Entrance to the Hall of Archives

Shukra watched enthralled as the atma dived towards the scene of the battle. He could see what the spirit was trying to do. It was headed for the group of defenders who were in front. It was aiming to thwart the vikritis or battle the pretas and pisachas. Or both.

He was impressed. It would take great power to accomplish any of those objectives.

Who was this?

Shukra closed his eyes and focused on the vibrations emanating from the spirit.

Suddenly, his eyes flew open.

He knew.

The living room in Maharishi Dhruv's house.

The girl in the study.

Maharishi Dhruv's daughter.

It couldn't be!

And yet, he knew he couldn't be wrong. It had to be her.

But she was a child. A sadh! He had sensed her total lack of powers when he had encountered her on that fateful day. There was no way she was capable of atma travel, leave alone what she was trying to accomplish now!

How could he have been so wrong?

In the microseconds that it taken him to identify her, the girl's atma had dived from hundreds of kilometres above them and was on the verge of clashing with the two opposing groups that were locked in battle.

Then it happened.

Chapter Sixty-six

What Happened?

Near the Entrance to the Hall of Archives

Don't stop. Don't give up. Kanakpratap exhorted the young Kshatriyas. Giving up now would be suicide. They had to resist, even though the odds looked impossible.

Arjun tried desperately to push away the feeling of hopelessness and thoughts of imminent death from his mind. He tried to focus instead on attacking the pisachas even more viciously than before.

We can do it, Arjun. He heard Adira's voice urge him on and took strength from her conviction.

He could not know that she too was afraid; terrified to the core of her being. But she was determined not to show it. She was a Kshatriya. And Kshatriyas did not show fear. Only courage.

The three groups of vikritis had encircled the defenders by now.

Agastya and Sonali stood prepared, still muttering the mantras against the pretas and pisachas.

Arjun heard Vishwaraj's voice rise above the din of the battle.

'Now!' he yelled.

Fireballs raced towards the besieged defenders from three sides.

But there were only two Rishis to stop them.

The third flank was unguarded and defenceless.

Arjun felt tears rolling down his face as the flaming spheres arced towards him and Adira.

There was no hope left.

Near the Entrance to the Hall of Archives

Shukra stood transfixed.

He couldn't fathom what was happening.

He had been watching Vishwaraj adeptly organise the vikritis into a fighting formation. Shukra's young acolyte had made his moves well and he could see that he was now in a winning position. For now, one of Shukra's questions had been answered, a doubt removed.

The young man had demonstrated, quite ably, his competence to lead on the battlefield. Leading off it was another matter, of course, but it wasn't something that some training couldn't fix.

But another question had entered Shukra's mind. One that he needed to explore.

Not a new question.

An old one, a niggling doubt that he had pushed away, ignoring it. It had resurfaced tonight.

But it could wait for now.

It was what was happening on the battlefield before him that puzzled him.

The atma of the girl had dived at high speed, clearly meaning to enter the fray.

Abruptly, just as she reached the scene of the action, she had stopped.

And disappeared.

Chapter Sixty-seven

Oh No!

Near the Entrance to the Hall of Archives

Sonali and Agastya whirled their brahmadandas, intercepting every missile from the vikritis, their weapons absorbing the energy of the fireballs.

On the third flank, Arjun braced himself for the inevitable.

Would it be an explosion, blowing him and the others to pieces?

Or would they all go up in flames?

In the Skies above the Bhimbetka Caves

Maya's atma raced towards the groups led by Jignesh and Usha, covering hundreds of kilometres in a matter of moments.

She hadn't really thought through her plan.

Actually, she didn't have a plan.

She was going to wing it. Quite literally.

Suddenly, she felt it.

A sudden surge of energy.

Where was it coming from?

She could feel it as strongly as if she was in her physical body and it had brushed past her.

Maya was confused. It felt vaguely familiar. She had felt this sensation before, when she was in her physical body.

But where?

When?

Then it came back to her.

In her father's study in Delhi.

When she had been trying to escape with the diary.

Shukra.

He was here!

Near the Entrance to the Hall of Archives

To Arjun's surprise, the fireballs arced towards him and Adira and then mysteriously died out just a foot or two away from them.

What was happening?

The vikritis continued hurling fireballs at them, but the flaming spheres never reached the two Kshatriyas. They seemed to hit an invisible wall that snuffed them out.

At least, that was the way it seemed to Arjun.

He redoubled his efforts against the pisachas. Adira, watching him, followed suit. Together, they dispatched several dozen pisachas more to the realms of the spirit world where their souls could move ahead in their cycle of rebirths.

The Gurukul
Panna

Maya sat on her bed, back in her body, hugging herself, trembling all over. Tears rolled down her cheeks as she wept uncontrollably.

She was still deeply affected by the trauma of the battle, the shock of seeing her friends in danger and the uncertainty of knowing what had happened.

When she had sensed Shukra's presence at Bhimbetka, she had hovered uncertainly for a few seconds, confused. Then a voice had intruded into her consciousness.

It was Satyavachana.

'*What are you doing here, child?*' the Maharishi had demanded. '*Leave immediately! You are in danger every moment that you tarry here! Begone!*'

The urgency in those words had struck her deeply. She had returned at once to the Gurukul and to her slumbering body.

But it troubled her that she was safe while her friends were still in danger.

How would they extricate themselves?

Chapter Sixty-eight

Shukra's Move

Near the Entrance to the Hall of Archives

Vishwaraj couldn't believe his eyes.

His plan had been perfect. The execution had been impeccable. The vikritis had encircled the defenders and attacked them from three directions.

It was the perfect set up. And he should have won.

But something had happened that he had not anticipated.

The undefended flank of defenders had been an illusion. None of the missiles had been able to get through.

Something was absorbing their energies before they reached their targets.

But what was it?

The mystery was solved before long.

But Vishwaraj could not understand why he had not been able to detect the new arrival on the scene.

Near the Entrance to the Hall of Archives

Arjun stared as Satyavachana as he suddenly appeared on the unguarded flank and launched a counter attack against the vikritis.

'*Agnichakra pariveshtyati*,' Satyavachana intoned and a circle of fire engulfed three of the vikritis, immediately putting an end to their assault.

'*Vidyutate.*' A sphere of light appeared above the Maharishi and he winked at Arjun and Adira before swiftly crossing over to the other side.

'*Agnichakra pariveshtyati.*' Another circle of fire appeared around the second group of vikritis, pinning them where they stood.

Near the Entrance to the Hall of Archives

Vishwaraj prepared to launch a counter attack. Whoever this newcomer was, he was not going to let him snatch victory from the jaws of defeat. Until now, he had been content to let the vikritis do all the fighting.

Once he unleashed his powers, he knew that even the Sangha could not stop him, leave alone these students. But even as he prepared to launch his counter offensive, he heard Shukra speak to him telepathically.

'*You have done a great job, my son. But I have got what I wanted and learned what I needed to learn. Now you must withdraw. I have a task to complete and the longer the battle continues, the more it will delay me.*'

'*Yes, Poorvapitamah.*' Vishwaraj gnashed his teeth with frustration but the Son of Bhrigu had issued his command.

And he had to be obeyed without question.

'*Samastrnute!*' he intoned. The circles of fire that had pinioned the two groups of vikritis following Satayavachana's attack were snuffed out. Simultaneously, the attack of the pisachas and pretas suddenly intensified.

This was his parting shot. He wanted his opponents to know that he was not retreating in fear. That he had the ability to parry every move they made. That *they* were helpless in the face of *his* powers.

Near the Entrance to the Hall of Archives

They're getting away! Arjun complained to no one in particular.

But there was no option.

The numbers of pretas and pisachas had suddenly multiplied manifold and all thirteen defenders found themselves struggling to cope with the sudden surge, even as the vikritis regrouped. Only, this time, they were clearly not planning to attack.

The battle continued for a while, mantras and swords striking at the pretas and pisachas. Then, suddenly, they were gone.

As were the vikritis.

Where the sounds of battle had raged just a few moments ago, the silence of a cold winter's night descended.

Chapter Sixty-nine

Shukra Acts

The Bhimbetka Caves

Shukra stood before the rocky outcrop that he now knew was the entrance to the Hall of the Archives.

His ploy had succeeded. True, an unexpected hiccup had occurred, but it had ended up being even more effective than his original plan.

Vishwaraj had been sent here by him to try and smoke out the Akshapatalikas from their concealed hideout. He had counted on the fact that the vikritis, by destroying parts of the landscape, would either hit upon the entrance by chance or destroy the rocks concealing it, which would surely bring the Akshapatalikas out, thus revealing the entrance.

That plan had gone awry because of the sudden and unexpected appearance of the Sangha members, but he didn't regret that.

In fact, it was a good thing that the battle had taken place. Shukra didn't know how the Sangha had got wind of the movements of Vishwaraj and the vikritis, but that didn't matter. Their appearance had given him a glimpse into their readiness to fulfil the prophecy.

He now knew for certain that the One was still woefully weak and totally unprepared to face him. He could focus on what he needed to do, rather than waste his time and energy on trying to kill the boy. It just wasn't worth it.

It was also interesting to see that the Sangha did have some power that it could wield. It was not, after all, as helpless and frail as he had thought it to be. And they did have a powerful Maharishi on their side. Someone he had not been aware of earlier.

Shukra had been impressed by Satyavachana's prowess and mastery of the siddhis. And the ease with which he had countered the vikritis within a few moments of joining the fray.

He belonged to an age where power was respected, even in adversaries. He had bowed his head silently in acknowledgment of Satyavachana's abilities even as the battle raged, and issued instructions to Vishwaraj to conclude the battle from his side. There was nothing left to fight over any more. And there was no time to waste.

As Shukra had anticipated, after the vikritis and their frontline of creatures had disappeared, the Akshapatalikas had emerged from the rocky outcrop that he now stood in front of, revealing the exact location of the entrance to the Hall of Archives. Thanks to his powers of illusion, none of them had the slightest inkling that he was around.

A brief conversation had followed in which the defenders from the Gurukul had briefed the Akshapatalikas on what had happened.

Then the defenders had vanished.

Shukra's admiration for Satyavachana had gone up several notches after that. He knew that instant travel was not something everyone was capable of. Even in his own time, thousands of years earlier, in the golden yugas, there were few who could master it. If the aged Maharishi was capable of transporting not just himself but also twelve others, he deserved respect.

Shukra hoped that he would never have to battle the Maharishi directly. It would be a shame to have to destroy him.

But now, he had a task to complete.

He chanted the mantra that Vishwaraj had passed on to him. The mantra that would open the entrance to the Hall of Archives.

The mantra completed, Shukra walked through the rock and into the Hall of Archives.

Inside the hall, he stood quietly, watching and listening. There didn't seem to be any movement. Everything was still. The Akshapatalikas were probably pottering around, busy with their work, now that the attack had been contained and the defenders gone.

Even if someone was around, it didn't matter. They wouldn't see or hear a thing.

A mantra silently unfolded in his mind and hundreds of clones emerged from his body and spread out silently into the archives. They would be invisible to any onlooker, just as he was. And each one of them was endued with his intelligence and capabilities.

Swiftly, Shukra's clone army browsed through the archives, searching and sifting through the documents and scrolls, taking care to ensure that no one could detect any unusual movement that would give their presence away.

The hours passed as the army worked.

Finally, Shukra found what he had been looking for.

He grasped the bunch of ancient manuscripts in his hand and recalled his army. The clones silently merged back into his body.

Shukra smiled with satisfaction.

He would finally be able to move ahead with his plan.

Chapter Seventy

Return

The Gurukul
Panna National Park

Maya couldn't bear it any more. Just looking at Adira's empty bed was upsetting.

Careful not to waken the other occupants of the dorm, she padded out of the room and down the stairs. Silence and darkness greeted her.

She opened the door of the cottage and peered outside.

There was silence and darkness outside as well.

Deeply disturbed, Maya shut the door and entered the common room. She didn't bother to switch on the light, but sat in a chair that gave her a clear view of the entrance.

She would wait for Adira.

The Assembly Hall

The group of weary defenders assembled in the hall. '*Prakshalayati kavach.*' The Kshatriyas intoned the mantra to rid their armour of the signs of battle—the blood of the pisachas and their own sweat.

Usha and Kanakpratap then led the girls and boys back to their cottages. They would return to join Jignesh, Parth and Satyavachana to discuss and analyse the events of the night.

Maya's Dorm

The door of the cottage opened and Maya rushed towards it, engulfing Adira in a huge, warm embrace.

'I … I was so worried!' she sobbed, unable to contain her tears.

Adira hugged her back. 'It's okay,' she said. 'It was a tough battle, but we made it.' She looked happy.

'No.' Maya stepped back and looked Adira in the eye. 'You don't know the danger you were all in. I was there.'

'You were?' Adira was puzzled, then she realised what Maya meant. 'You saw it all then!'

Maya nodded. 'Yes. And Shukra was there!'

Adira's looked horrified. 'No. That can't be.'

'He was. I sensed it. I'm sure of it.'

'What was he doing there?'

'I don't know, but he was watching it all.'

'And we didn't even guess.' A thought struck Adira. 'Why didn't he attack us then? He could have put an end to the battle single-handedly. Why did he allow the vikritis to fight us?'

Maya shrugged. 'I don't know. I don't like Shukra. He is cunning and scheming. He scares me.' She smiled at Adira. 'But what is important is that all of you are back.' She paused. 'How's AJ?'

Adira flushed. 'Oh, he's fine. He did well. We were fighting side by side towards the end. For a moment there, I thought we were going to die together, but then Maharishi Satyavachana appeared and I think the vikritis realised they had bitten off more than they could chew.'

'Thank god for that!' Maya laughed happily. Her friends were safe and they were back home. That was all that mattered.

For now.

The Assembly Hall

'What did the vikritis want with the Hall of Archives?' Jignesh demanded. 'That's the question I want an answer to. I don't think there is any need to speculate on how they got there. Clearly, they used the Akshapatalika in Delhi, and Vishwaraj, to get the information required to locate the entrance to the Hall of Archives. But why? What did they hope to achieve?' He looked at the others. 'Any opinions?'

'The knowledge of the Sangha,' Kanakpratap suggested. 'Isn't that what they have always been after? We doubted earlier that the vikritis had the ability to possess Diya's body, but it was always obvious that they had someone on their side who had the power of the siddhis. After seeing Vishwaraj there tonight, I think we have our answer. And that makes the vikritis more dangerous than ever. For thousands of years, they have had a purpose but not the means. If they finally have the means to achieve their purpose, then the Sangha needs to ensure that it is capable of stopping them.'

'It is meaningless to speculate on what they wanted tonight,' Satyavachana said calmly. 'Speculation will get us nowhere. What is important is to stay focused on the tasks ahead. Our defences are better. Our weapons are better. Our armour was tested in battle today. But we still need to find the remaining parts of the prophecy.'

'And the *Ranakarman Parva*,' Jignesh reminded him. 'We need that. If Shukra opens the gates to the other levels of Pataala-lok, nothing else can help us.'

Satyavachana nodded. 'I'm working on it,' he said with a touch of asperity. 'It will take time. It will happen when Maya is ready. Not before that. I cannot take the risk of having her enter the Mists without being fully prepared and capable.'

Chapter Seventy-one

Shukra's Cavern

Shukra's Cavern

Vishwaraj beamed as Shukra showered praise and blessings on him. He had been extremely cut up about having to abort what he felt was a successful mission.

Added to that was his chagrin at not being able to have a go at the One. Shukra had told Vishwaraj that the boy of the prophecy had been one of the defenders of the Hall of Archives. Nothing would have pleased him more than delivering the One on a platter to his glorious ancestor.

But now, after hearing what Shukra had to say about his performance, Vishwaraj was mollified. And delighted.

'Thank you, Poorvapitamah.' He bowed, with folded hands when Shukra finished his encomium. 'I feel blessed that I am able to serve you.'

'And I found what I sought in the archives,' Shukra told him, presenting him with the ancient manuscripts that he had purloined.

Vishwaraj could barely contain his excitement as he accepted the texts from Shukra. 'I will begin the search immediately, Poorvapitamah.'

'Go now,' Shukra commanded, 'and be successful.'

Vishwaraj bowed with folded hands and vanished.

Shukra sat ruminating. Things were definitely moving, but he was nowhere close to where he should have been. Even his discovery tonight, and the task he had given Vishwaraj, were just temporary diversions, to ensure that he would no longer be distracted from the main task at hand. He was done with attending to petty matters himself. The Sangha was no more than an irritant. But even an irritant cost time.

Time that he could not afford to waste.

He had already lost more than two months. He could not afford to lose any more time. And, while he knew that Vishwaraj's new mission would also take a while, it would free him from the mundane.

There was one more thing he had to do before he started the search for the mantras once again. He had to free himself from that old, niggling doubt once and for all. Shukra didn't quite understand what was troubling him. But the appearance of the girl—the atma of Dhruv's daughter—had brought it back to the surface; a doubt he had suppressed over two months ago.

But now, he had to be sure.

And that meant going back to where it had all started, almost fifteen years ago. To the city where he had appeared to the world, 5,000 years after his self-imposed exile.

Allahabad.

Chapter Seventy-two

Graduation Day

The Assembly Hall
The Gurukul
Panna National Park

Maya looked around, as she sat with Amyra, at the children streaming into the hall, chattering excitedly as they sat down to await the start of the ceremony. Today was a big day, one to which every student in the Gurukul eagerly looked forward.

In the centre of the raised platform at the far end of the hall were placed eight chairs. Arranged along the side of the dais were a few more, waiting to be occupied.

Chains of marigolds and rose petals festooned the hall to mark the occasion. Maya had never known it to be as vibrant as it was today. The very atmosphere pulsated with vitality.

In no time at all, the entire Gurukul had assembled in the hall. The chairs at the side of the dais were occupied by Jignesh, Usha and Parth from the Gurukul, Diksha and Anasuya from the Sangha Council, along with Satyavachana and Kanakpratap. Arjun, Agastya, Varun, Gopal, Anisha,

Tanveer, Sonali and Adira sat on the eight chairs in the centre, facing the audience.

A hush descended on the assembly as Jignesh rose and walked to the front of the dais. The moment had come.

'*Prapanchayati!*' Jignesh's intoned and his voice boomed out, amplified many times, over the heads of the children and the Mahamatis seated in the audience. 'Today is a big day for eight members of our Gurukul. As you all know by now,' Jignesh looked around with the hint of a smile, no stranger to the speed at which news spread among the children, 'they acquitted themselves with honour and courage, two nights ago, while defending the entrance to the Hall of Archives from the vikritis.' He had decided to omit any mention of Vishwaraj. 'That encounter was their final project to qualify for graduation to the ranks of the Gana. Even with death staring them in the face, these eight warriors of the Sangha did not falter. They did not cower or shrink back in fear. They stood tall and proud, and fought on regardless of the peril they found themselves in.'

Maya found herself brimming with pride for her friends, and tearing up a little as well. After all, she had been there and had watched them fight, surrounded by the vikritis, with little hope of surviving the battle. Jignesh's words were true. Her friends had not flinched even when they knew they were outnumbered. She knew they deserved every bit of his panegyric.

'Today,' Jignesh continued, 'they have demonstrated that age is no consideration for membership of the Gana. They have earned their way through hard work, discipline and commitment to their life's purpose. In accordance with the rules of the Sangha and the powers bestowed upon me as

Mahamatra by the Saptarishis, I formally welcome them into the Sangha as full members of the Gana!'

He turned to face the eight children and bowed to them, his hands folded, as the hall burst into thunderous applause.

Maya knew the significance of that bow. Satyavachana had explained it to her during their lessons together. In that moment, Jignesh was no longer Mahamatra. He was bowing to show his respect for the abilities of the children, for the powers they possessed and had honed, that made them eligible for the membership of the Gana. In the world of sadhs, what gained you respect was *who* you were: your title, your material possessions, your material power. The Sangha was founded on principles far older than those of Kaliyuga; in a time when you were respected not for who you were but *what* you were. A Rishi with mastery of the siddhis or a Kshatriya with mastery of the arts of war … Essentially someone who had voluntarily and deliberately renounced the sadh world and dedicated themselves to the service of humanity, to the development of powers that would protect those whom they served.

That, after all, was what the Sangha was all about.

Maya clapped until her hands hurt, beaming broadly as she shared in the happiness of her friends who now stood and acknowledged the rapturous applause with folded hands, bowing low multiple times to show their gratitude. They were now ready to take up their roles in the Gana.

She smiled at Amyra, who was clapping hard as well, and the novice smiled back at her, clearly delighted at the achievements of their friends.

Jignesh held up his hand and silence rushed to fill the vacuum as the applause died out.

'Now,' he said, 'for the hardest moment.' He looked around at the assembly. 'Parting ways.'

With a jolt Maya realised what he meant. The eight children would no longer be part of the Gurukul. Once they graduated, they belonged to the Gana and their place was in the outside world, among the sadhs. Not here, among the students.

'Varun and Adira will return to their home base in Mumbai,' Jignesh announced. 'Tanveer will return to Kolkata, Gopal to Chennai, Sonali to Jaipur and Anisha to Chandigarh. Admissions have been secured and they will leave within the next few days to start their new roles as their schools re-open after the winter break. Arjun and Agastya will not go back to Delhi just yet; they will stay at the Gurukul for a few more months. They have work to complete before they can join the Gana in their home locations.'

Maya's heart sank. It dawned on her that the Saptas, as the seven children had come to regard themselves, were being split up. They were all going in different directions. How would they fulfil the prophecy?

Or had they been wrong to think of themselves as the Saptas?

Suddenly she felt low, more depressed than she had ever felt in the last two months. It all seemed unreal.

Satyavachana's voice floated through Maya's mind, intruding on her thoughts. He was speaking to her telepathically. She almost jumped. She hadn't got used to this medium of communication yet, not having mastered it herself.

'*You will be up there soon, my child,*' Satyavachana said, '*with Jignesh praising you and your accomplishments.*'

Maya looked at Satyavachana, who gave her a broad grin and an almost imperceptible nod.

A deep sigh escaped Maya even as she was filled with joy by the thought that her guru had such immense confidence in her.

Amyra looked at her, concerned. 'Are you okay, Maya?'

'Yes, I'm fine, Amyra.' Maya smiled back at the novice. Deep down, the conflict continued to rage.

Was she really good enough for the Gana?

Chapter Seventy-three

Kapoor Takes Stock

Allahabad

'Turn up the bloody heater and bring it closer,' Kapoor instructed Mishra, suppressing a shiver.

This was his third trip to Allahabad. After Mirza had made a breakthrough in identifying Upadhyay at the stationery shop, Kapoor had flown back to Delhi and left Mirza to carry on the investigations with the help of the fourteen-year-old photographs. He had returned to Allahabad only today, after nine days.

It was cold—colder than Delhi, Kapoor thought—and it was also the last day of the calendar year. Some part of him was resentful that he would have to spend New Year's Eve alone in a strange city while his colleagues had warm homes and families to go back to.

Not that Kapoor would have spent his day any differently had he been in Delhi. His passion and commitment to his work had not only resulted in a separation from his wife and two children, but had also whittled down his social life over the years. And, quite frankly, he didn't care. He was quite happy by himself.

The perfect cop. The lone wolf. The solo player. That was him.

It was the slow progress in this case that was getting to Kapoor, not the prospect of spending 31 December alone. He had stocked up on rum and coke for his own little welcome for the New Year. It was one of the rare occasions when he allowed himself the indulgence of alcohol.

He was also conscious that he was keeping the other two men from their families.

Kapoor was not an insensitive man. Not that he had displayed much sensitivity towards his own family. But when it came to others, especially his fellow policemen in the rank and file, he was one of the more thoughtful senior police officers around.

'Thank you, Mishra,' he nodded to the STF driver. Kapoor had very quickly realised that the man was sharp and could go far beyond his prescribed duty. And he had put that intelligence to good use.

Yes, progress had been slow since he had first arrived in Allahabad, almost one month back.

But they were making progress nevertheless.

Finally.

In the past nine days, two breakthroughs had been achieved.

The first had come rather swiftly, to Kapoor's delight.

As soon as the stationery shop owner had identified Upadhyay's photograph and associated it with St. Joseph's College, Mirza had sought a meeting with the principal of the school. He had requested the principal to check with the teachers to see if anyone recognised the man in the photograph.

The principal had asked for some time, and then called back two days later. He had not only checked with the teachers but had also had someone go through old school magazines to see if there was a match between Upadhyay's photograph and faculty photographs in the school magazine.

Both initiatives had paid off handsomely.

In his second meeting with Mirza, the principal showed him photographs from the magazines where Upadhyay was clearly identifiable. A couple of teachers who had taught there fourteen years ago had also positively identified the passport photograph. They said it was of a history teacher who had taught the senior classes.

But the names didn't match.

The teacher whose photograph had appeared in the school magazine was Dhruv Srivastava. And that was also the name provided by the teachers who had identified Upadhyay's photograph when it was shown to them.

The realisation struck Kapoor like a flash of lightning. The man had changed his name upon leaving Allahabad and assumed a new identity in Delhi.

This only reinforced Kapoor's earlier suspicion that Singh and Upadhyay had been embroiled in something that had compelled them to leave Allahabad.

Upadhyay's—or rather Srivastava's—identification raised a second possibility: that Virendra Singh had also assumed a new identity. But they still needed someone to identify him so they could learn what his original name was.

And then, just yesterday, Mirza had found someone who recognised Singh's photograph, via the WhatsApp groups for the akharas he had been making the rounds of, for the last two-and-a-half weeks.

As Kapoor had expected, the names didn't match. The man said that the photograph was of someone called Kanakpratap Singh. Same surname, but a different first name.

According to him, Kanakpratap Singh was one of the strongest men in the akhara, second only to his brother, Rudrapratap Singh. Both men were well-respected and had the reputation of being decent folk.

On hearing the news, Kapoor had dashed to Allahabad once again, to take stock of the situation and plan ahead. It wasn't such a bad way to end the year, but he chafed at the fact that it had taken him so long to get to Allahabad, something he'd wanted to do almost two months ago.

At least, he consoled himself as he bade farewell to the two STF men, the new year would start on a positive note.

All they had to do was find out what had happened in Allahabad to make the two men flee to Delhi and assume false identities. They had not wanted to be traced. They had wanted to disappear.

Why?

This was bigger than it appeared. Kapoor could feel it in his bones.

And what was the nature of Vishwaraj's involvement in all this?

He was determined to find out.

Chapter Seventy-four

Arjun Broods

The Gurukul
Panna National Park

The last day of the year was a quiet affair. There were no celebrations or parties; nothing of the sort that Arjun was accustomed to in Delhi, where 31 December was a rambunctious affair, with the city lit up and crackers being burst to mark the start of the new year.

At the Gurukul, it was much more sedate. For one thing, the calendar that celebrated the end of the year was Western: the Gregorian calendar, introduced by Pope Gregory XIII in 1582 as a reform of the Julian calendar introduced by Julius Caesar in 46 BC, which in turn was based on the Egyptian solar calendar.

The Gurukul, on the other hand, followed the lunar calendar, and, in the tradition of diversity and inclusiveness that it had maintained for the last 5,000 years, it commemorated the New Year several times, in keeping with the differing traditions in different parts of the country.

The students at the Gurukul knew exactly why New Year's Eve had no special significance. Simply put, there was nothing remarkable about the date itself. All that it marked was the return of the earth, after one complete revolution around the sun, to the point where it had started from. And that starting point could be any point along the orbit of the earth around the sun.

What really mattered was the time when one yuga transitioned into another, because these transitions had a material and very real impact on the lives of people.

In any case, Arjun was not in the mood for any kind of celebration. It was more than a month and a half since his mother had left with the other Mahamatis for the Gandharva valley. In the intervening period, there had been no word from Gandharva-lok about the team or the progress of its mission. Neither was there any indication of when they would return.

Arjun knew that, in the Gandharva world, less than ten days had passed, so there was nothing to worry about. Ten days were hardly enough time for the prophecy to be found, considering it had been hidden away 5,000 years ago, with no clues to its location.

But he could not erase the worry from his mind.

He walked aimlessly in the forest surrounding the Gurukul, away from the dorms and the cottages where the Mahamatis resided, trying to find solace in the company of the grazing deer and his isolation from everyone else.

'Hi Arjun.' A soft voice intruded on his thoughts.

He whirled around, caught by surprise.

It was Adira.

Chapter Seventy-five

Farewell

The Gurukul

'Um …' Adira sounded tentative. 'Am I disturbing you? You seemed to be lost in thought.'

Arjun laughed, then immediately regretted it. It had sounded forced. It *was* forced. He was trying to hide his anxiety for his mother and act as if nothing was the matter.

'I was thinking about Mom,' he admitted, deciding to be honest. There was no point in pretending.

There was an awkward silence as Adira realised what Arjun meant.

'Did you want something?' Arjun could have kicked himself. Was this anything to say?

He was acutely aware that this was the first time he and Adira were having a conversation by themselves. Every time he had interacted with her, it was as part of the Saptas.

'Well,' Adira hesitated, sounding as unsure as Arjun was. 'I guess I just came to say goodbye.'

Arjun nodded, not knowing how to respond. Should he say goodbye? Would that sound too rude? Too abrupt? Too dismissive?

'Will we ever get the chance to meet again?' Adira continued, gaining confidence now. 'I mean, Mumbai and Delhi are so far apart and I don't think Gana members travel between cities. From what I've heard, their activities and responsibilities are restricted to their home cities.' She sighed. 'We had such a good time together.'

'Well, I'm not going to Delhi immediately,' Arjun responded, and bit his tongue. How did it matter whether he was in Panna or Delhi?

'I know.' Adira sighed again. 'But you'll go sooner or later. And even Panna isn't all that close to Mumbai.'

'We'll be in touch over WhatsApp,' Arjun said feebly. 'And email. And we can always call each other.' Again, he felt like kicking himself. WhatsApp and email would only be possible when he left the Gurukul for Delhi. Until then, even calling her would be out of the question.

Adira looked at him. 'You don't understand, Arjun. Maybe it hasn't sunk in yet, but the Saptas will never meet again. We may talk and message each other as often as we can, once you're in Delhi, but we'll never be together again.'

Arjun was silent. She was right. It hadn't sunk in yet.

Or, rather, he had not allowed the thought to take hold of him. He was fighting it tooth and nail, refusing to accept the reality of their situation.

'No,' he said, his innate stubbornness coming to the fore. 'We *will* meet again. I don't know how or when, but I can feel it in my bones. I just *know* it. We *are* the Saptas of the prophecy. And, somehow, somewhere, we will have to meet again if the prophecy is to be fulfilled.'

Adira shrugged, but said nothing. She knew it was futile to argue with Arjun when he was in this mood.

The silence hung heavy over them, only the chirping of birds and the monkeys rustling the leaves in the trees as they swung overhead penetrating its cloak.

Then Adira spoke, hesitantly. 'I'm going to miss you, Arjun.'

Arjun nodded, unsure once again. 'Um, yeah, me too.' Then, worried that his response may not have been adequate, he added, 'I'll miss you too.'

'Goodbye, Arjun.' Adira smiled wanly at him. 'Let's hope you are right about us meeting again. I would really like that to happen.'

She turned and walked away, leaving Arjun with his thoughts.

'Goodbye, Adira,' he said.

Why did he feel he had done something wrong?

Chapter Seventy-six

Parting

The Gurukul

The next day dawned cold and grey, the sun hidden behind a thick curtain of fog through which the students wended their way to the Assembly Hall for the morning assembly and prayers.

By the time they finished and emerged from the hall, the fog had dissipated somewhat, but it still clung to the trees as a thin veil, with wisps and tendrils curling around the branches and leaves as though seeking a place to settle down and stay.

The sun was still not visible but a weak brightness permeated the air, somewhat lending the scene an air of gloom and depression.

Which was quite appropriate for the occasion, and her mood, Maya thought glumly as she walked with Arjun and the other students towards the riverside entrance to the Gurukul. For today was the day when the six new members of the Gana would leave the Gurukul forever, and take their place in their home locations.

The entire Gurukul had turned up to see them off.

Last night, Arjun's Saptas had sat down to dinner together one last time.

It had been quite a lot of fun, actually, now that Maya thought back, and was a memorable one. They had laughed and cracked jokes, and recalled the many awkward moments over the years—the last two-and-a-half months, in the case of Arjun and Maya. By the time they finished, their faces ached from grinning too broadly and their stomachs were hurting from the non-stop laughter.

Maya stood now with Arjun, Agastya and Amyra, at the front of the crowd that had gathered around the six students and the Mahamatis, who were giving their final blessings to the new members of the Gana as they went around, touching the feet of their revered teachers.

Varun spotted Arjun as he finished his round of the Mahamatis and ambled up to him, followed at a distance by Tanveer.

Maya watched Varun walk towards them and remembered her initial meeting with him and the first time she had interacted with him on the night they had entered the Gandharva valley.

He had changed since then. Actually, they had all changed—Tanveer and Adira too. Ever since the episode at Bhimbetka, ten days ago, they seemed to have gained a new confidence, a new spring in their step. They strode rather than walked and their personalities had become more imposing somehow. They appeared to have grown ... older. Maya had noticed the change especially in Adira, since she shared a dorm with the Kshatriya.

Maya was also acutely aware of the change wrought in Arjun over the last two and a half months. He was no longer the boy who had entered the Gurukul with her. And, ever since the battle with the vikritis ten days ago, the change had become more pronounced. It wasn't just that he had grown in confidence. That was only natural, given the intensity of the practice he engaged in at the Gurukul—far more taxing than the regimen he had followed after school in Delhi—as well as the experience of having battled the vikritis and faced imminent death.

He had also grown in stature, Maya thought. Day by day, she had seen him morph from a scared boy into the One who would command the Sangha in the fight against Shukra. Whenever that happened.

Maya wondered if that change had been accompanied by other changes that she was not privy to. In Delhi they had been virtually inseparable, spending most of their free time in each other's company. At the Gurukul, however, over the last two and a half months, they had barely got a few minutes each day, usually at dinnertime, to catch up and talk.

Varun had reached them by now. He embraced Arjun warmly. Then he stood back, his hands on Arjun's shoulders— he was a good head taller than Arjun—and looked into the eyes of Yayati's scion.

'I guess we won't see each other for a while,' Arjun said, a weak smile on his face.

'You wish,' Varun retorted. 'I'll find a way for us to meet.'

Arjun nodded. 'You do that. And I will too.' He looked beyond Varun as if searching for someone.

'Oh, Adira's already in the car,' Varun said, guessing that Arjun was looking for his twin sister. He chuckled. 'Guess she's in a hurry to leave the Gurukul!'

'That's fine,' Maya said. 'We already said our goodbyes yesterday.' Adira and she had had a tearful farewell conversation last night before Maya left for her nocturnal lessons with Satyavachana.

'Cool,' Varun replied immediately. 'She said goodbye to Arjun too, yesterday.' He was going to say more but he saw Arjun's face and thought the better of it.

Maya kept a straight face, but inside, she was laughing. She had been observing Adira for a while and knew exactly what was happening.

Another warm embrace and a firm handshake and Varun moved to Agastya and hugged him as well, bidding him farewell as Tanveer came up to Arjun and embraced him.

'Farewell, archer,' Arjun told him. 'We had some good times together.'

Tanveer, not garrulous at the best of times, simply nodded and compressed his lips firmly. It was the only sign of emotion that he would allow himself.

As the archer walked over to Agastya and embraced him, Varun bade farewell to Amyra and approached Maya.

'Hey, Maya,' Varun said tentatively, unsure if he should shake her hand or give her a hug.

'Hey, Varun.' Maya noticed his hesitation and decided to resolve his dilemma. She stepped forward and gave him a quick hug, then stepped back.

Varun flushed. 'Now, you'd better learn everything you can from Maharishi Satyavachana,' he told her, 'and graduate to the Gana as soon as you can. Then you'll be posted to Delhi and we'll all find a way to be together again.'

Maya smiled at these words and nodded vigorously. 'I will, Varun. I'll do my best.'

They both stood for a moment, uncertain what to say or do next.

'All right then.' Kanakpratap's voice cut through the silence. He was driving Tanveer, Sonali and Anisha to Delhi, from where they would take trains to their respective destinations. Varun, Adira and Gopal were being driven by another Mahamati to Gwalior, from where they would catch a train to Mumbai and Chennai respectively.

'Let's go,' Kanakpratap boomed. 'We have a long way to travel.'

'Bye, then.' Varun smiled weakly at Maya.

'Bye Varun.'

Tanveer came up to her and nodded wordlessly. But Maya could see the unhappiness in his eyes.

They were all going through pangs of separation.

Varun and Tanveer turned and walked away, glancing back only once to wave goodbye to them.

Then, the six children were gone.

Chapter Seventy-seven

Update from Allahabad

Raman Kapoor's Office
New Delhi

Raman Kapoor listened intently to Ajit as he gave his report over the phone.

Ajit and Harish had arrived in Allahabad five days back to continue the investigation in collaboration with Mirza. They had spent the last couple of days consolidating leads and developing a plan of action. Today, they had begun meeting people and interviewing them.

Ajit had been telling Kapoor about their meetings with the teachers at St. Joseph's school and with the men in the akharas. Apparently, people had been very forthcoming with information and the investigative team had already begun piecing together a profile of Upadhyay, or Dhruv Srivastava. They had conducted a thorough investigation, talking to all the shopkeepers in the vicinity of the schools, including paanwallahs, who surprisingly were a storehouse of neighbourhood gossip.

'Hmmm,' Kapoor said thoughtfully, when Ajit finished his report. 'Good work, Ajit. Pass on my compliments to Harish, Mirza and Mishra as well.' He paused to think, then resumed, 'So something seems to have happened in Allahabad to make both men leave in a hurry. You guys need to find people who were close to both Singh and Upadhyay … I mean Srivastava. I want to know exactly what happened. I want to know everything about them—who they knew, who their friends were, where they went, what they did—all of it. That's the only way we'll figure this out.'

'Yes, sir,' Ajit replied. 'We're on it. The people here are extremely helpful. They are happy to talk. And we're getting some good leads. Every new person we speak to refers us to someone else, so it's just a matter of time before we reach someone who was close to the two men and can give us details of what happened to make them leave.'

'Very good.'

'And tomorrow, Harish is going to the Lete Hanumanji ka Mandir. Mirza says that's a place most Allahabadis visit often, and we may get some leads there.'

'I see.' Kapoor had a feeling that Ajit was holding something back. 'Okay, Ajit, what are you not telling me?'

'Sir,' Ajit replied hesitantly. 'I'm operating on a hunch here, so I might be wrong.'

'A hunch!' Kapoor snorted. He chuckled to himself. Maybe his modus operandi was rubbing off on his team. 'Go ahead and tell me. Don't you know by now? I operate only on hunches.' He chuckled aloud this time.

'Well, sir,' Ajit continued bravely, 'I think our elusive suspect from Delhi is also in Allahabad. Or, at least, he was here.'

Kapoor sat bolt upright. 'Our suspect? The guy with the eyepatch?'

'Yes, sir.'

'And why do you think that?' Kapoor frowned.

'Well … er …' Ajit fumbled, unsure now.

'Go ahead,' Kapoor pushed him. 'I'm listening.'

'Well, sir, some of the people we spoke to—the teachers, especially, told us that a news reporter had spoken to them just a few days back, asking questions about Dhruv Srivastava.'

'What? Another man enquiring about Dhruv Srivastava? That is quite a coincidence … So you asked them to describe him.'

'I did, sir. And they all described him as tall, well built, with an eyepatch over his right eye.'

Kapoor fell silent.

'Sir?'

Yes, yes. I was thinking. So here's what we'll do. I'll send you the portrait that the police artist made on the basis of your description of the guy. Make copies, distribute them to everyone on the team and, whenever anyone mentions the guy with the eyepatch, show them the portrait. Get a positive identification.'

'Yes, sir. Maybe we can nail this guy in Allahabad itself.'

'Oh, I wouldn't be so sure,' Kapoor told him. 'This man has managed to disappear and cover his tracks for almost three months. It's going to be difficult. But we have to try.'

'Yes, sir.'

'Great. Good job once again. Keep me posted if anything turns up.'

Kapoor signed off and sat looking into the distance.

Finally!

Finally, this case was beginning to yield clues that led somewhere. He had been right all along about Allahabad. It was the epicentre. Not just fifteen years ago, but even today. The fact that they may have found their suspect in the mysterious news reporter who was going around asking questions only reinforced his belief.

What had brought the man back to Allahabad?

And why was he snooping around asking questions about Dhruv Srivastava?

Chapter Seventy-eight

The Boatman

Lete Hanumanji ka Mandir
Allahabad

While Harish went inside the temple to try his luck, Mirza strolled along the banks of the Ganga nearby. He had contacted someone from the boat union, to whom he had given copies of the two photographs the previous day.

His mobile phone rang. It was the man from the union. He listened for a few moments, then said, 'Fine. I'll look for him.'

He pocketed the phone, a smile of satisfaction on his face. They were making progress. The boat union official had shown the photographs to the boatmen who moored there and one of them had recognised the photograph of Srivastava.

'Where can I find boatman Raju?' Mirza asked the nearest boatman he could see.

The boatman pointed out a boat with faded blue paint still visible around the bow, among the row of boats that lined the banks of the river.

Mirza walked along the river bank until he reached the blue boat.

A man was sitting in it, waiting for customers.

'Raju?' Mirza enquired.

The boatman looked up hopefully. 'Yes, sir. You want to go bathe in the Sangam?'

Mirza smiled. 'No, Raju.' He flashed his identity card. 'I'm from the police. Special Task Force.'

Raju froze, his face lined with fear. 'I haven't done anything wrong, sir. I'm just a simple boatman.'

Mirza winced; it always bothered him that the ordinary citizen's first reaction to the police was one of distrust and fear. 'No, no, Raju,' he hastened to reassure him. 'This is regarding the photograph that you were shown yesterday by Nitin. He told me that you recognised the man.' He took out a copy of Srivastava's photograph and showed it to Raju.

The fear disappeared from Raju's face and he nodded vigorously, anxious to be of help.

'Yes, sir,' he replied. 'I recognised him immediately. But as I told Nitin, I haven't seen him for many years. Maybe ten years or more. Perhaps even fifteen years. I don't know.'

'Tell me more about him,' Mirza urged. 'Anything that comes to mind.'

'Is he in trouble?'

'Not really. But what you tell us could be useful, and may even help us to help him.'

Raju nodded. 'In that case I will definitely tell you, sir. This man is a good man. Srivastavaji. That is his name. I still remember after all these years. He would come every Tuesday to the temple,' he indicated the Lete Hanumanji ka Mandir, 'and then go to bathe in the Sangam.'

He shrugged. 'For some reason, Srivastavaji developed a fondness for me and would only take my boat to the bathing spot. Since he was a regular and we had become friendly, I would wait for him every Tuesday. But then, one day, he disappeared. Just like that. I assumed he had fallen sick. I waited every Tuesday, for several weeks, but he never returned. After some time, I gave up. I feared he had died.'

'No,' Mirza reassured the boatman. 'He left Allahabad and went to live in Delhi instead.'

'But why didn't he say goodbye? He was such a nice gentleman, such a warm human being.'

Mirza nodded. 'Did he ever get his family along when he came here?'

'No.' Raju shook his head. 'But he told me about them. We would talk. When you meet someone regularly, once a week, for years, you do get to know something about them. He had a wife and a son. The son was born some months before he stopped coming here.' He looked at Mirza. 'Before he went to Delhi.'

'A son? I thought he had a daughter?'

'A daughter? No, sir, only a son. If he did have a daughter, he never mentioned her.'

Mirza frowned. This was at odds with the information he had. Kapoor had told him that Dhruv Srivastava had a daughter. Ajit had also testified to that. He had seen father and daughter enter their house in Delhi shortly before Srivastava was murdered.

Where was the son then?

'Is he happy in Delhi, sir? And his family? His wife and son?' Raju wanted to know.

'Yes, Raju.' Mirza pressed some money into the boatman's hand. 'Thank you. You have been very helpful.'

Raju smiled, showing discoloured teeth, stained with paan and tobacco, and pocketed the money happily. 'You are welcome, sir. And please give my regards to Srivastavaji whenever you meet him!'

Mirza nodded and made his way back to the entrance of the temple, where Harish was waiting for him.

'Anything?' Harish asked.

'Lots. DCP Kapoor was right. Something did happen here in Allahabad,' Mirza replied. 'Srivastava had a wife and a son. That's definite. But they weren't with him in Delhi. Only his daughter lived with him in Delhi.'

'So what happened to the wife and son?' Harish asked. 'Did he leave them behind? Did they separate? Divorce?'

'That's what we have to find out.'

Chapter Seventy-nine

Shukra Makes a Choice

Sadhu Mandali
The Sangam, Allahabad

Shukra sat in the shade of a tree, his eyes closed, arms outstretched and hands resting lightly on his knees, apparently deep in a meditative trance.

Around him, sadhus of various hues milled about, some arriving, others leaving. Yet others sat around talking.

Shukra had chosen the mandali since it provided him the perfect opportunity to stay in Allahabad without having to disguise himself or create an illusion to look different, and remain inconspicuous. Dressed in saffron robes, his hair bunched up in a topknot with sacred streaks of ash and a red tikka on his forehead, he looked like any other sadhu here.

Mandalis like this one were numerous and scattered all along the banks of the Ganga at the Sangam. Sadhus from all over India sought shelter here.

But Shukra was not meditating. He had had enough of that after 5,000 years of intense tapasya. He was reflecting on his two-week stay in Allahabad and the information he had uncovered.

His encounter with Maharishi Dhruv in Delhi had been extremely disconcerting. Too many things had happened that day that he had not anticipated and which seemed to be totally out of his control. Including the manner in which the confrontation had ended.

Too many questions had remained unanswered. Shukra had largely disregarded them after that fateful day; there were other, more immediate things on his mind. But there was something he couldn't overlook any more. He could no longer ignore the peculiar sensation he had felt that day. Especially now that he remembered when he had experienced it before. It had been thousands of years ago, when he had resurrected his disciple, Kacha—the son of Brihaspati—after the Asuras had killed him and mixed his ashes with Shukra's wine. Unknowingly, Shukra had drunk the wine and, with it, the ashes of Kacha.

Shukra had sensed something abnormal at the time, which he had never been able to explain.

Thousands of years later, something had happened at Maharishi Dhruv's home when he had come face to face with Dhruv's daughter, which, for some reason unknown to him, reminded him of that long forgotten sensation. He had been perplexed by it but had dismissed it from his mind as unimportant at the time.

But his observation of Dhruv's daughter indulging in atma travel at Bhimbetka had brought those questions sharply back into focus and made them relevant again.

Shukra had realised that night that he would have to seek the answers that had eluded him so far in Allahabad. He had arrived here immediately after concluding the mission at Bhimbetka and handing over the spoils of that intrusion to Vishwaraj. He had also left detailed instructions for the young man, on what he needed to do next.

The last two weeks had not been unproductive.

Shukra had meticulously set about seeking information, speaking to all manner of people. He had posed as a news reporter writing a story about people who had moved out of Allahabad to big cities, and had found it to be a convenient ruse for asking all sorts of questions, which the locals had been unusually eager to answer. He imagined that everyone wanted to be a celebrity and have their voice heard.

On these excursions to interview people, he had discarded his hermit's attire for a casual shirt and jeans with sneakers, to look the part he was playing. His eyepatch made him look alluringly rakish. No one suspected who he actually was.

No, the last two weeks had been far from fruitless. In fact, he had uncovered a goldmine of information.

He had learnt that Maharishi Dhruv had lost his wife and son almost fifteen years ago, after which Dhruv had packed up and moved to Delhi.

While Shukra had seethed at the memory of being outwitted fifteen years ago, this revelation had solved a mystery that had troubled him ever since he had discovered that the boy who was Yayati's scion—the One of the prophecy—was alive.

And that mystery was this: if he had not succeeded in killing the One of the prophecy, then whom had he killed?

He was sure that he had killed a woman and her son. There was no doubt about that. It was not an illusion woven by Dhruv. So who had it been?

Now he knew.

Maharishi Dhruv had sacrificed his own wife and son to save the scion of Yayati, who must have been smuggled out by his uncle and mother to Delhi. Oblivious to this deception, Shukra had departed, satisfied that he had achieved his objective and rid himself of his prospective foe.

For Shukra played by the rules. His objective was to kill the boy. Once that was accomplished, there had been no reason to stay on in Allahabad or kill anyone else. It would have served no purpose.

Shukra frowned as he thought of how he had been fooled by their plan.

In these past two weeks, he had also learned about Dhruv's daughter, Maya. He had had a brief glimpse into the girl's mind when he had encountered her at Dhruv's house in Delhi. He had seen enough to determine that she knew nothing of Dhruv's real identity as a Maharishi. Her mind had been a complete blank. No mantras, no powers that indicated that she had inherited Dhruv's Maharishi abilities.

What he had learned in Allahabad hinted at why that was so.

But it gave rise to other, equally perplexing questions.

Like the one he was pondering over now.

If Dhruv's daughter had no powers and knew no mantras, how was she able to travel as an atma?

He had witnessed this phenomenon for himself, but had no answers.

How important was it really?

And could it wait?

He wrestled with his thoughts, unable to reach a conclusion.

He had wasted two and a half months on what seemed to be a wild goose chase. Yet, he knew that he had to reconcile the obvious contradiction: Dhruv's daughter had no powers, yet she was able to travel outside her physical body as an atma. This was an impossibility that he could not understand.

He had an inkling of the possible explanation, and it was possible to validate his theory through a deeper investigation of the girl.

But that would mean spending more time finding out what this aberration meant. And this, at a time when every day that passed meant less time to do what he needed to do. He was also acutely aware that the peak of Kaliyuga was approaching and that time was running out for him.

Was it really worth his while to try and solve the mystery?

Even if his suspicions were correct, the girl had no powers. Of that, he was sure. She would take years to gain powers even if she was able to. There was nothing about which to be apprehensive where she was concerned.

Shukra knew he had to make a choice. He struggled with his thoughts, trying to cut through the confusion and arrive at a decision.

Enough of this. He had work to do.

The mantras had to be found.

Shukra's eyelids sprang open, his one good eye fixing the crowd around him with a piercing gaze. Inside the mandali, he did not need to wear his eyepatch. No one gave him a second look. He was just another sadhu in a crowd of sadhus.

He rose and strode towards the entrance.

It was time to leave Allahabad and revert to his original priority.

Chapter Eighty

Shukra Searches

Maya's House
New Delhi

It was past midnight. The streets were deserted. Under the streetlights, a lonely dog made his way across the road, sniffing around for food.

Shukra appeared on the pavement opposite Maya's house, materialising out of thin air. He looked around, then crossed the street to the front door of the house.

Standing before the door, which had been locked and sealed by the police, he closed his eyes. A mantra unfolded inside his mind.

There was a click as the lock slid back and the seal fell off. The door creaked open.

After another quick glance around, Shukra walked in.

As he entered the living room, he shut the front door and latched it from inside. A glowing sphere appeared at his shoulder, bathing the room in an eerie golden light.

Shukra knew exactly where to look.

The study.

That would be the best place to start. Surely Maharishi Dhruv would have hidden it there, among his books.

Another mantra silently unfolded in Shukra's mind and a dozen clones emerged from his body, just as they had in the Hall of Archives.

The clones quickly went to work, scanning the rows of books in the study, examining the ones that looked promising and discarding the others.

In a short while, the entire study had been combed—bookshelves, desk and all.

But what Shukra was looking for was nowhere to be found.

The clones made their way through the house, examining every room, every cupboard, every drawer.

Shukra waited.

It had to be here!

But, to his great disappointment, the extensive search yielded nothing.

For a few moments, he stood there, thinking.

It had been crystal clear when he had read Dhruv's mind. The Maharishi had desperately fought to shield his thoughts from Shukra's probing, but had not been entirely successful. Shukra had seen glimpses of the secret that Dhruv had tried so hard to protect.

It *had* to be here.

But it wasn't.

Which could only mean one of two things: Either it had not been hidden in the house at all or someone had moved it from here.

And there was only one person who could have moved it.

The girl whom Shukra had encountered the day Dhruv died.

Dhruv's daughter.

But he had examined her mind that day and found no knowledge of what he sought. She did not have it with her.

So where could it be?

Chapter Eighty-one

Recall

Police Commissioner's Office
New Delhi

Raman Kapoor fidgeted as he paced the small lounge outside Ramesh Vidyarthi's office. He had been making plans to visit Allahabad again; his team there, along with Mirza, had begun making good progress in collecting information about Singh and Srivastava. Kapoor had not been able to speak with them the last few days—the last report he had received was about Mirza's conversation with a boatman and Harish's success in talking to a couple of people at the Lete Hanumanji ka Mandir who recognised Srivastava.

And that had been a week ago.

In the midst of all his planning, he had received a sudden summons from the commissioner's office.

Kapoor always hated it when Vidyarthi did this. It meant that his boss was about to spring a surprise on him.

Just over two months ago, Vidyarthi had assigned the Diya Chaudhry murder case to him, while temporarily taking him off the Trivedi case. He wondered what lay in store for him today.

Well, he wouldn't have to wait too long. The commissioner's aide was indicating that Vidyarthi would see him now.

Kapoor knocked on the door.

'Come in, Kapoor!' Vidyarthi's voice boomed from inside.

As Kapoor entered, Vidyarthi beamed at him and gestured for him to sit down.

Kapoor took a chair and waited for the bombshell.

'Well, Kapoor? There's been total silence from you on the Diya Chaudhry murder case. Didn't your visits to Allahabad help you crack it?'

Kapoor knew he was being baited. He steadfastly refused to take the bait.

'We're getting leads, sir,' he replied, 'My men are following them up in Allahabad. We're getting there.'

'Getting there? In all the years I've known you, Kapoor, you've always got there. And no doubt you will in this case as well.'

Kapoor groaned inwardly. This was, he knew, where the 'but' was going to come in. He waited for it.

'But,' Vidyarthi continued, as Kapoor had predicted, 'it has been more than two months and no resolution in sight, eh?'

'No, sir. But I think it's just a matter of time now.'

'It always is, my man, it always is!' Vidyarthi's tone was too jovial for Kapoor's comfort.

The commissioner leaned forward conspiratorially. 'Look Kapoor, I know that, given time, you'll crack this one too. But, quite frankly, two months is just too long for a petty case like this. There are bigger fish to fry, more important cases that I need you on, here in Delhi. I can't have you disappearing to Allahabad ever so often, even if it's only for a day or two each time.'

Kapoor was silent. This did not bode well. Just when he felt his investigation was taking shape, too. He tried to contain his frustration.

'I'm pulling you off the case for now, Kapoor. There's an urgent new case that has come up. Involves national security. We've had a request from the Intelligence Bureau for one of our best men to work with them.' He beamed at Kapoor. 'Naturally, I thought of you.'

'But the media, sir? I thought the heat was on you to solve this case?'

'Ah, but we haven't solved it, have we? And it has been over two months since that poor girl's body was found.' Vidyarthi leaned back in his chair. 'In any case, the media has moved on. They have a very short memory. Just like the general public. Something happens, they flap around like mad, try to outshout each other on television, then something new comes along and they forget all about what they had been flapping about just minutes earlier.'

Kapoor gnashed his teeth. He knew Vidyarthi was right. Two months was just too long given the short attention span of the media and its audiences. Diya Chaudhry was a distant memory by now, if not totally forgotten, unless something dramatically new came up to merit attention all over again.

Something told Kapoor that he would get his big moment when he was able to piece together all the bits of the puzzle that lay scattered around him for now. But he needed time.

'What about the LG?' he asked, hoping against hope he could change Vidyarthi's mind. 'Isn't he putting pressure on you?'

'Not any longer,' Vidyarthi shot back. 'You see, the politicians have got involved. It's out of our hands now. The Delhi government and the Centre are trading accusations and counter accusations over the case. It is a political matter and we can't afford to sit back and wait while they figure out what needs to be done. We have a job to do and we're going to keep at it.'

Kapoor sighed. He knew when he was licked.

'You have a couple of men in Allahabad, don't you?'

'Yes, sir.'

'Well, recall them, then. Put a hold on the case. File it as unsolved if you want. Like the Trivedi murder case.'

'I didn't file that as unsolved, sir.'

'You didn't?' Vidyarthi looked puzzled.

'No, sir. The two cases are inextricably linked. We have uncovered tangible evidence of that in Allahabad. We solve one case, we solve both.'

'You still think you can solve those cases?'

'Yes, sir. I do. Given time.'

Vidyarthi nodded. 'Very well, then. I'm not going to be the one to put a blemish on your spotless record. Finish the job I'm giving you now and, if you aren't needed elsewhere by then, you can wrap those up too.'

'Thank you, sir. I appreciate that.' Kapoor was genuinely grateful. He didn't want these two cases to go down as the only ones he had been unable to crack. Especially not now, when he was so close to cracking them.

'No problem. Just make sure that no one is wasting any more time on them. I don't want anyone in Allahabad. Am I clear?'

'Yes, sir.' Kapoor realised that Vidyarthi knew him only too well. If his boss had not been so specific, Kapoor would have left either Ajit or Harish in Allahabad to continue the investigation.

But it didn't matter. As Vidyarthi had said, the two cases were not time critical. Nothing was likely to happen in the intervening months even if he didn't investigate further. He would pick up the threads later.

When he was done with the new assignment.

Whatever that was.

Chapter Eighty-two

New Information

Raman Kapoor's Office
New Delhi

Kapoor was taking the final debrief from Ajit and Harish, who had returned from Allahabad the previous day.

In the nine days since the last debrief, the team in Allahabad had covered quite a lot of ground.

After getting a positive identification at the temple, Harish had scouted around and managed to find someone who had known Kanakpratap Singh when he was a student at Allahabad University. According to the source, after attending classes, Singh would often cross the road to the Company Bagh, the gardens where the young revolutionary Chandrashekhar Azad was famously martyred. Apparently, in the days when Singh was in college, the freedom fighter was an icon for the pehelwans of Allahabad, who used to gather there. Singh had often been seen in the area, sitting beside the statue of Chandrashekhar Azad and discussing politics.

Ajit had also made inroads into finding out more about Srivastava. He had, on Mirza's advice, made the rounds of the Coffee House in Civil Lines. Interviews with the waiters, some of whom had been working there for decades, had also yielded results.

Apparently, many of the people who patronised the coffee house were vociferous and had strong political leanings. Among them, Srivastava had stood out for two things. First, his quiet, unassuming nature, quite unlike that of the other patrons. Second, he was a calming and sensible influence, intervening in the heated debates and injecting a healthy dose of logic and rationalism into fiery arguments which were often punctuated by emotional outbursts.

According to the waiters, some of whom were retired, Srivastava had been respected for his knowledge and demeanour. People listened to him.

The waiters, at any rate, remembered him. Like the boatman, he was known to have been a warm human being, kind to everyone he met and respectful to the waiters as well; something they did not often see in the patrons of the coffee house.

There was not much of an update on Vishwaraj, though. The team in Allahabad had failed to find his parents. Apparently, they had suddenly disappeared over two months ago. Ajit, Harish and Mirza had been able to find only a few people who claimed to have known Vishwaraj, and even they had little information to offer about the boy.

Apparently, he had been a loner in school and made few friends. The police team had met no one who claimed to be a good friend of his. Enquiries had revealed that the boy had been adopted by a childless couple when he was a child of three or four years. But there was little more to be discovered about the enigmatic Vishwaraj.

But the biggest discovery had been made by Mirza, who had chanced on someone who had told him of the tragedy that both Singh and Srivastava had been involved in almost fifteen years ago.

'The person we spoke to knew both Singh and Srivastava,' Ajit explained to Kapoor. 'He wasn't a very good friend, so he didn't have a lot of details. But he did tell us that the two families—the Singhs and the Srivastavas—were very close. Singh had an elder brother, Rudrapratap Singh, who was married to a woman called Yajnaseni. Singh was unmarried and had no children. Rudrapratap had a son called Arjun.'

'Isn't that the name of Singh's nephew?' Kapoor asked immediately. 'That's the name we got from the school, when we checked with them after Singh left town, isn't it?'

'Yes, sir,' Harish confirmed. 'I had gone to the school to check. I remember the name.'

'So,' Kapoor said thoughtfully, 'Singh's sister Pramila is not his sister but his sister-in-law. She too changed her name after coming to Delhi.' His razor-sharp mind was quick to connect the dots.

Harish nodded. 'Seems that way, sir.'

'Anyway.' Kapoor gestured to Ajit. 'Go on. What happened?'

'Well, sir, Srivastava had a wife and two children. A son and a daughter. Both were little, less than a year old.'

'So the boatman knew what he was talking about,' Kapoor murmured.

'Yes, sir,' Ajit resumed. 'And, according to this source, Srivastava and his wife did not divorce or separate. And he did not abandon his son. They were both murdered.'

'What?' Kapoor straightened up and leaned forward, his eyes shining. This was the big break he had been searching for—a piece of information that could be at the heart of this whole mystery. He had known there was a deep, dark secret that was waiting to be revealed.

'Not just that, sir,' Ajit continued, 'but Singh's elder brother Rudrapratap was also murdered around the same time. Unfortunately, this is all the source could tell me. Since he was not close to either family, he didn't know much more.'

'But both families lost someone,' Kapoor said thoughtfully. 'And it was murder in all three cases. This is no small coincidence.' He looked at Ajit and Harish in turn. 'What about the suspect? The guy with the eyepatch. Any leads?'

The two men shook their heads.

'No, sir,' Harish replied. 'The people we met didn't seem to have seen him. They were probably not contacted by him.'

'I think we need to talk to more people. Those who were close to the family,' Ajit said. 'Only they can fill us in on the details of what exactly happened.'

'Well,' Kapoor's exasperation was evident in his tone, 'we can't do that. At least, not just yet.' He clenched his fists with the frustration of a man who knows he has something within his grasp but has to turn away from it. 'Allahabad isn't going anywhere. It can wait. We'll get back to the case as soon as my new assignment is over.'

He looked at the two men. 'And then we will solve the mystery behind all three murders.'

Kapoor's phone rang.

'DCP Kapoor?' There was an authoritative ring to the voice on the line.

'Yes, sir.' Kapoor motioned to Ajit and Harish to leave the room and shut the door behind them.

'This is Imran Kidwai from the Intelligence Bureau.'

Chapter Eighty-three

A Walk in the Twilight

The Gurukul
Panna National Park

Arjun and Maya strolled together in the gentle twilight, among the trees of the Panna forest, beyond the cottages where the Mahamatis resided.

There was a slight nip in the air. The forest would grow increasingly cold as the dusk faded into night. Winter was on its last legs, but it was still making a stand.

More than a month had passed since Varun, Adira and Tanveer had left the Gurukul. The four remaining Saptas had become closer than before. Well, at least three of them— Agastya still stayed a bit aloof, though he was much warmer towards, and more accepting of Maya than he had been earlier. Maya guessed the fact that she was being coached by Maharishi Satyavachana had something to do with it; she knew Agastya would have given an arm and a leg to be in her place.

But Arjun, Maya and Amyra hung out together when they were not busy with their lessons, practice or homework. It wasn't often that all three of them were free at the same time, but evening walks like this one had become quite commonplace. Sometimes all three were able to make it, and at other times the two who were free would pair up.

Maya was happy to get more time with her childhood friend. Having been virtually inseparable from Arjun since they were toddlers, she had missed spending time with him and had disliked the fact that they only got to meet briefly at dinner, and that too not every day, in the first two months of their stay at the Gurukul.

For Arjun, it was a great way to keep his mind off his mother's absence. Not one day went by when he didn't miss her. He remembered the days in school when he would chafe at her constant presence—and his uncle's—wherever he went, even for his classmates' birthday parties. He had fervently wished them away, wished to be free of their constant attention. Now, he couldn't understand why.

You really don't know what you have until you no longer have it, he thought grimly.

His intense practice sessions with Agastya, Kanakpratap and Usha, with Parth joining in quite frequently, kept his mind distracted. And though he missed Varun and Tanveer, these moments spent with his friends also helped drive away the deep loneliness he felt with his mother away.

Around them, birds chirped hysterically as they settled down for the night. The call of monkeys echoed across the sparsely wooded forest and the occasional deer ambled through the undergrowth, presumably on its way back to the herd after a satisfactory session of grazing.

'I wonder what those three are up to,' Arjun speculated about his missing friends, as he watched a squirrel scurry across a branch, stopping now and then to dart its eyes around nervously and sniff the air. 'It must be strange to be back in school after spending so much time at the Gurukul.' He turned up his nose. 'Studies, cycle tests and all that sort of thing.'

'Sumitra!' Maya laughed.

Arjun joined in. They had almost forgotten about their old history teacher. Even though they had been at the Gurukul for almost four months, so much had happened during their stay here that it seemed much longer.

'It is a different life,' Maya agreed. 'It must be difficult to pretend to be ordinary and also ensure that the other students in the school don't get to know who they really are.'

Arjun nodded. 'Yeah. Well, you and I are going to face the same situation someday.'

'AJ, what are they keeping you and Ags back for? I don't get it. Wouldn't you be more useful out there? You're already one of the best warriors they have!'

Arjun shrugged. 'Beats me. I'm raring to go. I want to be out there, part of the Gana, outside the Gurukul. The purpose for which they brought me here has been served. In the last four months I have learned more than I learned in the last seven years. My technique, my speed, my skills have all improved exponentially, even without the use of mantras. And, *with* the use of mantras, the last seven years feel … I don't know … amateurish? You know what I mean?'

Maya nodded. She knew exactly what he meant.

They walked along in silence, enjoying each other's company and the soothing tranquillity of nature around them.

'Hey, AJ,' Maya said after a while. 'Can I ask you something?'

Arjun glanced at her curiously. 'What's up with you? You've never asked me for permission before.'

Maya didn't know how to tell him that he had grown so much faster than she had at the Gurukul that there were times, however rare, when she hesitated to ask him stuff outright. Especially when it was something personal.

'Well,' she smiled, 'I was wondering if you miss Adira.'

Arjun flushed, caught off guard by the question. 'What do you mean?' he demanded, recovering his composure a bit.

'I mean,' Maya chuckled at his reaction, now more at ease with the subject, 'that I think you have a crush on her. I've been watching you two.'

Arjun laughed sheepishly. 'Nothing escapes the eagle eye of Maya.' He looked at her. 'Okay, you got me. Can't hide it from you. I guess … I do have a crush on her. How did you know?'

'Well, for starters, considering you are the scion of Yayati and the One, and all of that, you act pretty silly and weak-kneed around her,' Maya said, arching an eyebrow. 'So, it's pretty obvious.'

'Do you think Varun knows?' Arjun enquired. 'And Tanveer and Ags?'

'Of course, silly,' Maya laughed. 'They all have eyes, you know!'

'Damn!'

'But don't worry your head about it,' Maya reassured him. 'Adira likes you too.'

Arjun looked at her in surprise. 'Really? How do you know?' He checked himself. 'Of course.' He grinned and executed a mock bow, his arms outstretched. 'The all-seeing one has observed Adira as well.'

Maya slapped him lightly on the back in feigned indignation. 'Of course,' she said. 'It's pretty obvious with her as well. I was her dorm-mate, remember? But I think she's had a crush on you for a long time, maybe ever since we arrived at the Gurukul.'

'Really?' There was scepticism in Arjun's voice. Suddenly he slapped his forehead as he remembered something. 'Ohh … now I get it.'

Maya looked at him enquiringly.

'What happened in the dorm—Adira's dorm—on the night we went to the Gandharva valley,' Arjun told her. 'Don't you remember? Oh, wait, you weren't there. You were waiting for us at the Gurukul entrance. At the rock.'

Maya remembered that night well. She had told Arjun about her plan to visit the Gandharva valley and he had insisted on accompanying her. They had arranged to rendezvous at the entrance to the Gurukul. To her surprise, however, Arjun had turned up with Varun, Adira, Tanveer and Agastya in tow, and, after some discussion, they had ventured forth together.

'Varun was telling me how Adira had insisted on coming along. I had no idea why, and I still recall he was about to say something when Adira shut him up. I think he knew even back then.' Arjun held his head in his hands as they walked. 'Oh gosh. I don't believe it. I've been so stupid! I missed so many clues.'

'Yes,' Maya replied drily. 'It is amazing that it was so obvious to everyone else except the two of you. I don't think Adira knows how you feel about her.'

'What about you?' Arjun changed the subject. 'Who do you like?'

Maya made a face. 'No one,' she said. 'I haven't found anyone in school in Delhi or here at the Gurukul who is worth having a crush on.'

'Come on,' Arjun pressed. 'Surely you don't still have a crush on David Tennant?'

'Ooh! His hair …' Maya sighed. 'But no, I'm over David Tennant. Though I still love *Doctor Who*.'

'Yeah, great series,' Arjun admitted. 'But I never figured out what you saw in Tennant. Or his hair.' He looked at her mischievously. 'Do you remember the time you squealed in delight when we were watching *Harry Potter and the Goblet of Fire* and David Tennant appeared?'

'Yeah, I remember,' Maya said sheepishly. 'It was so embarrassing. Everyone in our row and in front of us turned to look at me. But I'm over that now.'

'There must be someone here who has caught your fancy?' Arjun persisted.

Maya shook her head. 'I would tell you if there was, AJ. You know that. Maybe I'm growing up.'

'Hey!' Arjun protested as the implication of her remark sank in. 'What d'you mean? I'm growing up too!'

Maya laughed and he put his arm around her, both of them forgetting their cares and worries for the moment.

Chapter Eighty-four

Amyra

The Gurukul

The weather had begun to turn. It was more temperate and pleasant as winter gave way to spring. Amyra and Maya walked together along the bank of trees that lined the river Ken, providing shade and a barrier that, along with a mantra for illusion, hid the Gurukul from prying eyes.

'I've always wanted to ask you this,' Amyra said suddenly. 'I've been ever so curious. Why do you call Arjun "AJ"?'

Maya laughed. 'Yes, it is odd, isn't it?' She was silent for a few moments, her eyes misting over with the memory. 'It was Dad,' she said finally. 'It was his idea. Arjun and I became friends before we knew what it even meant; we were less than a year old, I think. When we first began to speak, Arjun was able to say "Maya" quite easily, but I would struggle to pronounce his name. The "r", the "j" and the "un" made it too complicated for me. And I'd sulk because he could say my name and I couldn't pronounce his. At least, that's what Dad told me.'

Amyra laughed.

'Yes, it's funny now, but I believe I was most upset about it,' Maya said. 'Then Dad asked me if I could pronounce "AJ". I proudly did. And the name stuck. I've called him that ever since.'

Both girls laughed again. 'I knew there had to be a story,' Amyra said. 'But I never knew how to ask.'

She felt a lot closer to Maya than she had before. It was like there was some invisible bond that had grown stronger over time.

Three months had passed since the departure of the six new members of the Gana. Amyra was no longer a novice. She had graduated to being a full-fledged member of the Gurukul. Psychics were rare, especially those with her special ability, and she was now being tutored in the development of her psychic powers to expand the boundaries of what she could accomplish.

'How are you progressing, Maya?' Amyra asked.

'I don't know,' Maya replied. 'It's hard to tell. Since December, Maharishi Satyavachana has been focused only on thought control. He has been putting me through exercises, practice sessions and tests to build my ability to control my thoughts. He says it will be useful in any situation I find myself in. I can think of only one where it will help; when I am travelling as an atma. That's when I need to be able to control my thoughts, both for controlling my ability to travel as well as ensuring that no one can hear my thoughts. I think I've been getting better, based on the tests, but until he allows me to practice some mantras and actually apply thought control, I won't know if it's really working. He keeps telling me I'm getting the hang of it, but he's such a sweet person, he would say that just to keep me from getting discouraged.'

Maya sighed. 'How are your lessons going?'

Amyra shook her head. 'Not great. I'm terrible at learning stuff. I only got by at school because of my psychic abilities. Actually, that's how I discovered I was psychic.'

'What do you mean?' Maya asked. She had assumed that Amyra had always known about her abilities.

Amyra smiled. 'Well,' she replied, 'one day, a few years back, quite by accident, I slipped into a self-induced hypnotic trance kind of state, while reading my textbooks. Weirdly enough, I discovered that, in that state, I was able to absorb a lot of stuff without too much effort. And when I did come out of the trance, I was able to remember everything.'

'Amazing,' Maya breathed. 'You must have topped the class.'

'I did,' Amyra admitted, looking embarrassed. 'And then I realised that I could control the trance and bring about that state whenever I wanted to. I used it a lot to study. It was during one of those times that I discovered I could see the past. I was studying in the library when one of my friends came up to me to say something and, during our conversation, I was able to see exactly what she had been doing before she met me. She was freaked out when I told her.'

'You mean you were conscious of your surroundings while in the trance?'

'Yes. You see, going into a trance is nothing like what you see on television or the movies or how fake psychics pretend to do it. It was like … an altered state of mind, an altered state of consciousness in which I was fully conscious and able to move and talk normally, but my mind was somehow … different … if you know what I mean.'

Maya shook her head. 'Actually, I don't understand. Never had such an experience myself, so I guess I never will understand. But it sounds pretty cool.'

'Yeah.' Amyra shrugged. 'Except I can't do it here because there really isn't anything to be learned from textbooks and stuff. I need to understand new stuff, techniques and all that kind of thing.' She sighed. 'And I'm not very good at that.'

'You'll pick it up,' Maya reassured her. 'Look at me. I'm a sadh. I'm not even someone like you, with some kind of power. All I have are my genes from my dad. But I'm working hard to ensure that I don't have to leave the Gurukul. If you put your head down and focus on what you need to do, you'll pick it up, don't you worry!'

'I guess.' Amyra smiled at her. 'But you're so wrong about yourself, Maya.'

'In what way?' Maya said, as they walked on.

'I mean, maybe you are a sadh. I don't know. I have no way of figuring out who is or isn't a sadh,' Amyra explained. 'But there is something about you that is …' She paused, struggling to find the right word, 'different, I guess? You're different. No, the word is "special". That's it. You're special.'

Maya laughed warmly. 'That's so sweet of you, Amyra. That's what I love about you, you're so nice to everyone.'

Amyra shook her head. 'No, Maya, I mean it. I'm serious. You really *are* special. I can sense it. I knew it from the day I first met you. Don't ask me how, maybe it's part of being psychic.' She paused. 'To be honest, that's why I wanted to be your friend. Because I knew you were special. But don't hold that against me, please! I agree it was childish. I really like you for who you are now. And I'm being open with you.'

Maya stopped and turned to face Amyra. She held her arms gently and looked at her. 'Never, Amyra. You are a very dear friend. It doesn't matter why you first approached me for friendship. What matters is that you were one of the very few people who wanted to be my friend. And you have stayed with me right through, protected me when I travelled to Dwarka to seek Garuda's help and encouraged me at every step. That's what true friends do. You've been there for me and that's what matters.'

She embraced Amyra. 'Come on, it's getting late,' she said. 'Let's go for dinner. Arjun and Ags must be waiting for us.'

Chapter Eighty-five

The Test

The Forest
Unknown Location

It was somewhat cooler in the shade of the trees, but only somewhat. Above them, the sun beat down mercilessly on the treetops, blazing with an unbearable intensity. Summer had the land well and truly in its grip.

Maya kept wiping the sweat from her brow as she followed Satyavachana's instructions. The Maharishi, on the other hand, was cool and composed, with not a drop of perspiration to be seen on his face.

Satyavachana had explained to Maya that his siddhis enabled him to weather the most extreme temperatures. 'A powerful yogi can brave the extreme cold and sweltering heat,' he had told her. 'When you are able to tap into your powers, you will be able to do the same. Until then, I'm afraid you will have to endure the heat and suffer like all sadhs do.'

Maya had nodded. But, as she stood now in the oppressive heat, she didn't understand how she was supposed to focus and concentrate.

'You can do it,' Satyavachana said, as if divining her thoughts. 'You have spent more than seven months practising and training since I first started teaching you. You have worked hard and you have done well. Now, remember that you need to tap into the inner power that you have been building up over all these months. Don't allow your external environment to distract you. Stay focused.'

Maya mopped her brow once again. 'Yes, Mahamati,' she said. 'I will try.'

'Don't try, Maya. *Do* it.'

Maya nodded.

The Maharishi disappeared and Maya began walking alone through the forest.

As she walked, she fought to keep at bay thoughts of the heat and the sultriness, the perspiration, the stickiness of her clothes. To her surprise, though it took some effort, it didn't take her too long to find her centre, a pool of tranquillity filled with a calmness that pulsed with energy. Satyavachana had been teaching her to create and find this calm centre since he had started working with her on thought control, the day before her fifteenth birthday. How time had flown. Seven months had already passed since the attack of the Nagas on the Gurukul in Panna.

Maya immersed herself in the pool of tranquillity, allowing it to overwhelm her mind completely. She lost herself in the energy that pulsed through it, revelling in the amazing sensation flowing through every fibre of her body, every nerve, every cell, until she was completely focused.

It was only when she had begun attaining this state of mind, with considerable effort at first, that she had understood what

Amyra had told her three months ago, about the trance that helped her to focus on her studies while remaining conscious of her surroundings.

For Maya was now keenly aware of the rustling in the bushes around her; a sound that grew in intensity as she walked. It started on her right in the undergrowth beyond the trees that lined the narrow path along which she strode, then spread to the bushes on her left, and ahead and behind her, until it was coming from all directions.

Above her head, the leaves whispered and the branches groaned with the weight of something that was as yet invisible, keeping pace with her and surrounding her from all sides.

Maya immersed herself deeper into the pool of energy and allowed her mind to soak it in. She focused her thoughts, emptying herself of all emotions until her mind was blank. She could still hear the sounds around her; in fact, her hearing was keener now, but she was not reacting to the sounds.

Deep within her, a single note resonated.

It was the sound of the universe.

She allowed her mind to drift, floating on the resonance, feeling her being vibrate in sync with the note.

She was one with the universe.

Her walk slowed. There was no longer any haste in her stride, no hurry to get anywhere.

Maya didn't *need* to get anywhere.

She was where she should be.

Abruptly, without warning, the creatures began to appear.

They emerged from the bushes on either side, rushing onto the path directly ahead of her, dropping from the trees around her.

Maya stopped and looked around.

She was surrounded.

Chapter Eighty-six

Attack

The Forest

Maya stood still. She could sense rather than see the creatures that surrounded her.

They were of all kinds.

Pisachas of different varieties—some winged, some horned, some thin, others deformed—mingled with other creatures from the bhutagana. Pretas hovered in the air along with fearsome looking creatures with bloodshot eyes, whom she identified as Panis—the cattle-stealing creatures mentioned in the Rigveda.

And that was not all. There were invisible creatures circling above her and around her. *Bhutas.* The spirits of the dead who were yet to be given another body for rebirth.

They set up a din, with howls and roars and grunts, creating a cacophony that seemed to silence every other inhabitant of the forest.

Maya stood still, but for once, it was not out of fear. She was not rooted to the ground as she had been on earlier occasions when Satyavachana had tested her.

Something had changed.

A thought briefly crossed her mind.

She did not know the mantras to destroy these creatures.

She swiftly pushed that thought away and it disappeared into oblivion.

Another thought crossed her mind, this time with a tinge of panic.

There seemed to be hundreds of these creatures, some of whom were visible on the path. More lurked in the forest beyond the path. She could not see them, but she could sense them.

How would she defend herself against so many?

There was the briefest disruption of her focus as this thought flitted through her mind. Then she dismissed it and sought the vibration of the universe again.

But the damage had been done.

The multitude of creatures, sensing her loss of focus, charged at her.

To Maya's surprise, she reconnected with the vibration almost instantly. Then she attempted to do something she had never done before.

She began chanting the *Narsimha* mantra. She knew from experience that the mantra would keep the creatures at bay, even if it didn't destroy them. She felt its power course through her body, amplifying in strength as it touched the resonance of the strange note that had sounded within her from out of nowhere.

The creatures stopped in their tracks, as if they had come up against an invisible barrier.

Maya continued reciting the mantra, but deep in her mind, she was now reaching out to them.

Become one with them. They are part of your universe. They are a part of you.

She closed her eyes and, without stopping the recitation of the mantra, reached out to each of the forms that she could sense.

To her great surprise, even though her eyes were closed and there was a physical distance separating her from the creatures, she could *feel* them.

Maya reached out, further afield, searching out the creatures, feeling them, trying to be one with them.

Then something strange happened.

Something strange and horrifying.

Chapter Eighty-seven

Something Strange

The Forest

As she connected with the creatures, trying to become one with them, she began to absorb and experience strange new feelings.

Pain, sorrow, guilt, grief, regret, remorse, contrition, repentance, shame, misery, anguish, distress and despair filled her mind, spreading like darkness.

Maya started shivering with the burden of the emotions that were flooding her mind. Her eyes were tightly shut, and yet tears began streaming down her face.

But she was oblivious to it all.

The only thing she was capable of sensing was the torrent of emotions.

Then, suddenly, it was gone.

The darkness that had enveloped her mind vanished.

Silence reigned around her.

Maya sensed another presence. But she could not make out what or who it was.

She opened her eyes. Tears continued to stream down her face and she was shaking like a leaf.

Satyavachana stood there with a worried expression, clasping his brahmadanda. Seeing her open her eyes, he seemed to relax and a smile lit up his face.

'I thought I had lost you there, my child!' he exclaimed. 'How do you feel now?'

Maya ran a hand across her forehead. She was drenched in perspiration and her clothes were sticking to her. Gradually, the shivering subsided and the flow of tears dried up.

'I ... I think I'm fine,' she said. 'But what happened? I could feel so many dark emotions, so much despair; what happened to me?'

'Come,' Satyavachana said, 'let us walk together.' They began walking down the path and Maya looked through the trees on either side. Nothing was visible. The creatures had all disappeared.

She realised that Satyavachana had put her through a rigorous test this time. One pisacha had not been enough today.

'I was observing you,' Satyavachana told her, 'though you could not see or sense me.'

'How did I do?' Maya was now more concerned about her performance than the explanation for what she had experienced.

'You did well, child. And you are stronger than I thought. But something strange happened. Something that shouldn't have.'

Maya waited for the explanation.

'You did well. Too well, actually,' Satyavachana resumed. 'All the dark feelings you experienced came from the creatures whose souls you touched. You didn't just feel one with them; you *became* one with them. You touched the depths of their souls, attracting and absorbing all their suffering. No doubt you gave them some relief, but it was dangerous. You could have been overwhelmed by all that guilt, remorse and despair. It is their burden to bear; the price they must pay for the karma of their previous births. It is not possible to take on the burden of so many creatures and survive. That is why I was worried for you.'

'I ... I don't understand. Why should it not have happened?' Maya wanted to know. 'You told me that I had to be one with them.'

'No, child. I told you to move closer to oneness with them. I asked you to feel compassion for them. Empathise with them. Not become one with them. That should never have happened. You should never have been able to become one with them, to feel their suffering the way you did. If I'd had even an inkling that it was possible, I would never have put you through the test.'

Satyavachana smiled at Maya's confused face. 'But you did pass the test with flying colours. You didn't even know the mantras to destroy the creatures of the bhutagana, but you didn't let that stop you. It was a masterstroke to recite the *Narsimha* mantra. And you recited it beautifully. There was no way any of those monsters could have harmed even a hair on your head the way you invoked the power of Narsimha. And, at the same time, you were able to reach out to them. Marvellous!'

'So I'm ready to learn some new mantras?' Maya asked anxiously.

'Not yet, my child. First, I need to teach you a few more things that will help you prevent this situation from ever recurring. You need to be able to protect yourself, control the flow of emotions from any creatures you face, if you happen to cross the barrier and touch their spirits. Otherwise, you may get overwhelmed, and we can't have that happening, can we?' He smiled at her again.

'Can we start today?' Maya felt ecstatic.

Satyavachana shook his head. 'You have been through a lot today. The techniques I have to teach you are strenuous. We will start tomorrow, when you are fresh and have recovered. Go now, back to the Gurukul. I will meet you tonight.'

Maya folded her hands and bowed. '*Pranaam*, Mahamati.' She disappeared.

Satyavachana stood for a while, lost in thought. Now that Maya was gone, the worried frown returned to his face. What happened with her today was totally unexpected. He had not been prepared for it. He was surprised that it could have happened at all, especially to Maya.

But of even greater concern was the implication for her if she entered the Mists. If she absorbed the energy of the Mists or from anything she came across in the Mists …

The success of his entire plan depended on Maya weathering the Mists and succeeding in the mission that he had planned for her.

He shook his head. There wasn't much he could do except teach her greater control over her defences. It would not take long. Maybe another month. Or two.

He wasn't sure if it was going to be enough.

But it would have to be.

Chapter Eighty-eight

Shukra Wonders

Mayurbhanj
Odisha

Shukra made his way determinedly through the dense forest cover. This was one place where he could not use his yogic powers to instantly transport himself to his destination.

For he had no idea where his destination lay.

It was rough going, but it didn't matter. He was made of sterner stuff than the weakling humans of Kaliyuga. And he had his yogic powers. The stifling heat and oppressive sultriness of the forest, the buzzing of flies and other insects, mattered little to him as he stalked through the undergrowth, between the trees, following no path, for none existed here. Not that that posed an obstacle, for he could manipulate matter using his thoughts—an outcome of his strength in the siddhis—so trees parted and bushes made way for him as he steamrolled his way through the dense forest.

What did matter to him were the changes that had occurred in Bhu-lok during the 5,000 years he had been away, immersed in meditation, and the complications caused by the events that had transpired in these 5,000 years.

When his meditation had been interrupted upon the birth of the child—the One of the prophecy—he had set about finding the means to make his mission successful. He had known that part of what he sought was in Deva-lok and part in one of the levels of Pataala-lok, but he had no idea in which level it was.

Consequently, his first priority had been to try and work out where he should search.

And he had started with Deva-lok. After all, that was also where one part of the prophecy was hidden, according to legend. That much he had got to know before he had disappeared on his self-imposed exile and tapasya.

His enhanced powers had aided him in gaining access and ensuring that the Devas had no inkling that he was travelling to and from their world. It had come as a bit of a surprise to him to learn that the Devas had blocked all access to their world to humans, save for the exceptional yogi who had the ability to pass unscathed through the barriers they had erected around the portal that led to Deva-lok. But then he had learned the reason why the Devas had acted so strongly against the humans.

It had taken time to obtain this information, but it told him why he had failed in his efforts to find what he sought in the world of the Devas.

His multiple visits to Deva-lok had not been futile, though. He had found the means to locate the gates to the five levels of Pataala-lok. That was something.

So, Shukra had returned to Bhu-lok and begun his search anew. He had lost fourteen years in the bargain, but it didn't matter at the time. He had thought he had plenty of time to find what he needed to execute his plan.

Now, things were different. The power of Kali was peaking. The events taking place in Bhu-lok were evidence of this. The sadhs were turning on each other, erecting imaginary barriers to separate groups based on tenuous notions of kinship. They were destroying their own progeny, in a matter of speaking, through illusory incentives that led to suicides and depression. Just as it had been foretold.

It was just a matter of time. It would not be more than a few years before the time was ripe for him to put the final part of his plan into motion. That was all the time he had.

And he was still searching.

For the location of the secrets he sought had been hidden away almost 4,000 years ago by a leader of the Sangha, a Maharishi called Tribhuvan. In order to succeed in his quest, Shukra had to first find the manuscripts that described the locations where the secrets were hidden.

And then he would have to find those locations to unearth the mantras and other resources he needed for his plan to be successful.

That was the other complication.

Bhu-lok had changed beyond recognition in the last 5,000 years. Bharatvarsha was no longer the land it used to be, in almost every way.

Today, he was pushing through this dense forest, climbing mountains whose slopes were covered with closely packed trees and dense undergrowth, making it all but impossible for anyone without his powers to reach the site that he had been directed to.

He was searching for a temple, an ancient ruin that was thousands of years old. No one knew how old it really was. He had seen a glimpse of the temple when he read Maharishi Dhruv's mind. And he had been hunting for it for five months now, ever since he had left Allahabad. Something told him it was crucial to his search for the mantras.

Yesterday, he had chanced upon someone who told him about an ancient temple that was rumoured to be in these parts. He had been pointed to some archives and temple inscriptions that described it.

Shukra had studied the inscriptions and the manuscripts in the archives. The description of the temple matched what he had seen in Dhruv's mind. Finally, he thought, he was getting somewhere.

He had set out for the forest immediately and had spent the day hiking through it. But he still had no idea how far he had to go.

Suddenly, he stopped and stood still.

He had felt something.

A great rage rose within him.

Someone was meddling with the bhutagana. He could sense it. Lord Shiva had, at Shukra's request during his meditation, given him complete command of the bhutagana; their services would be at his disposal, to aid him in his search. The only time Shukra had relinquished that control was when he had temporarily given the command of the bhutagana to Vishwaraj in Bhimbetka.

Now, someone had breached the barrier. He didn't know how, but someone had gained control over a small segment of the spirits and creatures that made up the bhutagana.

Shukra stood, his eyes closed, trying to sense who or what was toying with his forces.

It was a yogi, in another forest, not far from here.

Who could it be?

Shukra couldn't make out the identity of the yogi. Nor could he tell what purpose was being served by this unnecessary trifling with the creatures under his command.

He continued to concentrate, trying to reach out, to understand, but it seemed that the yogi had put up a protective barrier that even he could not penetrate.

Shukra was perplexed.

Then, suddenly, the creatures that had been commandeered by the yogi were returned to the bhutagana.

It had lasted just a few moments. A temporary breach.

But a breach nevertheless.

Still wondering who the yogi might be, Shukra pressed ahead.

He had to find the temple. Everything else would have to wait.

Chapter Eighty-nine

Second Test

The Forest
Unknown Location

Maya stood, gazing at the immense cleft that had opened up before her. It hovered in mid-air, stretching from a foot above the ground to three feet above her head.

It was a portal.

But a portal to what? To where? Maya had no clue.

How had it even come to be there?

One moment, she was walking along the narrow forest track, alert to rustles in the undergrowth and whispers among the leaves that would indicate the presence of monsters, like those she had battled in her last test three months ago. The next moment, a yawning gap in the forest had opened up, swallowing up the trees and everything else that had stood there just a moment before.

She realised that this was her test. She had to pass through the portal.

What would happen next?

She reached into her core of calmness, feeling the pulse of the subtle energy that swirled around there. She immersed herself in its glow. This time she had used the new mantras that Satyavachana had taught her, to fortify her inner pool of tranquillity and protect it from external influences.

Taking a deep breath, Maya stepped through the portal, unafraid.

A deep blackness enveloped her. She could see nothing, not even her hand when she held it in front of her face.

Maya had never seen such utter, black, darkness before.

She quickly pushed herself deeper into the pool of energy within and heard the note again. It was the same note as last time. She recognised its timbre, its frequency.

The sound of the universe.

Maya allowed herself to synchronise with the note, her entire being resonating at the same frequency as that of the universe.

She moved ahead in the darkness, trusting her senses and her oneness with the universe to protect her from harm.

What was this place? Where was she?

There was complete and total silence all around her.

Slowly, confidently, she made her way forward.

The darkness seemed to part before her as she advanced, but immediately coalesced around and behind her as she passed through.

Then, without warning, it hit her.

Chapter Ninety

Inside the Portal

Inside the Portal

It came at her in waves, one after the other, each subsequent wave crashing against her mind even before the earlier one could subside.

Maya couldn't fathom what it was. It felt alive—was it one or many? But there was no shape, substance or form to it—or them. But whatever it was, and however many, she could feel them, sense them, as clearly as if they were material, substantial, physical.

Thoughts, a profusion of them, swarmed into her mind, all at once, as if trying to burrow into her very being and consume her. There were positive thoughts and negative thoughts, happy emotions and depressing emotions, all battering her consciousness ceaselessly.

Even without thinking, Maya recited the mantras to fortify her inner calmness, her centre, reinforcing the barriers. She had to keep these thoughts out. There were too many of them and of too many shades, for her to allow them through. If they did slip through, they would devour her inner energy and she would succumb to their sheer force.

She would not allow that to happen.

She knew that the Maharishi was not with her. He had not entered the portal. He was waiting outside, counting on her to get through this test on her own.

His confidence gave her fortitude.

Maya began reciting the *Narsimha* mantra, alternating it with mantras to keep at bay the impact of the waves pounding her mind.

She didn't know how long she stood there chanting, immersed in her inner pool of energy, ensuring that her synchronisation with the sound of the universe was not disrupted. It seemed like an eternity. But she did not stop to think. She carried on, not missing a beat, just as she had been practising for the last three months.

And then, just as suddenly as the waves had materialised, they ceased.

Silence reigned once more.

Silence and stillness.

No waves.

No thoughts.

No emotions.

Just the darkness.

Chapter Ninety-one

Briefing

The Forest
Unknown Location

Satyavachana gazed at Maya thoughtfully. 'Hmmm,' he said, without taking his eyes off her.

Maya stood before him, nervous, wondering what that meant. Had she passed or not?

After her last test, Satyavachana had told her that she needed to build her defences against attracting the thoughts and emotions of her opponents. It might prove to be a weakness for her in the event of an actual encounter with the creatures he was testing her with. That had been over ninety days ago. Since then, the Maharishi had put her through some gruelling new exercises, new mantras and techniques that left her mentally drained by the time she returned to the Gurukul every evening.

Too drained for even the customary evening walks with her friends.

Today, after all those months of toil, Satyavachana had assessed her once more. He had felt confident that she was ready for the test.

But he had created a new illusion for her. An illusion that was far more powerful and perilous than facing the bhutagana.

Maya had survived unscathed. But she still didn't know if she had managed to do it by herself or if Satyavachana had helped her along.

She was awed at the Maharishi's power and ability to create the illusion that he had tested her with. It had seemed so real. And so menacing.

Finally, after what seemed like a very long time, Satyavachana smiled broadly at her. 'You did it, Maya! You passed the test. And not a mark on you. I just wanted to be sure that there was nothing I needed to do to help you recover. But you need no help at all. You're just fine! Well done!'

Maya could barely contain her delight. She didn't know if the other Rishis in the Gurukul were made to undergo this test, but surely, if she had emerged victorious here, she had a good chance of making it to the Gana.

'Can I start learning mantras now?' she asked.

'But child, you did learn mantras. You used them in the portal, didn't you?'

'Yes, Mahamati, I did.' A note of desperation crept into Maya's voice. 'But I want to learn the other categories of mantras. The offensive mantras, the ones to create illusions, like the one you just created. I've never been able to master those!'

'In time, child, in time,' Satyavachana said soothingly.

'I'll never make it to the Gana at this rate,' Maya sulked.

'Now, now,' Satyavachana said sternly. 'Just when I thought you'd grown up a bit, you go throwing a tantrum.'

'Sorry, Mahamati.'

'It's all right.' There was a twinkle in Satyavachana's eye.

Maya cheered up on seeing it. It meant that the revered Mahamati was going to teach her something new. Something unexpected.

'I'm going to tell you about something that few people even in the Sangha know about,' the Maharishi said to her. 'Come, let us walk.'

Maya wondered what it was that he was going to share with her. By now she knew he was a repository of knowledge. And she was appreciative of the fact that he had chosen her to share much of this knowledge with. It could have been Ags he had chosen to teach. But, no, it was Maya. She felt lucky.

She looked at him expectantly.

The Maharishi held her gaze. 'I'm going to tell you about the Mists of Brahma.'

Chapter Ninety-two

About the Mists

The Forest

'The Mists of Brahma,' Satyavachana continued, 'were created 5,000 years ago by the Saptarishis, when they withdrew from Bhu-lok along with the Devas. The Mists were primarily a means for the Devas to keep in contact with humans even in Kaliyuga, without having to set foot on Bhu-lok. The idea was that the Devas could continue to preserve the balance in Kaliyuga, and advise and oversee the nascent Sangha without having to exercise their own powers. Thus, the power of Kali could be counteracted by the Sangha, aided by the Devas.'

He glanced at Maya to make sure she was paying attention, then resumed.

'The Mists were the conduit to Deva-lok for selected humans who were permitted entry. These humans, who were powerful Maharishis, could travel instantly between Deva-lok and Bhu-lok through the Mists.' Satyavachana paused, as if considering what to say next.

'The Mists had another attribute. One that was both beneficial and fraught with danger. And that was their ability to transport anyone who entered them to a different place and time before the start of Kaliyuga; that is, before the Mists were created. Since the only people who were allowed entry were powerful Maharishis from the Sangha, they were able to use their thoughts to either enter Deva-lok or to transport themselves to a place and time of their choice; much like we use our thoughts during atma travel. This allowed the Sangha members to go back in time before the start of Kaliyuga, observe the ancient Rishis, Saptarishis and Kshatriyas of yore, and learn from them.'

Maya wondered why Satyavachana was telling her all this. The Maharishi never indulged in idle talk, so he must be leading up to something. She had never heard or read of the Mists of Brahma, either at the Gurukul or in any of the ancient texts that her father had got her to read. All that she *had* heard since joining the Gurukul was that humans could travel to Deva-lok in the earlier yugas but not in Kaliyuga. She was surprised to hear that a means for entry into Deva-lok still existed.

'So why am I telling you all this?' Satyavachana glanced at her.

'We're going to Deva-lok to look for the part of the prophecy that is hidden there?' Maya guessed.

Satyavachana laughed heartily and clapped his hands in delight. 'Just the kind of answer I should have expected from you! That's what I love about you, my child!'

His face took on a sober expression as he turned to face her.

'Unfortunately, that is not the reason,' he told her. 'Humans are not permitted to enter Deva-lok any more. Not for the last 3,500 years has a member of the Sangha set foot in that world. Maharishi Tribhuvan was, as far as I know, the last to enter.'

They had reached a small clearing in the forest, a few feet across, where the forest floor was covered with a thick carpet of lush green grass.

'Let's sit, shall we?' he asked her and led the way into the clearing.

Maya sat facing him and waited.

'You had asked me for help in translating the verses in your father's diary, remember?'

Maya felt a thrill course through her at these words. Did the Mists of Brahma have something to do with Brahmabhasha? Was that why the Maharishi was telling her about them?

'I strongly believe,' Satyavachana continued, 'that the key to deciphering the verses lies in the Mists of Brahma.' He looked at her gravely.

'And we'll go into the Mists and find the key?' Maya suggested tentatively.

'Not "we", Maya.' Satyavachana fixed her with a serious gaze. '*You* will enter the Mists of Brahma and find the key. That is what I have been training you for all these months.'

'But how will I manage?' Maya wondered aloud. 'I mean, you just said that only powerful Maharishis were allowed to enter the Mists. I am not even a Rishi!'

Satyavachana shook his head. 'No, you are not. But you have demonstrated over the last eight months that you have the capability and the strength to navigate the Mists. I always knew you could do it, but you have proven it. The test you underwent today was designed specifically to see if you could withstand entry into the Mists.'

Maya thought back to her experience within the portal. Did she really want to go through something like that again?

'It's up to you, my child,' Satyavachana said gently. 'I can take you there and I can advise you on how to navigate the Mists. But I cannot accompany you inside, nor can I compel you to enter. You have to be willing and must agree to enter them of your own free will. It will not work otherwise.'

'Oh.' Maya pondered this. While the Mists seemed wholly unfamiliar and somewhat terrifying, they also offered an opportunity. This could be her key to gaining admission to the Gana. If she could find the means to translate the verses in her father's diary, surely it would count for something? And the fact that she could enter the Mists, which only the powerful Maharishis of yore were capable of doing—wouldn't that be a qualifying factor? She was quite sure, after her latest test, that the Mists would not pose a significant barrier. Also, she did really want to know what the verses in her father's diary were about.

Were the Mists going to be all that dangerous? After all, she thought, Satyavachana would guide her about what she needed to do once inside the Mists.

'I'll do it,' she said, making up her mind. 'I'll go into the Mists and find the key.'

'Thank you, my child,' Satyavachana said softly. 'But do not take the decision in haste. You must know the perils of entering the Mists before you agree. It is a dangerous mission. The Mists also have a dark side!'

Chapter Ninety-three

The Dark Side

The Forest

'The Mists are alive,' Satyavachana explained. 'In order for them to work as they do, they delve deep into your inner consciousness. As long as you are able to control your thoughts, as you are trained to do, the Mists perform as they should. They will take you to the place and time of your choosing—as long as it is before the start of Kaliyuga—and return you to the present without a problem. But they present a danger for people who cannot control their thoughts. They can easily overwhelm them. They can draw out thoughts and qualities from your subconscious mind that you probably never knew existed. They reach down to the core of your individuality and create an experience in response to that which exists locked away in the recesses of your being. You may be surprised at how much there is within the human mind that we are not aware of; thoughts, plans, deeds in the making, and traits that shape our inner beings. It is these that lie revealed through the Mists of Brahma. Anyone who is unable to control their thoughts will come face to face with their true self and that will change them. Not all of us are ready to confront new truths about ourselves.'

Maya remembered the sensation of endless waves crashing against her consciousness. As if the waves were alive and probing, trying to get into her mind and overwhelm her. She now realised why the trip through the portal had been necessary. She had to be strong enough to withstand the onslaught of the Mists.

'You must also remember that what transpires within the Mists is very real. The touch of a blade there will make you bleed as much as it would in the world outside. They are not illusory, though they are not real either. So you must treat everything that you see, hear and feel as the truth and act accordingly.'

Maya kept her eyes fixed on Satyavachana, trying to digest everything he had told her.

'Another thing, Maya. You must remember that, in the last 3,500 years, only one person has entered the Mists. No one from the Sangha will ever do so. That is because, when the Devas decided that humans were no longer allowed in Deva-lok, they strengthened the power of the Mists to keep unwanted people out.' Satyavachana paused.

'Does that scare you, my dear?' he asked, seeing Maya's face.

Maya shook her head numbly. She was unsure of how she felt. The disclosures Satyavachana had just made were overwhelming. Was she ready to enter the Mists that even members of the Sangha avoided?

'You don't have to do it if you don't want to,' Satyavachana repeated. 'If you enter unwillingly, the Mists will play games with you.' He smiled at her. 'Don't you want to know who the one person is who entered the Mists?'

Maya looked at him enquiringly. 'My father?'

'No doubt Maharishi Dhruv could have entered the Mists had he wanted to. He was an immensely powerful Rishi. And young too. But, as far as I know, he never did. *I* was the one who entered the Mists two hundred years ago.'

Maya didn't know if that made her feel better or worse. On the one hand, the fact that only a powerful Maharishi like Satyavachana had dared to enter the Mists, and return unscathed, unnerved her. On the other hand, the fact that he had first-hand experience of being in the Mists gave her confidence. If anyone could guide her, it was Satyavachana.

She gathered up her resolve. Her father had given her a responsibility. He had trusted her with the diary and had believed that she would do everything it took to decipher the verses in it. The realisation had struck her when she had hovered over Dwarka almost a year ago, in the grip of indecisiveness and a sense of hopelessness. It had been that realisation that had driven her to push ahead and seek out Garuda.

She had come a long way since then. And she was not going to let her father down.

Not now. Not ever.

'I will do it, Mahamati,' she said firmly, all doubts erased from her mind. 'I will go into the Mists and I will find the key to deciphering the verses in my father's diary. And I will not fail in this task.'

'Very good.' Satyavachana smiled at her. 'I expected nothing less from you. But I had to give you a choice; I had to tell you what you would be up against.'

'Where are the Mists located?' Maya asked.

'Beyond Gangotri is Gomukh, where the Ganga flows into Bhu-lok. It is the terminus of the Gangotri glacier. Further beyond Gomukh is a place called Tapovan—you have to trek through ice to get there. The Mists of Brahma lie beyond Tapovan, at the point where the Ganga descends to Bhu-lok. Sadhs do not know the location of the Mists. Only members of the Sangha do. I will take you there.'

'When do we leave?' Maya asked.

'Immediately.' Satyavachana smiled at her. 'Are you ready?'

Chapter Ninety-four

The Mists of Brahma

Beyond Tapovan
Uttarakhand

Satyavachana and Maya stood on the glacier beyond Tapovan. Ordinarily, this would have involved an arduous trek over sheer cliffs, a moraine strewn glacier and a rocky landscape, but the two of them had a better option.

It was cold at this height, but Satyavachana had used his powers to create an insulating bubble around them, so that Maya was not troubled by the cold.

'This is where I must leave you,' the Maharishi told her. 'From here, you must travel by yourself.'

Maya looked around at the bleak landscape. There was ice all around. Satyavachana had briefed her before they left the forest, on how she could get to the Mists of Brahma and what she was to do once she entered them.

Maya would have to follow the course of the Ganga, which was ice from this point till the location of the Mists. There was no other way to travel to her destination. Satyavachana had told her that he would use a mantra that would make her body dissolve into the ice so that she could enter the Ganga and follow it backwards to its celestial origins.

'It will be a bit disconcerting,' Satyavachana told her, 'since you will be in your physical form but within the ice. Apart from that, it is exactly like atma travel. Control your thoughts and guide your movements so that you flow upstream along the Ganga and you will emerge in the Mists of Brahma.'

'I'm ready,' Maya said. She reached within to her calm centre and all traces of anxiety and apprehension disappeared. She was in control of herself now.

Satyavachana nodded. 'Bless you, my child. May you succeed in your mission.'

Maya closed her eyes as Satyavachana chanted the mantra.

'*Sampraliyate hima!*' the Maharishi intoned.

Maya felt herself slowly sink into the ice that she had been standing on just a few moments ago. Only, this was not like sinking into water. She was entering the ice, being absorbed by it. She was dissolving in it.

She maintained her control over her thoughts and kept reciting the mantras that fortified her inner calmness. She had now melted completely into the glacier and looked around in wonder at the glassy interior of the frozen river of ice.

The Maharishi had been right. This was exactly like atma travel, except for the fact that she was still within her physical body. Strangely, she didn't feel cold at all despite being enveloped in the ice. Or maybe, she thought, it was because she *was* part of the ice now.

There was no time to wonder. Maya pulled her thoughts together and focused on eliminating all distractions. She concentrated on the direction in which she had to move.

Upstream. Towards the celestial origin of the Ganga.

To her surprise, she began moving through the ice at top speed, gliding smoothly through the frozen river. It was a weird sensation.

In a matter of moments, she came to a stop. Was this where she had to emerge from the ice?

Satyavachana had taught her the mantra for reversing the effects of dissolution. She would have to articulate it in her mind, in the same manner that she had recited the Garuda mantra in her atma form while seeking Garuda.

The mantra unfolded in her mind and she slowly emerged from the ice, only to be engulfed by a thick white shroud.

She was in the Mists of Brahma.

Taken by surprise, Maya fought to keep her thoughts in control, even as she felt the tendrils of the Mists reach into her mind, seeking out her innermost thoughts and feelings. She closed her eyes and reached for the pool of calm. Then she listened for the sound of the universe and allowed herself to synchronise with its frequency.

Only when she knew she was one with the universe did she open her eyes.

White.

White and smoky. In every direction she looked, all she could see were the Mists.

She held out her hand in front of her face. It disappeared beyond the elbow.

Maya shook her head, recalling Satyavachana's instructions.

The wisps of fog floated around, encircling her. She recited the mantras to reinforce the barriers against them, keeping them at bay, not allowing them to sink into her subconscious mind.

Deliberately, she focused her thoughts on the diary. On Brahmabhasha. That was what she was here for. To find a way to decipher the words in her father's diary.

Her father.

The Mists suddenly surged around her as if agitated by something.

Then, abruptly, they began to thin. She sensed a presence in front of her.

The fog disappeared altogether, as if it had never existed.

But the presence remained.

With a shock, Maya realised that she could see who it was, not just sense the presence.

She was standing face to face with her dead father.

Chapter Ninety-five

Unexpected Meeting

The Mists of Brahma

'Dad!' Maya stepped forward to embrace him, but her father smiled and held up his hands.

'No, Maya,' he said, 'you cannot touch me, though I would love to hold my daughter one more time. I am here in my spirit form. It is your mind that has made the Mists present me in the form that you knew and loved. But it is not substantial. It cannot be. I left that form back in Bhu-lok.'

Tears welled up in Maya's eyes. 'Dad! I've missed you so much! I ... I ...' Words failed her and sobs racked her body as she stood there, longing to hold her father but knowing that she could not do so.

Her father waited.

Finally, Maya pulled herself together and wiped her eyes dry. 'How ... how did this happen?' she asked.

'You mean our meeting here?' her father asked.

Maya nodded tearfully.

'Well, I guess you were thinking about me when you entered the Mists,' he said, 'but that's not all. My atma resides in Tapalok—it's where Maharishis go after death—and I sensed that you were in the Mists. There is much that I wanted to say to you, so I too willed us to meet.' He smiled again. 'I am so proud of you, Maya. You understood what I wanted.'

'The diary?'

'Yes, Maya, the diary. I was hoping you'd understand that I wanted you to take care of it and get it deciphered. I was sure that you would eventually seek out Satyavachana and end up here in the Mists of Brahma. Of course, I took a chance that someone would tell you that the undecipherable verses are in Brahmabhasha. I relied on Kanakpratap bringing you and Arjun straight to the Sangha, where I knew they would definitely guess its origin.'

Maya wondered how her father had known all this, how he had been so sure she would enter the Mists when even he knew that she was a sadh but before she could ask him, he was speaking again.

'Time is short, Maya. The Mists do not permit long conversations. I have a lot to tell you but very little time. Let me say what I can before we are separated again. I had come up with a plan to stop Shukra. The diary was a part of it and you had a part to play in putting the plan into motion. Your being here is a part of that too. I cannot go into details now, there isn't enough time. It's up to you to ensure that my plan does not get derailed. If it does, terrible things will happen.'

'What do I need to do, Dad?' Maya asked, wide-eyed. All this was part of her father's plan? But how? She was a sadh! How could she help him, a Maharishi, with his plan?

'I will tell you,' her father said. 'Listen closely.'

Chapter Ninety-six

Last Instructions

The Mists of Brahma

'So that is what I had in mind,' Maharishi Dhruv concluded.

Even as he spoke these words, Maya could see the Mists approaching them, advancing rapidly, a few wisps and tendrils scooting ahead of the pall of white that moved like a great white beast towards them.

'I know I haven't been able to give you details and explanations,' Dhruv said hurriedly, 'but we don't have much more time together. Remember two things: first, don't question anything. Just do what I've told you. Second—timing is crucial. Everything should happen as I have instructed and at the right time.'

The advance wisps now curled around them, sweeping over their feet at first, then rising rapidly until there was a fine white veil between Maya and her father's spirit.

'And one more thing,' her father said. 'Do not share what I have told you with anyone in the Sangha. Tell no one, not even Satyavachana. Not even that you met me in the Mists today!'

'Not even Maharishi Satyavachana? But why, Dad?

'There is a traitor in the ranks of the Sangha,' her father told her, his face beginning to dissolve and fade away. 'Someone has been helping Shukra, telling him about our plans. He has known what we are planning to do all along. We cannot risk sharing the plan with anyone if it has to work.'

'Dad, wait!' Maya cried out in dismay as her father's form began to lose itself in the Mists.

'Go on,' her father instructed. 'Focus on the source of the verses. The Mists will guide you onward.'

'That's what Maharishi Satyavachana told me.' Maya's voice trembled as she realised that her father would be gone in a few moments.

'You focused on me,' Dhruv explained, 'as the source of the verses. You were thinking of my diary, weren't you?'

Maya nodded. 'Yes, Dad.'

The veil between her father and her had begun to thicken as the mantle of the Mists began to descend upon them, obscuring their view of each other.

'That isn't the source.' Maya could not see her father any more. Even his voice had begun to grow faint. 'Remove all thoughts of me from your mind. Focus your mind on the real source!'

'Dad!' she cried, tears welling up again.

'You have to find the source!' Her father's voice faded away, as the thick fog rolled around Maya. Once again, she could see nothing.

'Dad!' she wailed in despair. 'Don't leave me!'

But the dense fog around her was impenetrable.

There was no reply.

Her father had gone, leaving her alone once more.

Maya wept.

Chapter Ninety-seven

Onward

The Mists of Brahma

Maya had never allowed herself to feel the grief of losing her father. But meeting him here brought it all back. She allowed herself to break down, feeling his loss all over again.

On the day of his death, she had suppressed her emotions, concentrating on getting the diary to Arjun's uncle. And then, she had immersed herself in her lessons at the Gurukul, focussing on her ambition to graduate to the Gana.

There had been no time to grieve.

After meeting him here, in the Mists of Brahma of all places, the hurt, the grief, the pain all came flooding back. They had never really gone away. She had numbed herself, but had never really got over his death.

Today, seeing him again, unable to even touch him, the painful reality had finally sunk in. And even hearing his plan to counter Shukra had not assuaged the aching pain she felt; the pain of having lived without him for almost a year, of only being left with happy memories of moments shared together, of their special bond.

Within moments, she felt the Mists begin to penetrate her consciousness. She could feel their energy as the wisps of fog touched her mind, probing, extracting. She knew she was distraught and vulnerable. Satyavachana had warned her.

She could not allow the Mists to overwhelm her.

Not now.

There was too much at stake.

Maya wiped her tears and struggled to focus again on her mission. The Mists continued to tap into her despair and grief while she desperately tried to reconnect with the sound of the universe.

For a few long moments she grappled with her thoughts, reciting the mantras that would fortify her inner centre of peace, driving all thoughts of her father out of her mind, creating a vacuum that could be filled by the pulsating energy of her core.

Slowly, but surely, Maya drove back the tendrils that were swarming into her mind, penetrating deep into her subconscious.

She was chanting the mantras non-stop now, willing the Mists to lead her to the source of the verses.

Maya had understood what her father had been trying to tell her as he vanished into the Mists.

He was not the source of the verses. He had simply copied them into his diary. He had duplicated them, preserved them. But they had originated elsewhere.

She now knew where she had to go.

What she didn't know was how to get there. But she left that to the Mists.

As she slowly gained control, the Mists gave up the struggle, withdrawing from her mind, realising the power that she had within.

Finally, they bowed to her will.

The fog around her began to swirl violently as if disturbed by a strong gust of wind. It began to thin.

Slowly, as if in a haze, a scene began to form before Maya's eyes, materialising out of the white wall that she had confronted until now.

She had not moved a step but she had been transported somewhere else.

To a different place.

And, possibly, a different time.

The sun shone in the sky, beating down upon the carpet of grass under her feet.

In the distance, she could see figures—human forms—engaged in some kind of activity.

Had she found the source?

Was this her destination?

Chapter Ninety-eight

The Source of the Verses

The Mists of Brahma

The last vestiges of the fog disappeared and Maya could see clearly.

As she advanced towards the distant figures, Maya saw that they were clustered around some kind of a structure that rose out of the ground, towering over them.

The faint sounds of a low chanting came to her ears.

A thrill coursed through her. Had she really done it?

Were these the Devas?

And was this Deva-lok?

It couldn't be, because Satyavachana had clearly told her that humans were no longer welcome in the world of the Devas.

Wherever this was, in whichever time, it was beautiful. Lush grasslands stretched around her as far as the eye could see. She was on a plateau and, in the distance, she could see two lakes, their surfaces shimmering in the noonday sun. Rocky knolls, some as high as 100 feet, dotted the landscape, rising out of the grassy carpet.

One such rocky mound lay directly in front of her. It was the focus of all the activity.

As she neared the cluster of people, the chanting grew louder. The people congregated at the hillock were building a wall around it. But that was not the amazing bit. It was the manner in which the wall was being built that was stupefying.

There were hundreds of enormous stone blocks lying around, some of them easily twenty or thirty feet in height and an equal length and breadth. As she walked towards them, one of the gigantic blocks of stone rose into the air, seemingly of its own accord, and landed on the topmost layer of the stone wall that was being built, nestling snugly into place, jammed tight against the blocks adjoining it.

What was happening?

Maya looked on as another block repeated the process, accompanied by chanting.

A thought occurred to her. Were these people chanting mantras? And were they using the power of mantras to lift the blocks and get them into position?

But the mantras were being uttered in a strange tongue that she did not recognise.

Could they be chanting mantras in Brahmabhasha?

Maya had focused strongly on the source of the verses, the creators of the language in which the verses were inscribed.

And the original creators were the Devas.

Maya was now close enough to be able to observe the figures. She barely glanced at the wall, though the brief glance she gave it rang a bell somewhere in her mind—why did look so familiar?

But she quickly pushed the thought away. She was not here to wonder about a wall. She needed to find a way to understand Brahmabhasha; to translate the verses in her father's diary.

And she knew that she had a limited period of time in which to accomplish this. It would not be long before the Mists crept back. She didn't know if she was strong enough to be able to return here, to this place, to these people, a second time. The Mists had already taken a toll on her and exhaustion was beginning to overcome her. She longed to return to her own world.

Maya focussed on the scene ahead. She observed that, while the group of people building the wall looked human, they were in fact quite different.

For one thing, they were significantly taller—each one was at least seven to eight feet in height. And their faces shone with a strange radiance; it was as if their skin glowed.

She remembered then that the word 'deva' also meant 'shining one'.

Her heart skipped a beat. So these *were* the Devas.

Maya was now nearly upon them.

They had been so intent on the construction activity that they had failed to notice her. Now, however, her presence became obvious.

The chanting immediately ceased and a silence fell over the plateau. One of the Devas turned and walked towards her with measured steps.

Maya's throat was dry and her palms clammy.

She was going to meet a Deva! What was she going to say? How did one greet a Deva?

The tall, radiant being came to a halt before her. He was so close that Maya could have reached out and touched him.

He smiled and spoke softly to Maya in a strange tongue that sounded soft and musical.

Maya bowed. It was all she could think of doing. Then, straightening, she shook her head to indicate that she could not understand.

The Deva smiled at her again and raised his hands to touch her forehead, as if in benediction.

Maya felt a strange surge of energy course through her body as his hands touched her forehead. She swayed slightly, feeling a bit dizzy.

Then, the nauseous feeling cleared, and she could focus once more. The Deva was speaking to her.

'Welcome, child,' he was saying. 'We have been expecting you.'

Maya recoiled in shock and took two steps back. The Deva was still speaking in the same tongue he had used earlier, with its musical tones and soft inflections, but now she could understand what he was saying! Her mind unconsciously warmed to the sound of the language, as if it were welcoming a new friend.

She shook her head to clear it, unable to understand what was happening. Had the Mists finally got to her?

Chapter Ninety-nine

Maya Asks for Help

The Mists of Brahma

The Deva smiled warmly. 'Do not worry, child. I am Indra. What you are hearing is the language of the Devas. We do not teach it to your people, but you are different. You have a need, which is why you are here. And we will help you.'

'How … how did you know that I would come here?' Maya stammered, unable to believe what was happening. She was amazed to find herself responding in the same language. 'How am I able to comprehend what you are saying? And how am I able to speak your language?'

Indra smiled. 'So many questions, and so little time to answer them all. I fear your time here is not long and you will need to leave soon.'

Indra held out his hand and Maya hesitatingly accepted it. He smiled once again and led her towards the other Devas, who set up a chant as she approached.

'Blessings upon you, child from Kaliyuga!' they intoned together.

Indra let go of her hand and joined them, facing her.

How did they know she was from Kaliyuga?

Maya gazed curiously at them, trying to identify them by their appearance. She would have loved to know who among them was Agni, Surya and Varuna. But they made no attempt to introduce themselves and she did not dare ask.

She had a more important question.

'Indradeva,' she addressed Indra, 'I need the help of the Devas to be able to translate Brahmabhasha. I need to be able to read some verses written in your language. Please help me. Bhu-lok is in great danger.'

'We know,' Indra replied calmly. 'But we cannot help you with your request.'

Maya despaired. 'But why? You have enabled me to understand you, to speak Brahmabhasha. Why can you not teach me to read it?'

'There is not enough time for that, child,' Indra replied. 'You must seek out the energy of the Saptarishis. It lies upon Bhu-lok. Only then will you be able to read Brahmabhasha.'

Maya was nonplussed. 'Where do I find the energy of the Saptarishis, O Deva? How do I locate it?'

Indra shook his head. 'I'm sorry, my child. That is all I can tell you. Even the Saptarishis cannot give you the answer. If you truly are who you are, you must find it yourself.'

Maya didn't understand a word of what Indra was saying. Her heart sank, but she refused to give up. 'You said you were expecting me, Indradeva. You have advised me to find the energy of the Saptarishis. If you know all this, then surely you know how I can find what I need?'

'My child,' Indra said gently but firmly, 'we cannot see the future. We expected you because we know the prophecy. It told us that you would come back in time, all these thousands of years, to us, seeking our help. It told us that the energy of the Saptarishis is what you truly seek. But the answer to your problem lies in the future. That is why even the Saptarishis cannot help you. The location that you need to seek out will be determined in the future, when Kaliyuga begins. That is all we know. And as I said, if you truly are who you are, you will find your way.'

'Who am I?' Maya demanded, confused now, desperate for some answers before she was forced to leave. 'How do I know that I can find what I need by myself?'

'You ask for answers that I cannot give you,' Indra said with a sigh. 'You have reached us, travelling thousands of years back in time. That is not something an ordinary human being can do. But how can I tell you how to find out if you are the one who can find the solution to your own problem? That is something you need to discover for yourself.'

Maya stood there for a moment, unsure. Out of the corner of her eye, she could see the fog beginning to return, the advancing tendrils dragging the ponderous weight of the Mists behind them. They would be upon them in a matter of moments.

'It is time,' Indra said. 'You must leave now. It is dangerous for you to stay here any longer. Go, my child. Our blessings go with you. Look deep within yourself for the answer and you will find it!'

As Maya looked at him, she realised to her horror that Indra and the other Devas were slowly dissolving, fading away into nothingness. As she looked on, the Mists came up again and the lakes in the distance, the lush grasslands, all disappeared behind a white curtain.

Soon, all that she could see was a thick white wall of swirling fog, just as it was when she had first entered the Mists.

Recalling her experience after her encounter with her father's spirit, Maya immediately reached out to control her thoughts.

It was difficult. Dozens of questions swirled inside her head, just as the Mists swirled around outside.

What had just happened? What was she going to do? Had she come all this way only to fail in her mission?

Maya dispelled these thoughts with a conscious effort, and focused instead on the glacier from which she had emerged into the Mists.

She was growing weary of grappling with the power of the Mists, but she managed to focus by reciting the mantras that kept them from gaining control of her thoughts, her mind.

The Mists began fading again and she found herself standing on ice.

The glacier.

'*Sampraliyate hima!*' Maya intoned and once again felt herself sink into the ice, absorbed by it, dissolving in it. Once she had melted completely into it, she turned her thoughts to where she had left Satyavachana, gliding swiftly downstream through the ice until she came to a stop.

The mantra to emerge from the ice unfolded in her mind and she slowly rose, gaining her physical form, shivering in the cold, bereft of the protection Satyavachana had offered her when they had first arrived at this very spot.

The Maharishi was waiting. He hurriedly advanced towards her as she emerged. Maya stumbled and almost fell, suddenly feeling extremely weak, her strength drained from her as if by some enormous exertion.

Satyavachana quickly muttered some mantras to protect her from the bitter cold. Night had fallen and the stars were out, twinkling in a clear sky overhead. He led her to a large rock and sat her down beside him, still supporting her with one arm.

Presently, the feeling of weakness passed and Maya felt better. She sat up straight, rubbing her temples and forehead. It felt as if there was something inside her head that she couldn't purge.

Satyavachana sat patiently, waiting for her to recover. He knew that her journey through the Mists had been arduous, but he was prepared to wait until she was ready to talk about it.

Finally, Maya spoke. 'I have had the most bizarre experience,' she began, her voice tremulous.

But Satyavachana hushed her immediately. 'I can sense your fatigue and confusion,' he said gently. 'You need to recover before we discuss what transpired in the Mists.'

He helped her get to her feet. 'Come,' he said, 'we must get you back to the Gurukul. You need rest and a good night's sleep before we speak of this again. We will not practice atma travel tonight. You can tell me everything tomorrow.'

As Maya and the Maharishi began their journey back to the Gurukul, Maya wondered how she was going to break the news to him that she had come back empty-handed.

How was Satyavachana going to react to her failure to accomplish her mission?

Chapter One Hundred

Maya Tells Satyavachana

The Forest
Unknown Location

The next day dawned pleasant and clear. Fluffy white clouds scurried across a clear azure sky, powered by a western breeze, as Maya arrived at the forest where Satyavachana was waiting for her.

'Ah, my child!' he beamed as Maya appeared. 'How did you sleep last night? Did you rest well?'

Maya nodded, smiling at his genuine warmth and concern. 'Yes, Mahamati,' she replied.

'Good. I didn't want to tire you out yesterday, but perhaps now you can tell me what happened in the Mists of Brahma!' Satyavachana gripped his brahmadanda with both hands and assumed an air of anticipation.

Maya started her story hesitantly, skipping the part where she met her father. Her father's instructions not to disclose their meeting or their conversation to anyone were fresh in her mind, and she was not going to disobey.

But she left out no details of her encounter with the Devas. When she finished, there was a look of disappointment on Satyavachana's face.

'So,' he remarked, 'you did not get the key to deciphering the verses.'

'No, Mahamati.'

'I suppose that means I was wrong,' the Maharishi muttered, sounding a bit despondent.

'But I did learn to speak and understand Brahmabhasha,' Maya said, by way of consolation.

'Indeed. But that doesn't help us at all, does it?'

'No, Mahamati.'

'I wonder what Indra meant by his last words to you,' Satyavachana said thoughtfully. '"Look deep within yourself for the answer and you will find it."'

'I have no idea,' Maya replied. 'He told me I had to find the energy of the Saptarishis. What does that mean, Mahamati?'

'I have to admit, I am quite clueless,' Satyavachana admitted, as he stroked his beard. 'I have never heard of the energy of the Saptarishis, let alone know what it means. It just show how little we know.' His eyes flashed. 'And the Sangha believes that with just one part of the prophecy, they know everything that is required to counter Shukra and defeat him. Ridiculous!'

'Indra did mention a prophecy,' Maya reminded Satyavachana. 'Do you think he meant the part of the prophecy that is hidden in Deva-lok?'

'Hmmm. Let's see,' Satyavachana mused. 'You went quite a long way back in time. Indra mentioned thousands of years.

And he did seem to indicate that Kaliyuga was yet to start. If that is the case, he could not possibly be referring to the part of the prophecy which we believe is hidden in Deva-lok. The prophecy we seek was, according to legend, created by the Saptarishis at the start of Kaliyuga and hidden by them in Deva-lok. The Indra you met lived in a time far before Kaliyuga started, so he was referring to a different prophecy.' He paused, lost in thought.

'You mean there was a different Indra later?' Maya was confused.

'It is possible,' Satyavachana replied, a faraway look in his eyes. 'Even the Devas could not escape death. What is interesting is that there seemed to be a prophecy even back then, in the yuga you visited. That too, a prophecy about Kaliyuga. I wonder what *that* prophecy said.'

'But that doesn't help us at all.' Maya was not interested in the older prophecy. 'How am I to find the energy of the Saptarishis?'

'It doesn't make sense,' Satyavachana agreed. '"If you truly are who you are …"—isn't that what Indra told you?'

Maya nodded.

'What did he mean by that?' Satyavachana muttered, rubbing his chin. 'I can only think of one interpretation,' he said finally. 'If you could make it back in time through the Mists to meet the Devas, you can find the energy of the Saptarishis. Whatever that is. And you need to find the answer deep within yourself.'

The Assembly Hall
The Gurukul
Panna National Park

'So you were wrong, Maharishi,' Jignesh addressed Satyavachana.

The group—comprising Jignesh, Kanakpratap, Parth, Usha and Satyavachana—had assembled in the hall on Satyavachana's request. He had just finished briefing them on Maya's journey into the Mists of Brahma.

Everyone was impressed that Maya had not only survived the Mists, but had also travelled back in time and met the Devas.

But the fact that the trip, however impressive, had not led to any tangible results could not be ignored. It was a definite setback.

'Not entirely,' Satyavachana protested, but his remonstration lacked conviction. 'We did learn about the energy of the Saptarishis,' he offered.

'Not very useful though, is it?' Jignesh retorted. 'And Maya is supposed to find that, is she? Just the way she found the answer to translating Brahmabhasha?'

For once, Satyavachana was silent.

'It seems to me,' Parth said, 'that we need to pin our hopes on the success of the team that is searching for the prophecy in the Gandharva valley. Clearly, the *Ranakarman Parva*, if it does exist, is beyond our reach, since we cannot read the verses in the diary.'

'There has to be a reason,' Satyavachana persisted, 'that Maharishi Dhruv copied those verses into his diary. How he found them, I have no way of knowing. Having found them, he could have still discarded them. But he clearly thought they were important.'

'Well,' Jignesh retorted, 'Maharishi Dhruv is dead. If there was something important there, he has taken it with him. And we have no way of finding out what it was.'

'How is Maya holding up?' Kanakpratap asked quietly. He had not spoken until now. 'The journey must have been difficult for her.'

'She'll be fine,' Satyavachana replied. 'But we should give her a chance to find out what Indra meant by the "energy of the Saptarishis". Surely there may be some hope for us there?'

'Maybe we shouldn't send her away from the Gurukul just yet,' Usha suggested. 'She may not be much more than a sadh, but she does have some abilities. I cannot think of anyone from the Sangha who would have had the courage to do what she did. And that means something.'

'Not just courage,' Kanakpratap added. 'From what I understand, no one can just waltz into the Mists and expect to be entertained by the Devas. The fact that she held her own and actually managed to meet the Devas and find her way back qualifies her to continue her lessons with Maharishi Satyavachana.'

'Very well, then,' Jignesh conceded. 'She stays for now. But we will continue to evaluate her progress. And if she does not make further progress with her siddhis, she must leave the Gurukul.'

Chapter One Hundred and One

That Strange Feeling Again

The Gurukul

A week had passed since Maya's journey into the Mists and her subsequent return to routine.

By now she was beginning to get the hang of the basic mantras that Satyavachana had started her off on. She was already quite good with the *shaanta kaaram* mantra and the *Narsimha* mantra—mantras for peace and calm and for protection, respectively.

The Maharishi had told her that he wanted her to master the first two categories before learning the offensive mantras—the third category that was used by the Rishis of the Sangha and the Gana.

Meanwhile, for most of the last nine months since Maya's terrifying visit to the Dandaka, the strange tug that seemed to originate from the forest had been barely perceptible. Whether it was the lessons in thought control that enabled her to keep the inexplicable attraction at bay or something else, she didn't know. But it had faded to an irritating background noise, nothing more. The strong urge to go to the forest never recurred. And Maya had also consciously steered clear of the Rishi practice field and the Dandaka.

But something strange had happened ever since she returned from the Mists. Every single day of the week that she had been back, the call was back too, stronger than ever.

Maya could feel it deep within her, a dreadful urge to go back to the forest. It was almost as if the forest were calling out to her.

She couldn't understand why she felt this way. Why had that feeling returned?

It became an effort to repress the urge to go to the forest, day after day, with each day that passed making it more difficult to suppress or ignore it.

On the seventh day, after returning from her lessons, she finally succumbed to it.

As the sun sank behind the trees, she walked briskly down the Central Avenue, past the classrooms. Then she cut across the Rishi practice field and made for the forest.

As she squeezed through the hedge that separated the field from the grassy stretch of land that led to the forest, she felt again the familiar, almost magnetic tug. In spite of her misgivings, she kept walking.

This time, she did not stop a few feet away, as she had done on the previous occasion. Even though she slowed her pace somewhat, she did not try to fight the force that drew her on.

When she finally reached the trees that lined the edge of the forest, she halted, wondering how she would enter. She could see no path leading into the woods.

To her amazement, as she drew to a halt, the trees in front of her parted, revealing a gap between them. Maya was stunned. She couldn't believe her eyes.

She stood there, staring at the path between the trees, undecided. She was calm, unlike the last time she had stood here; her training for the Mists had ensured that she could now control her thoughts and emotions. But there was still a measure of uncertainty.

Was entering the forest the right thing to do?

After all, it would mean flouting the rules of the Gurukul.

Maya made up her mind.

She took a deep breath and entered the forest.

Chapter One Hundred and Two

Inside Dandaka

The Dandaka Forest

It was hardly a path, more a narrow space between the trees, but as she advanced, the trees up ahead seemed to move aside too, leaving just enough room for her to pass through.

Bewildered by this bizarre phenomenon, Maya moved cautiously through the forest, taking care not to touch the trees on either side of her.

The sequence was repeated as she progressed through the forest. The trees that stood a few paces ahead would part at her approach and allow her through, closing in behind her as soon as she had passed.

As she advanced steadily through the forest, she was struck by the apparent lack of life within the Dandaka. No animals scurried away at her approach. No birdcalls broke the silence in the branches above. It seemed that the forest was dead but for the trees that seemed to move with a life and a mind of their own.

Maya didn't know how long she had walked, but presently she came to a large, circular clearing deep within the forest.

The branches of the trees around it stretched overhead, forming a dense canopy. The soft light of the gloaming was too weak to penetrate the foliage, resulting in near darkness.

At the centre of the clearing was a pond, its waters still in the absence of any kind of breeze. Its surface was almost completely covered by a carpet of green—probably a kind of moss.

Clearly, the pond had suffered extreme neglect for a long time, which was not surprising given the proscription of entry into the forest. Maya was sure that even members of the Sangha never entered the Dandaka.

She gazed upon the pond, wondering why it lay abandoned deep within a forest that no one was permitted to enter.

And why was entry into the forest proscribed anyway? No harm had come to her so far.

She approached the pool. Was there life within it? It seemed unfathomable that anything could lurk beneath its placid surface. Like the rest of the forest, it too appeared to be dead.

Unless one counted the trees. That, Maya could not explain. They did seem to be alive.

Though the inexplicable urge to enter the forest had waned, there was still something tugging at her. What it was, Maya couldn't say, but she could feel it.

She kneeled beside the pond and gingerly lowered her hand towards the water.

A small ripple broke the surface at the touch of her fingers and the carpet of moss parted.

The water was cool to the touch and felt pleasantly energising.

Maya's senses were fully alert. She began to chant the mantras that would help control her thoughts. She was taking no chances. What if this was place like the Mists?

Gradually, Maya's thoughts faded, replaced by a vacuum.

She was one with the universe.

One with the pool.

She could feel the frequency of the pool's vibration. It was a slow, languid pulse, not exactly matching her frequency, but close.

Maya closed her eyes, enjoying the peace and tranquility.

One.

Suddenly the pool exploded, its frequency exponentially increasing, throwing her off balance, catching her unawares.

Maya stared in shock at its surface, which was placid once again, save for the gentle ripples where her hand had emerged, dripping water.

What just happened?

A cool darkness enveloped her.

Maya collapsed on the grass, beside the pool.

Chapter One Hundred and Three

Missing

The Forest
Unknown Location

Satyavachana looked up at the sky, frowning.

It was late. Where was Maya? In all these months that he had been teaching her, she had never been late. What could have happened today? He decided to go over to the Gurukul and find out.

In the twinkling of an eye, he was there. The Gurukul was abuzz with activity. Maya was missing and almost everyone was looking for her.

Adira had reported her missing first thing in the morning. Her bed had not been slept in and they had not seen her all evening since her return from her lessons.

The Mahamatis knew that Maya was close to Arjun and Amyra and had questioned both children. But neither of them had any idea where she was. Both reported that they had not seen Maya on the previous evening either.

Fearing the worst, the entire Gurukul had begun looking for her, combing the forest in search parties of three.

Satyavachana was flummoxed. What could have happened to Maya? The Gurukul was the safest place, unless ... A terrible thought crossed his mind.

What if Maya had decided to go off by herself? After all, she was the only one in the Gurukul who had the ability to leave the premises whenever she wanted, not just in her atma form but also physically. He fervently hoped she had not done anything foolish to put herself at risk. He knew her to be strong-willed and persistent, not easily swayed from a course of action once she had decided on it.

The sun had climbed overhead and it was almost noon when the Maharishi suddenly remembered Maya telling him about her friend Amyra. She had psychic powers and was able to see into the past.

Would she be able to help?

Amyra was quickly summoned with Jignesh's help.

'Can you find her?' Jignesh demanded.

'Yes, Mahamati,' Amyra replied. She had been distraught since the news of Maya's disappearance but it had not occurred to her that her special powers could help in the search.

As the Mahamatis, accompanied by Satyavachana and Kanakpratap, set off with Amyra, Arjun accosted his uncle.

'I'm coming with you,' the young Kshatriya told Kanakpratap.

'No, you're not,' Kanakpratap retorted. 'You're going to stay here. We have no idea what kind of trouble Maya may be in. Let the elders handle it.' Seeing Arjun's downcast face, he added, 'Look, Arjun, if you were needed, I would have asked you to come along anyway. But right now, I don't think there's anything you can do that we can't.'

Arjun recognised the truth of his uncle's words. But that did not stop him from fretting as he watched the five elders follow Amyra, who was walking slowly away from her dorm and towards the Assembly Hall.

A sense of déjà vu embraced Amyra as she tracked Maya's presence from her dorm cottage, past the Assembly Hall, the classrooms, and across the Rishi practice field. As she crossed the field, accompanied by Satyavachana, Jignesh, Kanakpratap, Usha and Parth, she paled as she realised that the tracks led only in one direction.

Towards the Dandaka.

But this time, unlike the last occasion, there was no sign of Maya outside the forest.

'Dandaka?' Jignesh was incredulous. 'She's gone into the Dandaka? Despite knowing that it's against the rules?'

'If she's in there, we have to hurry,' Satyavachana muttered. '*Udnayate!*' he intoned, and floated over the hedge and across the patch of land separating the Gurukul from the forest. He was closely followed by the other Mahamatis.

If Maya had not returned at night, it meant that she had spent it in the forest. The mood was grim as the group advanced towards the forest and halted at its edge.

'How do we enter?' Kanakpratap asked.

'We can't,' Jignesh replied. 'At least, not on our own. We use a mantra. Then it is up to the forest.'

Kanakpratap frowned. 'What does that mean, "up to the forest"? It's just a forest, isn't it?'

Jignesh didn't reply. '*Dandaka krpya vishto!*' he intoned.

'Not this patch of Dandaka,' Usha said to Kanakpratap. 'This is possibly the only surviving portion of the original

Dandaka forest. At some point in antiquity, a set of powerful mantras was used to give the forest a life of its own. We don't know who did it or why, but it was discovered centuries ago, when a student from the Gurukul wandered in by mistake. No one knows how or why the forest allowed him in, but it did.'

'I've heard about the case,' Satyavachana muttered. 'He died.'

'What's inside the forest that can kill someone?' Kanakpratap asked, his face lined with anxiety. With Dhruv dead, he felt Maya was his responsibility.

Usha shrugged, glancing towards the forest to see if there was a response to the mantra. 'Nothing that is obviously dangerous. Just trees, bushes—the usual fauna. And a pond at the very centre.'

Jignesh repeated the mantra, his voice urgent.

'So, nothing that can kill.' Kanakpratap frowned.

'I've heard,' Parth added, 'but I don't know how true it is, that since the Dandaka was created by Shukra, mantras were used to cleanse and protect it; at least, this part of it. The process gave the forest life. And maybe the power to take away life as well. Who knows?'

'That's the reason no one is allowed to go in there,' Jignesh said, sounding impatient. 'We don't know what power the forest has and what it is capable of. It has never been a problem, ever since the rule was instituted after the student perished inside. Remember, it protected us against the Nagas.'

Kanakpratap remembered Parth and Jignesh being confident that the reptiles from the netherworld would not cut through the Dandaka to attack the Gurukul. They had been right. That was the only flank the Nagas had not attacked. Now he realised why. The Nagas feared the forest. Even they knew.

Then why had Maya gone in there?

An eternity seemed to pass as the group waited, with Jignesh chanting non-stop.

Finally, the trees before them bowed and parted, revealing a gap.

'Come on,' Jignesh said. He rushed into the forest, followed closely by the others.

Chapter One Hundred and Four

The Consequences

The Assembly Hall
The Gurukul
Panna National Park

Maya stood before Usha and the four men who had rescued her from the forest—Satyavachana, Jignesh, Kanakpratap and Parth.

The five of them had walked swiftly through the forest, the trees parting before them, until they reached the pond in the clearing. Beside the pond, they had found the prone body of Maya. She was still breathing, but when they turned her over, they found that her lips were turning blue. Her right hand had already gone blue and was cold to the touch. There was also a lump on her head where it had struck the ground.

The group had wasted little time in getting her back to the Gurukul where two Mahamatis who were part of the Bhisaj Varga immediately set to work on reviving her and attending to whatever affliction she had suffered in the forest. The Bhisaj Varga were the Healers of the Sangha, who specialised in mantras and the use of herbs for healing.

For three days, the Healers worked round the clock, taking turns to treat Maya for the shock and trauma she had undergone in the Dandaka, as well as the strange condition of her hands and lips.

Much to the despair of her friends and teachers, Maya's progress had been negligible on the first day. But on the second day she began responding to the treatment and mantras, and by the third day, she had recovered enough to stand and walk a little.

Today was the fourth day. Seeing that Maya was strong enough to return to her daily routine, with the exception of lessons with Satyavachana—the Maharishi had suggested she take a week off and regain her strength before they resumed their classes—Jignesh had summoned her to appear before those members of the Mahamati Council who were in the Gurukul at the time. Kanakpratap and Satyavachana, as the two people who were closest to her among the elders in the Gurukul, were present too, but they were not to be part of the proceedings; only observers.

'You know that your actions contravened the law laid down by the Gurukul, by the Sangha.' It was a statement, not a question. Jignesh's voice was flat, hard, and bereft of emotion. But Maya could sense the anger and disapproval simmering behind his words.

'Mahamatra,' she began, 'I am sorry ...'

Jignesh held up a hand to cut her off. 'I have not summoned you here for an apology. Nor do I wish to hear an explanation for your actions. There can be no excuse and there will be no apology.' In his eyes, Maya saw his self-vindication, an affirmation of what he had said when she first arrived at the

Gurukul: that she was not fit to be admitted and that she would never be a member of the Gana.

She shrank back at the thought of what he might say next, though she maintained her composure, just as Satyavachana had taught her. She didn't want to even speculate about what Jignesh might say. All she could do was hope.

But what he said next dashed all her aspirations to the ground, shattering her dreams.

'There is no place for you here,' he told her pointedly, 'in this Gurukul. There is no room for you in the Sangha. You have demonstrated that you are incapable of following the rules laid down by us. There are reasons why these laws were made. They have kept the Sangha from disintegrating for thousands of years.' He paused and looked at the others.

No one spoke. Kanakpratap was silent. Even Satyavachana, who was usually the first to leap to her defence, was subdued.

Maya realised the gravity of her indiscretion. She was angry with herself rather than with Jignesh or the Sangha. What he said was true. She should have controlled the urge to enter the Dandaka. If she had the ability to control herself while travelling through the Mists, she should have been able to resist the lure of the forest.

Maya realised that, for the first time, Jignesh was questioning not her ability but her will.

For, Maya realised with a shock, she had *wanted* to enter the Dandaka. It wasn't that she was unable to hold back; she had not even tried.

'And this isn't the first time,' Parth added, a tinge of regret in his voice. 'You violated the rules once before, when you went to the Gandharva valley last year.'

'You were forgiven then,' Usha added, 'with the hope that you would learn from your mistake. But clearly you have not learnt anything at all from that misadventure.'

Maya stood, trembling with fear and fury. How could she have been so careless? She could not blame anyone for what was happening now.

The law of karma. She had acted in a manner that invited consequences. And now she would have to take responsibility for her actions and face those consequences.

Whatever they were.

Jignesh's voice boomed in her ears and his next words fell like bombs, each one blasting her dreams and ambitions to smithereens.

'You are hereby expelled from the Gurukul and from the Sangha. You will have nothing more to do with any of our Gurukuls or the Gana network. You will return to Delhi by yourself. Since you have no one to take care of you, Maharishi Ratan will be your local guardian until you reach an age when you are able to be on your own. You will leave tomorrow morning.' Jignesh looked at Kanakpratap. 'Will you drop her at the Gwalior railway station and make sure she takes the train to Delhi?'

Kanakpratap nodded. 'I will, Mahamatra.' His voice was low and sad.

'Go now. You may say farewell to your friends in the Gurukul,' Jignesh said. 'You have our blessings.'

For a few moments, Maya stood rooted to the spot, transfixed by the sentence that had been pronounced. A storm of emotions raged within her. Hurt, rage, disappointment, regret, all swirled together, making her head spin.

She suppressed her emotions and went up to each of the elders in the room, touching their feet and obtaining their blessings. But she could not meet their eyes.

When she was done, she turned and walked out of the hall, looking more frail and vulnerable than she had ever appeared.

Chapter One Hundred and Five

Exile!

The Gurukul

Maya sat back against the trunk of a tree and hugged her knees, as she allowed the reality of the situation to sink in. Her right hand had not completely recovered all its functions yet and was still weak. She clasped it around her knees with her left hand.

When she had entered the Gurukul almost one year ago with so many hopes, she had never, in her wildest dreams, imagined that a day like this would dawn.

Her lower lip trembled with emotion as she contemplated a future without the Gurukul or the Gana. She had been banished to the sadh world.

And she had only herself to blame for it.

Maya allowed herself to wallow in self-pity for a while. There was nothing she could do to reverse the sentence that had been passed on her. Nothing she could do, or promise, would make amends for what she had already done. It was too late for remorse.

She pulled herself together. Why was she going to pieces? The law of karma worked in more ways than one.

Sadhs often used it to explain why bad things happened to good people. To explain concepts like destiny and fate. And how one's actions in a past birth were responsible for all that happened to them in their lives. But Maya knew that this explanation was effectively an abdication of accountability. This simplistic interpretation of the law of karma effectively took away the onus from a person for what happened to them in their current lives.

Sure, she reflected, our past life and our actions in it do influence the circumstances of our birth and some of the things that happen in our present life. But many things that happen in our lives are a result of the choices we make and the decisions we take. Very often, luck—whether good or bad—can be attributed directly to these.

And Maya was keenly aware of this. It had been her decision to enter the forest. It was that action of hers that had led to the situation in which she found herself now.

But that didn't mean all was lost. There was always something one could do, no matter how hopeless the situation. Maya was sure that there was some way in which she could redeem herself; something she could do to prove to the Sangha Council that she was, in fact, worthy of being re-admitted to the Gurukul and deserving of a place in the Gana.

The question was: what?

Long moments went by as Maya pondered the question.

Then she rose. She had made a decision.

Maya knew what she was going to do. And nothing was going to sway her from her course of action.

Chapter One Hundred and Six

Plans

The Gurukul

Arjun opened the door of the cottage and stuck his head out.

Darkness cloaked the Gurukul. No one was about. The moon lit up the Central Avenue, giving it a silvery sheen.

Good.

He slipped out, followed by Agastya.

'Okay,' Arjun whispered, as he shut the door of the cottage, taking care to ensure that it didn't slam shut and wake someone. 'Let's go.'

The two boys made their way down the Central Avenue and past the Assembly Hall, heading for the Kshatriya practice field, along the river Ken.

Just as they were crossing the classroom blocks, a dark form disentangled itself from the shadows and stood in front of them, barring their way.

Instantly, Arjun's sword appeared in his hand and Agastya's brahmadanda was in his grasp, both boys ready to attack or defend as required.

'It's me,' a familiar voice said.

'*Vidyutate.*' Agastya created a glowing ball of light that lit up their features. Arjun's uncle stood before them, a stern expression on his face.

'And when were you going to tell me about this little expedition of yours?' he demanded.

Arjun looked downcast. He hadn't expected this.

'I'm sorry, Uncle,' he said, unable to look Kanakpratap in the eye. 'I didn't think you would allow me to go if I told you. We were planning to be back in a couple of days. I left a note for you in the dorm with an explanation.'

Kanakpratap said nothing but studied the faces of the two boys.

'And where were you going?' he asked finally. 'I presume this has something to do with Maya's exile?'

Arjun nodded. 'Maya came to see me earlier today. To say goodbye. She told me that she wasn't going to wait until morning to leave the Gurukul.' He hesitated. Maya had confided in him about her encounter with her father's spirit in the Mists. Dhruv had told her not to reveal their meeting to anyone in the Sangha. But Arjun was not part of the Sangha. And if she couldn't trust Arjun with the information, there was no one she could trust. She had made him promise that he would not tell anyone, even his mother or uncle, about it.

'And you decided to go with her,' Kanakpratap said.

'Well, someone has to accompany her. She's going to need help,' Arjun said.

'Where does she plan to go?' his uncle asked. 'What is she going to do that she needs help?'

'I don't know exactly,' Arjun admitted, 'but she wants to try and find the means to translate the verses in the diary.'

'And how does she plan to do that?'

'I don't know, Uncle. But I trust Maya. And the Sangha Council isn't exactly going to allow her to present her ideas. So she's decided to do it without their help or approval.'

When Maya had met Arjun earlier in the evening, she had been hazy about her plan. All she was willing to share was her objective. And the fact that the meeting with her father in the Mists had given her some direction. Maya hadn't told Arjun that it was her father's plan that she was going to put into motion. Nor had she revealed exactly what her father had told her. That was between her father and her. But she knew she needed help, and had, therefore, approached Arjun.

'I will understand if you say no,' she had told Arjun. 'After all, I am asking you to do exactly what I had refused to do for you earlier, when you wanted the Saptas to embark on a search for the prophecy. It's strange how the wheel turns. Then, I preached to you about respecting the rules of the Sangha. Now I am asking you to break them. So feel free to refuse. I am already an outcast. What more can the Sangha do to me? But you have a great deal at stake.'

'Don't be silly,' Arjun had replied immediately. 'When I insisted that we leave the Gurukul, I had no plan in mind. Just a vague desire for us to prove ourselves. In hindsight, it was silly and impetuous of me. But you ... you know what you are doing. That makes it different. And if we succeed, we will have given the Sangha something to make them proud of us. I'm coming with you. And I'm going to ask Ags as well.'

Maya had been grateful for his help and they had agreed to meet at midnight in the Kshatriya practice field.

Kanakpratap sighed. 'Well,' he said, 'I'm not going to stop you. You are old enough and, after all, both you and Agastya are now Gana members. You can take decisions by yourself. You don't need me chaperoning you around.'

Arjun looked at his uncle in surprise. He hadn't expected this.

Kanakpratap smiled at his shocked face. 'Remember all those times when you asked to be allowed to do things on your own and kept trying to shake off my presence, and I would tell you that someday it would happen? That you would take your place in the world and face it?'

Arjun nodded. He remembered how frustrated he had been, badgering his uncle and mother in vain.

'Well,' Kanakpratap said, 'that time has come. The time to be independent, to take charge of your life and take your place in the world. I believe that you are now prepared to face the dangers of the world outside the Gurukul.'

Kanakpratap held out his hand. He was holding a sheathed sword.

Arjun gasped as he set eyes on it. The golden metal scabbard had intricate carvings along its length and shone as if it had been polished yesterday. A magnificently carved hilt completed the picture, embellished with precious stones. In the centre of the pommel was a small cartouche, which Arjun did not recognise.

Kanakpratap drew the sword and held it aloft in the light.

Arjun was captivated by the fine lines of the weapon and longed to touch it, to hold it and wield it, just once.

'I wanted to give you this,' Kanakpratap said as he twisted the sword this way and that so its blade caught the light and gleamed. 'This is your father's sword, inherited from our father, going back I don't know how long. I have been keeping it safe till the time you were ready.' He sheathed the sword and held it out.

'Here,' he said. 'Take what is yours. And wield it wisely.'

Arjun couldn't believe his eyes and ears. With trembling hands, he took the sword and unsheathed it, marvelling at how well it fit his grasp.

'Thank you, Uncle,' he said gratefully, as he slid the sword back into its scabbard. 'Thank you.' He was at a loss for words.

'May you succeed in achieving whatever you set your mind to doing,' Kanakpratap blessed them as both boys touched his feet. 'I will try and explain this to the Sangha Council so that you do not get into any trouble when you return!'

Without another word, he left them and walked away, back towards the cottages.

The two boys looked at each other. Arjun's eyes were shining with excitement as he uttered the mantra to stow his sword away. 'Fancy that!' he told Agastya. 'Let's go. Maya must be waiting.'

They hastened towards the rendezvous point.

When they reached, Maya was already there, with Amyra.

'Is she coming with us?' Agastya asked in surprise.

'Of course!' Amyra said fiercely. 'I'm not going to stay behind! And you will need me more than you can imagine.'

'Thanks, friends,' Maya said, almost formally. 'I really am grateful to you all for coming along.'

'Right,' Arjun said, wanting to get on with their adventure. 'What's the plan? Where are we going from here?'

'We're going back to where we started,' Maya told him. 'Hold tight!'

Chapter One Hundred and Seven

The Search Begins

Shukra's Cavern

Shukra appeared in the cavern, materialising out of thin air. A globe of light materialised next to him, lighting up the closed space. He closed his eyes and concentrated, then opened them slowly.

It would not take long.

Barely a few minutes had passed, when Vishwaraj appeared. He bowed with his hands folded.

'*Pranaam*, Poorvapitamah,' he greeted Shukra. 'You summoned me? I have not yet completed my task, but am very close to accomplishing it.'

'That is not why I called you here, my son,' Shukra told him. 'I too was elsewhere, engaged in my search, when I received news from Panna, from our spies in the bhutagana there. They tell me that the boy, Arjun—the One of the prophecy—has left the Gurukul, along with a few other children.'

Vishwaraj looked surprised. 'No one from the Sangha is accompanying them?'

'Apparently not.'

Vishwaraj smiled. 'What is your command, Poorvapitamah? They will be easy pickings for me.'

Shukra shook his head. 'No, Vishwaraj. Remember my principles. We are not savages. It is in Kaliyuga that people kill each other wantonly under the influence of Kali. Our target is the boy. None of the others are important for us. Why waste lives when it is not required? And I don't want you to kill the boy either. Not unless it is absolutely essential.'

Vishwaraj's face fell. 'Then what would you have me do, Poorvapitamah?'

'Watch them. If they have left the Gurukul, it is possible that the Sangha has tasked them with something important. Possibly something that concerns my plans. And I need to know what that is.'

Vishwaraj bowed. 'I understand. Where are they now? I will go immediately.'

'New Delhi,' Shukra told him. 'The house of Maharishi Dhruv.'

Maya's House
New Delhi

Arjun, Maya and Amyra watched with interest as Agastya tried different mantras on the locked door of the house. So far, nothing he tried had worked.

'Come on, Ags,' Arjun goaded him, 'surely you can't let a locked door defeat you?'

Agastya gave him a withering glare in the light of the streetlamps. 'This is not what I do for a living, you know.'

Arjun chuckled.

'Don't mind him,' Maya said. 'I'm sure you can do it.'

Agastya nodded and tried another mantra. '*Visramsate taalayantra!*'

This time it worked. They heard the sound of the latch unfastening, and the door hung loose on its hinges.

'You did it!' Maya said excitedly. 'I knew you could!'

'Yeah,' Arjun said drily. 'Great to have you along, Ags. This is what we needed you for.'

Agastya frowned at him. 'Yeah, right. You needed someone to pick locks, right?'

'Come on, guys,' Amyra said, unable to contain her excitement. 'Let's go inside!'

Agastya pushed the door open and led the way into the living room. '*Panchataya Vidyutate!*' Five globes of light spread out, illuminating the room and the study adjoining it.

Immediately, Arjun and Agastya stopped in their tracks, struck with horror at the sight before them.

Maya gasped as she saw the bloodstains on the walls and the furniture. She had seen this room when she had travelled as an atma for the first time, a year ago, while staying in Ratan Tiwari's house. But seeing it in what she had assumed was a dream, at that time, and seeing it in reality were two different things. She shuddered and closed her eyes, trying to keep out thoughts of what Shukra may have done to her father. Instinctively, she reached within herself to keep at bay the black thoughts that threatened to invade her mind.

It was even worse for Amyra. She had not imagined that she would be able to feel the horrifying reality of what had happened here, so keenly, almost a year after the tragedy.

But it hit her like a ton of bricks.

She screamed.

Maya clapped a hand over the younger girl's mouth, afraid that the sound would draw attention to their presence in the house. Amyra broke down, sobbing in her arms. Maya suppressed her own emotions and held her, comforting her.

Meanwhile, Arjun and Agastya walked on through the living room. Arjun was familiar with the layout of the house, having once been a regular visitor, and they both knew that the study was where Maya had been headed.

Arjun walked into the study and looked around in the light of the globes that hovered above him. A thick coat of dust covered everything. All Maya had said was that they were going to her house in Delhi to look for something. She hadn't specified what they would be looking for. And yet, Arjun had the feeling that she knew exactly what she wanted to find here.

'Hey, Maya!' he called out to her. 'What are we looking for?'

Maya was still in the living room, sitting with Amyra, who had calmed down by now. 'I'm fine,' she told Maya, 'thanks a lot. I … I just felt overwhelmed. The enormity, the ghastliness of what happened here was too much for me.'

'I know, I know,' Maya murmured. 'You rest here for a bit. I'll be right back.' She gave her a pat on the back and went towards the study.

Amyra watched Maya walk away. She felt miserable. But how was she to tell Maya the truth? Maya had said she knew about the savagery, the awfulness of what had transpired in this room between Shukra and her father.

But tonight, as she had walked into the room, Amyra had realised that Maya *didn't* know what had happened here.

Neither did anyone else. They all seemed to think that Shukra had tormented Maya's father and then ripped him apart; the bloodstains bore mute testimony to that.

How was she to tell Maya that she, Amyra, was the only one, apart from Maya's father and Shukra, who knew exactly what had happened here on that fateful day?

Chapter One Hundred and Eight

A Dead End

Maya's House

'It doesn't seem to be anywhere in the study,' Arjun said in exasperation. They had been searching for over half an hour without success. 'Are you sure it isn't in some other room?'

Maya shook her head firmly. 'No, AJ. It should have been under the desk. I remember it well. It had slipped out of Dad's diary and fallen under the desk.' She looked at Arjun. 'There's no way a sheet of paper could have relocated itself.'

'Well, is it so important?' Agastya wanted to know. 'I mean, did we really come all the way here to look for a sheet of paper?'

'Don't be silly, Ags. It's not the sheet of paper but what is written on it that's important,' Arjun said. 'But Maya, what exactly *is* on that sheet of paper that's so important? Isn't there anywhere else we can get the same information?'

Maya hesitated to respond. How was she to tell them? She knew that Agastya would be the first to pooh-pooh it if she revealed what was on that sheet of paper. Though she hadn't seen it herself, her father's spirit had told her. And even Maya had found it difficult to believe what she had heard. If she hadn't heard it from her father, she too would have refused to believe it.

'Inscriptions,' she said simply, not being untruthful but not revealing the entire truth either. The sheet did have inscriptions on it.

'Oh great,' Agastya said. 'We don't seem to be able to rid ourselves of inscriptions, do we?'

'We're searching for something that was hidden away more than 5,000 years ago,' Maya told him. 'It won't be easy to find, but there is a trail of clues that my father had found that can lead us to it.'

Agastya fixed her with a sceptical look. 'And what exactly is it that we are looking for?'

Maya was silent. She didn't trust anyone with the story of her encounter in the Mists. Definitely not Agastya. He would be the first one to disbelieve her and maybe even mock her for hallucinating while in the Mists. Worse, he was capable of running back and squealing to the Sangha.

'Does it matter?' Arjun interjected, realising Maya's quandary. 'We'll find out when we locate it. Whatever it is, it must be important for it to have been hidden away, with only cryptic inscriptions left behind as clues.'

'How will we know we've found it if we don't know what it is?' Agastya sounded exasperated.

Maya didn't know how to respond. But before she or Arjun could say anything, Amyra spoke up. 'If I could see what happened in the living room a year ago, perhaps I can see what happened here too.' She placed a hand on Maya's arm. 'Let me try.'

Maya nodded. She could think of no other way to learn what had happened to the sheet of paper. And her father had told her that it was important, even essential, for countering Shukra.

Amyra closed her eyes and concentrated.

There was silence in the room as the other three children waited.

Finally, she opened her eyes.

'Well?' Maya demanded before Amyra could speak. 'Did you see anything?'

Amyra nodded. 'I did. The paper was taken away by the police.'

'Oh great,' Agastya rolled his eyes. 'That's all we need.'

'We'll never be able to find it,' Maya said glumly. 'How will we ever know who took it or where they took it?'

'Actually,' Amyra replied, 'I saw who took it.'

'You did?' Hope shone in Maya's eyes.

'Yes. There was just one man in a police uniform who came into this room, looked under the desk and retrieved a sheet of paper. He put it in his pocket. I saw the name on his nameplate. Raman Kapoor.'

'Great,' Agastya groaned. He looked at Maya. 'Now you'll want to go and search for this Raman Kapoor, right?'

'I would like to,' Maya said, 'but we don't know how to find him. He could be in any of the police stations in this part of the city.' She sighed. 'I really thought we could pick up the trail from here.'

There was silence for a few moments as they considered what could be done next.

Did this mean they would have to return empty-handed to the Gurukul?

Chapter One Hundred and Nine

Books

Outside Maya's House

Vishwaraj stood outside the front door of Maya's house. He had made himself invisible using a mantra for illusion that Shukra had taught him. It was simple yet effective, and Vishwaraj had wondered why he had not been taught it earlier, in the Gurukul. But it didn't matter now.

'Prapanchayati svara kutigata!' The mantra instantly amplified the voices inside the house.

So, he thought, *the children from the Gurukul have arrived.*

He didn't need to go inside. He could hear every word just as clearly as if he was standing next to them. Shukra had asked him to watch them and see what they were up to.

He was going to do exactly that.

The Study

'Well,' Agastya said, 'I guess we're done here.'

'Not so soon, Ags.' Arjun glared at him. 'Let's look around a bit more. We've been trying to find that damn sheet of paper all this time. Now that we know it's not here, let's see if there's something else we can find that can help us.' He looked at Maya. 'Is there anything else you remember from that day?' Even as he spoke, he cringed at the terrible choice of words. Maya's memories of that day would be horrific.

He hurriedly went on, hoping she wouldn't notice what he'd said. 'Like these books, for example?' He quickly picked up the two books that were lying on the desk and dusted them off. A cloud of dust rose into the air and he coughed.

'*Mysteries of the Indus Valley Civilisation.*' He read aloud the title of the first book, then looked at the cover of the second. '*Mysteries of the Great Pyramid.* Uncle must have been really interested in ancient mysteries.' He opened the book on the Great Pyramid and began leafing through it with interest.

Agastya moved a globe of light closer so he could read with ease and Arjun smiled his thanks at the young Rishi.

'Dad taught history, remember?' Maya didn't seem to have noticed Arjun's faux pas.

'Yes, but these aren't the kind of books he would have used for reference,' Arjun said, his eyes glued to the book. 'This, for example, theorises that the Great Pyramid was engineered to resonate using sound waves and that the internal chambers of the pyramid could concentrate energy.' He looked up from the book with a frown. 'Not exactly the kind of thing you'd teach in a history class.'

'Let me see that.' Maya held out her hand for the book. Knowing her father, he wouldn't have entertained such theories, at least not for use in his classes. And she had never known him to have had any inclination for the so-called alternative theories on history either.

As the book changed hands, something fluttered to the floor.

'What's that?' Amyra bent to pick it up. She squinted at the black sheet of paper with white inscriptions on it. 'It looks like Hindi, but I can't make sense of it. Weird.'

'Here, show me.' Agastya stretched out his hand and took the sheet of paper. 'Hey, this is in Sanskrit! I can read it.'

'Tell us what it says,' Arjun said.

'Sure. I'll read it out to you.' Agastya transferred the sheet to his other hand and examined his fingers. 'This paper has black ink on it!' he complained.

'Doesn't matter,' Arjun said impatiently. 'Read it out.'

'Fine, fine.' Agastya turned his attention back to the sheet of paper. 'It appears to be a note written in the first person. It says: "I, Tribhuvan, have realised that there will be a time to come when the Son of Bhrigu—the great Asura Guru, Shukracharya—will return."'

He looked up. 'Who is Tribhuvan?'

Arjun shrugged. Amyra looked blank.

Only Maya knew. Maharishi Satyavachana had told her on the night they had both travelled as atmas to Bhimbetka. More recently, and more importantly, her father's spirit had mentioned the name to her when they met in the Mists of Brahma.

'He was the first Mahamatra,' she informed the others. 'Maharishi Satyavachana told me that he lived around 4,000 years ago and organised the Sangha into what it is today. Apparently it was quite different before that.'

'You mean this is a note from 4,000 years ago?' Arjun was awestruck.

'This paper certainly isn't 4,000 years old. It must be a copy of the original. But how did your father get hold of it?' Agastya asked Maya.

Maya shrugged. 'Dad travelled a lot. Maybe he picked it up on one of his trips?'

'Doesn't matter,' Arjun said, impatient to know what the inscriptions said. 'Go on, Ags.'

Agastya continued reading aloud. '"It is written in the prophecy of the Saptarishis, which was divided into three parts and hidden away. I do not know what the entire prophecy says, since I have only been able to find one part of it. But I have the means to discover the other two parts and I am securing their location. I am concealing a key in the archives of the Sangha. The Akshapatalikas, whom I have created for this purpose—though they do not know it yet—will protect this key until it is ready to be discovered according to my plan. For I have set in motion a series of events that will foil the Asura Guru's various attempts. The One of the prophecy will be determined by me and will be recognised by ..."'

Agastya broke off suddenly as the sheet of paper was rudely snatched from his hand and floated away from him, through the air, seemingly by itself.

'Whoa! What's happening?' Arjun asked, puzzled.

'We're not alone,' Maya said quietly. She was looking straight at the sheet of paper, which was making its way into the living room and out of the front door.

Chapter One Hundred and Ten

Confrontation

Outside Maya's House

Vishwaraj listened intently to the conversation that was in progress inside the house. It seemed that the children had discovered something. Inscriptions, from the sound of it.

Vishwaraj paid close attention. A tingle ran down his spine as he heard the words being read aloud. He knew about Tribhuvan. It seemed that Maharishi Dhruv had somehow come into possession of an ancient document, dating back almost to the early days of the Sangha.

Vishwaraj immediately realised that it was an important document. He had to get his hands on it. But Shukra had told him only to spy on the children.

There was one way, though, that he could get the sheet of paper out of their hands. He was invisible after all. All he had to do was enter the house and make away with the inscriptions.

It would be easy.

Slowly, carefully, he tested the door handle.

It was unlocked.

Good.

He twisted the handle and the door opened silently. Thankfully, the hinges were oiled, even though the house had not been maintained for almost a year.

Vishwaraj walked into the house. He calmly grabbed the sheet of paper from Agastya's hands and headed towards the front door.

The Study

'*Virachayati kavach!*'

Even as Maya spoke, Arjun was sheathed in his armour and his new sword appeared in his hand, gleaming brightly in the light of the globes that floated overhead.

Agastya's brahmadanda appeared in his grasp.

Maya too summoned her brahmadanda. She caught Agastya's look of surprise, but she was beyond caring. She was anyway out of the Sangha. And she was not going to just stand by and watch.

To Maya's surprise, she could see the intruder. Although, she was the only who could. She had watched, stunned, as Vishwaraj walked in and grabbed the sheet from Agastya, and then turned to leave. It was only when he had almost reached the front door that she had recovered her composure and revealed his presence to the others.

'*Lochanagocharamya!*' Agastya yelled, brandishing his brahmadanda, breaking through the illusion surrounding Vishwaraj and rendering him visible.

Vishwaraj realised that the group could see him now. Whoever this young Rishi was, he was well trained.

He pivoted to face them.

'I was trying to leave without harming any of you,' he said coldly. 'Why did you have to do this?'

As Vishwaraj turned towards Agastya, Maya gestured to Amyra. 'Take cover!' she whispered. The younger girl nodded and hid behind the desk in the study, trembling.

'You're Vishwaraj, aren't you?' Maya asked the young man, drawing his attention back to herself.

Vishwaraj smirked. 'I see you know who I am. Then you should fear me. Don't try to stop me and I will reciprocate by letting you all live.'

Arjun advanced a few steps. 'You're not leaving with those inscriptions.'

'Arjun,' Maya said softly. 'Let him go. Let it be. It isn't worth it.'

'Arjun,' Agastya said in a beseeching tone. 'She's right. Listen to her. Back down.'

But Arjun was in no mood to listen. If the inscriptions had been written by the very first Mahamatra of the Sangha, they had to be important. Even though they had stumbled upon it quite by chance, the discovery vindicated their decision to leave the Gurukul without permission and come here tonight. More importantly, while it was definitely of use to the Sangha, it represented their only chance to have Maya reinstated. After all, this had been her idea.

There was no way he was going to allow Vishwaraj to walk away with a document that was so important to them all. There was a cold fear deep within his heart, and he trembled internally with an unknown dread, yet he stood there, steady in his resolve, determined to fight.

No matter what it took.

'Give that paper back,' he demanded.

Agastya moved forward to stand with Arjun.

Maya realised what he was doing. Agastya was Arjun's Rishi partner. If Arjun had decided to be aggressive, then Agastya was going to be by his side.

The die had been cast.

Maya stepped forward and joined them.

Agastya gave her a sideways glance. 'Hide, Maya,' he whispered. 'You cannot fight him.'

Maya realised the truth of his words, but she could not leave Arjun and hide like a coward. He was her childhood friend and she would do whatever she could to protect him. She was hoping the sight of her brahmadanda—and the fact that there seemed to be two Rishis against one—would make Vishwaraj reconsider.

Would her bluff succeed?

Chapter One Hundred and Eleven

Shock!

Maya's House

'I know you,' Vishwaraj told Arjun. 'Poorvapitamah told me about you. You're the One, aren't you?' he sneered. 'They were grooming me to partner with you. That's what I was told. But I guess I've left you way behind, haven't I?'

Maya didn't like Vishwaraj's tone. It was condescending and indifferent.

Like he didn't care. He didn't seem to be bothered that he was outnumbered.

His next words confirmed her fears.

'Two Rishis with brahmadandas against one,' Vishwaraj mused. 'Not fair, huh? Shall we lessen the odds?' His own brahmadanda appeared and he planted it firmly on the ground. '*Pavanaghata pratisphurati!*'

He pointed at Maya and to her shock and horror, a strong gust of wind blew her brahmadanda clean out of her hand. It flew through the air and fell clattering to the floor after smashing into the bookcases at the far end of the study.

'So,' Vishwaraj smirked. 'Quite the fraud, aren't you? Where did you get a brahmadanda from if you don't know how to use it? Stole it, huh?'

Maya should have felt embarrassed at being openly ridiculed for her lack of powers, but she was too terrified right now to feel any other emotion.

What was Vishwaraj going to do? Was he going to kill her?

But Vishwaraj had already decided not to waste any more time on her. He turned his attention to Agastya. 'So you're my replacement, huh? Let's see if you're any good with that.'

Before any of them could react, he was spewing mantras.

'*Banavrishti praharati! Agnichakra pariveshtyati!*'

A shower of arrows appeared out of nowhere and streaked at lightning speed towards Arjun, followed immediately by a circle of fire that surrounded both the boys.

Maya screamed as the flames licked her arm. Arjun turned and pushed her away from the flames, sending her crashing to the ground.

But Agastya was lightning quick. He stepped in front of Arjun, his brahmadanda held aloft. The arrows disappeared before they could reach their target. Even as he moved, he uttered '*Samastrnute!*' and the circle of fire was immediately extinguished.

But Vishwaraj was not done yet.

'*Vidyutprapatana praharati!*' he intoned and a bolt of lightning shot its way towards Arjun.

Once again, Agastya stepped forward and his brahmadanda absorbed the attack.

Maya watched, fascinated, despite her terror and fear for Arjun's safety, as Agastya effortlessly wielded the brahmadanda. If there was anything that could protect them today, it was this.

She noticed that Agastya did not launch a counter attack, hoping that his defence would convince Vishwaraj to leave them alone. Perhaps he knew that in a direct confrontation with Vishwaraj, the young Rishi who had gone over to Shukra would prevail. Agastya had seen him in action during the siege of the Gurukul and had watched as the young apostate had demolished the defences of the Gurukul to allow the Nagas through. He knew he was no match for Vishwaraj.

'Impressive,' Vishwaraj said, 'but still below par, my friend. You have much to learn before you can effectively defend the scion of Yayati. Oh, by the way, did you know that I too am a scion of Yayati?'

His face grew serious. 'I'm done playing games,' he said. 'I warned you. I gave you the option to save yourselves. I had promised Poorvapitamah that I would not hurt you if I could help it. But you took it upon yourselves to provoke me.' He pointed at Arjun. 'You, scion of Yayati, I concede you are brave. We are cousins after all. But if you are no match for me, how do you expect to stop the all-powerful Son of Bhrigu? I think I need to put you in your place. And we have witnesses. How nice. They can go back and tell the rest of the Sangha about how "the One" could not stand up to young Vishwaraj, let alone defeat the great Shukracharya!'

Arjun's eyes widened with fear and Agastya immediately stepped in front of him to protect him.

Vishwaraj pointed at Agastya. '*Apasaarayati!*'

Agastya had raised his brahmadanda in defence, but to no avail. He went flying to one side, ending up in a heap on the floor.

He lay there, watching in horror at the scene that unfolded before his eyes.

In a fraction of a second, it was all over.

Chapter One Hundred and Twelve

No!

Maya's House

Arjun's blood ran cold as he heard Vishwaraj's threat and saw Agastya flung away from him, helpless as a leaf caught in a strong gust of wind.

Time seemed to stop as he looked into Vishwaraj's eyes and saw his intention there.

There was only one thing Arjun could do. It was the only thing that was left in his control.

Futile, perhaps, but still in his control.

Raising his sword above his head, he charged at Vishwaraj with a warcry.

Vishwaraj stood unmoving and chanted in a calm voice: 'Mahamaya prajvalati. Vadabamukha!'

Arjun didn't recognise the mantra but he felt an unbearable heat suddenly pour out of every pore in his body, mere milliseconds before his body spontaneously burst into flames. He cried out in anguish for one brief moment before collapsing to the ground.

Vishwaraj glanced at him once, then turned and walked out of the house, carrying the inscriptions with him. The others didn't deserve his attention. But he had finally delivered his ancestor from the threat that had been hanging over his head. Not that it had turned out to be much of a threat. But at least it didn't exist any more.

The One was dead.

Inside the house, Agastya scrambled to his feet. He had recognised the mantra that Vishwaraj had invoked. It was a very difficult mantra to master, combining the power of illusion with the power of igniting fire.

Everything had happened so fast that by the time Agastya got to his feet, Arjun was already engulfed in flames. And, in any case, he did not know the mantra that could counter the one Vishwaraj had used.

He knew there was nothing he could do to help Arjun.

From the other side of the room, Maya rushed towards Arjun, but the the flames were too strong to allow her to get close.

Amyra crept out of the shelter of the desk, also in a state of shock.

'Isn't there something we can do?' Maya pleaded, tears streaming down her face as she looked at Agastya, who was on the verge of tears himself. 'Please, Ags, do something! How can we save him?'

Agastya shook his head numbly. The mantra was a powerful one. Everyone present could see Arjun burning, including Arjun himself. It was an illusion, there were no flames in reality, but Arjun would die believing that he was, indeed, alight. He would feel the pain of being burnt alive. Even his armour would not be able to protect him from the illusion.

And all three of them—Maya, Amyra and Agastya—would watch Arjun burn alive.

It was over in a matter of seconds. The fire had disappeared and all that was left of Arjun, to their eyes, were ashes on the floor of the study.

And his sword, which had clattered to the floor when he collapsed.

Chapter One Hundred and Thirteen

Grief

Maya's House

Maya sat next to Arjun's ashes and wept bitterly, her body racked by huge sobs.

'It's all my fault!' she wailed. 'All my fault. I asked him to come with me. If I had left the Gurukul by myself, this would never have happened!' She buried her face in her hands and bawled her heart out. Her closest friend, the only one she considered family, the only one she had trusted after her father's passing, was dead.

And it was all because of her.

Agastya sat in silence. He had his own demons to battle. When it had come to the crunch, he had failed. There was no way a Kshatriya like Arjun could have taken on a Rishi like Vishwaraj, who was so much more powerful than any of them could have believed. More powerful than any member of the Sangha, in fact. Vishwaraj had not merely created an illusion of fire. He had summoned *Vadabamukha*, the powerful fire that resided under the ocean, making it a part of the illusion. It was this melding of *Vadabamukha* with the illusion that made the mantra he had used so deadly. The resulting blaze was both real and unreal at the same time. A power that no one alive could wield. Except Vishwaraj, as they had witnessed today.

Amyra sat in stunned silence, unable to believe what had just happened. It seemed so unreal, so unfair. It was difficult to believe that the One, the boy whom she had looked up to ever since he entered the Gurukul almost a year ago, had been reduced to a pile of ashes.

For an hour or so, they sat around the ashes, struggling to come to terms with their loss.

Maya's tears seemed to dry up at last and she just sat there, staring into the distance, saying nothing.

At length, Agastya came and sat next to Maya. 'We need to get help,' he told her. 'We need to get out of the house.'

Maya shook her head. 'No,' she said. 'We can't leave without his ashes. We'll take them with us.'

'We can't,' Agastya replied. 'We're part of the illusion.' He explained what Vishwaraj had done, the mantra he had used, and its effect on Arjun and the three of them.

'So you see,' he concluded, 'we can't see anything but ashes, whereas, in reality, Arjun's body is lying right here. As long as the illusion is in our heads, we will see nothing but his ashes, even if we know it is an illusion. But if we can get someone else to come here, someone who has not been subject to the mantra, they will see Arjun and not the ashes and can help us take his body from here.'

Maya started sobbing again at the reference to Arjun as a corpse and not a living person.

'We need to hurry,' Agastya said gently. 'Soon, it will be dawn and the neighbours will begin stirring. We can't afford to have anyone find us here with Arjun like this. It will compromise the Sangha.'

Maya nodded and wiped her tears. 'Maharishi Ratan ... I will go and fetch him,' she said. 'I know where he lives.'

'We'll stay here till you return,' Agastya said. 'Come back quickly. Time is running out for us.'

Chapter One Hundred and Fourteen

Help Please!

Ratan Tiwari's House
New Delhi

Maya stood outside Ratan Tiwari's door and rang the bell. There was no response. She rang the bell again.

She heard footsteps approaching.

The door opened a crack and Tiwari's sleepy face appeared. His eyes widened and all traces of sleep vanished when he saw Maya standing there.

'Maya! What are you doing here?'

The door was flung open and Maya rushed in and started sobbing again.

'Now, now,' Tiwari said comfortingly as he led her to the sitting room and made her sit down. 'What's the matter? What happened?'

Megha, Tiwari's wife, came bustling into the room, wearing a floral nightgown. 'My goodness!' she exclaimed, shocked to see Maya with her dishevelled hair and tear-stained face. 'What happened to you, child?'

In between sobs, Maya narrated the entire tale to Tiwari and Megha. She told them about her ill-advised adventure in the Dandaka forest, her expulsion from the Gurukul and their unfortunate expedition to her old house in Delhi, concluding with a summary of the one-sided battle with Vishwaraj.

There was silence when she finished. Tiwari and Megha were aware of Maya's expulsion from the Gurukul. But the chilling encounter with Vishwaraj came as a shock.

'Dear God,' Megha breathed, 'I cannot fathom what you have been through.' She looked at Tiwari. 'Ratan, you'd better go with her.'

Tiwari nodded. 'Give me five minutes,' he told Maya.

Exactly five minutes later, he was dressed and ready. 'Will you take us there?' he asked Maya. 'It will be faster than driving.'

Maya nodded, and in a matter of moments, they were standing outside her house.

Tiwari hurried in and stopped short on seeing Arjun's body on the floor. Despite knowing what had happened, the sight of the One of the prophecy lying lifeless on the ground shook him.

He knew he had to first rid the three children of the illusion that they had been subjected to.

'Stand before me,' he instructed them, then intoned, 'Nirvyajikrta bhavati.'

Instantly, a film seemed to lift from Maya's eyes and she saw Arjun lying there, his eyes closed, his visage peaceful.

'Help me,' Tiwari said. 'We have to carry Arjun outside and lock the house behind us. If we leave it open, there could be trouble. As long as it's locked, no one will bother. Maya, will you take us all back to my house?'

Maya nodded and the three children helped Tiwari carry Arjun out of the house. The door had a self-locking mechanism, which Tiwari activated. It would be enough to secure the house for now.

Soon they were back in Tiwari's house. Knowing they were out of immediate danger, and exhausted after all that had transpired, the small group felt quite overwhelmed in this very normal setting. Amyra shed silent tears while Agastya barely spoke a word. Tiwari realised the only way to help them out of their daze was to lay out a plan.

'I know this is hard to think about, but we will need to take Arjun back to the Gurukul,' he said. 'The Sangha Council needs to know about all that happened and they will decide where the last rites will be conducted.' He placed a comforting hand on Maya's arm as she broke down again, at the mention of last rites. 'Will you take us there, Maya?'

'I will,' Maya said, 'but I will not stay. I will transport you all there and leave. I cannot stay at the Gurukul. Not just because they have expelled me. I cannot bear the thought of seeing Arjun like … like this.'

'Where will you go, child?' Megha asked. 'Why don't you come back here? In any case, the Sangha had wanted you to come to us in Delhi. We've been appointed your local guardians, after all.'

'Thank you,' Maya replied, grateful to have somewhere to stay. 'I will come back here.'

Where else could she go? Who else did she have left in this world?

'Let's go then.' Tiwari nodded to the three children.

Chapter One Hundred and Fifteen

Farewell to Arjun

The Gurukul

The eastern sky was beginning to banish the darkness and a pre-dawn glow was spreading across the horizon as Tiwari and the three children, carrying Arjun's body, appeared in front of the Assembly Hall.

'This is where I say goodbye.' Maya's voice was lifeless and dull, as if something or someone had crept up in the night and robbed it of all zest and cheer.

And life.

Tiwari nodded. 'I'll see you back in Delhi in a few days,' he said.

Amyra stepped forward and gave Maya a big, warm hug. She knew how close Maya and Arjun had been and sensed, rather than knew, the extent of her loss. Moreover, Amyra could see that Maya still held herself responsible for Arjun's death.

'Take care, Maya,' she whispered. 'I hope we will meet again.'

Maya returned her embrace wordlessly and shook hands with Agastya, who returned the handshake silently. He hadn't spoken much since the events of the night. The trauma was still etched in his eyes.

Ratan Tiwari's House
New Delhi

'Okay,' Megha said to Maya, 'you go straight to bed and try and get some rest. You've been through a lot and I'm sure you want to be alone right now.' She smiled at Maya and led her to the guest bedroom.

Maya was grateful for the solitude and Megha's kindness. But sleep would not come to her. She felt like she had lost a part of herself. Like something inside her was missing. And she knew it would never come back.

How would she cope for the rest of her life, knowing that she had led her dearest friend to his death?

Maya knew that Time was a great healer. At least, that was what everyone said. But Time could not take away the sense of loss; it only made it easier to cope with it. She had only just begun to come to terms with her father's death. And now she had one more loss to bear.

She didn't want to use the *shantaa kaaram* mantra to calm herself down and fall asleep. She didn't think she deserved the peace and rest that the mantra would give her.

She sat lost in thought until the sun had risen in the east.

This was what life was going to be like for her, she reflected. There would be no peace for some time. Maybe forever.

Finally, out of sheer exhaustion, she fell asleep.

Chapter One Hundred and Sixteen

Maya Gets an Idea

Ratan Tiwari's House

Maya awoke with a start. The curtains were drawn and the room was in darkness, but she was sure she had slept much of the morning away since she had fallen asleep only after sunrise.

She slid out of bed and pulled the curtains apart, allowing the bright sunshine to stream into the room, flooding it with light and dispelling the darkness. For just a few moments, the memory of what had happened the previous night stayed away from her.

Then it hit her with full force. The image of Arjun going up in flames, the horrified faces of Agastya and Amyra, her own helplessness at being unable to save her friend; it all came flooding back, along with the guilt, the remorse and the self-flagellation.

But she also realised what had woken her up.

She had been dreaming.

It had been an amazing dream. It had featured her father, the Devas, who were building a strange wall, and a sheet of black paper with white inscriptions on it. It was when she came to the part where she was speaking with her father that the words hit home. Her father was telling her a story about Shukra, going back thousands of years, and something that Shukra had said or done then. It was a story from the Mahabharata.

Maya struggled to recollect what it was that had struck her during the dream and had caused her to wake up so abruptly.

What had her father said to her?

And why had it roused her from sleep?

Still thinking, she went into the bathroom to brush her teeth.

It was then that she remembered.

In no time at all, Maya had finished washing her face, showered and donned the fresh clothes that Megha had thoughtfully laid out for her. Then, emerging from her room, she looked for Megha. She couldn't leave without letting her know. She found Megha sitting with her laptop, working in the living room.

'You're up! Let me whip up something for you to eat, child,' Megha said.

But Maya could not stop for food. She knew she was running out of time. She had to leave now. She bid a hasty goodbye to Megha and before the woman could react, she was back in her room and shutting the door.

Then she vanished.

The Gurukul
Panna National Park

The residents of the Gurukul had gathered in mourning, outside the Assembly Hall. Arjun's body lay within, as the Mahamatis discussed the arrangements for his funeral.

Kanakpratap's face was black as thunder. When Arjun had left with Maya and the others last night, he had thought he would only have to explain to the Mahamati Council about Arjun's sudden departure and convince them to wait until the children returned to see what they had accomplished.

Little had he known that, before the night was through, before the Council had a chance to question him, his nephew would return. But not in the manner he had expected.

He didn't blame anyone, least of all Maya. Agastya and Amyra had given a full account of all that had transpired in Maya's house last night. Even though Jignesh had felt that Maya should not have asked Arjun to accompany her, he had agreed with the others that it would be unfair to blame the children in any way. They could not have been expected to stand up to Vishwaraj. Agastya's graphic description of the manner in which Vishwaraj had attacked them had convinced the Council that, in addition to his existing strength in the siddhis, Vishwaraj's powers had been enhanced by Shukra's mentoring. They had already witnessed his extraordinary abilities during the siege of the Gurukul by the Nagas almost a year ago.

'He died bravely,' Kanakpratap said finally, when the analysis and discussion were done. 'Like a true Kshatriya, he did not flee when the odds were stacked against him. He attacked with his last breath. I am proud of him.'

But that did not change the fact that Arjun was dead.

And the Sangha had lost the One who was destined to lead them against Shukra.

Chapter One Hundred and Seventeen

Maya Confides

Satyavachana's Cottage

Maya appeared in front of the cottage, having transported herself from Tiwari's guest room in Delhi. Satyavachana's dog, Maharaja, who had grown to recognise Maya, barked happily on seeing her. She stroked his head gently and ruffled his fur before knocking on the door.

She heard the Maharishi approaching the door.

He threw it open and stared at her in surprise. 'Maya! What are you doing here?'

'I need your help, Mahamati.'

'Of course, child. Tell me what I can do for you. Does the Sangha know you are here? You were supposed to be in Delhi!'

Maya told him everything. But this time, she did not break down. A hard lump seemed to have formed deep within her; a cold knot that seemed to have soaked up all her emotion. It allowed her to think more clearly. She needed to, if she was to carry out her plan effectively.

Satyavachana shook his head when she finished. 'A great tragedy,' he said. 'I don't blame you for going there. But I wish you had told me. I would have come with you. You know that.'

Maya nodded. But there was no time for regrets.

She told Satyavachana what she planned to do.

The Maharishi's bushy white eyebrows shot up in surprise as he listened to her.

'Audacious,' he said when he had heard her out. 'Audacious. No other word describes what you wish to do. It has never been attempted in the history of the Sangha. Child, you want to play with fire. Are you sure you really want to do this?'

'I see no other way, Mahamati.'

Satyavachana nodded. 'Yes, of course. Given what you want to accomplish, there is no other way. But there is also no guarantee that you will succeed.'

'I have to try, Mahamati. There are no guarantees in life. You have taught me that. You have also taught me that if I want to achieve something, I have to take the initiative.'

'Yes, child, but what you plan to do is not what I had in mind when I said that. Your plan is downright dangerous.'

Maya shook her head. 'No, it isn't,' she said stubbornly. 'We all know the story, Mahamati. And it does not involve a teenage girl in any way. So I know I will be able to do it.'

Satyavachana sighed. 'I know I cannot dissuade you, child. You are obstinate. That can be a strength, but I hope in this case it will not be a weakness for you.' He looked at her. 'You are sure you will be able to remember the mantra?'

'Yes, Mahamati. I am confident.'

'Then will you accept one piece of advice from me? It does not involve abandoning your idea. But it will help you accomplish your purpose.'

'I always value your lessons, Mahamati. There is no one in this world that I trust more.'

'Good. In that case, travel in your atmic form, not your physical form. You have learnt by now to cloak your thoughts so no one can sense them. I have also taught you to disguise your atma so no one can detect it. I have tested you, and you were able to hide your atma from my eyes every single time. If you go in your physical form, you are doomed to fail. But if you travel as an atma, there is a chance you might succeed.'

Maya recognised the wisdom in his words and nodded. 'I will do that, Mahamati. But can you please go to the Gurukul and manage things there while I travel? You're the only one they will listen to.'

'I will. But hurry back, Maya. There is a limit to how long even I can hold them off without an explanation.'

'Maharishi Ratan will understand, Mahamati. And so will Arjun's uncle. I am fine with your sharing my plan with them. But no one else.'

Satyavachana bowed. 'Your wish is my command.' But his tone was not mocking. He looked at her, his expression grave. 'Take care, my child. I want to see you back unharmed.' He shook his head. 'Only you could have come up such an idea. But I will say this: if there is anyone who can pull it off, it is you, Maya. I always believed in you and I still do, no matter what the Sangha says. But be careful.'

'I will, Mahamati. Thank you so much!' She bowed, her palms folded in a namaskar.

'Come inside the cottage. You can leave your body here while you travel. Maharaja will ensure that no one disturbs you. I will leave him loose to prowl around outside. He is very fond of you anyway, so he will not stray too far from your side.'

With these words, Satyavachana vanished.

Maya looked at Maharaja, who stood beside her, gazing at her affectionately, his tongue lolling out. 'Maharaja,' she said softly, 'watch over me, won't you?'

The dog wagged his tail happily and barked. Maya took that as a yes and went inside the cottage.

She lay down on the rough wooden platform that she had noticed on her first visit here as an atma.

Satyavachana had been right. What she was attempting to do was almost unthinkable. But it was the only way she could atone for her mistake. She had been responsible for Arjun's death. And this was the only way she could make it up to him. She knew the risks. But she was going to do it.

Maya uttered the *shaanta kaaram* mantra and closed her eyes. Soon, she was in a deep sleep.

Her atma emerged from her body and rose into the air, passing through the walls of the cottage to the forest outside. Maharaja stared at her atma and barked at it, then whined. He much preferred her when she could pet him and play with him.

Then Maya rose above the treetops and was gone.

Chapter One Hundred and Eighteen

The Journey

Beyond Tapovan
Uttarakhand

Maya hovered above the glacier, at the exact spot where Satyavachana and she had stood two weeks ago.

Without another thought, she dived into the glacier. This time, she didn't need a mantra to dissolve her physical form in the ice. As an atma, she could travel freely through the ice at top speed.

She focused her thoughts on the Mists of Brahma and, in an instant, had reached the spot where the glacier met the Mists.

Emerging from the ice, she found herself surrounded by the familiar white fog, but it was very different now that she was in her atmic form.

For one thing, she could see in all directions and right through the fog as well. Maya realised that the fog was absolute. It was not a screen, concealing events and periods of time behind it, as she had erroneously believed on her last visit here. All that existed here were the Mists. Nothing else.

For another, the manner in which the Mists interacted with her atma was entirely different. In her physical form, she had felt the tendrils swarming over her consciousness, trying to extract thoughts from deep within. As an atma, she felt the Mists attempting to merge with her consciousness, but in a more subservient manner. The power of the atma, she realised, was something that even the Mists recognised. Maya herself had come to appreciate, if not entirely understand, the power within each human, sadh or otherwise. She knew now that sadhs remained the way they were because they either refused to tap into their inner power or were simply ignorant of it.

But there was no time for reflections like these.

Maya expanded her consciousness, seeking the oneness with the universe that Satyavachana had taught her to achieve. It was easier to do this as an atma, she knew, without the constraints and emotions associated with her physical mind.

It wasn't long before she felt the connection, and her consciousness expanded in a manner that she recognised from the innumerable practice sessions with Satyavachana. It was a curious yet comforting feeling, losing herself in the vast expanse of the universe, while being aware that she was much bigger than just an individual soul on a journey of rebirths.

One last thing. She had to cloak her thoughts and make her atma invisible even to the eyes of the most powerful yogi.

For she was about to meet one of the most powerful yogis to have ever lived.

Now settled with her thoughts, cloaked and invisible, Maya turned her attention to her objective, the purpose for which she was here.

The Mists immediately sensed her desire and made way for her, directing her consciousness to the place and time that she sought.

The white fog around her began to thin and fade and Maya knew that she was approaching her destination.

She floated along until the scene began to unfold before her.

Maya had heard her father narrate the story from the Mahabharata many times before, but seeing it actually play out before her was an entirely different experience.

Chapter One Hundred and Nineteen

Waiting for Maya

The Gurukul
Panna National Park

'We have to leave now,' Jignesh told Satyavachana. 'In a few hours, the sun will go down and it will be too late to reach the cremation grounds. We cannot wait any longer. We have humoured you so far and acceded to your request to wait, but I must ask, why are we waiting? What are we waiting for?'

'Mahamatra,' Kanakpratap spoke up. He had been briefed by Satyavachana as Maya had requested. 'Just a while longer. It is my responsibility to get my nephew's mortal remains to the funeral pyre in time.' He wished Yajnaseni was here, but there was no way of getting word to her in the Gandharva valley in time. He thought of how protective she had always been of Arjun and it saddened him to think she wasn't here right now, to attend to her son's last rites. Kanakpratap knew the news would shatter her.

Jignesh sighed impatiently. He didn't understand why Tiwari, Satyavachana and Kanakpratap were so keen to wait until the very last minute.

'Very well,' he said. 'Half an hour. And no more.'

Kanakpratap nodded and joined Satyavachana and Tiwari in a discussion conducted in hushed voices.

The entire community was waiting. Classes had been suspended for the day. Arjun had become quite popular in the months he had spent at the Gurukul and, of course, everyone knew that he was the One of the prophecy. The students and Mahamatis alike had turned out to bid him goodbye. Only, no one knew why they were lingering instead of proceeding for the funeral as originally planned. The Mahamati Council—or what remained of it at the Gurukul, with two members still in the Gandharva valley—had not shared any information other than the announcement that the departure of the funeral cortege had been delayed for a while.

The minutes ticked by. Satyavachana looked around, an anxious look on his face. His concern was less for whether Maya's plan had succeeded and more for her safe return from the Mists. Despite the abilities she had demonstrated, she was no Rishi and she was attempting a very dangerous manoeuvre. Not since the time that the Sangha had been originally set up had Maharishis travelled through the Mists with a purpose similar to Maya's today. And he had never heard of an instance when anyone had entered the Mists as an atma. The sole reason why Satyavachana had suggested it was because it was the only way Maya could accomplish her objective undetected.

'It's time,' Tiwari said despondently, looking at his watch. 'We cannot hold on any longer.'

As if on cue, Jignesh came up to them. 'Well?' he said, looking at each of the three men in turn.

Satyavachana shrugged. 'It seems that our expectations have not come to pass,' he said cryptically. 'You may proceed.'

Jignesh turned on his heel and stalked away, issuing instructions to the Mahamatis to begin preparations.

The three men looked at each other, the same question foremost in their minds.

What had happened to Maya?

Chapter One Hundred and Twenty

A While Longer

The Gurukul

It did not take more than fifteen minutes or so for the preparations for the funeral cortege to be finalised. Most of the work had already been done while they were waiting and all that was required was to put things together once Jignesh gave the permission to proceed.

With Jignesh at their head, a procession of Mahamatis moved up the stairs that led to the Assembly Hall, chanting mantras and prayers as they walked.

Suddenly, a ripple ran through the crowd.

The procession stopped. The chanting ceased. Silence fell over the gathering.

Maya had suddenly materialised out of nowhere and was standing at the doorway to the Assembly Hall. She was pale and looked exhausted.

But she was here.

Satyavachana swiftly pushed through the Mahamatis and made his way up the stairs to where Maya stood, followed closely by Kanakpratap and Tiwari.

'Maya!' Satyavachana breathed as he reached her. 'Are you okay?'

Maya nodded, swaying slightly. Kanakpratap caught her and steadied her.

'Did you get it?' Tiwari wanted to know.

'Yes, Ratan,' Maya replied with the shadow of a smile. 'I got it.' She looked at Satyavachana and smiled at him. 'I did it, Mahamati. I succeeded.'

'I knew you would do it,' the Maharishi told her quietly. He looked at the other two men. 'We have to stand back. She must do this by herself.'

Jignesh came up, scowling. 'What's going on here?' he demanded. 'What is *she* doing here? We need to move quickly!'

Satyavachana held out a hand. 'We have waited so long,' he told Jignesh calmly, 'a while longer will not hurt. We were waiting for Maya. Now, we must allow her to do what she needs to do. And, for the good of the Sangha, let us hope that her plan works!'

Jignesh's face darkened, but he didn't try to stop Maya as she entered the Assembly Hall and shut the door behind her. 'I demand an explanation,' he told Satyavachana, his voice hard. He looked at Tiwari and Kanakpratap. 'The Maharishi is not a member of the Sangha, having renounced it of his own will. But you both are. Whatever the three of you have been conspiring about, it is time that you told me. I have been patient for far too long. Do not test me any further!'

Tiwari nodded and looked at Kanakpratap, who nodded back. 'As you wish, Mahamatra,' he said. 'We will tell you everything.'

Chapter One Hundred and Twenty-one

Maya's Test

Inside the Assembly Hall

Maya shut the door of the hall and slowly walked to the centre, where Arjun's body lay on a makeshift platform. For a few moments, she stood and gazed at his face. He looked peaceful.

Was it worth doing what she was about to do next?

But she had to.

She sat down on the floor next to Arjun and reached into her inner consciousness, becoming one with the universe. Somehow, it was becoming easier for her to do this. Earlier, it took time, there was a bit of a struggle, but over the last two weeks, she had found herself able to do it effortlessly.

Maya threw her mind back to the scene she had witnessed in the Mists. She had carefully memorised the mantra, every word, every syllable, the intonation, the speed. It was critical to get everything absolutely correct.

She began reciting the mantra.

Outside the Assembly Hall

'You can't be serious!' Jignesh declared. 'There's no one in Bhu-lok who can pull this off. There never has been! Not since Shukra!'

'We'll see about that.' Satyavachana's face was grim.

Jignesh shook his head. 'You put too much faith in that girl,' he told the Maharishi.

'So tell me this.' Satyavachana fixed Jignesh with a hard gaze. 'If she does succeed, will you admit her back in the Gurukul?'

Jignesh paused to consider this. 'Yes,' he said finally. 'If she succeeds, she will not only have done the Sangha a big service, but she will also have proved herself to be worthy of the Gurukul once more. It does not exonerate her for her past transgressions, but I will accept her back.'

'Good,' Satyavachana replied. 'There is still a lot that I have to teach her.'

A pall of silence had descended on the gathered assembly. Initially, there had been whispered conversations as the students speculated about what was going on. The message had quickly gone around that Maya had entered the Assembly Hall by herself, but no one knew why.

Suddenly, a loud gasp went up from the crowd and everyone looked at the entrance to the Assembly Hall.

The door of the hall had opened.

Maya walked out slowly, her gait unsteady. Her head hung low and she was dragging her feet.

Satyavachana gazed at her anxiously.

Was she just exhausted?

Or had she succeeded?

Chapter One Hundred and Twenty-two

What Next?

The Assembly Hall

As Maya reached the topmost step of the short stairway that led down from the upper hall, she glanced back.

A murmur went through the crowd.

What was happening?

To the astonishment of everyone gathered there, a second figure emerged from the open door of the hall.

Arjun!

He was alive!

Arjun walked stiffly, blinking as he walked out of the dark interior of the hall into the sunshine outside.

A loud roar went up and the crowd gathered outside burst into applause.

Arjun smiled weakly at the rapturous welcome.

Jignesh looked on, amazed, then he too smiled and started clapping. This was a moment to celebrate. The unthinkable had happened!

No, the impossible had happened.

Arjun had come back from the dead.

Kanakpratap bounded up the stairs and put an arm around Arjun, even as Tiwari rushed to Maya's side. Both children looked like they were ready to collapse.

Then Arjun held up a hand, requesting the crowd to quieten down.

There was pin drop silence.

'*Prapanchayati!*' Tiwari intoned, as he realised Arjun wanted to address the crowd.

'Thank you all,' Arjun said, his voice amplified by the mantra to the gathering below. He looked up at the sun, then at the trees, and the crowd assembled in front of the hall. 'I can't tell you all how great it feels to be alive. But more than me, you should be applauding Maya. If not for her, I would not be standing here before you.'

He took Maya's hand and raised it high. 'Thank you, Maya,' he said. 'I owe you my life. Literally.'

Maya smiled wanly as the assembled crowd clapped enthusiastically. They didn't know what Maya had done or what had happened. But if Arjun was saying it, it must be true.

'Let's get you two to the Bhishajs,' Kanakpratap said. 'They will nurse both of you back to health in no time.'

Chapter One Hundred and Twenty-three

Maya's Story

Three Days Later

The Hospital
The Gurukul
Panna National Park

Loud peals of laughter floated to the ears of Satyavachana, Kanakpratap and Tiwari as they approached the room where Arjun and Maya were waiting to meet them.

'The children got here before we did,' Tiwari smiled.

Agastya and Amyra had come to meet their friends as soon as they heard that they were allowed visitors. Until now, they had been kept in isolation to allow them to recover properly.

The three men stood at the door and watched the children double up with laughter as one joke after another was cracked.

'So,' Arjun said, tearing up with mirth, 'Maya was diagnosed as having low energy, low blood pressure, some kind of chemical imbalance and severe exhaustion, bordering on a breakdown.' He chuckled. 'See, I got it down pat. But that's not the reason they weren't allowing her visitors. She was just plain grouchy!'

There was another round of laughter.

'And Arjun had been … well, Arjun had been dead for quite a while, so they wanted to ensure that he was really alive before they allowed anyone near him,' Maya retorted as the others convulsed with laughter.

Satyavachana cleared his throat and the laughter subsided.

'Can we come in?' the Maharishi asked, a twinkle in his eye.

'Come in, come in!' Maya waved the three men in. 'Join us!'

Agastya and Amyra quickly fetched three additional chairs from elsewhere in the cottage and the three men sat down.

'I'm not going to ask how you both are feeling,' Tiwari smiled, 'because the answer is pretty obvious.'

Arjun laughed. 'I'm fine! Never felt better in my life. Thanks to Dr Maya!'

Laughter followed again.

'I wanted to know,' Satyavachana looked at Maya, 'what happened in the Mists of Brahma. Is this a good time for that story or should I return later?'

'Yes, Maya!' Agastya and Amyra chimed in.

'We also want to hear what happened,' Amyra added with a smile, looking at Satyavachana.

'Very well then,' Satyavachana said, 'that's settled. Tell us.'

Arjun had by now heard the story from Maya a few times, but he too listened with interest.

With a deep breath, Maya began. She told them about gliding through the glacier, arriving at the Mists, and then willing the Mists to lead her to the time, thousands of years ago, when Kacha, the son of Brihaspati, had been accepted by Shukra as his disciple for one thousand years.

'I had read, in the Mahabharata,' Maya said, 'that Kacha had come to Shukra to obtain the knowledge of resurrecting the dead. But when the Asuras learnt that he was the son of Brihaspati, they decided to kill him, to thwart his plans. Thrice they killed him and each time, Shukra resurrected him.'

'So you got the idea that you might be able to learn this art from Shukra.' Agastya smiled. 'Clever. But ambitious. How were you going to get this knowledge? Shukra wasn't going to teach you.'

'"Audacious" is the word I used,' Satyavachana said with a smile. 'Go on, Maya.'

'That's correct,' Maya said. 'That's exactly what I planned to do. There is a common perception that the *Sanjeevani* mantra is all that is required to bring someone back from the dead. I had thought that as well. But when I experienced the entire ritual for myself, I realised that while the mantra was essential— even crucial—it was just one component of the ritual. After watching Shukra resurrect Kacha for the first time, I went back and saw what happened on the next two occasions as well, including the time when the Asuras mixed Kacha's ashes with wine and gave it to Shukra to drink. That was very useful, for that was when Shukra actually taught Kacha the ritual and the mantra and Kacha used the knowledge to bring Shukra back to life after emerging from his body.'

'So, since Shukra was actually teaching Kacha on the last occasion, it was easier for you to follow the instructions,' Kanakpratap said, finally understanding how Maya had carefully planned out the entire thing.

'Yes, Uncle,' Maya replied. 'It was exhausting, but worth it. I was not sure it would work, but then I came back and applied what I had learnt, and well, here we are, with Arjun alive and well!'

'Did Shukra know you were there?' Tiwari asked.

'I don't think so,' Maya said. 'There was a moment, though, on the third occasion, when he was teaching the ritual to Kacha, that I thought he felt something. He stopped midway and looked at where I was standing, but after a pause, he just frowned and continued. I was travelling in my atmic form, as Maharishi Satyavachana had suggested, and I had cloaked my thoughts and concealed my atma. I've been practising this for close to a year now, so I managed to not give my presence away. Otherwise I am sure he would have stopped me.' She shuddered. If Shukra had indeed stopped her, she would have been trapped in the Mists forever.

'There's some good news for you,' Tiwari said to Maya. 'Mahamatra Jignesh has reinstated you in the Gurukul.'

Agastya and Amyra cheered and Arjun sat up, a broad grin on his face at the news.

'He has?' Maya's eyes shone with delight. 'Oh boy, that's the best news I've heard in a long while!' She looked at Satyavachana. 'When do we start our lessons again?'

'As soon as you get out of here!' Satyavachana laughed at her enthusiasm.

'I think we should all leave now,' Kanakpratap stood up. 'These two need to rest!'

Satyavachana smiled and rose. 'Rest well, both of you. There is a lot of work to be done. Shukra thinks he has killed the One. But he doesn't know what Maya has accomplished.

When he does, there will be trouble for sure. And we need to be prepared.'

There was a chorus of goodbyes as the three men, followed by Agastya and Amyra, left the room and made their way out of the hospital.

Arjun looked at Maya. 'Well?' he said. 'The adventure continues, doesn't it?'

'It certainly does.' Maya smiled at him and ruffled his hair. 'See you later, AJ.'

Epilogue

In the Air between Allahabad and Delhi

Kapoor sat back in his seat and stared out of the window at the clouds that stretched away into the distance, looking like a smooth white floor ready to be walked on. How deceptive that was, he thought. Much like the case involving Trivedi and Upadhyay ... no, Srivastava.

After more than eight months, he had finally been able to turn his attention back to the two unsolved cases that he had vowed to crack. He had sent Ajit and Harish to Allahabad a couple of weeks ago to work with Mirza, interviewing people and ferreting out the information that he needed.

Yesterday, he had flown to Allahabad himself for a debriefing. He was now on his way back to Delhi.

He went over the facts in his mind. When they had abandoned the case eight months ago, they had made little headway with information about Vishwaraj, though some interesting facts about Singh and Srivastava had come to light. But not all the new information was edifying. Some of the facts they had uncovered only raised further questions.

One such piece of information had been troubling Kapoor for a long time now: the testimony of the boatman who had said that Srivastava had a son and no daughter.

The team had learned that, a short while before leaving for Delhi, Srivastava and his wife had adopted a baby girl. That could be why the boatman didn't know about her. Maybe Srivastava never spoke to the boatman about his newly adopted daughter. On the other hand, if he had been so garrulous and had liked the boatman so much that he had shared details of his personal life with him, wouldn't it have been natural to share a major development like the adoption of a child? Or had he kept the fact hidden on purpose?

Despite this mystery, there had been other significant gains made by the team, especially regarding the murders in the Singh and Srivastava households.

Kapoor had instructed Ajit and Harish to concentrate on finding out more about these murders. He was sure that there was more to them than met the eye.

And he had been right.

Deeper investigations had unearthed more people who knew either one or both families well, and it emerged that Srivastava's wife and son had been killed at the house of Rudrapratap Singh, the elder brother of Kanakpratap Singh, alias Virender Singh.

What was more, all three victims had been murdered on the same day.

This was no coincidence, Kapoor realised. While police cases had been registered, they had been shelved as unsolved. And, after that, both Singh and Srivastava had disappeared from Allahabad. Most people had thought that they had decided to leave the city to leave their unpleasant memories behind and start life afresh in a new place.

Little did they know, Kapoor mused, that the two men had actually started new lives, with new names and new identities.

And there was one more thing.

Ajit, Harish and Mirza had shown around the police portrait of the suspect from Delhi, who had been seen entering and leaving Srivastava's house around the time of his murder. Quite a few of the people they interviewed had claimed that a man of a similar description—tall, well built and with an eyepatch over his right eye—had met them as well, posing as a news reporter and asking questions about Srivastava and Singh.

Kapoor cursed. They had been in the same city as the suspect eight months ago. It was futile to hope that the man would have hung around all this while, waiting for them to return.

No, the man had clearly been after something. He had probably got it in the meantime and left town.

But Kapoor had tasted blood. The scent of a trail was clearly discernible now and he had left Allahabad after clear instructions to Ajit and Harish to dig deeper.

Where there was smoke, there was fire. And there was a great deal of smoke now.

He was determined to find the fire.

Author's Note

While this is a fantasy and therefore completely fictional, there is much in the book that is based on extant verses in the Mahabharata, the Srimad Bhagavatam, the Bhagavad Gita and the Puranas, as well as some real-world science—you should know me by now! I thought I should help readers understand which parts of the story are products of my imagination, and provide references for the parts which are based on, or sourced from, other texts.

This may also be the appropriate place to mention that all the laghu mantras (i.e. shortened mantras) in this book are completely fictional and invented by me. What is important, though, is that the words in the laghu mantras are not made up at all. They are real, Sanskrit words and the mantras are not a random jumble of Sanskrit words but have a meaning that is directly connected with the result that the mantra is intended to achieve. For more information on laghu mantras, please log into The Quest Club.

The list below is organised by order of appearance in the story, as far as possible. All references to the Mahabharata are based on the M.N. Dutt translation. Here we go…

Vartika: There are very few detailed descriptions of pisachas or any other non-human creatures in the ancient texts. But the Mahabharata has a very clear description of a vartika in the Vana Parva, Chapter 179, Verse 42: *'And facing the sun, the ugly and dreadful looking vartika, having only one leg, one eye and one wing, was seen to vomit blood.'* Of course, everything else about the pisacha, including the way it walks and shrieks, is fictional.

Pratismriti **mantra:** In the Mahabharata, Vana Parva, Chapter 36, Verse 30, Vyasa tells Yudhishthira: *'Accept from me this knowledge called Pratismriti'.* It is this mantra that enables Arjuna to travel for the acquisition of his weapons. In Chapter 37, verses 16–17, Yudhishthira passes on the knowledge of the mantra to Arjuna, who then proceeds to meet Indra: *'having said this, the lord Dharmaraja (Yudhishthira) imparted to him (Arjuna) the knowledge. The elder brother communicated with due rites the knowledge to his heroic brother whose speech, body and mind were all under complete control. He then commanded him to go.'*

Possession of other humans: In this book, Vishwaraj is shown possessing the bodies of Diya and the Akshapatalika. This is not a fictional concept but something that accomplished yogis can achieve. I based this on the description of one of the ten secondary siddhis in Canto 11, Chapter 15 of the Srimad Bhagavatam.

For those readers who may wonder if I am dabbling in the supernatural when Suresh voices his theories about the soul being sucked out of Diya (Chapter 5) and the attempt to suck the soul out of the Akshapatalika found in Vishwaraj's apartment (Chapter 36), allow me to clarify that Suresh's response is not an unusual one. There are a lot of superstitious people who would think exactly like him, even if they have been trained in science. I have attempted to depict Suresh as a normal human being, vulnerable to his beliefs in the face of a phenomenon that cannot be rationally explained. I am not promoting superstition at all, but only being realistic. And, of course, as we know from the book, no souls were sucked out; both Diya and the Akshapatalika were possessed using a siddhi that is clearly explained in the Srimad Bhagavatam, as mentioned above.

The Akshapatalikas and the Shastrakars: There will be more details on these at The Quest Club (in coming times) and in future books. Watch this space!

Karna's kavach: In Chapter 25, the Mahashastrakar says that the Sangha has rediscovered the secret of Karna's kavach or body armour. I should clarify that the armour developed by the Shastrakars of the Sangha is not the same as Karna's armour in one critical respect. What the Mahashastrakar is referring to is not the material that the armour is made of, but the fact that it is a part of the body, just as Karna was born with the armour which literally grew on his body, and which he had to cut away when Indra asked for it (along with his earrings) in the guise of a Brahman. This story is narrated in the Mahabharata, Vana Parva, Chapter 310, Verses 30, 31, 35–38. The material of the armour, however, is a different matter. The Sangha could not possibly have replicated the material that Karna's armour was made of because his armour was made of *amrita*. This fact is clearly explained in the Mahabharata, Vana Parva, Chapter 307, Verse 18 and Chapter 310, Verse 10. It is for this reason that the armour made Karna indestructible, such that Lord Krishna says in the Mahabharata that even He, armed with his Sudarshana Chakra, cannot defeat Karna while he is clad in his armour. This assertion is made in the Drona Parva, Chapter 181, Verse 17.

On a related note, for the curious reader who may question the practicality of the armour emerging from the skin of the Kshatriyas and covering them from head to toe while they are fully clad, I would like to clarify that the armour is a liquid that emerges from the pores of their skins as microdroplets (quite like perspiration) and can, therefore, seep through their clothes. The concept of liquid armour is not far-fetched. It is rooted in scientific fact. There are several materials being experimented with, in laboratories around the world, which are liquid but harden when exposed to the air. There are also materials that can change state (from liquid to solid and back to liquid) under different conditions. I was inspired by the fact that Karna's armour was made from amrita (which is also a liquid) and used that knowledge, along with recent scientific advances in materials, to create a fictional liquid armour that emerges from the body, seeps through the clothes and then solidifies or hardens to protect the Kshatriyas. More on the armour at The Quest Club.

Mention of Visvavasu in the Mahabharata: In Chapter 26, Kanakpratap informs Arjun that Visvavasu is thousands of years old and is mentioned in the Mahabharata. While his name comes up in several places in the epic, I am listing only a few where he is specifically referred to as the leader or king of the Gandharvas: Shalya Parva, Chapter 37, Verse 10; Shanti Parva, Chapter 29, Verse 76 (where he is described as the 'great Gandharva'), Chapter 318, Verses 31, 36, 84; Adi Parva, Chapter 8, Verse 5.

Yayati and Devyani: In this book I have revealed that Vishwaraj was a descendant of Shukra through his daughter Devyani, who was married to Yayati, thus making Vishwaraj a scion of Yayati. For more information on Yayati and Devyani, please see the Mahabharata, Adi Parva, Chapter 75, 78, 81.

Brahmadanda: This is mentioned (but never described in detail) in the story of Vashishta and Vishwamitra, which is narrated in the Valmiki Ramayana, Bālakānda, Chapter 56.

Bhimbetka: A large complex of naturally occurring caves near Bhopal in Madhya Pradesh. Please log into The Quest Club for a detailed photo tour of the parts open to the public, from my visit to Bhimbetka.

Mantras used in the Battle of Bhimbetka: These are all real mantras.

Allahabad: All locations in Allahabad, like the Lete Hanumanji ka mandir and Company Bagh, are real locations.

Imran Kidwai and his call to Kapoor: For those who have read The Mahabharata Quest series, Imran Kidwai is a familiar name. I want to clarify that I was just having a bit of fun while writing this book and thought I'd mention him in passing. There is no plan to make the two series converge in any way.

David Tennant and Doctor Who: 'Doctor Who' is a popular and long running (more than 50 years old) British serial. David Tennant is a Scottish actor who plays the tenth Doctor.

Panis in the Rigveda: Mentioned in Chapter 86 and portrayed as cattle thieves, they appear in the following places in the Rigveda: 1.83.4; 1.93.4; 2.24.6; 4.58.4; 6.13.3; 6.20.4; 6.33.2; 6.39.2; 6.44.22; 6.45.31; 6.51.14; 7.9.2; 8.26.10; 9.111.2; 10.67.6; 10.108.2, 4, 6–8, 10–11.

The description of Kaliyuga in the Mahabharata: In Chapter 88, Shukra muses that events in Kaliyuga are coming true, as foretold. The description of Kaliyuga and the foretelling of events can be found in the Mahabharata, Vana Parva, Chapter 190, Verses 11–87, where the sage Markandeya narrates his view of what Kaliyuga will be like. Do read these verses. Markandeya's forecast is chillingly accurate.

Kali: I want to emphasise that the Kali referred to in Chapters 16, 20, 55, 88, 92 and 107 of this book is not the goddess Kali, but the Kali after whom Kaliyuga is named and who is the personification of Kaliyuga. For more details, please refer to the story of Parikshit (Arjuna's grandson) and Kali, which is narrated in the Srimad Bhagavatam, Canto 1.

Dandaka: The story of how Dandaka was created (by Shukra) can be found in the Puranic Encyclopaedia, pages 46 and 200. Please refer to the Author's Note in *Son of Bhrigu* for more information on Dandaka. The pond is fictional, as is the concept of the trees seeming to be alive.

The Mists of Brahma: These are completely fictional. For those readers interested in how I came up with the concept, please see my post at The Quest Club. The location of the Mists is also fictional, but details about the river Ganga are geographically accurate (Gangotri, Gomukh, Tapovan are all real locations). For more information about the mythology of Ganga, please read my post at The Quest Club. Also, to know more about the topography, including maps and other details, please log into The Quest Club.

You will find yogis meditating at Tapovan—it is a sacred place. And for those who wonder how Maya can melt into the ice, all I can say at the moment is that the explanation involves quantum physics. For more on this, you will need to keep reading the series.

The Devas and immortality: In Chapter 100, Satyavachana tells Maya that even the Devas could not escape death. For those who are surprised by this assertion, please refer to the Mahabharata, Drona Parva, Chapter 52, Verse 11, where Vyasa tells Yudhishthira, '*Death takes away all; Devas, Danavas and Gandharvas (without exception)*'.

The paper with black ink and white inscriptions: What Vishwaraj snatches away in Chapter 110 is a rubbing. It is a method by which inscriptions on stone or metal can be copied accurately. For more information on rubbings, please log into The Quest Club.

Vadabamukha: The story of Aurava and the fire that resides under the ocean can be found in the Mahabharata, Adi Parva, Chapter 180, Verse 22.

If the concept of the illusion of being consumed by fire (which killed Trivedi in Book 1 and Arjun in this book) is confusing, there is a more detailed explanation available at The Quest Club. Do look it up.

The story of Kacha and Shukra: You can read the entire story in the Mahabharata, Adi Parva, Chapter 76. However, the sensation felt by Shukra while he is teaching Kacha the Sanjivani mantra—which is a result of Maya watching him as an atma, having travelled back in time through the Mists—as mentioned in Chapter 76, is fictional.

Pronunciation Key: If you would like to know how to pronounce the Sanskrit words and mantras that have been used in this book, please log into your account at The Quest Club, where you will find a detailed Pronunciation Key under the section dedicated to *The Mists of Brahma*.

Chronology of events in this book: The events in this book have been spread over a period of almost one year. For those readers who would like to have greater clarity on the chronology of events and the time gap between events, please log into The Quest Club, where a detailed chronology has been provided.

Acknowledgements

The book you hold in your hands, dear reader, is the result of teamwork. There are so many people who have contributed to give the book its final shape and I would like to acknowledge and appreciate their efforts and contribution.

As always, my biggest appreciation and gratitude goes out to my wife Sharmila and my daughter Shaynaya. They have supported and encouraged me throughout the time I spent writing this book, even though it took away from the time that I could have spent with them. Moreover, Sharmila, as always, was the first to read the first draft of the manuscript and give her feedback and Shaynaya, being a teenager herself, gave me some valuable tips on teenage behaviour in different situations. I am also deeply grateful for Sharmila's valuable contribution in spearheading the marketing and sales efforts for this series.

It is extremely difficult to write a book using, as a base, ancient texts that are revered and followed even today. If I had been writing on Egyptian or Greek mythology, it would have been much easier. But the Vedas, the Puranas, the Srimad Bhagavatam and the Bhagavad Gita are all texts that are as relevant today as they were when they were composed thousands of years ago. As a result, while creating scenes, ideating or inventing fantasy elements, I wanted to stay true to the texts. This could not have been possible without the constant guidance of Shubha Vilas, who ensured that I stayed true to the texts and accurately reflected their teachings. Shubha Vilas has been studying and teaching Vedic texts for the last two decades and is also the author of the *Ramayana: The Game of Life* series, *The Chronicles of Hanuman* and *Open Eyed Meditations*. His expertise in Sanskrit was also invaluable in validating the mantras that I invented.

My thanks go out to Artika Bakshi, who read the first draft, as always, and gave me her valuable feedback.

Anand Prakash, my friend and designer extraordinaire, continued his tradition of designing brilliant covers for my books by creating a cover that was in keeping with the very different theme of the book, while visualising some of the key plot elements. Ishan Trivedi did the cover illustration and brought Anand's vision to life, for which I am grateful.

I am also indebted to my good friend Ashish Gupta, who helped me detail many of the plot elements pertaining to Allahabad, including names and locations, as well as small details that make a big difference in terms of authenticity. His tips on police related matters also helped me ensure that I did not stray from reality while portraying the scenes involving police procedures for investigation, the STF and other details.

My thanks go out to Patricia MacEwen, Patricia Burroughs, Madeleine Robins, Phyllis Irene Radford, John C. Bunnell, David D. Levine and E. M. Prazeman, fellow scribes in my writers' research group, who answered questions on key research topics that I struggled with at times.

A big thank you to all the people at Westland, especially Gautam Padmanabhan, Krishna Kumar Nair, Nidhi Mehra and the entire marketing team, who have been tremendously supportive with this book.

As usual, Sanghamitra Biswas, my editor, did a wonderful and very thorough job of polishing my writing and making changes that ensured that the narrative was smoother and true to the plot. I am also deeply appreciative of the time that Karthika V.K. took out from her schedule to do a final edit and polish and tighten the narrative.

Finally, I am deeply grateful to my parents for encouraging me to read and write from an early age and provided me with all the books I wanted to read as I grew up. It is only due to their encouragement and blessings that I have been able to fulfil my childhood dream of becoming an author.

While I acknowledge the contribution of everyone who has supported me, I take full responsibility for any errors and omissions of fact or detail.

Have You Joined the Quest Club?

A word about the Quest Club, in case you haven't registered as a member yet. Membership is free and gives you access to Quest Club events—where readers interact with me both online and offline—that are held all over India. There will be free ebooks over the coming years, in addition to quizzes, puzzles, contests and exclusive previews of my future books for members of the club. Finally, you can join me, as I research my books, and gain free access to images, videos and my research notes. You could even learn more about characters, locations and events in my books. An exciting journey filled with adventure and mystery beckons all Quest Club members. You can register at: www. christophercdoyle.com/ the-quest-club right away for free.